JOHNNY APOCALYPSE

AND THE NUCLEAR WASTELAND

MARK ROBIJN

Blue Forge Press

Port Orchard ✲ Washington

Johnny Apocalypse and the Nuclear Wasteland

First eBook Edition
March 2019

First Print Edition
March 2019

For information about film, reprint or other subsidiary rights, contact: blueforgegroup@gmail.com

Blue Forge Press
7419 Ebbert Drive Southeast
Port Orchard, Washington 98367
360.550.2071 ph.txt

DEDICATION

To my son Isaiah, my best bud and companion
in many adventures.

ACKNOWLEDGEMENTS

I'd like to thank all the great writers and friends who gave me feedback and encouragement over the years, especially my good friends Carl Palmer and Rob Miller, who sadly is no longer with us. I'd like to thank Blue Forge Press for believing in me and my stories enough to take a chance on my novels. I'd also like to thank all the great authors who fueled my imagination through the years, including Jack London, Isaac Asimov, Ray Bradbury and Sir Arthur Conan Doyle. Without their great examples and inspiration, this series of books would probably not exist.

JOHNNY APOCALYPSE

AND THE NUCLEAR WASTELAND

MARK ROBIJN

CHAPTER I

The Elders of the Tribe tell tales of the days when war came, and the Mushroom Monsters filled the sky with fire and smoke. Cities melted into piles of rubble. People turned to ash or turned into ghost shadows on the walls. Metal melted like hot wax. Almost all who lived during those times died. Then to those who were still left came the Sickness. Many developed terrible sores and died. Babies were born deformed or missing arms, or legs, or eyes, some looking like monsters.

Now one hundred years later, only a few survivors remain. Nature has reclaimed the empty gray ribbons where men once drove their metal machines and the twisted skeletons of steel where men lived. Beasties run in the streets now, rat-beasties, and dog-beasties and other Beasties larger and much fiercer.

Next to one of the abandoned, decaying cities stands

a group of one-story square buildings huddled together, as if for protection. The buildings are surrounded by a sea of flat, cracked, and broken stone men once called concrete. The concrete is littered with rusted hunks of steel that man used to call cars. The buildings were once called a "Shopping Mall." Now, the tribe of humans living there in the dark, dirty interior who make it their home call it simply, "Sanctuary."

Sanctuary has one long, large area in the middle that goes the length of the whole place. The people call it the "Main Hall." On either side of the Main Hall are rooms, some small and some big where the people of the "Tribe" lived. They used to be called "stores," but now are just called "dwelling places."

Johnny Apocalypse lived on the third floor of a large dwelling place shared by many families of the Tribe. It had strange, silver letters on it that spelled, "J.C. P nn y" on the front, though no one could read the ancient text anymore, no one except the wise old man Misterwizard.

Johnny's room was in the back of an area of rooms with the letters "Employees Only" on the door. He lived there with his father Foodcourt, his mother Teavana, his sister Carny, who was heavy with a wriggler, and her mate Buildabear.

This morning Johnny heard a voice and woke up, for he'd trained himself to be wake at the slightest sound. He opened one eye and listened. It was his sister Carny, whose full name was Carnivalsintown, moaning in her sleep in the next room. Johnny frowned at her, unhappy to be taken out of a nice, deep sleep. He sat up anyway and scratched his dirty, short blond mop of hair that stuck up in the air like spikes to knock the bug-beasties out. Johnny wore the black leather pants he always wore, a shirt with the picture of some weird creature Misterwizard told him was a "Wookie," and his leather vest. They were favorite clothes, ones he'd found on his secret trips out to the Forbidden City. He slept in them every night. Why take them off? The only things he ever removed were his black leather boots, and that was just because Carny complained he moved his feet and made noise at night.

Johnny was tall, big and strong for a boy of only fifteen seasons, as big as most men. It was why people often turned to him for help or advice, that and the fact that Johnny was always friendly, willing to help or be kind to anyone. With a cheerful smile and a way of talking that made it seem like he wasn't afraid of anything, people in the Tribe almost treated him like he was one of the leaders.

Johnny's room was just big enough for his bed and a small table, and to Johnny it always felt like he was in a box, but it had one good thing that Johnny liked. It was next to the outer wall of Sanctuary with a window. A metal sheet covered the window to keep the Bad Air out, but against the rules Johnny had bent the metal up in the corner large enough so that if he tilted his head and put one eye near the hole he could see outside through the cracked glass beyond.

Johnny put his eye to the hole now. The window glass was cracked and covered with grime, but Johnny could still see through it. The Red Eye hadn't risen over the distant hills yet and the world was still bathed in shadow. It was way too early to be waking. But he smiled, because it was the perfect time of day to sneak out on an adventure.

Johnny moved back and started to put his shoes on

as fast as he could. Johnny's room was covered in paper with flowers on it, another reason Johnny hated it. The wallpaper hung down in many places, and most of the ceiling tiles were gone, leaving gaping black holes to the metal ceiling far above.

The room smelled too, in fact all of Sanctuary smelled. No matter how much people cleaned and swept, spider-beasties still made webs everywhere, rat-beasties crawled all throughout the rooms and the old, decaying junk from before the Great War still gave the place a rotten odor.

An unlit oil lamp sat on the table. Two faded and rotted pictures also hung on the walls. One showed a man with a big smile in a blue suit standing next to a white metal box. The other pictured a woman holding a cup in her hand and gazing at the black liquid inside as if it was something wonderful. Most tribe members spruced up their rooms with things they found around Sanctuary like old bits of gold string with rocks attached to it or one of the old, moldy chairs, but Johnny didn't bother. He hated Sanctuary and wanted more than anything in the world to convince the Tribe to leave it. To him it was nothing but a dark, depressing prison.

Carny walked into Johnny's room looking sleepy. She was twenty seasons old with long brown hair. Like most people in the tribe, Carny was born with a deformity. Hers was a right hand with only three fingers and a misshaped left ear, but otherwise she was beautiful. With soft brown eyes a, large but attractive nose and a big mouth, Carny was only of the prettiest girls in Sanctuary. Most of the men looking for mates had wanted her, which was why Johnny couldn't understand why she chose the lazy, good for nothing Buildabear.

Carny looked down at her belly. "Oooh. You stop kicking, Miracle." It was another thing that annoyed Johnny. She asked Misterwizard to name her wriggler already, even though it wasn't even born yet. Misterwizard named Carny's baby, "Miracle." The name made Johnny angry. Why bother? Miracle would probably die before it was born, just like the last one did. Only a lucky few made it to the breathing, let alone the walking. So why talk to it until came out? Even more, why name it?

Johnny thought back to the last wriggler Carny had. It was two full summers ago, when Johnny was only thirteen. He remembered how excited everyone was, and how he looked forward to having a scrabbler to play with. Then when it was born, it was dead. He could still remember how sad Carny and the Tribe had been, and how he snuck away and cried where no one could see him. It made Johnny wonder if he should ever love anyone too much, for they all died, sooner or later.

Johnny lay back down quickly, one shoe on, hoping she would think he was still sleeping.

"Johnny!"

Johnny groaned. It wasn't fair, just because he was young they all treated him like a Slavey. Johnny couldn't wait until one more season passed, for then he would be sixteen seasons old and be considered a man. He would have the right to pick his own space in Sanctuary and have a family of his own. And something even more exciting would happen: he would be old enough to choose a girl to be his mate, and he already knew who he wanted it to be.

Carny looked cross. "Johnny! I know you're awake! Go get me water. I need it bad!"

Johnny scowled and pulled his blanket over his head. "Water is spendy. Cannot waste water."

Carny took a step further into Johnny's room. "Get up now, Lazy Bones! Or I'll tell Foodcourt where you was the day before."

Johnny sighed, lifted his head and propped it on his hand.

Carny smiled, knowing she had him. "I know you snuck out to the Forbidden City with your friend Starbucks, even though Leader Nordstrom has forbidden anyone leaving Sanctuary. You do all kinds of scary things out there, even fight with Gangers and Wildies. One day you will come back with the Sickness and infect us all. I bet you and Starbucks go visit Misterwizard at Castle too, where he fills your mind with all sorts of strange ideas. He's teaching you how to use the forbidden things from before the Great War, isn't he? I've heard you and Starbucks talking about those things you ride, and the places you've been. And I know he's teaching you to read the ancient words. I saw that thing you hide under your mattress and look at when no one is watching you."

Suddenly Johnny realized by the sound of Carny's voice, she wasn't angry at him, she felt bad she couldn't go too. It made Johnny feel sad. He sat up and smiled at her. "It's called a 'book,' Carny. The words on the outside say, 'The Cat in the Hat.' It's very funny, about a cat-beastie that can talk just like a person. You're right, Misterwizard teaches me lots of amazing things. And one day, I'll teach you, and Miracle."

Carny smiled with affection, then quickly hid it and frowned crossly, but not before Johnny noticed and smiled wider. Carny rubbed her belly with one hand and pointed an accusing finger at Johnny with the other.

"You know what Leader Nordstrom says. He says we don't need the ancient words, they don't mean anything anymore. And he says the things from before are just junk now and give people strange, bad ideas. He says Misterwizard is just a crazy old man because of the Sickness."

"Then why does Misterwizard help when someone is sick and deliver all the wrigglers and give them all the ancient names? It's because Leader Nordstrom knows Misterwizard is smarter than anyone else, including Leader Nordstrom."

Carny frowned and didn't reply, proving to Johnny that she knew he was right. She continued talking, but Johnny could tell she knew she was losing the argument. "You're going to get caught and Leader Nordstrom will throw us all out. Then we'll all die! We'll be eaten by Beasties or attacked by Wildies, or even worse, be captured by the Gangers. Why couldn't I have normal brother like Onsale? He's not so high and mighty. He doesn't act like he's smarter than everyone else. He's willing to obey the rules. He's not strange, like you."

Johnny stuck out his tongue and made an ugly face and Carny did the same back at him. Onsale was born a half-wit, and he beat up his own little brother. Onsale wanted to join the Gangers. If Carly only knew what Onsale was really like, she'd be glad Johnny wasn't like him. Misterwizard said it was safe to go outside now. If only he could convince Leader Nordstrom and the Tribe! Each time Johnny had to come back to Sanctuary after an adventure outside, it felt more and more like a death sentence.

"Maybe you wish I was like your mate Buildabear. All he does is lie around, like a lazy cat-beastie, and eat. Why you not ask Buildabear to get you water?"

Carny didn't answer, and Johnny knew why. Her man Buildabear did nothing but sleep, eat and complain. He was weak, with fingers of his left hand fused together, thin like a beanpole, and lazy. Johnny sneered with contempt when he looked at him. And worse, he was mean to Carny. That made Johnny's blood boil. When Buildabear yelled at Carny, Johnny got so mad it was all he could do to keep himself from going over and beating Buildabear until he died. Someday, Buildabear would go too far, and Johnny would make him pay.

Johnny sat up and started putting on his other shoe as Carny walked over and sat on the edge of his bed.

"You can go out too. You don't need to be scared. Misterwizard says the air is fine, the water is fine. Long ago the 'radiation reached its half-life,' Misterwizard says, whatever that means. People here get the Sickness from sitting and doing nothing but breathing bad air. They drink nasty rain water from the rusty pipes or for from the stale old well in the middle of Main Hall. They eat nothing but mush from the tiny garden or rat-beasties. People here are all dying, Carny!" Healthier than all of them. Johnny ran and played, He ate meat from the Beasties he shot with his slingshot or stabbed with his sword and cooked over an open fire. He drank cool, clear water from the flowing river. He had even stayed out all night once, and watched the little lights in the blue sky, and the big Yellow Eye that rode the sky at night.

Carny looked at Johnny, her voice full of confusion. "Leader Nordstrom says the air is bad! He says Misterwizard is bad in the head. He says the Book of Law says to stay in Sanctuary until we get the "all clear," when the voices from the Magic Talking Box says it's safe to leave."

Johnny snorted with disdain as he stood up and tied his shoelaces. "The Magic Talking Box. Humph! Misterwizard says Magic Talking Box needs 'lectricity and will never say anything ever again, because anyone who spoke to it is long dead. Leader Nordstrom won't listen. Leader Nordstrom keeps that big dwelling place where he was named all to himself, though it's big enough for the whole Tribe. He wants everybody to treat him like he is a king. Misterwizard wants to move the Tribe to a new place, a better place, but Leader Nordstrom won't listen."

Johnny walked to the door. "I'm not staying in Sanctuary to die. I'm going to live and feel the heat from the Red Eye on my face and see the white lights in the sky at night. And when I leave, I'm taking all of you with me."

Carny smiled with affection, nodded sadly, turned and walked back to her room. The bad thoughts of Buildabear and the idea of going on an adventure had driven the idea of sleep from Johnny. A small, shaft of light from the crack Johnny opened in the window played across the room, illuminating dust motes in the air. Clothes lay all over the floor, and rat-beasties crawled through them and slept on them. No matter what you did, you couldn't get rid of the rat-beasties or the bug-beasties. They seemed to think *they* owned the World, not people.

Johnny peered out the crack in the window again. The Red Eye peeked over the distant hills. He had to hurry before others started waking up. He and Starbucks could sneak out before the rest of the Tribe were up, and if anyone asked where they were they would claim they were playing games in areas of Sanctuary where no one ever went, just like they always did. It always worked, because most of the Tribe were superstitious and believed some places in Sanctuary were haunted.

Johnny reached under his bed for his two most prized possessions, his sword and his slingshot. He put his slingshot on his belt then lifted his sword up and gazed at it lovingly. He swung it in an arc and heard its quiet whistle as it cut the air. Silver but with a gold handle adorned with fancy curls and colorful gems, its blade was as long as Johnny's forearm. Johnny sharpened it to a razor point with a special stone had found in the same old place full of weapons where he found the sword. It was in a dwelling far away on the other side of the Forbidden City, on the bottom floor of a huge building that shot up into the sky like a huge building block. The building had rooms like Sanctuary but right in the middle of the Forbidden City. Only he and Starbucks knew of the place, and they blocked it off so no Gangers or Wildies could find it, because it had lots more cool weapons in it, even some very rare and magical things Misterwizard called "guns." Johnny brought one to Misterwizard and he trained Johnny on how to use it. After that, Misterwizard brought a few to Sanctuary and helped train the men on how to use them, but most of the men were too afraid of them to touch them.

Johnny slipped his sword in its leather scabbard on his waist and tiptoed over to the door. He quietly opened the door and entered a much larger area where many of the Tribe slept, some in separate rooms, others in corners sectioned off with old racks and shelves. He walked quietly through the big, dark space, for the oil lamps were still unlit. The musty air he walked through was like a wall, stale and smelly and hard to breathe through. Like Johnny's room, most of the ceiling tiles were gone, exposing long unused wiring and ragged insulation. Metal racks lay in pieces everywhere, most shoved into the corners making what looked to Johnny like giant metal spider-beastie webs. Some still had ragged bits of clothing from before the Great War hanging from them, though most of that had rotted long ago. A layer of dust covered every surface, and in the corners squeaks and scrabbling came from the rat-beasties.

Dark shapes loomed in the twilight like silent ghosts. The Fake People watched him, like they always did. Even though some had no hands, arms or even heads, they still looked so real they gave Johnny the creeps. When he was a scrabbler, he'd been so afraid of them he wouldn't walk in front of them because he could feel their eyes watching him. When he grew older he realized they weren't alive, but they still sent chills up his spine, like a spider-beastie crawling up his back. Johnny wished the Tribe would gather them up and get rid of them, but some who were superstitious said it would bring bad luck because the Fake People were there first.

Johnny heard snores as he passed Tribe members and their families sleeping on the floor behind makeshift partitions. Some families had only a corner of the room for their dwelling place. Johnny didn't know why he and his family got actual rooms, but he was glad they did.

Johnny passed a door that read, "Changing Room,"

where Microsoft, his wife Abercrombie and their daughter Sephie lived. A small figure peered at him out of the dark. At first, he thought it was just another one of the Fake People, but then he saw it was Sephora, Microsoft and Abercrombie's little girl, or Sephie, as everyone called her. Five seasons old, Sephie had long brown hair and a big mouth that was missing a tooth on the bottom row. Sephie thought the Red Eye and the Yellow Eye rose and fell on Johnny, and her most favorite times were when Johnny would sit down and tell her about his secret adventures. She smiled at Johnny now with her arms open wide waiting for a hug. Johnny stopped and frowned, trying to be irritated, but inside, warmth and affection filled him. Johnny didn't want to admit it, but he had a special place in his heart for the Sephie too.

Johnny tried to look cross. "What are you doing awake? I don't have time for you. You just going to die like the rest of the scrabblers."

Sephie's smile faded awat. Her eyes started to tear up and she dropped her arms.

Johnny sighed, knelt down and opened his arms. "Okay, come here."

Sephie's smile returned and she ran to Johnny. As she grabbed him in a big bear hug, a lump grew in Johnny's throat and he scowled harder, forcing it down. He pushed her back, so he could look in her face. She grinned, showing really had two missing teeth, one on top as well. Johnny glanced around to make sure no one else was awake. "Can you keep a big secret?"

Sephie nodded, instantly excited.

"Come with me but be quiet."

Johnny took Sephie's hand and led her down the hall

to a room with a door labeled, "Men's Room."

Johnny turned to her and knelt down. "Wait here." Sephie bobbed her head up and down so fast she looked like she was going to lose it, and waited expectantly. Johnny slipped into the room quietly. Though it was pitch black inside Johnny moved confidently and swiftly, having done it a thousand times. In the back corner he removed a metal panel revealing a hole in the wall. This was where Johnny hid his treasures, all the things he found on his secret trips into the Forbidden City.

Johnny felt around and found what he was looking for. He pulled out a shiny red apple. He found it and a few more on a tree in the Forbidden City in a small patch of grass in the courtyard of a tall building. He fought a raccoon-beastie for it, but it was worth the effort. The apples were small, but delicious. He gazed at it and grinned. Then he ran back to Sephie.

Johnny knelt in front of Sephie again. "Here."

Sephie grabbed the apple, with wide eyes, smiled and put it to her mouth. Then she took a bit bite and started eating it eagerly.

"That's called an apple. Can you say apple?" Sephie kept eating and nodded again, her eyes bright. "Don't eat the middle, just the outside." She nodded.

When she was almost done Johnny led her back to her room. "Give me what's left." Sephie handed it to Johnny. Then she hugged him again. Once again Johnny had to choke back the feelings that came bubbling up and mentally he scolded himself angrily; he was supposed to be tough, not soft like his sister Carny.

He looked Sephie squarely in the eyes and in a cross tone said, "Listen to me. Don't you die, you hear me? You grow up to be big and strong and have lots of wrigglers of your own."

Sephie put her head on Johnny's chest. "Love Johnny."

Johnny frowned, his heart warm inside. "Johnny love Sephie too, even if she is a little annoying scrabbler. Now go back to bed."

Sephie gave Johnny one more good look then ran back into her room.

Johnny watched her for a moment, grinning. Then he headed to the metal stairs that led down. Siding down the metal ramp on the side to the next level, he turned and did the same to the next set of stairs until he was on the ground floor.

From here on, Johnny knew he had to be cautious, for the Tribe's Enforcers roamed the halls, listening for Gangers, Wildies or Beasties trying to break in or any other trouble. The Enforcers were mostly old men wearing red capes, but If they caught him he'd have a lot of explaining to do, and probably get in big trouble with Leader Nordstrom.

Johnny walked to the large opening that led to the Main Hall. Keeping a watchful eye open, he crept out, feeling the cool night air on his face.

CHAPTER 2

Johnny looked down the large, dark hallway in the middle of Sanctuary. Not seeing anyone nearby, he ran, careful to be quiet.

Johnny's thoughts turned to the one person that occupied his mind the most, and it instantly made his heart beat faster. It was Little Debbie, the girl that Johnny loved. Little Debbie was Johnny's girl, or she would be if Johnny had his way. Deb, as everyone called her, had long blond hair and the softest blue eyes Johnny had ever seen. She had a cute turned up nose and a sharp chin. Before he saw Deb, Johnny didn't know girls could look so lovely, and it was all Johnny could do to keep from looking stupid every time he was around her.

Best of all, Deb had no missing parts, like so many other people did. She was perfect in every way. Misterwizard said that the way her and Johnny being born with no deformities showed the world was getting better. Johnny hoped that was true. But Deb being so perfect made Johnny afraid, for all the men in the Tribe wanted her, even the oldest ones of nearly forty seasons. Deb's father, Thegap, would not give her to just any man, he was keeping her for someone special. Johnny vowed that someday he would prove to Thegap that he was that man, though he knew on the day he declared his love for her, he would have to fight for her. He didn't know if he would want to live if he had to see her with another man.

Johnny passed by the gardens in the middle of Sanctuary. Here the hard floor had been broken up long before Johnny was born, and crops planted. It was a good place for this, for it was under one of the glass domes at the top of Sanctuary that let the light in. Metal mesh attached to the ceiling kept anyone from using it as way to get in or out, which created a cross-hatched shadow on the floor from the Red Eye's light during the day. Johnny spent many an hour as a scrabbler working in the garden, and it was another thing he hated about Sanctuary. The vegetables were always mushy and small, and before he started sneaking out on adventures, he was always hungry. It made him feel sad for the rest of the Tribe, who had almost nothing else to eat.

As Johnny crept along he passed a shop with a sign labeled, "Sharper Image." From inside it he heard a hissing sound. Johnny stopped and grinned, for he knew instantly who it was. Out of the darkness strolled Johnny's best friend in the whole world next to Misterwizard, his friend Starbucks.

"Hey Stupid, where you going in such a hurry? The Necessary Place is the other way."

"You're Stupid," Johnny whispered back with a grin.

"Don't talk so loud. Enforcers will hear you and kick you in your sitting place."

Starbucks walked out of the store and put out his arm. Johnny slapped it with his, hard. It was a game they played, to see who would flinch. Neither did, though both had to grit their teeth. Starbucks was older than Johnny, almost sixteen seasons, shorter but strong. Starbucks and his family were one of only two black families in the Tribe, though there were two families with slanted eyes who Misterwizard said were of Korean descent, and one brown-skinned family Misterwizard said that in the old days were called Hispanic. There were some that disliked the people who had different colored skin saying they were different because they were cursed by the Sickness, but Johnny knew that was nonsense. It made him furious when he heard them talking like that.

Starbucks' hair was black, short and curly. The corner of Starbuck's left eye drooped and one of his arms was shorter than the other. He was strong though, and not afraid of anything and he liked to make jokes, just like Johnny. Johnny even wondered if Starbucks wasn't just a little crazy.

"Going over to make silly over Deb I bet."

"Naw," Johnny said, sorry that Starbucks had caught him, because that was exactly what he had planned on doing. "Going on an adventure to see Misterwizard. It's a good day for an adventure! You in?"

"Of course. Somebody has to protect you from the Wildies, the Beasties and the Gangers." Starbucks lifted up his own sword, shorter than Johnny's, but more curved and mean looking. Johnny raised his sword and they softly clinked them together.

Starbucks said, "But you mean going on an adventure

so see Merlin, don't you?"

Johnny smiled. "I've heard you call him that before. Who was Merlin?"

"He was a wizard from long ago in a story Misterwizard read to me and some other scrabblers when I was little and he visited Sanctuary. I think the real Merilin is dead, but I'll bet Misterwizard is his son, though."

They put the swords back and ran off into the dark together. Johnny and Starbucks no longer looked at the "stores" they passed, for the rooms had long ago been picked over for anything useful. All the wearable things, interesting knick-knacks, safe food in cans and pretty pictures were gone. What was left consisted of weird junk like little round shiny discs, metal boxes with wires, and more Fake People. Misterwizard told Johnny a lot of the old junk in the stores took 'electricity' to use too, so it was useless.

The boys kept low and moved as silently as they could to avoid the Enforcers. Johnny saw one sitting on a bench, and he motioned to Starbucks. Dressed in the usual long, red robe made out of old curtains and carrying a long, pointed stick, the Enforcer looked like some kind of huge, dark, sleeping Beastie.

Johnny and Starbucks began to tiptoe past, but then Starbucks smiled and relaxed. He bumped Johnny's arm and pointed. The Enforcer was asleep. His soft snores echoed in the vast chamber. Both boys grinned with humor.

Starbucks whispered, "Leader Nordstrom catches him sleeping, it would be ten hits with the Cane of Correction."

Johnny nodded and whispered back. "It's good we

saw him though. If he catches us later, we can use it to bargain with him."

Starbucks nodded in approval. "Smart!"

The boys approached a store with a sign that said, "Macys" on it. Johnny's heart beat fast again, for it was where Deb lived with her parents.

Johnny stopped in front of the store and peered into its black interior. The empty shelves loomed like dark monsters. On top of one, a rat-beastie stared back up at him. Johnny picked up a piece of glass to throw at it. Johnny hated rat-beasties because they were disgusting, and the rest of the Tribe was forced to eat them. They also stole food.

"Why are we stopping here, Johnny?" Starbucks teased. "Hoping Deb is awake and will give you a big kiss? Johnny's getting gooey. Johnny's getting gooey." Starbucks grinned in the darkness.

Johnny punched him on the arm and Starbucks yelled, "Ow!"

"Just like Starbucks gets around Super," Johnny shot back.

Super was the girl Starbucks liked. She had long black hair and blue eyes and was almost as pretty as Deb, but no other men dared try to romance her, because she was tough and wild. Her real name was very long and funny and made no sense, a name Misterwizard had picked out: "Supercalifragilisticexpialidocious." Nobody could say it or even remember it, so they just called her Super. Super was smart and not afraid of anything, and she liked to crack jokes. Johnny thought that she could even be a Ganger girl if she wanted to.

Starbucks scowled for he knew Johnny had gotten him back. From the dark interior of Macys someone coughed. Johnny peered into the dark, wondering who it was. The sound instantly set off alarms in Johnny's mind, for coughing was a bad sign. I might mean nothing, but it could mean someone had the Sickness. Then Johnny heard a new sound that made him forgot all about the cough.

"Johnny Apocalypse!" A soft, melodious voice floated out from the dark interior. It was Deb! Johnny's insides turned to goo and he smiled wide before he could stop himself. Deb strolled out of the darkness, her blue eyes twinkling. Johnny stopped smiling and put on a tough look, but his face colored. Behind him Starbucks laughed quietly, which only made it worse.

Deb looked at Starbucks. "And Starbucks! What are you two troublemakers up to? Why aren't you sleeping like good little boys? Because Johnny and Starbucks are going on an adventure again, against the rules."

"How do you know we go out?" Starbucks said, and Johnny slugged him in the arm again, making Starbucks wince.

"Everybody knows, silly, except Leader Nordstrom. They don't tell, because they want Johnny and Starbucks to bring back something good, like food or special magic things from the time before. Maybe even something that will prove we can leave this dark place."

Deb walked over to Johnny and smiled at him, making his legs feel weak. "You are going out, aren't you?"

"Maybe, maybe not." Johnny flipped the piece of glass in the air and catching it and yawned, trying to look uninterested. Deb's eyes seemed to look right into Johnny's soul, to know just how Johnny felt, almost like Carny. It made Johnny uncomfortable.

"What is Deb doing up so early? Little girls need to sleep too."

Deb moved closer and sweat broke out on Johnny's forehead, even though the air was cool. She moved so close he suddenly found it hard to breathe.

"Maybe I want to catch Johnny and Starbucks being bad, so I can tell Leader Nordstrom, and see them get twenty hits with the Can of Correction."

Deb smiled and tilted her head to one side, making her long blond hair fall straight down. "Or maybe I'm tired of this dark terrible place too and want to go with Johnny and Starbucks on their adventure today."

"Yes!" Starbucks whispered excitedly, saying out loud what Johnny instantly thought secretly. "It's about time you came along! We can show you amazing things, things you won't even believe! We'll take you to see Misterwizard's Castle!"

Johnny tried not to show in his face how excited he was at the idea of Deb joining them. He shrugged and nonchalantly replied, "Okay, but it can be dangerous outside. There are Wildies, and Beasties, and even Gangers. And if Leader Nordstrom catches us, you'll be in big trouble too."

Deb touched Johnny's hand with hers, making Johnny feel faint. Then she looked him in the eyes, making Johnny's mind go blank. "I'm not afraid of Leader Nordstrom any more than Johnny and Starbucks are. And I know Johnny will protect me from the Wildies, the Beasties and the Gangers."

Johnny gazed into Deb's eyes and they stood still

smiling at each other. Finally, Johnny realized how silly he looked. He yawned and looked away, trying to act cool. "Okay, but Johnny and Starbucks have no time for slowpokes. You better be able to keep up."

"I can run faster than either of you, and you both know it. Well, what are we waiting for? Let's go!"

The adventurers, now three, walked down the hallway together. Johnny couldn't keep his eye of Deb, but he tried not to show it, looking away any time she looked his direction. She caught him many times though, and he didn't really mind. He smiled at her and she smiled back.

"You're gonna have lots of fun, Deb!" Starbucks whispered, looking at her with excitement as they walked. "Get ready for the time of our life!"

Then Starbucks stopped. Johnny and Deb stopped too and looked at him, curious.

"Wait a minute! If you get to take Deb, I should get to take Super too."

Johnny shrugged. "Okay by me, if she's willing to risk getting into trouble too. Go get her. We'll meet you by our secret door out."

Starbucks whispered, "Yippee!" and ran off towards the place where Super and her family lived, the store labeled, "feugo." Johnny and Deb kept walking.

They were alone! Johnny couldn't keep his eyes off Deb. She noticed and smiled at him. Once Johnny had given her one of the bottles with the smelly water inside as a present. She was wearing it now, and it made her smell so good Johnny almost felt woozy.

"Is it true what everyone says, Johnny?" Deb asked, glancing at him coyly.

"What's that?" Johnny replied, trying to sound casual.

"That Johnny is in love with Deb and wants her all for himself?"

Johnny stopped and looked at Deb, his insides suddenly all tied up in knots. He tried to answer, but his tongue stuck to the roof of his mouth. Finally, he croaked, "Deb's very pretty."

Deb moved closer, until her face was just inches from Johnny's. Johnny felt his knees go weak.

"Just pretty?"

"No," Johnny said, "the prettiest girl in Sanctuary." Deb smiled with triumph, and Johnny felt like he floated on one of the white puffy things he saw in the sky.

Starbucks and Super joined them. Starbucks held Super's hand. Johnny wished he was that bold with Deb, but he was too much of a cowardie.

Super was a tall full-figured girl, and Johnny really liked her. Her ears was shaped funny and came to points at the top, but it wasn't very noticeable because of her long hair.

Super was always ready for adventure, just like Starbucks and she had hinted before she wanted to go with Johnny and Starbucks. Johnny thought maybe she was a little crazy too, so her and Starbucks fit together well.

"Hi Johnny and Little Debbie. It's about time you stupid boys stopped being afraid us girls would show you up and let us go with you on an adventure!"

Somewhere in the dark, far away and faint, glass shattered, echoing through the gloomy hallway. They all stopped talking and turned towards the sound, instantly alert, for it meant only one thing.

"Shhh!" Johnny whispered. "Somebody is breaking in!"

"It could be a Wildie, or even the Gangers!" Starbucks whispered back.

"Let's go find out," Johnny said, taking out his sword.

CHAPTER 3

Johnny pointed to a store nearby. "You girls stay here while Starbucks and teach them a lesson."

Super crossed her arms grumpily. "We're not scared. We can fight too, you know."

"Four is better than two," Deb added.

Johnny grinned at Starbucks and they both just shook their heads. Then he said, "Okay but let me and Starbucks and fight first."

The four friends ran through the dark towards the place where they thought the sound came from. "Johnny!" Deb whispered back. "What if it's Ripper and his whole gang? Maybe we should go tell Leader Nordstrom first."

Johnny scowled and tried to look more confident than he felt. "Then Leader Nordstrom will find out about us sneaking around. Besides, Starbucks and me can take them all on."

"That's right!" Starbucks agreed, though he didn't sound as confident as Johnny did. "We'll teach those Gangers Sanctuary belongs to us!"

As they grew close, they heard more glass breaking. Now they could tell where it came from; the store with the big, yellow 'M' on it, the one with the funny statue of a man in big red shoe, a white face and a red nose. As they ran inside, Johnny and Starbucks looked around, swords ready. From the back room came soft voices. There were two of them, at least. Johnny looked around for something else to use as a weapon. He saw something interesting on the counter. He grinned and picked it up.

A whisper came from the back: "Hurry up Leaker or I break your jaw. Then you won't be able to stuff that fat faced of yours and you'll die!"

Johnny knew Leaker. He acted tough, but he was weak and a cowardie. He was also terrified of Johnny, though he tried not to show it. Johnny beat him good every time he saw him, because Leaker was a sneak and a thief. Leaker didn't worry Johnny, but the person who spoke, that was a horse-beastie of a different color. It was Ripper. Ripper was the leader of the Gangers, and he was mean as an old dog-beastie, and tough. Johnny had tangled with Ripper many times, and each time they fought they both left bruised and bloody, but Johnny had always escaped before Ripper could call the Gangers to help hm. Ripper and the Gangers called themselves the Doomsday Prophecy, something they heard Misterwizard say once, though Johnny was sure they had no idea what it meant.

A whispered reply came in a whiny voice that Johnny

knew was Leaker's. "I'm trying. Johnny's gonna hear us."

"Johnny. Someday I'll cut his heart out. Then I'll take that girl he likes. She'll make a good slavey for the whole gang."

Johnny's insides burned with anger at what Ripper said. He turned to Deb and Super. "You girls wait here. If we need you, we'll holler." The girls nodded and hid behind a plastic booth. Johnny and Starbucks climbed over the counter and hurried into the back room.

As they grew close to the source of the sounds they crouched and slowed down. As Johnny came around the corner to the back of the room, he saw them!

At the very bottom of a window, a beam of sunlight made a red line across the floor where the metal plate bent inwards. Behind it the glass window made a spider-web pattern and a large portion was gone.

As Johnny and Starbucks watched, a hand snaked in holding a metal tool with loops for the fingers that gripped the metal in a pincer-like grip. The hand grabbed the metal in the tool's teeth and pushed on it, trying to bend it in further.

Johnny crept up as softly as he could and hid next to the opening.

A loud 'smack' came from outside, and Leaker yelped. "Hurry up!"

"Ow! What'd you do that for? You cut my leg!"

"I'll cut off your leg off and change your name to Crawler! The Red Eye is rising. The whole gang is waiting. Get that thing open!"

The whole gang was there! That meant over a hundred men, and half as many women. For the first time, Johnny felt uneasy and unsure. Maybe he should run back and tell Leader Nordstrom. The Tribe had over two hundred people, but most of them were weak from malnutrition and no exercise, and a lot of them were women and children who couldn't fight. Still, if the Tribe had to, it would fight and defend their home. Johnny was only fifteen, but he was big and a good fighter. Most of the Gangers were not much older than him, and he could take any one of them, one by one, but all at once? Johnny was no crazie. He knew that would be suicide.

The spot of light from the Red Eye grew bigger. They almost had the metal plate off!

Leaker's head slipped in and turned up towards the ceiling. Dirt and sweat covered his long, thin face, pointed nose and toothless mouth.

Johnny was ready for him. He turned to Starbucks, grinned and whispered, "Watch this!"

He tipped the plastic box he'd found on the counter upside down right, the one filled with huge roach-beasties! They all fell on Leaker's face!

Leaker screamed in terror and tried to pull his head back, but his chin caught on the edge of the metal plate. He squirmed back and forth in torment as the roaches crawled up his nose and in his open mouth. His chin bled from the sharp edge of the plate, and he screamed in terror.

Ripper yelled, "What's going on?"

Leaker thrashed about, blood dripping onto the floor. Johnny and Starbucks laughed so hard they had to grab onto a wall to keep from falling. Then Johnny glared down at Leaker. "That'll teach you, Dumb-head."

Leaker's eyes opened wide in fear and the roach-beasties crawled into his hair. "It's Johnny and Starbucks!"

From outside they heard Ripper curse. Johnny took

out his sword. He lowered it to Leaker's face and put the blade right next to Leaker's nose. Leaker's eyes moved as far down as they could, trying to watch it. Johnny smiled, and his meaning was all too clear.

Leaker smiled entreatingly. "Hey Johnny. What's up?"

"Get out of here," Johnny whispered fiercely, "and don't ever come back. Tell Ripper the whole Tribe is here, and if you try to get in again, we'll kill all of you." Johnny nicked Leaker's nose. Blood gushed from it and Leaker howled.

Johnny and Starbucks weren't done. Starbucks spotted a square pan on a metal box with metal legs. He ran over, looked inside it and smiled.

Starbucks picked it up and carried it over. As Leaker watched in horror, Starbucks tipped it upside down over his face. It was full of congealed goo that had been sitting in the pan forever. It dripped slowly, a thick rancid goo that snaked down like maple syrup. Soon it covered Leaker's face. Leaker instantly threw up, but since he was looking up, he swallowed some and the rest splashed all over his face. Johnny and Starbucks laughed until their sides ached as Leaker moaned.

Finally, Leaker was able to pull his head back out. Johnny and Starbucks heard Leaker moaning and retching, surrounded by angry whispers from the others.

Johnny and Starbucks held their swords ready, just in case.

Ripper spoke again from outside, his voice full of venom. "You win this time, Johnny. But I'm gonna get you someday, you and your whole Tribe. You're gonna regret crossing the Doomsday Prophecy. We're going to kill all your men and make your girlies our slaves. The day is coming soon, so get ready."

Then there was silence. Ripper and the Gangers were gone! Johnny and Starbucks had won! Johnny's heart soared with pride. He turned around, triumphant and slapped Starbucks' hand. Deb and Super joined them. Deb's eyes shone with pride. Johnny was sure now she was gooey for him too. Johnny felt ten feet tall and he stood up to his full height, chin held high.

Deb moved forward purposefully. Was she going to kiss him?

Johnny's toes tingled in anticipation. But she passed him by and strode to the opening, and Johnny felt disappointment.

"We have to block the hole up good, so the Gangers can't come back this way."

As Johnny and Starbucks bent the metal back in place and tried to fasten it closed, Deb looked around. Seeing a large metal box in the corner of the room, she walked over and tried to push it towards the opening. It was too heavy for her and her feet started to slip. Johnny, Starbucks and Super ran to help her. Together they moved the large metal box in front of the hole. Then they stood back, surveying their work. If the Gangers tried to come through again, they'd have to push the metal box away from the wall, which would be almost impossible from the other side. The hole was sealed as good as Johnny and the rest could make it.

As they walked back toward the Main Hall, Johnny and Deb gazed at each other. Her eyes bored into Johnny again, searching. It made tingle all over with happiness and his head buzz. Deb reached over and touched Johnny's hand. A shock of pure pleasure traveled up his arm and all through his body. He almost tripped and fell and made sure to concentrate on his walking after that.

Starbucks, meanwhile, spoke angrily. "We have to tell Leader Nordstrom. Enforcers are not doing their job, sleeping mostly. The Gangers are going to get in and kill all of us."

Johnny turned to answer, but with surprise ran right into Deb's lips! It was so dark, Starbucks didn't see and kept walking. Deb leaned forward and pressed her lips against Johnny's. Johnny's mind went numb with shock and pleasure, but before he could gather his wits, she pulled away again and walked away as if nothing had ever happened.

Johnny watched her go, out of breath and full of wonderful sensations. When he could move again he walked out of the "M" Store to join Deb, Super and Starbucks. Johnny frowned. It was lighter now; they didn't have much time to get out, before the Enforcers would definitely see them.

"What's wrong, Johnny?" Deb asked, mirroring his frown.

"The Red Eye is in sky now. If we want to get out before everyone is up, we have to go fast."

"Well, what we waiting for?" Starbucks said. "Let's go!" Starbucks took off running and Super joined him.

Johnny started to follow too but Deb didn't. He turned to her. She held out her hand.

Johnny looked at it. It was soft and slender, like a girl's hand was supposed to be. Gingerly he took it. It felt warm and wonderful. Once again, the blood in his body ran faster, as if it was in a race.

Sanctuary fell away. It was just him and Deb, alone. To Johnny, nobody else existed; he was king, and Deb was his queen. It was their job to build a whole new tribe of their own, and go off on exciting adventures, far away from the miserable, dark and stuffy place. Gazing into each other's eyes, Johnny and Deb ran to catch up to Starbucks and Super and find Johnny's Secret Way Out.

Soon Johnny, Deb, Starbucks and Super stood in the dark interior at the back of the store with no words on the front, just a picture of an apple. They walked through a door and into a thin, long back room. Johnny walked over to a wall panel. As Super and Deb watched, Johnny and Starbucks smiled with pride and each grabbed hold of a metal box with wheels on it. Together they pushed it a few feet. Behind it there was a metal grate. Johnny and Starbucks unscrewed the bolts that were already loose and lifted the grate off, revealing a metal tunnel inside.

Johnny turned to Deb and Super. "We have to crawl out this tunnel for a little way. It's pretty tight, but if we can fit, you girls should be okay."

The girls nodded. Johnny went first. He slipped into the tunnel and crawled on his hands and knees down it. Quickly the rest followed. Starbucks went last, after moving the metal and glass object close enough so that it hid the opening.

When Johnny reached the end of the tunnel there was another grate. This one led to the outside, and bright sunshine streamed through it invitingly in long strips of light. Johnny pushed the grate open and fell onto the concrete outside. In front of the grate on the outside, he and Starbucks had rolled a large green metal box on wheels. Johnny bumped his head on it when he landed.

He stood up, rubbed his head and rolled the box far enough away to let the others get out.

Johnny looked up at the sky. The Red Eye was just coming up over the distant mountains; it was going to be a beautiful day. He looked around at the sea of concrete and old piles of steel that littered it as far as Johnny could see. Looking past the concrete and cars, Johnny could see tall, dark shapes looming on the horizon. They were the old buildings of the Forbidden City. Seeming to hold menace and the promise of adventure at the same time, the buildings looked like the black, twisted skeletons of old men. They sent a thrill of fear and joy through Johnny; he couldn't wait to reach them and start exploring again. And to think this time, he was going to get to share it with Deb! The thought made Johnny's heart leap with excitement. And he had another surprise to share with her. He couldn't wait to see her reaction when she saw it.

They were on the opposite side of Sanctuary from where the Gangers tried to get in, and there was no sign of them. They were safe, for the moment. Deb, Super and Starbucks crawled out of the hole, and Johnny quickly placed the grate back in place.

Starbucks raised a fist. "Woo-hoo! You're free from Sanctuary!"

The girls blinked from the sun and looked around, scared and thrilled at the same time. It was the first time they'd been outside Sanctuary. They both breathed slowly, making sure the air was safe. Then they both smiled. Debbie closed her eyes, breathed in deep and sighed with pleasure. Joy filled Johnny's heart as he watched, but there was a tinge of anger as he thought how she'd been cooped up in Sanctuary all her life.

Deb looked at Johnny. "It's like that mythical place Misterwizard talks about, Heaven, where everything is wonderful and magical." Deb gazed around and smiled with excitement. "Oh, Johnny, look at all the space! And the Red Eye feels so warm! Why have we never come out here with you before?"

Super scowled. "And to think we've been locked in that dirty, dark place all over lives, when we could have been enjoying this. All because of Leader Nordstrom."

Starbucks shrugged. "I don't think Leader Nordstrom knows any better. I sometimes think he is only trying to do what he things is best. Nobody in the tribe knows."

"Only because they won't listen to Misterwizard!" Johnny said frowning.

Deb shaded her eyes with her hand. She and Super gazed around at the world that they'd never seen before. Deb looked at the sea of concrete around them and the rusted hulks dotting it. Beyond the concrete lay a ribbon of gray, and on the other side of that she saw smaller one-story buildings, empty and decaying, somehow sinister with dark holes where windows had once been, now looking like eye sockets without eyes, and dark interiors beyond. She turned and gazed at the city in the distance that looked like a mirage, shimmering in the morning heat. Its broken buildings looked sinister, but exciting

Deb grabbed Johnny's arm. "The Forbidden City! Johnny are we really going there?"

"We sure are," Johnny said, putting an arm around her. "Just wait until you see it, Deb. You'll never want to go back to Sanctuary again."

Super shaded her eyes and looked at the city too. "Aren't there Wildies and Beasties there?

"There sure are," Starbucks said.

"And the Gangers. Isn't that where they live?" Deb asked.

"It sure is," Johnny replied.

The girls looked at each other and grinned. Then Super turned to Starbucks.

"Well, what are we waiting for? But it looks so far away. How do we get there?"

Johnny and Starbucks grinned at each other. "That's the best surprise of all," Johnny said.

Suddenly Deb put her hand to her mouth and coughed. Everyone looked at her, their smiles turning to looks of concern. Johnny's heart, which seconds before soared in the clouds, sank to his shoes, and fear entered his chest like a hungry Beastie looking to devour him. So, it was Deb Johnny heard coughing. Coughing was bad, a sign of bad things, and most times meant the person had the Sickness. Johnny studied Deb intensely, worry making his heart beat like a drum. She saw his look and smiled. "It's only the dust from that tunnel, silly. Don't be such a worrier. I'm fine."

Johnny tried to smile back. He hoped she was telling the truth; but she had been coughing before the tunnel, in Sanctuary. Johnny forced the worry away, though it was like beating back a raging Beastie. A fleeting thought of Deb sick and dying came to his mind and he forced it away, for it was too terrible. He managed to put it in the back of his mind, but it stayed there, just out of the firelight of his conscious mind, biding its time.

Starbucks and Super seemed to believe her more than Johnny. Starbucks did a little jig. "Come on, what are we waiting for? Wait until you girls how we get to the Forbidden City!"

Deb frowned, but underneath she there was a smile of curiosity. “Ride?”

Johnny took her hand and pulled her towards a tall, long metal box nearby. Deb watched it warily.

Super grinned and pointed. “What is that?”

“That’s called a ‘truck’” Starbucks said, beaming with pride. “Misterwizard says it used to move and carry things. It’s where we hide our metal-beasties.”

“Metal-beasties?” Both Super and Deb in unison and looked at each other then back at the boys.

Johnny nodded, forgetting for a moment about Deb’s cough in the excitement of the moment. “Misterwizard taught us how to use them so we could get from Sanctuary to Castle fast. Misterwizard teaches us all kinds of wonderful things. He found these and fixed them up, just for us, as a present. These metal-beasties have a name. They’re called ‘Harleys.’ Wait until you ride one!”

Super giggled. “You ride them?”

“It’s like being on a bird-beastie and flying!” Starbucks said.

“What’s a bird-beastie?” Deb asked.

Johnny and Starbucks frowned, her sad question temporarily spoiling the mood.

“You’ll see, Deb. And lots of other things, too.”

The old, rusted metal box seemed to stretch on for miles. As Deb and Super watched with interest, Johnny grabbed a piece of leather attached to the back. As if by magic, the back wall rolled up with a loud rumble to expose a dark, empty interior, except for two metal objects with rubber wheels way in the back. Johnny pulled a metal ramp out that was hidden in the floor and it extended to the ground.

Deb peered into the dark interior. "Those are metal-beasties? Are they asleep?"

Johnny laughed. "They're not really alive, Deb, like real Beasties. Wait until you see them!" Johnny climbed in. Starbucks waited with the girls, grinning and enjoying their reactions as they experienced all the wonderful things he and Johnny had gotten to enjoy for a long time.

Soon Johnny appeared again, rolling one of the metal-beasties next to him. He rolled it down the ramp and Starbucks grabbed it. Then Johnny went back inside for the other one.

Deb and Super gazed at the Harley with wonder, walking around it with mouths open. "It's beautiful," Deb said, "and so big and shiny."

The Harley was black, with black fenders and the words, "Harley Davidson" on the black gas tank.

"Wow," Super said. "This is way cool. Look at the silver pipes coming out and the seats!"

"They're so big. How do you and Johnny ride them?" Deb asked.

"It's easy," Starbucks said. "Johnny's bigger than me, but once you get the hang of it, it's not that hard. You'll see once we get going."

"Which one is yours, Starbucks?" Deb asked.

Starbucks laughed. "This one. Just wait until you hear them roar!"

Johnny came out with a second one. His had a red tank, red fenders and a red cowling on front. The coolest thing about Johnny's was the front of the cowling was shaped like a skull. He hopped on the seat and held out a hand to Deb "Come on!" Hesitantly but with a smile of wonder, Deb walked over, took Johnny's hand and let him help her on. Johnny moved his sword, so it wouldn't be in the way, and as if she'd done it a thousand times, Deb laid her head on his back and put her arms around his waist.

Starbucks leapt on the other one and helped Super on behind him. Super let out a whoop of excitement. Starbucks and Johnny grinned at each other.

"Ready?" Johnny said, grinning at the girls. Deb and Super smiled, looked at each other and shrugged. Then they both nodded.

"Scrabblers, start your engines!" Starbucks yelled.

As one, Johnny and Starbucks started their Harleys. Two loud roars filled the air. Deb and Super covered their ears, big grins on their faces. Super yelled, "Their roar is loud!"

Johnny and Starbucks revved their engines, enjoying the girl's reactions. The sound echoed off the empty parking lot, off the walls of Sanctuary, and into the open air.

"Let's go, before the Gangers hear us!' Starbucks yelled over noise of the Harleys.

Johnny nodded and turned his head towards Deb. "Hold on tight." Deb nodded, closed her eyes and tightened her grip on Johnny. Johnny looked down at her hands on him, extremely pleased. Today was going to be the best day ever.

Super grabbed Starbucks. "Why didn't we bring you girls along sooner?" They took off in a roar, and Deb gave an involuntary squeak. They sped across the parking lot as the heat from the Red Eye rising in the sky washed over them like a wave. Johnny started out slow to make sure Deb got the hang of holding on, but soon sped up, enjoying the rush of wind, the feel of Deb's head on his back and her soft hands around him. He felt ten feet tall, and couldn't remember feeling so alive, or happy.

Ahead of them, the abandoned city loomed large and empty, like a concrete and steel skeleton, beckoning with untold adventures and hidden treasures. Johnny gave the Harley gas, and just like Starbucks said, it was just like flying.

CHAPTER 4

It wasn't long before the tall buildings of the city grew close and towered above them. The girls stared up at them with looks of amazement, excitement, and a little fear.

"Johnny, it's so wonderful!" Deb said. "It's like a magical land."

Johnny just smiled and kept going.

Before they reached the city, they had to cross the river, a thirty-foot wide expanse of rushing water. Every half mile or so a bridge crossed it, but many of them had crumbled and the middles of the bridges were gone. Johnny and Starbucks drove to a bridge they knew was safe. When they reached the start of the bridge, Johnny stopped his Harley. Starbucks, seeing him, stopped too.

Deb raised her head and looked down at the rushing river. "Look at all that water!"

"It's beautiful!" Super said. The boys looked at each other and grinned, thoroughly enjoying watching the girls experience it for the first time.

Johnny looked over his shoulder at Deb. "This is it. You know entering the "Forbidden City" is against the rules. If you girls go any further than this and Leader Nordstrom finds out, you will get in lots of trouble. You and your families may get kicked out of Sanctuary. You sure you don't want to turn back?"

Deb laid her head back down on Johnny's back and smiled. "Where Johnny goes, I go." Johnny looked ahead, touched, until he saw Starbucks watching him, and then he put on a tough look. "Okay but we warned you." He started off again slowly and Starbucks fell in behind him again.

The bridge rose high enough that they could see a long way into the abandoned city ahead. Clear, blue water flowed below them. Good, clean water, Johnny knew, all the water you could drink. It made only a few clicks on the Misterwizard's machine and it 'flowed,' which Misterwizard said meant it was safe.

From the bridge as far as they could see, nothing moved. It was as if they had the whole world to themselves, though Johnny knew it wasn't true. Somewhere among the ruins, Ripper and the Gangers had their hideout. The city also held Wildies, people crazy from the Sickness and from being alone all the time. There were also Beasties, lots of them. Now that the city was mostly empty, the Beasties came more and more. Some were small and made good food; others were big, with sharp teeth and appetites of their own.

Johnny thought back to a time when he was only fourteen seasons, and the first time he snuck out. It was the most wonderful day of Johnny's life, when he realized there was a world outside of Sanctuary to explore. It was also almost Johnny's last day alive, for he faced a danger worse than any Ganger or Wildie.

Back then, Johnny didn't have his Harley, and Starbucks wasn't with him, Johnny was all alone. He found the secret passage out and crawled outside on his own, and having a spirit of adventure, he naturally took off for the tall buildings on the horizon, beckoning him to come explore. It was on that day that he found Misterwizard's Castle, but before that, he ran into something else, something terrifying.

Johnny had been walking along, looking up at the tall, twisted skeletons of the buildings and peering into the old junk cars, which were mostly empty rusted old heaps. He saw a building that still had a few sheets of glass on the front with the door wide open. Johnny decided to explore inside.

He walked in the dark, cool interior to find a long hallway with a white stone floor. On either side of the hallway were stores, just like Sanctuary. Johnny's eyes lit up, for here were tons of more places to explore!

He walked in and saw a set of metal stairs, just like in Sanctuary at his dwelling place, going up to a second floor full of more stores. Johnny walked into the wide-open hall and gazed around, trying to decide which store to go in first. He finally decided the store with a shelf of what looked like toys in the front window looked most promising. It was on the second floor so Johnny walked up the metal stairs, over to the store and inside.

The store was filled with all kinds of fun things, though they were all buried in a layer of dust. Stuffed animal toys of all kinds of Beasties sat on one shelf, but most looked like the bug-beasties had been eating them, so Johnny didn't touch them. Another shelf held all kinds of gadgets with loops and handles and pieces of metal. Johnny thought how he cold spend days just trying to figure out what they all did.

Then he heard the growl. Johnny's heart leapt into his throat. Johnny was big for his age, and even at fourteen seasons was strong, but he was still just a boy and he was all alone. Fear gripped him with its icy hand. A cat-beastie was outside, and it sounded hungry!

Johnny crept over until he could see out the door. There it was, not just a cat-beastie, but a tiger-beastie! Big and lean and menacing, it paced by outside, its eyes looking bored but ready to attack at any second. It was surely hunting for food. If it saw Johnny, he was dead for sure!

Even in his fear, Johnny couldn't help but feel pleasure at seeing such a beautiful animal. Its orange and black fur shone in the darkness and its soft, big paws padded on the stone floor. Its mouth was open, and it panted, showing sharp white teeth. Johnny thought of what to do. Could the tiger-beastie smell him? Could it hear him? He suspected that if he made any sound at all, it would. How could he get out without getting eaten? Would he be trapped in the store for the rest of his life?

Johnny backed up slowly, his heart in his throat, wondering if he really should have left Sanctuary after all. If he died there at the store, no one would ever even know what happened to him. He wasn't looking where he was going, so intent on watching the door, that he backed into a shelf of boxes. With a crash, half of the boxes fell on the floor. The floor had the soft stuff on it, so the noise wasn't very loud, but would it be enough for the tiger-beastie to hear?

To Johnny's dismay, he saw the tiger-beastie come back and peer in the door. Its black eyes scanned the interior, looking intelligent and keen to see in the darkness. Johnny froze, wishing the tiger-beastie away. But it didn't go away, it walked inside!

Now what? thought Johnny. *The moment it sees me, I'm dead*! Johnny watched carefully to see which direction the tiger-beastie walked. Luckily it walked on the opposite side of the aisle Johnny stood next to, his first big break. Johnny slowly, every so slowly, crept towards the door, fear almost freezing him in place.

He was almost at the door. He turned and looked. The tiger-beastie was standing there, looking at him! Johnny ran, faster than he'd ever run in his life, out the door. He ran so fast that he ran right into the railing at the edge of the big hole in the middle of the hall. He doubled over the railing and his head and the top part of his body dangled over the edge, looking down at the hard stone ground of the first floor below.

Johnny knew he had seconds to get back up. In his mind he could feel the tiger-beastie's claws on his back already. He pulled himself back off the ledge and turned around. The tiger-beastie was running right for him!

Johnny yelled and dove. The tiger-beastie leapt at him and missed, and it went over the edge! Johnny jumped up to see it lying on the floor below. He smiled, amazed at his luck, fully expecting to be the tiger-beastie's meal. He didn't wait to find out if the tiger-beastie was dead or not. He ran away, his heart still in his throat and his stomach in knots from the fear.

Somehow Johnny made it out of that building and found his way to Misterwizard's. Johnny always wondered what happened to that tiger-beastie. He hoped it wasn't still roaming around the city, waiting to attack them. He especially hoped they wouldn't meet it now that they had the girls with them.

They reached the other side of the bridge, where the real city started. Misterwizard told Johnny that the Forbidden City had not taken a 'direk hit' from a 'nukleer bom' whatever that was but suffered only 'residooal damaj.' Misterwizard said other types of 'boms' fell, though, destroying most of the city, and there was enough 'fallout' to kill most of the people in the city, ages ago.

Johnny and Starbucks stopped for a moment next to a green sign that stood on the side of the bridge. Deb raised her head and peered up at it. "What does it say, Johnny? Misterwizard has been teaching you the ancient words, hasn't he? Can you read it?"

"Show her, Johnny," Starbucks said.

Johnny looked at the letters. It was true, Misterwizard was teaching Johnny but long words still were difficult, and Johnny still couldn't read this sign. He tried to fake it.

"It says, 'We come to—" Johnny sounded out the letters, the way Misterwizard had taught him; "pilla... dep-a."

"What's a pilladelpa?" Super asked.

"What does it mean, Johnny?" Deb asked.

"It's the name of the city," Johnny said with a superior air, "Welcom Pilladelpa."

Deb laughed. "That's a silly name."

Starbucks looked at her with a grin. "Johnny can read all kinds of weird stuff, like books and even posters on the walls. Misterwizard is teaching me too."

"Only he's so dumb it is taking Misterwizard twice as long," Johnny quipped.

"Says you," Starbucks shot back.

The four teens looked ahead at the city that sprawled out before them. Empty buildings lined the streets, covered with vines and choked with weeds. Some buildings were broken and crumbling, others nothing but piles of bricks with the outline of a shape, and some were almost totally untouched, rising up into the sky like towers. Most of the windows in the buildings were gone, making them look like empty shells. Rusted piles of steel lay about the streets, old cars, buses and trolleys, most so eaten by time and weather that they resembled nothing more than shapeless hulks. The sidewalks and streets were broken and uneven, filled with tree roots and weeds. Here and there rat-beasties scurried through the streets, along with an occasional cat-beastie or raccoon-beastie. Bird-beasties roosted on every ledge and flew from building to building, giving the city the feeling of a giant aviary.

There were also skeletons of people from before. After a hundred years many had rotted away, but there were still some in the cars and in dark places in the buildings. Sometimes when Johnny and Starbucks would be exploring, they'd come upon one that looked more gruesome than the others, and even though most of them no longer scared Johnny, that one would give Johnny a start. Johnny hoped the skeletons wouldn't scare Deb and Super too much if they saw some.

Johnny and Starbucks started again, going slow. They rode down a trash lined street, weaving between the rusted hulks, tree roots and broken pavement. The girls made excited sounds and pointed, asking questions.

Some of the buildings were nothing but twisted hulks of steel with chunks of concrete attached. But even in the ones that looked intact, Johnny had never been brave enough to go higher than the first few floors. The thought of going up to the top in one of them and being that far off the ground scared him, but thrilled him too. Someday he vowed he would go up to the top of the tallest one he could find. Then he would truly be King of the World.

Deb saw something and pointed. "Johnny, look!

In the ruins of a collapsed building a man of about thirty seasons wearing ragged clothes and with long, matted hair rummaged through a pile of trash. He mumbled to himself in an angry voice.

Deb's eyes went wide. "Johnny, is that a Wildie?"

"Yes," Johnny answered, watching the man warily.

"Are they all crazy, like Leader Nordstrom says?" Super asked.

"Most of them," Starbucks replied, "They don't have a tribe. They fight each other for food and the treasures they find."

"I feel sorry for them," Deb said; "all alone with no tribe. It must be lonely."

"Most of them are crazy, like Starbucks said, and not very friendly. We should get moving before he sees us." Johnny took off and Starbucks followed.

They drove along for a while, enjoying the sights and the clean, fresh air. "Johnny, it's so wonderful, but scary, too." Deb pointed at one of the rusted hulks they passed. "What are those, Johnny? They were all over outside Sanctuary too."

Starbucks answered with an air of superiority. "They're called 'cars.' Misterwizard says people used to ride in them, just like we're riding our Harleys."

"How could they ride in those dirty, filthy things?" Super asked.

"Well they looked a lot nicer before the Great War, I bet," Johnny said.

"What's that?" Super pointed at a long, yellow hulk.

"That's a 'bus,'" Johnny answered. "And see that over there, with the weird metal thing coming off it? That's called a 'streetcar.' It used to run on lines in the sky."

"Lines in the sky," Super said, skeptically. "Are you sure you're not making all this up to impress us?"

Johnny shrugged. "Don't believe me if you don't want."

"I believe you, Johnny," Deb asked, resting her head back on Johnny's back. "Misterwizard has taught you lots of things, hasn't he?"

"He'll teach you, too, Deb. All kinds of wonderful things."

A raccoon-beastie peered at them from the second story of a building. It held some kind of vegetable in its paws. Johnny saw a group of Wildies a few blocks away, fighting over a blanket. He drove a little faster.

Super asked, "Are we going to Misterwizard's place first, or are you going to take us exploring?"

Starbucks looked at Johnny, to see what he thought.

"Let's go to Misterwizard's first," Johnny said. "I want you to see Castle!"

"I've only seen Misterwizard a few times," Super said. "Only when he comes to Sanctuary to help someone who is sick or delivers a wriggler. I can't wait!"

"How far to Wizard's, Johnny?" Deb asked.

"Not far," he answered. "Look!" Johnny pointed to

one of the buildings still standing in the near distance, a huge white building that stood above the rubble. A single square tower rose from its center into the sky, and on top of it was golden metal dome with a stick. The stick had a smaller stick near the top crossways. "There it is!"

Both Deb and Super stared with wonder, mouths open. "It's beautiful!" Deb said. "Johnny, why did I wait so long to let you take me outside? I never want to go back. I want to stay out here forever."

"Me, too!" Super said.

Johnny frowned, sad. "I wish we could. Sanctuary is nothing but a rotten, dark, tomb. But the tribe refuses to listen, they're too afraid."

Deb looked serious. "We have to convince Leader Nordstrom."

"Good luck with that," Starbucks said. "He's even more stubborn than Johnny."

Suddenly Johnny heard something that made his heart leap into his throat, for he instantly recognized it. It was a low, deep growl from behind a nearby building.

Starbucks heard it too. "Oh, oh, we got trouble. Barkers!"

"Barkers?" Super asked. "Are they Beasties?"

"Yes," Johnny said. "Dog-beasties. Some are nice, but the ones that run in packs are not."

From behind the building the first one padded out. Its gleaming eyes shone with hunger. Its lip curled, showing sharp fangs. It was thin, its rib bones showing, and its fur was matted and dirty. It was a huge with black curly fur.

Soon another came up behind it, a shorter one, and another, shorter but thick and strong looking. Then two more came out. They scanned the horizon, and then they spotted the teens.

Deb raised her head and looked towards the sound. "What do we do, Johnny?"

"We ride, fast!" Johnny replied. He gunned the engine and took off towards the Misterwizard's castle, Starbucks right behind him. Deb almost fell off, and Johnny had to grab her and hold her on.

The Barkers yelped with excitement and took off in pursuit, barking and snarling with excited hunger. Because of how big the Harleys were, Johnny only being fifteen and his attempt to go fast, he had trouble driving around all the rusted cars in the street and slowed down. Starbucks had the same trouble. Johnny knew if they didn't put some distance between them and the Barkers soon, the hungry Beasties would be on them.

They came to a tall building, with a roof different than the rest, full of weird rounded yellow shapes. The outside of the building was covered with glass. Johnny rode up the steps, jarring and bouncing himself and Deb, who almost lost her grip but held on. Starbucks followed. Johnny drove through the huge open doors of the building. As they entered the dark, cool interior they were instantly plunged into darkness.

Johnny chose the building because he'd been in it before and knew his way around, even though he didn't like to go in it much; it was full of weird things and it smelled. It had a real long name that ended with M-U-S-E-U-M. Johnny had no idea what the word meant.

"Johnny! I can't see!" Starbucks yelled. "They're right behind us!" Starbucks' Harley slipped on the dusty floor and he went down in a heap. Johnny turned to see what happened and ran into a tall, white column. It stopped him and made the engine shut off.

The Barkers reached the door and stopped, sniffing, looking for a trap, but they didn't hesitate long before taking off in pursuit again. Their eyes could see better in the dark, and they ran swiftly through the dusty interior.

"Hurry! Run!" Johnny grabbed Deb's hand, and with the other one grabbed Starbucks' coat and dragged him up. Starbucks grabbed Super and all four ran off into the dark as fast as they could.

Dark shapes layered in dust filled the interior, and the dust made it hard to breathe. Johnny knew from looking at the shapes up close that they were people made of white stone that never moved. The walls held huge paintings, but they were so faded and peeled that he couldn't even tell what was on most of them. In the center of the room stood the giant sticks of some weird Beastie that existed before the Great War. It was as big as a house and Johnny was glad he'd never met whatever it was, for it looked fierce, with teeth as long as Johnny's arm.

Johnny led Deb and Starbucks into a second room. It was full of glass cases and phony men frozen in place wearing strange furs from some kind of Beastie. Some of their faces were half gone, rotted from age. Some of their clothes had mold growing on it. Johnny didn't stop, for not only did this room make Johnny's skin crawl, he could tell the Barkers were not far behind, for he heard their barking. They entered another room full of frozen Beasties and plastic vines. The words on the wall said, "A-F-R-I-C-A."

A Barker grew close and leapt at Johnny. Deb

screamed. Johnny turned and swung his sword and the Barker yelped as the big knife found its mark. Blood splattered on a glass display case and the Barker fell to the floor. It rose up and limped away, its front leg bleeding.

But now the others had arrived. They surrounded the teens. Deb strained to see in the dark. "Johnny, we're trapped!"

"No, we're not!" Johnny smashed the glass of one of the cases with his sword and it shattered. He pulled Deb inside the display case and Starbucks and Super followed. They stood next to two mangy lion-beasties, half-eaten by bug-beasties, their phony snarls looking sad and pathetic. Johnny picked up one of the lion-beasties and threw it outside the case. The Barkers dove for it, growling and snapping their jaws.

"Run!" Johnny pulled Deb out of the case and made for the door with Starbucks and Super right behind them. The Barkers reached the lion and began biting it, but soon realized quickly that it was too old and rotten to eat. They turned to pursue, but Johnny's trick had worked. The teens reached the door while the Barkers were still half a room away.

Johnny pulled the door shut, trapping the dog-beasties inside.

"Yahoo! We beat 'em!" Starbucks yelled, and hugged Super, who jumped with joy.

Deb gazed at Johnny with admiration. "You did it, Johnny! I thought we were goners. You are the bravest man I know."

Her words filled Johnny with joy and pride. He puffed out his chest and tried to look nonchalant, but his face colored again. He decided to quickly change the subject.

"We have to hurry. The Barkers will find the other door out soon and be here."

"Back to the Harleys, quick!" Starbucks yelled with glee. He ran back for his bike.

Deb grabbed Johnny's hand. Johnny looked in her eyes and saw something that made his insides feel like they were turning to jelly. Strange emotions tumbled around and mixed together inside him. He didn't want to stop staring into her eyes, but he forced himself to look away. He realized he was still holding Deb's hand. He didn't want to let go. And she didn't take her hand back. He pretended not to notice and started pulling her along again.

They reached the Harleys and Johnny had to let go of hand as she climbed on, but his disappointment was quickly replaced with happiness as she put her arms around him and laid her head down on his back again. Johnny realized that he had never loved anyone the way he loved Deb; that he would die for her a thousand times, if only she promised never to look at anyone but him.

Starbucks picked up his Harley, helped Super on and started its engine.

Johnny started his Harley, and he was about to give it gas, when from behind him, Deb spoke in a throaty voice that made Johnny's insides melt like ice cream left out in under the Red Eye. "I love you Johnny. I will be Johnny's, forever."

A lump suddenly appeared in Johnny's throat. He tried to fix his voice before he spoke, so she wouldn't know what he was feeling, but finally gave up, for it was a lost cause. "I guess Johnny loves Deb, too. But don't go getting all mushy-mushy." Deb squeezed her arms tighter around Johnny, and he found it hard to breathe, but not because her arms were too tight.

The rode out the doors and back down the steps and soon the Barkers were forgotten. As they rode along Johnny and Starbucks started pointing out shops they'd been in to the girls, telling them about their adventures and some of the crazy things they'd found. The girls listened eagerly, eyes wide with excitement, asking questions or making comments as they went. Johnny felt like a king showing his queen his domain.

Deb coughed again. It was a hard, thick sounding cough. And then she coughed again. Johnny's heart stopped for a second, then beat faster. He looked at her over his shoulder. Deb saw his expression and smiled. "Johnny worries too much, just dusty in that old place."

Johnny nodded and turned around again, but a cold dread enveloped him. Deb was coughing too much. It wasn't the dust; something was wrong. The memories of people in the tribe getting sick and dying came to him, and he tried to push them away. Sometimes people were forced to leave Sanctuary, out of fear they would infect others. *Why,* Johnny thought, *on this day of such joy and fun, did Deb have to cough?* For Johnny it put a darkness and sadness on the whole adventure. He tried to believe she was okay but kept it in the back of his mind. He would have to ask Misterwizard about it.

With a sense of relief Johnny saw that they had finally reached Misterwizard's castle. Large steel fences surrounded it, adorned with old skulls and dead animals. Misterwizard lived alone in the abandoned city and so he had to defend himself against the Gangers and the Wildies. Luckily, many of them were simple minded or superstitious. The skulls and dead animals scared most of them away. Barbed wire also covered most of the fence, with bits of clothing and fur where Wildies and Beasties had tried to climb in and found out the hard way it wasn't a good idea.

Despite his worry for Deb, excitement and happiness filled Johnny, for visiting Misterwizard was the greatest pleasure in Johnny's life. Not only was Misterwizard Johnny's best friend, but his castle was filled with strange and wonderful things from the time before the Great War, and Misterwizard was always showing Johnny and Starbucks something new.

Deb stared up at the castle, her mouth open with wonder. "It's beautiful, Johnny. Are you sure he won't be mad at us coming?"

Johnny grinned. "Don't be silly. Misterwizard is the nicest man in the whole world, and Johnny and Starbucks' friend. Wait until you see inside, Deb."

Johnny and Starbucks stopped the Harleys and all four got off. Johnny led them to the secret gate that only he and Starbucks knew about. On one spot on the fence, a picture of a funny looking black mouse with red shorts and big white shoes concealed a latch. Johnny found the picture and lifted it up. As he pulled the latch, a small section of the gate popped open. He led her inside and Starbucks and Super followed. Then Johnny closed the gate again, and it locked with a clicking sound.

Johnny and Starbucks led the girls to a strange opening into the building. It was round, surrounded by glass and with one opening into it in the front.

"What it that, Johnny?" Deb asked, looking at it warily.

"Misterwizard calls it a 'revolving door.' It's magical. Come inside, and I'll show you."

"Are you sure it won't eat us?" Super said.

"Don't be silly," Starbucks said. "It's not alive."

Johnny led Deb and the others through the opening into the revolving door.

"Now watch." Johnny pushed on the glass of one of the plates inside the glass circle and it began to move. The girls stared, mouths wide open, as Johnny and Starbucks walked into the open space between the glass panels. Johnny held his hand out to Deb, who tentatively walked inside. Starbucks motioned for Super to join him, but she shook her head. Starbucks rolled his eyes and grabbed her hand. He pulled her inside as she squeaked.

Laughing, Johnny and Starbucks pushed on the glass panel in front of them. "Start walking!" Johnny said. The panels started to move. The girls saw the glass panel behind them start to come towards them and they hurriedly started walking. As if by magic, the panel in front of them moved and suddenly they were inside the building.

"That was fun!" Super said. "Can we do it some more?"

"Maybe later, but there's too much other fun stuff to see." Starbucks crowed. "You're about to see things you never even imagined."

CHAPTER 5

A cool breeze wafted over them from the dark interior. They entered a small room, only five feet across and twenty feet long. It was empty except for two paintings on the wall and two figures, one painting and one figure on either side of an archway that led into a much larger room beyond.

The paintings always fascinated and terrified Johnny, for they were very strange. One showed a man falling as he was being eaten by a frightening looking bird-beastie. Misterwizard said the painting had a name. It was "Prometheus Bound," whatever that meant. Johnny just knew it scared him.

The other painting was just as strange. It had lots of people in it, all without clothes and all looking like they were drowning in a giant pool of water. Little people with wings flew in the air, and there was even a Beastie

Misterwizard called a "cow" in the water. Misterwizard said this painting was called, "The Abduction of Europa." It scared Johnny too, but there was something magical and beautiful about it too.

The figures were made of metal and stood on wooden pedestals.

"What are those?" Super asked pointing at the metal figures. "They look scary."

"They're called 'suits of armor,'" Starbucks said. "People wore them for clothes when they protected fair maidens in the days before the Great War."

"People did so many strange things back then," Deb said. Johnny and Starbucks laughed.

"They're made of metal," Johnny said. "Misterwizard let me try one on once. They're super heavy. I couldn't even move."

"Look at those paintings, Johnny!" Deb said, her eyes wide. "They're not faded and rotted, like the ones in Sanctuary. They're beautiful!'

Johnny nodded, somehow disappointed that she wasn't as scared of them as he'd been.

They walked through the doorway into the larger room. This room was so large the other side looked like it was a long way away. It had wooden floors filled with strange, beautiful and fascinating objects.

Display cases full of swords, ribbons and strange objects filled the room. Colorful paintings filled the walls. One had three women with no clothes on in it. Super looked at it and giggled. Another had just a display of yellow flowers in a vase.

More dead Beasties stood around the room, but these were not rotted or moldy, in fact they looked like they could come to life at any moment and attack them.

The four teens walked slowly through the room gazing at the objects and sights they saw.

Deb pointed at a gleaming metal object in the middle of the floor and asked, "Johnny, is that a 'car'?"

The teens gathered around the object. It was shiny and bright, a bright red color with black tires. There wasn't a spot of dust on it.

"Yes. It's what they looked like before they got bad."

"No wonder people rode in them," Deb said. "They're beautiful."

"This one is called a 'corvette,'" Starbucks said. "Misterwizard has a whole collection of them in here, all different shapes and sizes. But they're all super wonderful to look at."

"Does Misterwizard ever drive them?" Super asked.

"I don't think so," Johnny said. "He just rubs them with a cloth and sits in them."

The teens walked on. They came to a door that said "Choir Room" on it.

"Is that the way to where Misterwizard is?"

"Yes, he lives on the very top floor."

"And you're sure he won't mind us coming?" Deb asked.

"Of course not. I bet he's going to be happy when he sees we brought you girls along. Come on, we have to through that door and then walk up for a long way. "

Johnny took Deb's hand and led to the door as Starbucks and Super followed.

"On to Misterwizard!" Starbucks cheered.

As they passed through the door to the staircase, Deb, who was holding Johnny's hand, stopped and peered up at the stairs leading up into what looked like impenetrable darkness. "It's so dark, Johnny. Don't we need a torch?"

"Sorry, Deb," Johnny said, "I forgot you and Super have never been here before. Starbucks and me are used to the stairs," Johnny said. "I know it's dark, but there's nothing to be afraid of. There's nothing here, just stairs, lots of 'em. I'll hold your hand, you'll be all right."

Deb and Super both looked nervous, but let Johnny and Starbucks lead them as they started climbing. Soon they were totally enveloped by the darkness.

"I can't see my hand," Super said.

"Hold the rail," Starbucks said.

"It's cool here," Deb said. And then she coughed, just once. In the dark, Johnny squinted at her, trying to see her in the dark, but he couldn't. "How far do we have to go, Johnny?"

"A long way. Misterwizard's place is at the very top. But it won't take us long."

"Pretty soon, you'll be glad it's nice and cool, long before we get to the top," Starbucks said with a laugh.

"Johnny, it's been a long time since I saw Misterwizard too. The last time seemed so long ago," Deb said. "When Fuego had the Sickness, remember? Last year during the hot months. He started shaking and nobody would go near him. They made him live on the far end of Sanctuary, and finally Fuego had to leave."

"I remember," Johnny said, his mind thinking about Deb's cough again.

"I was sad when Fuego had to leave," Super said, her voice somber in the darkness. "I wonder what happened to him."

"Probably died, get eaten by Beasties or got killed by Wildies," Starbucks said. Starbucks felt a punch on his arm. He yelled and peered in the dark, wondering why Johnny hit him.

"How much longer, Johnny? This darkness, it feels like it's alive, like it's touching me." Suddenly as if by magic at the sound of Deb's words, the stairway filled with light. They all stopped and stood still, blinking in amazement and happiness. They looked at each other with big grins.

"What happened, Johnny?" Deb asked.

"I don't know! Misterwizard must have done it."

"Johnny," Super said, her mouth open with wonder, "there are no torches. Look, just little round circles on a string!"

The teens stared at the lights with wonder. "I told you Misterwizard was magical," Johnny said in a hushed whisper.

"Maybe we should turn back, Johnny," Deb said, looking fearfully up the stairs.

"Don't be silly. Come on!" Johnny pulled Deb and started walking quickly up the stairs. She laughed and tried to keep up. Starbucks and Super followed right behind them.

They finally reached the top and a door marked, "Choir Room." They all stopped for a second. Johnny began to move again, but Deb didn't move, and Johnny had to stop. He turned and looked at her. She stared at the door, looking frightened.

"Don't be afraid, Deb," Johnny said. "Misterwizard is wonderful. Just wait until you meet him again!"

Finally, Deb let Johnny pull her forward. Johnny

opened the door to Misterwizard's home.

They peered into the room from the doorway, four heads peeking out, eyes wide open. Strange sounds assailed them, buzzing noises and beeping, and something whirring. Smells filled their noses as well, strange but wonderful smells, and some not so nice, that made their noses wrinkle. Somewhere in the room, they also heard humming. Misterwizard!

They tiptoed into the room, looking about. A rich red carpet covered the floor, elegant with dragons and knights portrayed on it. Every wall was lined with tables, each holding strange objects or glass cases. The walls held beautiful paintings, cloth banners in bright colors, and glass displays with swords or busts of people in them.

They crept into the room further, and even Johnny and Starbucks seemed a little frightened. They passed a cage with a beautifully colored bird-beastie in it. It squawked loudly, ruffled its feathers and tilted its head. Then it said in a voice just like a person, "Pieces of eight! Pieces of eight!"

"Johnny!" Deb said, her mouth open with amazement. "That bird-beastie spoke words!"

"I told you Misterwizard knew magic," Johnny said boastfully.

"I think we should go now," Super said, pulling back.

"Don't be a scaredy," Starbucks said. "You haven't seen nothing yet!"

They walked on, and suddenly saw a pot on a stove with something bubbling in it. Whatever it was smelled delicious. They came to an elegant dark wooden table with high-backed chairs with velvet seats. On the table there was a table setting for one.

"Misterwizard! Hello, Misterwizard!" Johnny called out.

"Shhh, Johnny!" Deb whispered. Johnny chuckled.

"Hello, Misterwizard, come meet our chicken-beastie girlfriends!"

Johnny and Starbucks laughed, and the girls looked annoyed.

Suddenly from around a corner Misterwizard appeared. Misterwizard was short, only five feet two inches tall, with a round boxy shape and a round, bald head. He also had a short white beard, bushy white eyebrows and a big nose. He reminded Johnny of an old picture Misterwizard had on the wall of a little funny yellow creature Misterwizard called a "minion." He typically wore funny shirts with flowers or seashells on them, shorts and shoes with no fronts Misterwizard called "sandals." At this moment, Misterwizard wore a white lab coat and a strange pair of green goggles. Misterwizard peered at them. In one hand he held a glass beaker and in the other he held a long, glass rod.

Even though he'd been at Misterwizard's Castle a dozen times, Johnny was nervous for some reason. He grinned lopsidedly. "Hi Misterwizard!"

Misterwizard raised his goggles to reveal intense but smiling brown eyes. Misterwizard grinned hugely and spread his short arms out. "Johnny! Salutations and solicitations, my brave and stalwart adventurer! How indescribably gratifying it is to have you arrive at this precise and monumental moment!"

Johnny just nodded. Usually half the words Misterwizard said Johnny didn't understand, so he'd learned simply to nod and smile. He was able to make out enough of what Misterwizard said to know what he meant most of the time, and Johnny liked trying to learn new words.

Deb wasn't used to it, though. "What did he say?" she asked.

Misterwizard saw Starbucks and the girls for the first time, and his smile grew twice as large. "Ye-gats! How amazingly splendiferous! You've not come alone or simply with your stalwart companion Starbucks, but have brought two fair maidens with you, charming and beguiling members of the fairer sex! How utterly delightful!"

Super giggled. "You talk funny!"

Misterwizard walked closer, the smile still radiating from his face. "If I'm not mistaken, you are the lovely and mischievous Supercalifraglisticexpialadocious!"

The teens laughed. "That's me, all right," Super said. "But nobody can say that name you gave me, so they only call me Super."

Super fidgeted with her hands and looked nervous. "I've always wondered, I mean, Misterwizard can you tell me—"

"What your name means?"

Super nodded.

"Not at all." Misterwizard walked up to stand in front of her. "It is a magical name. It means you are super and fragile, and listic and espially and docious. Put together, it simply means you are special and unique, a young woman who will one day do amazing things."

Super smiled, flushing with embarrassment and nodded, though she still had no clue what her name meant.

"Just like Johnny's name. Johnny Apocalypse. His name is the symbol of the new world coming, as we move out of the shadows of destruction left by mankind's foolishness into what I hope is a new era of peace and hope.

"And you," Misterwizard said, turning to Deb, "are, unless my memory fails me, are Little Debbie, the sweet little progeny of your father, Thegap, and Bathanbodyworks, your kind and somewhat unattractive mother."

"Yes, Your Wizardness," Deb said, bowing slightly, though she didn't know why.

"Well, well, well, welcome dear friends, to the humble abode of the man your tribe has given the unlikely moniker of Misterwizard. I am no wizard, but I am, technically a mister. I know some things, but have no magical power, or at least none that I'm cognizant of. I am so overjoyed that you made the arduous journey to visit me. I am both honored and flattered."

"Misterwizard," Johnny asked, "why did you say this was a special moment?"

Misterwizard pointed to the ceiling and around at the electric lights. "You have arrived at precisely the moment when I rediscovered the scientific principle of electricity. I've been researching it for quite a spell but couldn't figure out how to make it a reality. And then I read about something called a 'generator,' that runs on fossil fuel instead of a turbine engine powered by wind or the movement of water through a dam. And low and behold, here we are!"

Johnny nodded, frowning, sorry he asked.

Starbucks said, "Something smells good, Misterwizard. Are you making something?"

Misterwizard grinned impishly "I most certainly am, a delicacy that I'm sure you fine Sanctuary dwellers have never had the pleasure of sampling before. But now you shall! I am so happy to have someone to share my simple repast with. The food is called, 'Spaghetti," Starbucks, and I endeavor to say you will find it quite a treat. It is made with wheat I grew in my very own garden, spices I managed to fabricate from old recipes, and meat of a hapless deer-beastie who lingered too long while attempting to eat my roses."

The teens grinned at each other with eager anticipation.

Then Deb saw something in the corner, something beautiful and amazing. "Misterwizard, may I ask you what that is?"

Misterwizard looked to the corner to see what she was looking at. There in the corner stood a tall black wooden chair in front of a strange set of keys set in a half circle. Behind the keys, long, tall silver pipes reached up to the sky.

Misterwizard smiled at Deb and his eyes twinkled. "That, my dear Deb, is my most cherished possession. It is called a 'Pipe Organ.' I carried it here piece by piece from Saint Peter's Cathedral almost a half mile away. It took many an arduous trip to retrieve all of it, but it was most sincerely worth every muscle ache and drop of perspiration."

Misterwizard and the teens walked over to stand in front of it. "What does it do, Misterwizard?"

"Do? It makes melodious melodies, dear little girl, wonderful, joyous sounds to lift spirits to the skies above. Attend, and I will demonstrate!"

Misterwizard sat in front of the organ. He pushed a petal on the floor and placed his fingers over some keys. Then he grinned at the teens, who watched with rapt attention.

Suddenly the air filled with beautiful, amazing sounds that seemed to shake their bones and rattle their teeth but fill them with pleasure at the same time. It made Johnny feel the way he did when he stared up at the night sky and watched the stars, or when he gazed into Deb's eyes.

All four of the teens grinned at each other as Misterwizard continued to play beautiful music. Finally, he stopped, and all four teens clapped.

"I've never heard anything so beautiful!" Deb said.

Misterwizard grinned, very pleased. "Thank you, my dear. I'm so pleased it met with your approval."

Misterwizard stood up. "But, let's head to the dinner table and begin our feast. I can't wait until you sample my spaghetti sauce. It is from tomatoes I grew myself as well."

Misterwizard led the teens to the table and had them sit down. He placed dishes and silverware in front of them and began preparing the spaghetti. As he did, the teens continued to ask him questions.

Deb gazed around at the room, her eyes wide. 'It's so wonderful out here, Misterwizard. Johnny always told me it was, and how much fun he had, but until now I was too afraid to join him. I'm glad I finally did."

Misterwizard heaped spaghetti on each of their plates. "I'm so glad you overcame your trepidation, Deb. The world is no longer a place to be feared, for as I've told Johnny, the radiation's half-life is now to the point where normal life can once again resume, except in certain isolated areas where the bombs actually impacted the surface."

"What happened, Misterwizard? To the Old World?"

Super asked. "Some in the tribe say huge monsters roamed the Earth eating everyone."

Misterwizard chuckled and went to get the sauce. "What you're relating to me is a perfect example of how ignorance and fear breed strange traditions. No, my dear, radiation was not a monster. It is simply a physical reaction caused by the intentional combination of certain elements together that then react violently. It actually occurs naturally, though not in the degree that caused the Great War. And over time, its effect lessens as the reaction runs its course."

"I'm sorry I asked," Super said.

Misterwizard laughed. "In plain terms, the people before created the bombs. Those bombs killed everyone in a certain area and left what are called 'radiation' and 'contamination' in a much larger area. The effects of the radiation are the cause of the birth defects, and what your tribe calls the Sickness. But as I've told Johnny, it has been one hundred years since the bombs fell, and the world is slowly returning to normal. It is relatively safe to venture outside now, and even safe to eat the plants and animals."

Super asked, "So why did they drop the bombs, Misterwizard? What made them do such a terrible thing?"

"You see, dear children, back before the Great War, the tribes were much bigger, and they were called 'countries.' Unfortunately, all the countries were not led by men of good character, though some were. Those countries with evil leaders wanted to take what other countries had, and many simply refused to trust their neighbors. It came down to a time when peaceful men could no longer prevail, and evil men attempted to force their will on others.

"The President of this country known as the United States, was not a good man either, though the country itself was the greatest and most democratic in the world. From what I understand, when the bombs began to fall, he seized power and tried to change the country from a democracy into a dictatorship. It is thought that our own leader was the cause of the beginning of the destruction, a sad story to have to tell.

"The Great War was caused by men fighting for freedom from other men bent on destroying any who opposed them, one of those men our own President. And the whole world paid the price. Eventually every country became involved. When it was all over, there was no countries left, only what we have now, no law or order, only the strong taking what they want from the weak. That's why the world needs a Leader Nordstrom now to bring us back to civilization." As Misterwizard said this last, he glanced at Johnny meaningfully, but Johnny didn't notice.

There was a moment of silence as the teens thought about what Misterwizard said. Then Johnny said, "I think Leader Nordstrom is like those evil men. He refuses to listen to anyone. I think it's because he has the power and doesn't want to lose it."

"If we could only convince Leader Nordstrom to listen to you," Starbucks said, "the whole tribe could come with us."

"He is a seemingly insoluble conundrum, indeed," Misterwizard said. "A man of resolute resistance to change, and I fear a man frightened of it. But let us talk of more pleasant things, sealing wax and dragon's wings. It's time to eat!"

The teens each picked up a fork and looked at their food. None of them had ever eaten spaghetti before. Johnny dug his spoon in and lifted it up, only to watch with confusion as the noodles fell back down, leaving only sauce on his fork. The other teens were having trouble as well.

Misterwizard watched them with eyes twinkling in amusement. He lifted up his fork and looked at them. "Watch, and I'll show you how it's done." Misterwizard dug his fork in and spun it around, looping the noodles around it. Then he lifted it up and took a bite. He sucked the spaghetti in his mouth with a big slurp, and the noodles disappeared. The teens all laughed and then imitated him. Soon they had the hang of it.

"This is wonderful!" Super said. "It's amazing!"

"I've never tasted anything so wonderful!" Deb said, as she stabbed a meatball and popped it in her mouth.

Johnny looked at her, feeling bad, thinking how she and the rest of the Tribe had to consist on rotten vegetables and meat in Sanctuary. He vowed to himself that he would find a way to get them all out, where they could all enjoy spaghetti.

He tried to put his dark thoughts aside and enjoy the meal. "Mmmm," Johnny said, slurping noodles into his mouth and getting spaghetti sauce on his cheek. "Wow, we have to come here and eat with you more often, Wizard!" Starbucks said.

Misterwizard smiled, imminently pleased. "I'm overjoyed you're finding it satisfactory. My garden grows in the sun in the courtyard, unlike the scrawny patch you have in Sanctuary that only gets sun through the skylight. It also has the benefit of good deer meat and fresh pasta made from wheat."

Misterwizard and the teens continued to make small talk as they finished their meal. Then when they were done, they all stood up.

"Don't worry about the dishes, I'll take care of them later. Girls please feel free to explore my domicile to your heart's content. I'll be glad to tell you about anything you see here. It all has a purpose, or should I say, had, at one time."

Deb and Super squealed with joy and took off to explore. Soon they were looking at the displays and gazing at the paintings throughout Misterwizard's home.

CHAPTER 6

Misterwizard motioned to Johnny. "Come Johnny, I have something to show you. You too, Starbucks." Johnny and Starbucks followed Misterwizard as he walked over to a large chest of drawers by the bed.

Misterwizard led Johnny and Starbucks to a big, black square object on the floor with black tubes sticking out of it and running across the floor. Wizard's picked up a can filled with something that had a strong odor.

"Look at it, Johnny? Do you know what it is?"

Johnny glanced at Starbucks and then said, "No, Misterwizard."

Misterwizard grinned. "This is the 'generator.' It runs on the same substance as your Harleys, and my Moped. Now we can have electricity, Johnny. No more living in the Middle Ages!"

"Generator," Johnny parroted. "Electricity."

"That's right! Electric lights! Convection heat! Television and internet! Then it's back to the exploration of outer space!"

"So that's what happened on the stairs coming up!" Starbucks said.

"Why, yes. You must have been coming up the stairs just as I turned the lights on for the first time. And now that I have electricity, let me show you something else."

Misterwizard hurried over to another side of the room, and Johnny and Starbucks followed. Deb and Super joined them, eager to see what he was going to show them. This time Misterwizard stopped at a table in the corner on which sat a funny box with a round black disk in the middle and one arm that rested on stick. Johnny and Deb hurried over, eager to see what was going to happen next.

Wires from the noisy machine ran to another flat thing on the floor. From that thing other wires ran out and around the room. One ran to the strange box.

"Are you ready?" Misterwizard winked at them. Johnny held his breath, for he knew something special was about to happen.

Misterwizard flipped a little switch on the box, and the black disc began spinning! Misterwizard's eyes twinkled with joy as he raised the little arm and placed it on the spinning black disc.

Sound came out of the box! Beautiful sound, not as nice as the pipe organ, a little tinny, but still wonderful. The teens smiled at each other with wonder as the Misterwizard closed his eyes, reveling in the sound.

Then a man started singing!

"She loves the theatre, but never arrives late. She gets too hungry for dinner at eight. She but always arrives on time. That's why the Lady is a Tramp."

Johnny looked around for him, but there was no one there! He pulled out his knife, ready to fight the strange man singing, but Misterwizard put a hand on Johnny's arm.

"Have no fear, Johnny. There is no intruder on the premises. It's only a man's voice, on the record!"

The girls ran over and looked at the box too, eyes wide with amazement.

Johnny stared at the 'record.' What powerful magic! It made Johnny's head spin, trying to understand how it worked.

"It's something else, Misterwizard!" Starbucks said.

"Where is the man? Why can't we see him?" Super asked.

"I'm afraid the man is long deceased, dear Super. But his voice lives on, saved for posterity."

"Johnny, it's wonderful. " Deb's said, having the best time of her life.

Misterwizard picked up another black disc and blew on it, removing a layer of dust. Then he studied its label. "This is just the beginning, my dear friends. With Leader Nordstrom's acquiescence, we will soon have the lights working in the Shopping Mall again. No more need for those filthy old torches. And then we can get the furnace going. No more crowding around fire-pits to stay warm. We'll have to forage for fuel for the generator, but we're inching closer to modern living again!"

Suddenly Deb covered her mouth with her hand and coughed. The rest all looked at her. She looked back and smiled sheepishly.

Johnny looked at Misterwizard to see him frowning, just like Johnny was. Johnny was right to be afraid, for even Misterwizard seemed worried.

Deb smiled, trying to act as if nothing was wrong. “It’s all so wonderful, Misterwizard. I’m so glad we came.”

Misterwizard smiled, but the concern didn’t leave his eyes. “Thank you Dear.”

Misterwizard put down the disc and turned to Johnny. “How are your alphabet studies going, Johnny? And you as well, Starbucks.”

The ‘alphabet’ was a strange series of things called ‘letter’s Misterwizard was trying to get Johnny and Starbucks to learn. Misterwizard said they were the key to reading the strange things on the buildings and in the ‘book’s. Johnny tried hard to learn the ‘alphabet,’ even though it seemed a waste of time. He knew he tried harder than Starbucks, who called it silly.

“Have you finished “Finger, Finger, Toes Thumb?” Misterwizard inquired.

Johnny puffed out his chest and said proudly, “I read the first page.” Johnny had sounded out the letters on the first page. Putting them together was still a little hard.

“Finger, Finger, Toes Thumb” was a ‘book’ Misterwizard had given Johnny. It was tattered and some of the pages were torn. One of the pages had green mold on it and the picture had turned to mush, but it was still one of Johnny’s most prized possessions, for it was his first ‘book.’ It had funny pictures of creatures Misterwizard called ‘monkey’s’ in it. They were hairy and had funny faces.

“You have to learn to say the sound that goes along with each of the letters, Johnny, and then put them together. I’ll work with you some more today on it, if you like. But right now, let's add some more lights to the room, shall we?"

Misterwizard was off again to another corner, and once again the teens followed, reluctantly though, because it was hard to leave the magical spinning disc and the man singing.

When they reached the corner, they saw Misterwizard fiddling with a glass ball he was trying to twist into a hole on a long, black pole that stood on a stand.

"It's a lot harder than you think, finding a light bulb that isn't broken!" Misterwizard chuckled. "Mustn't twist too tightly. It's a long journey to a store for another one."

Misterwizard finished tightening the 'light bulb.' He walked over to the side of the long pole and grinned with a twinkle of mischief at them. "Ready? Here goes nothing!"

Misterwizard flicked a small switch on the side and suddenly, brightness like the sun sprang from the 'light bulb'! The teens "Oohed" and Aahed" and stared at it, amazed. It hurt their eyes. Deb shielded hers and looked scared. She felt heat coming from the light bulb.

"It's hot!" Deb said. "Is it going to burn us?"

Johnny walked over to her and put an arm around her. "Don't be afraid, Deb. Misterwizard's magic is always good magic. It won't hurt you."

Deb smiled, no longer afraid. "We should be getting back, Johnny, before they really know we're gone."

Deb was right; no matter how much Johnny hated to leave, if they didn't return soon everyone would notice. Then Leader Nordstrom would be very angry. Johnny didn't want to get Deb or Super in trouble or their families. He nodded and took her hand. He turned to say goodbye to Misterwizard.

A rock crashed through the window! The glass shattered with a loud sound and shards flew through the air. Deb screamed, and Johnny quickly covered her with his body to protect her from getting cut.

Misterwizard's face contorted with anger. "It's those ruffians again. Low intellect, testosterone driven thugs with no morals or common sense." He wagged an angry finger towards the rock throwers outside in judgment. "Louts like you are the ones that brought this world to its knees!"

From outside came a familiar voice that Johnny hated. It was Ripper. That meant the Gangers were all there too.

"Hey! Old Man! You still alive in there? Or did you finally do us all a favor and die?" Loud snickering and laughter followed Ripper's words.

Rage filled Johnny's heart. He put his hand on his sword and thought of Deb. They should be safe inside Misterwizard's palace, he thought, unless Ripper had found a way in through the hurtful wire.

Misterwizard seemed to read Johnny's thoughts. He put a hand on Johnny's shoulder. "Don't be apprehensive about our safety, young friend. My castle is fortified and impregnable. The delinquent denizens gather below to taunt me once a day. What else do they have to do? I'm a curious incongruity to them in their otherwise simple and understandable existence. Their inferior minds can't comprehend what I am, so they disparage me in order to counterbalance their own fear. It's the way of simpletons and fools."

Misterwizard walked over and stood on a stool so that he could see out the window and his tormentors. "Yes, I'm still here, you scurrilous scalawags. Now go find some hapless animal to torture or some other mindless cruelty to occupy yourselves, thank you."

Johnny climbed on another stool and looked out a different window but was careful not to expose himself. Deb stood below them, looking up nervously.

Ripper stood outside the barbed wire with the whole gang. Wearing ragged clothes made of animal skins and covered in filth, the Gangers made Johnny's stomach turn just to look at them. Their hair was dirty and tangled. There was dried blood on their skin and faces.

Ripper was the only one who looked different. His dark black hair was slicked down. He wore a black leather vest and black leather pants, like Johnny's, but his had skulls and monsters on them. He wore a gold chain around his neck and gold rings on his fingers. He held a club with nails stuck in it in one hand drooped over his shoulder. He wore the same cruel cocky grin he always wore, the one that said he wanted to kill or torture something. Just seeing him made Johnny's blood boil.

"Did you think about what we said, Old Man?"

Johnny looked at Misterwizard. "What did they say, Misterwizard?"

"Nothing worth repeating, Johnny. An empty threat and a poor attempt at extortion."

Johnny shook his head and wished sometimes Misterwizard wouldn't talk in so many riddles. Suddenly, he thought of something to teach Ripper a lesson.

Johnny smiled.

"I'm telling you Old Man; we can come in there any time we want. You start giving us some of that fancy stuff of yours or we're going to burn this place to the ground."

"I have nothing of the slightest interest to men of your ilk, you silly malcontents. All I have are knick-knacks and thingamabobs, items from the past to remind an old man of days gone by. Now go and do yourselves a favor. Take baths and brush your teeth, before vermin move in and take residence on your bodies and decay causes your teeth to fall out."

Leaker stepped forward and scowled. He pointed a finger up at the window. "Listen up, Old Man, who you calling 'malcontents'? You use all them fancy words, thinkin' we don't know what they mean, but we do. And maybe knicks and knacks are just what we're lookin' for. Don't you tell us what we want!"

Ripper turned to Leaker. Leaker smiled, expecting approval. Instead he got a cuff on the face. "Shut up, stupid."

Leaker slunk back, glowering but contrite.

Meanwhile, Johnny had taken out his slingshot. He scanned the room and found some old metal shards that looked good and sharp. While Misterwizard was distracted, he snuck over and picked them up. Then he returned to the window and loaded one of the sharp metal pieces in his slingshot and took careful aim.

Ripper grinned up like a wolf-beastie at them. "I got to wonder what you're doing out here, Old Man. Seems they don't like you in Sanctuary. You're all by yourself. But this here city belongs to us and we don't like you either. You got to start paying a toll, or we're gonna cut you in little pieces and let the Wildies fight over 'em."

Misterwizard put his hands to the sides of his mouth and said in a loud voice, "A storm is approaching, oh Minions of the Darkness. The Bad Air will soon arrive. I suggest you slink back to whatever den you crawled out of, err you get the Sickness. Be off!"

Before Ripper could reply, Johnny fired. A second later they heard Ripper yell and curse.

Misterwizard gave Johnny an accusing stare. "Johnny, did you fire a projectile at our enemies?"

"Just helped you get your point across. Is there really a storm coming Wizard?"

Misterwizard scratched his short beard with his fingers. "Not at all, dear boy. But a mind full of violence soon becomes a dull one, easily controlled by fear and superstition. Along the same train of thought, Johnny, you should not have shot him. Violence only begets more violence."

Johnny looked outside and grinned. Ripper held his neck with his hand where blood oozed out. "Maybe, but I got him good."

Ripper glared up at the window, his eyes full of fury. "Okay, Old Man. You just dug your own grave."

The Gangers glared up one more time then slunk away.

Misterwizard looked at Johnny with a mild look of admonishment. "Johnny, do you see what your action has wrought? You antagonized them. Now whatever little hope there was of negotiating a peaceful resolution has been significantly reduced. Though truthfully, the possibility of a détente with these fellows was remote at best, you still have lowered the odds of a favorable solution by a noticeable degree."

Johnny felt bad, unsure just what Misterwizard was saying. "I just wanted to stand up for you."

Misterwizard squeezed Johnny on the shoulder. "I appreciate the sentiment, Johnny, but if you are ever going to be a great leader, you must learn diplomacy. If you are one day to lead the people of this land, as I hope that you will someday with my tutelage, restraint is going to be a necessary evil. And besides, that was gold you shot at him, a very rare and useful commodity."

Once again Johnny didn't know half of what Misterwizard was saying, but he nodded anyway.

"Johnny, let's get to our Harleys fast, and get out of here, before Ripper comes back with even more Gangers," Starbucks said.

"Yahoo!" Super said. "I can't wait to ride those metal-beasties again!"

"But won't the Gangers be waiting for us?" Deb said.

Johnny just huffed. "Starbucks and me can ride faster than they can run, and we know all the shortcuts."

"And today, I'm going to accompany you on my own mode of transportation," Misterwizard smiled mischievously. "Just in case you need a little diversion. I might even have a surprise or two for our antagonists." Misterwizard picked up a green bag from a table and slung it over his shoulder.

The teens all looked at each other and shared a mutual understanding that none of them really understood half of what Misterwizard said. As Misterwizard led the way back to the stairs Johnny wondered what a diversion was, or antagonists, or even trans-por-tation.

Down in the courtyard, the teens saw Wizard's 'mode of transportation.' It turned out to be a little red machine, a tiny version of their Harleys.

"This is my Moped, "Misterwizard said, beaming with pride. "Isn't it just the most whimsical and enchanting of vehicles?"

"It looks... small," Starbucks said.

"It is, my boy, not nearly as intimidating as your powerful machines. But then it was made for utility, not impressiveness. It is just enough for an old, short man like me, fast and economical."

As the teens watched, Misterwizard straddled the Moped. Johnny and Starbucks mounted their Harleys and the girls got on the back of each Harley with smiles of anticipation.

Misterwizard put on a strange plastic strap with two round circles on his head and adjusted the circles in front of his eyes. "We're going to have to move at a fair rate of speed. I will egress first and lead them on a path of obfuscation. Then you may take French Leave at a more leisurely pace."

Johnny nodded, figuring he'd understand as they went along. He looked up at the sky. The Red Eye was high in the sky; almost half the day was gone.

"Now I open the gate, and off we go!"

"Misterwizard, what if the Gangers catch you?" Deb said. "You should not risk yourself for us."

"Ha, ha, don't worry about me. I think I can outwit some young men with low intelligence quotients. And by now they might have already moved on, found some poor rat-beastie to torture or Wildie to torment. Their type does not keep a thought too long in their heads."

With that Misterwizard turned a key and the Moped came alive with a buzzing sound, which sounded funny and weak to Johnny. Johnny and Starbucks roared their engines and Johnny smiled at how tough and loud their Harleys sounded in comparison. Deb and Super grinned at each other, held on tight and placed their heads on the boys' backs.

Misterwizard turned a handle and sped forward. He reached the gate and held up his hand.

He didn't move a lever at all, but simply said, "Open Sesame!" and the gate swung open!

"Just like the Bat Cave!" Misterwizard said with a big grin, and in a second, he and his moped sped through the opening. As Misterwizard sped off he yelled back, "Say the magic words "Close Sesame" to close the gate when you're through, Johnny!"

Johnny grinned and drove through the gate. When Starbucks was through too, he said, "Close Sesame!" He took off with Deb hanging on, Starbucks and Super followed right behind. As Johnny glanced back, he saw the fence move back into place. Johnny smiled, amazed again at all the magical things Misterwizard could do.

The buildings sped past in a blur. Though she held on tight, Johnny could sense Deb was having fun. It made Johnny feel a hundred feet tall. Johnny smiled with glee and raced down the street.

Then Johnny heard the Gangers yelling behind them! Johnny slowed down and turned his Harley so he could see what was happening. With dismay he saw the Gangers, a huge snarling mob, chasing Misterwizard down the street. Suddenly a bright yellow light flashed and there was the sound like thunder right in front of the Gangers. The Gangers stopped as if by magic and flew backwards, without even turning around. As Johnny, Starbucks and the girls watched open mouthed, it happened again, this time ten feet away from the

Gangers. The Gangers stopped, turned and ran away, looks of terror on their faces!

Johnny grinned at Starbucks, who grinned back. Starbucks said, "I'm sure glad Misterwizard is on our side!"

"Me too," Johnny said. "But let's get out of here!"

The Gangers saw Johnny and Starbucks and began to give chase, yelling louder, but Johnny and Starbucks gunned their engines, and all the Gangers could do was watch as Johnny and Starbucks left them behind.

Just before the Gangers disappeared out of sight, Johnny saw Ripper. Their eyes met for a split second before Johnny disappeared over the crest of a hill. Johnny had never seen such hatred on a person's face before. He knew that sooner or later, he and Ripper were going to come face to face in a fight, and only one would be left standing.

CHAPTER 7

When they arrived at Sanctuary, Misterwizard was there waiting for them as if nothing had even happened.

Johnny and Deb hopped off Johnny's Harley, and Starbucks and Super dismounted his. The teens walked over and Deb and Super both gave Misterwizard a hug.

"My, my, you are touching the heart of an old fossil like me. We did well, didn't we, lads? I love it when a plan comes together."

Johnny and the teens laughed. Then Johnny remembered how late they were.

"We'd better get inside. I think we may be in trouble."

"Dumb Leader Nordstrom," Starbucks growled. "If it wasn't for him, we could all live with Misterwizard."

"And Misterwizard wouldn't be alone," Johnny

replied. "I worry about you, Misterwizard. What if the Gangers finally get inside Castle? They could—"

Misterwizard chuckled good-naturedly and turned something on one of the handles of the Moped, making it buzz louder. "Tusk, tusk! I'm not afraid to die, Johnny. I've had a good, long life. I know things that no one on this World now can even understand. My grandfather and father survived the Great War, and I have seen a new generation spawn from the ashes and begin to flourish. And the fact is Castle is more secure than Sanctuary. If the rest of the tribe will not listen, at least you, Starbucks, Super, Deb and your families should come join me there. Wouldn't that be fun? You and I could study together, Johnny, and Starbucks too, all day and all night!"

Johnny couldn't believe his ears! Misterwizard was asking them to come live with him! He grinned with disbelief and happiness. "Could we really?"

"Of course, you could. And should. Sanctuary has too many entrances to protect; it's inevitable that the Gangers will find their way inside. When that happens, Leader Nordstrom won't be able to stop them."

"You are Johnny's best friend, Misterwizard," Johnny said. "Thank you."

"And Starbucks' ," Starbucks said.

"And Super's!" Super added.

"And everybody's!" Deb said at last.

"And you are all dear to my heart. I love you as if you were my own progeny."

Deb coughed again, just a little. Johnny spun around and stared at her. Misterwizard also looked at her critically. She saw them staring.

"It's just the dust from the place with the Beasties,

Johnny, I told you."

"That was a long time ago," Johnny said with worry in his voice. "How come you are still coughing?"

Deb shrugged meekly. "A lot of dust."

Misterwizard spoke. "You should get some rest today, dear, just in case."

Deb nodded and crawled back into the mall. Super followed her. Johnny and Starbucks put their Harleys back in the truck, then Starbucks went inside, leaving Johnny and Misterwizard alone.

Johnny looked at Wizard. Their eyes met in understanding.

"Don't worry, Johnny. The best, most rational explanation is the one she gave. There is a lot of dust in the old city."

Johnny turned to look at the opening into the mall. "What if it's not, Misterwizard? What if she has the—the—" Johnny couldn't make himself say it. "Misterwizard,—"

Misterwizard put up a hand. "Johnny, you really are scared for Deb, aren't you?"

"Misterwizard," Johnny said, fear and desperation creeping into his voice, "people who get the Sickness die."

"That has been true, in the past. But Johnny, as more time passes, the effects that cause the Sickness are lessening. Often people now mistake other maladies for the Sickness, and many people still die because of the lack of anti-biotics and medicine. I have been able to recreate some simple medicines, but they are but a drop in the bucket to what is really needed. I have been doing some research, some field trips, as it were, on my own, and think I have found a possible place where we might still find some medicines in useable condition.

"I still have quite a lot of field work to do, but if circumstances take a turn, such as Deb getting sick, well I may have to move up my timetable and find solutions to the remaining variables quickly. If that happens, you and I may have to go on a great adventure. But that is all speculation at the present. We'll believe that Deb was only coughing because of the dust, for the moment."

Misterwizard saw Johnny's puzzled look and patted him on the shoulder. "Don't try to understand everything, just have faith that I am working on a solution. For now, get inside before Leader Nordstrom notices you missing. I wouldn't like to see you get in trouble."

But as Johnny nodded and turned to go inside, Misterwizard remembered something.

"Oh, wait Johnny!"

Johnny turned to Misterwizard to see him digging through a bag on the back of the moped. "I almost forgot! I have a special gift for you!"

Misterwizard pulled out a new book!

Johnny walked over and joyfully looked at it.

"It's called, "Hop on Pop." I found it yesterday in my meanderings. I couldn't wait to give it to you. Here, take it!"

Johnny took the book gingerly, afraid that it would disappear as soon as he touched it. With a big smile, he studied the picture on front.

"When you can read this to me, I'll get you more advanced books, so work hard at it. You remember your vowels, don't you?"

"A-E-I-O-U. Yes. I've been repeating them every night. What do they mean, Misterwizard?"

"They are some of the letters that make up the alphabet, Johnny, and the alphabet is what we use to make up words. When you know what each letter sounds like, it will be much easier to read."

"Thank you. Misterwizard. You are my best friend of all time."

"Keep an eye on Deb, Johnny. She has a special place in your heart, doesn't she Johnny?" Misterwizard asked with a smile. "Shall we say, Cupid's Arrow has found its mark?"

Johnny looked back at Misterwizard with a frown of puzzlement. "Who's Cupid?"

"Cupido, as he is called in Latin, was the son of the love goddess Venus. In Greek mythology, he would shoot arrows at unsuspecting men, making them fall in madly in love with the first girl they saw."

"What is a goddess? What is Latin? How would shooting arrows make men fall in love?"

"So much to learn, Johnny, but I fear I will have to tell you at another time. I'm off!"

Misterwizard made his moped buzz again and took off in a flash. Johnny watched him leave, clutching his new prize with joy. When Misterwizard was just a dot in the distance, Johnny crawled inside.

As soon as Johnny entered into the dark, dusty interior, he knew something was wrong. Deb stood only a few feet away, waiting for him. The expression on her face immediately told him something bad was happening.

He looked past her and saw why. Leader Nordstrom stood behind her. A tall, thin man with a long, sad face and white hair that stood up like needles, Leader Nordstrom always seemed to be scowling and it made his face seem even more foreboding. Starbucks and Super stood next to him, and behind them were Buildabear, the Enforcers, and the whole tribe, including his father and mother.

They all stared at Johnny, looks of anger and fright on their faces. Johnny quickly hid his prized book under his shirt. He slowly stepped towards the group. Leader Nordstrom glared at him, a look of pure fury on his face.

"Aha!" Buildabear said. "I told you! I made Carny tell me where Johnny go."

"So, we finally caught you! Rebel! Defiler of our laws and home!"

Johnny strode up to Buildabear, a look of pure fury on his face. "If you hurt Carny, I will knock all your teeth out."

Buildabear blanched, and backed up, fear on his trembling face. "She is my mate. I did not hurt her. Just make her talk, that is all."

"I'll find out from Carny," Johnny said, his eyes full of anger. "Then you and I will talk."

Leader Nordstrom turned to address the tribe. "You see how he goes out in the Bad Air and brings back poison, him and his evil sidekick Starbucks? And now they are corrupting our young women as well! They will bring the contamination on us all. Johnny in league with Devil Misterwizard and the Gangers!"

"That a lie!" Johnny yelled; his lip curling in anger. "Don't talk about Misterwizard like he's Devil, whatever that means! Misterwizard is a great man!"

"Why won't you won't listen to us, Leader Nordstrom?" Starbucks said. "We only want what's best for the Tribe. The air is safe now. We can go outside, where the water is clean, and air is pure!" Starbucks said.

"You hear now how they do not respect your Leader Nordstrom?" Leader Nordstrom said. "Starbucks is disrespectful, but Johnny is pure evil! He looks normal, but you see how he's really bad in head, just like his father! And now he has even begun to lead our dear children," Leader Nordstrom put an arm around Deb and pulled her to him, "into danger with him."

Deb squirmed out of his grasp, and he glared at her.

"Don't touch her! And don't call my father bad in the head. He's a great man, just like Misterwizard!" Johnny knew he was not acting respectful, but he was having a hard time not losing control of his anger.

Leader Nordstrom's eyes flashed. "How dare you talk to me like that? Who do you think you are, boy? You think this girl is for you? Ha."

Johnny's face flushed, and he balled his hands into fists, getting even closer to losing control. "There is nothing wrong with the air. Or the water," Johnny said. "We can all go out. It is safe now. Misterwizard has a real Magic Box—"

"There, that proves it," Leader Nordstrom said smugly. "No one can use the boxes of old. The Bad Air has made that old fool crazy. It's why Gangers don't even bother him, because they know it. And it is affecting Johnny too. He should be banished, along with his family."

The Tribe all turned to look at Johnny's father. He turned to Johnny with a sad expression. Johnny felt shame that he'd brought trouble to his family, especially since his father didn't need any more problems.

Johnny's father stepped forward. Johnny noticed the confused look on his father's face. He knew his father was about to say something embarrassing. He felt bad that his father would have to speak in front of the Tribe and have them laugh at him.

Foodcourt glared at Leader Nordstrom. "Johnny is not evil. He is a good boy. He is only trying to help. He is busy finding a way to go to Australia."

All the Tribe laughed, and Leader Nordstrom snickered. Johnny grit his teeth in and tried hard to control himself. He wanted so much to fight them all, make them say they were sorry for making fun of his father.

"Yes, Johnny, say you will behave, until you and your whole family leave for Australia," Leader Nordstrom said with a mocking grin. "We'll even help you get ready."

Australia. It was his father's obsession, a mythical land where the bombs never fell and the machines all still worked. He was always planning their big trip there, collecting supplies and planning their route, but it would never happen. The whole tribe knew of his father's obsession, and they laughed at it behind his father's back. It made Johnny so angry he could spit. His father said what he wanted and didn't care what people thought, and it only made people think he was simple.

The Tribe waited. Johnny stared at Leader Nordstrom. Leader Nordstrom sneered at him.

"I feel sorry for Johnny, because look who raised him? It is not Johnny's fault, and I am feeling generous to day. I will forgive this incident, if you and Starbucks agree to obey my authority and have respect. And you must promise never to go out in the Bad Air again. If you're caught next time, you will be banished, you and your families!"

The Tribe waited to see what Johnny and Starbucks would say.

Johnny stared Leader Nordstrom in the eye, making Leader Nordstrom nervous. "I will stay inside and not go out any more, until the last time, and then I will leave for good, with my family. While I am here, I will respect your authority, though I don't agree with you.

"As for the rest of you, you can follow Leader Nordstrom if you like, but you should be listening to Misterwizard instead. There is a whole world outside, and it is ours to have, if we have the courage to take it. Leader Nordstrom is making you, all of you, into cowardies. You will all die in this dark place, living on mushy food from the garden and drinking stale water from the well when you could be outside enjoying the warmth of the Red Eye."

"I'll obey, too," Starbucks said, "but I agree with everything Johnny said."

Leader Nordstrom snorted. "You are both rebels, and I'm sure you won't be around for long. Now we must all leave, before the Bad Air affects us. Seal up that opening good!"

The Tribe turned as one and shuffled dutifully away, except for two men that began plugging up Johnny's secret opening as Leader Nordstrom grinned smugly. As Johnny and Starbucks left, Leader Nordstrom gave him one more parting shot.

"And boys," he said.

Johnny and Starbucks turned to him.

"Don't even dream of having Deb and Super for your mates. I will make sure they never see you again."

This was too much. Johnny balled up his fists, anger filling his mind, but luckily Starbucks held him back. "Don't listen to him Johnny. You know he can't stop Deb and Super from choosing us."

"Don't count on it," Leader Nordstrom sneered.

Johnny let Starbucks drag him away as he glowered at Leader Nordstrom, wanting with all his heart to grab Deb and take her away right then. But he knew he'd have to wait until the right time.

Buildabear waited until Johnny caught up to him and then he sneered at Johnny. Johnny gave him a look that said Johnny was in no mood to mess with. Buildabear's eyes opened wide in fear. He turned and hustled off. Johnny watched him go, his eyes slits. Someday, Johnny vowed silently to himself, he would take Carny and Miracle away when he left Sanctuary, and Carny would be free of Buildabear and his cruelty for good.

Starbucks caught up to Johnny, smiled at him and punched him on the arm. Johnny smiled grimly back. Then Starbucks left.

Johnny felt a squeeze on his hand. He looked up, surprised. It was Deb. She gazed at him with affection.

"Thank you for wonderful adventure, Johnny. It was the best day I've ever had. And I got to share it with you, which was the best part. I'm sorry about what happened."

Johnny squeezed her hand back as love filled his heart. "Leader Nordstrom says he's going to keep you from me."

"Nothing will keep me from you, Johnny, I promise. Don't you remember what I told you when we fought the dog-beasties?"

Johnny felt all soft and gooey inside, and for once he

didn't fight it. "Someday soon I will take my family and leave this place. We will go to Misterwizard's castle. Will you go with me?"

Deb looked up into Johnny's eyes. "I told you, wherever Johnny goes, Deb goes."

Johnny's heart filled with joy. Deb moved close to Johnny, so close that their lips almost touched.

"Deb! Get away from him, now!"

It was Deb's father Thegap. He glared at Johnny with fear and anger. Deb glanced up at Johnny one more time then let go of him and followed her father. They shared one more look of understanding. Then Deb and her father were gone.

Johnny reached his mother and father. His mother Teavana turned to him. "Johnny," his mother warned, "I know you right. But you must be careful. Leader Nordstrom has power. The Tribe will do anything he says. I think he could have you killed, if he wanted to."

"But Mother," Johnny said with frustration, "We are dying here. There are less and less wrigglers all the time. If something doesn't happen soon the Tribe will end. We will all be gone."

"I know, Johnny. But you must win the minds of the Tribe to the truth before you act, or you will never succeed."

"It doesn't matter," Johnny's father Foodcourt said. "We leave soon for Australia. Then Leader Nordstrom can just shut up and die."

"Father, we don't need go to Australia any more. We can live here, outside. It's safe."

"Nonsense," his father said. "Australia is where we must go. The Mushroom Monsters never came there. And we must leave soon. Today would be good."

Foodcourt stood only five feet tall, but he was strong and stout with large arms like tree trunks and stout legs that looked as if they could kick down a wall. His imposing strength would have made people afraid of him, if it wasn't for his brown curly hair and the impish grin he always wore, for Foodcourt was jolly man who liked to smile. His long nose and big ears added to his comical appearance, though anyone who talked to him knew he was a man who could be stubborn and determined when he wanted to be. This was part of the reason people thought he was crazy, always insisting the Tribe move to the imaginary place called Australia.

Johnny's mother Teavanna was just the opposite, tall and thin, with long black hair warm eyes. She reminded people of a wraith or a spirit, and some who happened to find her walking up behind them found the experience unsettling. But she smiled a lot and was friendly, and once people got to know her, they soon learned to like her and forgot her haunting appearance.

"Now, now, Foodcourt," Teavana said, putting a long thin hand on Foodcourt's arm. "Come along now. Let's go back and get you back in bed."

Johnny's mother led his father away as he protested weakly. Johnny followed as his mother led his father away.

"Johnny needn't worry," Foodcourt prattled on in a happy voice. "I heard it. I know they all think I'm not smart, just because I was sick that one time and said crazy things, but that was a long time ago. I'm all right now."

"Of course, you are, Dear," Johnny's mother Teavanna said, patting his father on the arm. "But we should listen to Johnny now, he knows best."

Johnny thought about the place his father was always talking about: Australia. Johnny had seen the big map in Misterwizard's castle. He asked the Misterwizard where Australia was once, and if what Foodcourt said was true. Misterwizard pointed to the spot where Sanctuary was and then to another small section no bigger than Johnny's finger away and said that to travel that far would take from the cold time all the way to the next cold time, if one were 'foolhardy' enough to try it, for there were not only 'miles and miles,' but also 'oshians' in the way. Misterwizard didn't seem to know for sure if Australia had not had been visited by the Mushroom Monsters, but he said that if it had, surely someone from there would have 'ventured' to 'America' to say 'hello,' or at least come and 're-occupied' the land, unless, Misterwizard said, they decided to be 'isolationists,' whatever that meant.

All Johnny really knew was that they were never getting to Australia, and they didn't need to. What they did need was to organize and learn the old ways again so that they could conquer the Gangers and the Wildies and the Beasties and be free to live in the air again without fear.

He followed his parents as they headed back towards their place. As Johnny walked down the cold, dark hallway of Sanctuary, he noticed Leader Nordstrom in a corner talking to two of the Enforcers. They were talking animatedly, and it made Johnny nervous.

A loud crash echoed through the hall. Johnny stopped in his tracks, instantly on alert. Leader Nordstrom and the Enforcers looked up towards the ceiling, and Johnny soon saw why.

Light sprang from overhead making a triangle on the

floor right in front of Johnny. Johnny looked up. There was a hole in the roof. Someone was breaking in!

Johnny leapt back just in time as a flaming ball of fire fell burst on the floor in front of him. Ripper and the Gangers were back, and this time it looked like all out war.

CHAPTER 8

Leader Nordstrom and the Enforcers yelled, like chicken-beasties with their heads cut off, turned and ran. Johnny noticed how scared Leader Nordstrom looked. Johnny had always suspected Leader Nordstrom was a cowardie at heart. Now he hoped he was wrong.

The fire on the floor danced, radiating heat and spreading an orange glow. Another crash sounded further down the mall, and another flaming ball fell, exploding on the floor, then another, and another. A dusty fake tree sitting in a square concrete display far down the hall burst into flame, smoked and crackled.

Clanging filled the air as the Enforcers banged pots and pans to sound the alarm. Johnny pulled out his sword, knowing that soon the Gangers would be dropping through the holes and he would have to fight. Just as Johnny thought the end of a rope fell from the ceiling and coiled onto the floor. Down the hallway, more fell. It was an invasion!

Johnny hurried to his mother and father.

"Mother! Hurry! Get Foodcourt to our room and bar the door."

Teavana turned to him her eyes open wide with panic. "Come with us Johnny! They'lll kill you!"

"I told you we should have left for Australia!" Foodcourt yelled. "Now it's too late!"

Dark shapes flitted by in the dark: other men of the Tribe wielding crude weapons made of table legs or lengths of metal with spikes tied to them running to the defense.

Johnny waved his hand at his parents. "Go! I have to fight."

Foodcourt and Teavana hurried off as Johnny turned and looked down the Main Hall.

Starbucks ran up to stand next to Johnny. "You mean we have to fight."

Johnny grinned, happy to have Starbucks by his side. Super ran up. "Girls can fight too."

Both Johnny and Starbucks smiled at her, liking her spunk. Starbucks smiled at Johnny with pride. "She can, too. I'm afraid of her."

"I bet she can, but Super we need someone to help get the families to safety. Can you do that for us instead?"

Super frowned grumpily. "Okay. But next time, I get to fight, too."

"That's a promise," Johnny said. Super ran off after Johnny's parents.

Johnny stood up to his full six feet and set himself, raising his sword. Starbucks took his out too, and with grim looks they faced the approaching Gangers. Johnny was shocked and dismayed at what he saw. There were so many of them! Like roaches they crawled down the ropes, ten, now twenty, now too many to count. There was no way the men of Sanctuary were going to stop them, but Johnny knew they had to try.

The fight started, and soon the air was filled with shouts of anger and screams of pain. Johnny and Starbucks ran out to join the fight, both with their swords held high. Soon in the confusion they were separated and lost track of each other.

Johnny saw two men surrounded by Gangers being beaten mercilessly. He leapt on the nearest Ganger and plunged his sword into his side. With a howl of pain, the Ganger fell to the floor. The rest of the Gangers, distracted, turned towards Johnny. The men of Sanctuary seized the moment to fight back, and Johnny helped by running to the next closest Ganger.

This Ganger's dirty face turned towards Johnny and Johnny saw the whites of his wild eyes shine in the semi-darkness of the Main Hall. The Ganger held up a long, metal stick, sharpened at the end, as long as Johnny's sword. Johnny circled him, being careful to watch the sharp end of the stick warily.

From the dwelling places flaming balls of fire flew into the middle of Main Hall. Tribe members were fighting back with the defenses set up just for such an attack. Soon Gangers became living torches. They screamed and ran, writhing in pain.

Arrows flew from the darkness. Gangers fell, pierced in the chest and neck, but more crawled down the ropes. Some men of the Tribe grew so desperate they put aside their fear and used the guns Misterwizard brought. Most of them were such bad shots they didn't hit anyone, except when they got really close to their target. The effect of the guns was good, for the Gangers retreated from the men with them, but bullets and gunpowder to power the guns were scarce, and wouldn't last very long. How many Gangers were there?

Suddenly an explosion rocked the mall and Gangers flew through the air, screaming in pain. The Enforcers had lit and thrown sticks of the special weapon Misterwizard had given them he called 'dyna-mite.' Johnny had always suspected they would be powerful weapons, but now that he saw them used, he was amazed at their strength and power. He realized Misterwizard must have thrown something like them when he was fighting the Gangers on his Moped. The Tribe only had a few sticks of the dynamite, but Johnny began to hope that they might drive the Gangers away after all.

The Ganger Johnny fought turned towards the sound, and Johnny smiled grimly. He struck fast, jabbing his sword into the Ganger's hand. The Ganger yelled, dropped his stick and took off running.

More explosions and more screams shook the Main Hall. The Enforcers, not careful where they threw the dynamite sticks were killing men of Sanctuary too. Soon chaos reigned as men ran everywhere and it was hard to tell the Gangers from the men of the Tribe.

Johnny scanned the dark interior, lit only by the slivers of light from the ceiling and small fires from the explosions. What he saw made his heart sink. There were not ten or twenty Gangers, but too many to count. Ripper must have been gathering strength for a long time, just waiting for the right moment.

Johnny took his slingshot off his hip, loaded a steel shot in it and prepared to aim. Then realized their only hope now was to gather the people together and flee. He had to get to Leader Nordstrom fast.

He couldn't find Starbucks anywhere. Everywhere he looked men fought in small groups, but they were being overwhelmed by sheer numbers. Johnny looked and looked but didn't see Leader Nordstrom anywhere.

From the dark a Ganger spied him. The Ganger yelled and ran towards Johnny. Johnny put his slingshot back on his belt and turned to face him. It was Leaker. Johnny's lip curled, and he raised his sword in a defensive position. Leaker ran up holding a wicked looking piece of ragged steel with a rag wrapped around the bottom for a handle. It dripped blood, a tribe member's blood. When he saw Johnny, he stopped and frowned with nervousness, but then his wild smile returned.

"Ha ha! Who's scared now? Not Leaker! Johnny better be, because Johnny's gonna die tonight!"

Anger filled Johnny like magma from a volcano and shone from his eyes. Johnny sprinted towards Leaker, sword raised, heedless of the danger.

Leaker yelped and ran. Despite the danger and the dire situation, Johnny couldn't help but chuckle. Johnny had bloodied Leaker's nose and Leaker knew not to mess with him. Even when it appeared the Gangers were winning, Leaker was still a cowardie.

Johnny saw Leader Nordstrom. He was curled up in a corner, hiding. Disgust and anger filled Johnny's heart. He ran over to Leader Nordstrom. "Leader Nordstrom!"

Leader Nordstrom didn't respond. His wide open eyes stared ahead, watching two Gangers beat up on a tribe member.

Johnny knelt down, grabbed Leader Nordstrom's arm and squeezed it hard. Leader Nordstrom finally seemed to be freed from his spell. He turned to look at Johnny.

"We have to leave, before we're all killed. You have to tell the men to get their families and run!"

In a faraway voice Leader Nordstrom responded "Where are we supposed to go? They're out there too. And the outside is death. We're doomed. There's no escape."

Johnny thought desperately. "Misterwizard's castle. We can go there."

Leader Nordstrom shook his head, in shock. "No. We can't leave. The Sickness outside. The bad air. And they'll catch us. We're doomed."

Leader Nordstrom sat, not moving.

"Leader Nordstrom! Leader Nordstrom!"

No response. Johnny gave up. He stood up. He turned, cupped his hand to his mouth and yelled as loud as he could.

"Listen! Everybody in the Tribe! Get your families and meet me where my family, Foodcourt and Teavana, live. We're leaving! Now, before it's too late!"

Johnny's words echoed through the mall. Soon he saw men nodding, turning and running away. *Good,* Johnny thought, *they were listening.*

"NO!"

Johnny spun around to see Leader Nordstrom standing up, his face full of fury.

Leader Nordstrom shook with rage and glared at Johnny. "We will not leave Sanctuary! I know what you're trying to do," Leader Nordstrom snarled. "You want to be Leader Nordstrom, you and your evil Misterwizard. But you won't be! I am Leader

Nordstrom!"

Johnny scowled back. "Don't be a fool. I'm trying to save the tribe. Can't you see what's happening?" Leader Nordstrom ignored Johnny and turned towards the dark interior. "Listen to me! Don't listen to Johnny! He is not Leader Nordstrom! Stay and fight!"

"No!" Johnny looked around desperately for a way to silence Leader Nordstrom before it was too late. Knowing what he was about to do might ban him from the tribe forever, Johnny slugged Leader Nordstrom in the face. Leader Nordstrom fell instantly, out cold.

Johnny frowned down at him. "I'm sorry Leader Nordstrom, but I had to do that." He turned and ran down the Main Hall, anxious to find his family and Deb.

Johnny hid as best as he could as he tried to make it back to the store where his family lived, but still had to scuffle with a few Gangers. He watched them with anger and sadness as they trashed everything in Sanctuary, setting fires and searching for Tribe members to attack. Johnny passed tribe members captured and being tortured by the Gangers. When he did he stopped and fought as much as he could, but he couldn't help them all. He had to get to his family and Deb and get them to safety.

As Johnny drew close to his dwelling place, he saw that the tribe had barricaded the front of the J C P nney store with shelves and boxes. They were trying to hold off the Gangers with arrows and the last of the bullets. Johnny looked around, looking for a way to help.

Then he saw something. In the corner of a store across the hall from Johnny's store a small fire burned. Johnny remembered something that Misterwizard had said: certain things made fire burn hotter. One of those things came in the bottles in the store where the fire was.

Johnny ran into the store and searched frantically. This store held spoons and plates, pans and 'lectric machines. It was a store for making food, and many of the items inside people in the Tribe used for cooking.

Finally, on a back shelf he found what he was looking for. It was a glass bottle with yellow liquid inside: he knew it was called cooking oil. It wasn't as good as the stuff Misterwizard put in his moped, but it was better than nothing.

Johnny grabbed as many bottles as he could carry and brought them to the front of the store. There he unscrewed the lids of the bottles and took old, dirty towels hanging on racks and stuffed them in so that they absorbed the oil. When Johnny had all the bottles ready, he carried a lit stick over from the fire.

He looked at the Gangers. It wouldn't be long before they breached the tribe's defenses. It was now or never.

Johnny lit the first rag with the fire and watched with pleasure as it flared brightly. Then with a mighty heave, he threw it at the nearest group of Gangers.

As it hit the ground behind them it exploded, just as Johnny hoped it would. Burning oil covered the ground, soon catching the Gangers on fire. They stumbled backwards, yelling and patting at themselves.

Quickly Johnny threw another and another. Gangers yelled and ran as small bonfires started everywhere from the burning oil.

When Johnny had only one bottle left, he made a run for it. He sprinted across the hall to the store. Ahead of him was a pile of broken shelves twice his height. Johnny hoped that he could get through them, or he'd be at the mercy of the Gangers.

As he reached the shelves, he looked around. The fires were dying, and the Gangers were coming back. Johnny tossed the last bottle and it exploded with a loud crash. Then he scaled the shelves.

After a few minutes Johnny realized that it was useless; he couldn't get through the tangle of steel any more than the Gangers could.

"Johnny! Over here!"

Johnny turned and looked. It was Deb! She stood in the corner of the storefront next to an opening.

Johnny leapt down and ran for it. He almost made it too, before-

"Got you!" A strong, cruel hand grabbed his leg. Johnny spun to see who it was.

Ripper, the Leader Nordstrom of the Gangers held onto him in a tight grip. He grinned at Johnny and held a gun level with Johnny's head.

"Today you die, Johnny, right in front of your girlfriend."

Johnny shook his leg, but Ripper held on tight. Johnny looked over Ripper. The rest of the Gangers were coming, very fast.

Ripper grinned in the dark. "Today I get revenge on Johnny! Today Johnny is going to die!"

"Johnny! Hurry! They're coming!" Deb yelled.

"I may die today, but it not be you that does it." Johnny reached down with his sword and hacked at Ripper's arm. Ripper yelled and let go, jerking his arm back in panic. Johnny smirked and ran away.

"That will not save you, Johnny. I going to kill you and have your little girlfriend for mine. All the Gangers will too!"

Johnny ignored Ripper and hurried to the opening. When he reached it, he saw Deb's look of terror, pricking his heart and energizing him with purpose. Her face was pale, and she looked faint. He crawled through the opening and they closed it as best they could, wedging pieces of metal around and against it.

Deb moved close to Johnny. "Johnny. I'm scared."

Johnny looked at Deb and saw she was trembling. He grabbed her around the waist and held her close.

Johnny turned and surveyed the men. Despite their best efforts to be brave, fear shone from their eyes. Johnny also read confusion on their faces, and the hope that someone would tell them what to do next.

Johnny spoke loudly. "We must leave Sanctuary. The Gangers have it now. It is no longer safe here."

A man in front spoke. Johnny knew his name was Richardmillhousenixon. A fat man with a bald, round head, he had a family of three girls, all slow-witted, and deformed. "Leave Sanctuary? You're insane just like Leader Nordstrom said! We will die out there! The Red Eye will burn us to a crisp! The poison will eat our bones!"

Johnny had to force the feeling of contempt he felt ring up inside himself for the man down, telling himself that the man just didn't know. "That's not true. It is safe outside. And we'll die here, now, if we don't leave. We will go to Misterwizard's castle. It has big, strong walls. We will be safe there."

As if to emphasize Johnny's point, a flaming ball smashed into the hastily erected barrier. Flames rose up, spreading quickly.

"Who gave you authority to make such a decision?" It was another that spoke this time, a short, stocky man named Dellcomputers.

"No one. But I know the way. Either follow me or die here. It's your choice."

The hastily erected wall shook; the Gangers were coming.

Johnny saw Deb watching him. He waited, holding his breath for the men's reaction. For a moment, no one spoke, or moved.

Another man whose name was Fuego, a short, thin man with only wisps of hair, big ears and a big nose, spoke. "What are we waiting for? The boy has a plan. Let's follow him!"

A woman spoke up, her voice full of fear. "But Leader Nordstrom said he was a rebel and a bad man!"

Deb answered this time. "That's nonsense. Johnny is smart, and he cares what happens to you. Listen to him, people!"

A loud crash sounded from the makeshift barrier. A large piece of metal fell inwards. They all turned to Johnny, waiting for orders.

Johnny smiled, relieved. "Get your families! Meet me on the second floor next to my family's dwelling place. Hurry!"

Finally, the men began to comply. They ran with their families into the dark interior to do as Johnny said. Johnny turned to Deb. "Deb, is your family still in their dwelling place?"

"I think so, Johnny. I can't leave without them. "

"But they're outside, down the Main Hall!"

"You go help the Tribe. We'll find another way out."

Johnny gripped her arm. No!" Johnny said. "I can't leave without you!"

Deb pulled away. "I'll be all right. I'm not as helpless as you think I am."

Johnny stared at her, worried. Deb smiled. "Don't worry so much. Didn't I tell you, where Johnny goes, I go?"

Johnny smiled. Deb turned to run away, but just then two round eyes appeared in the darkness. It was Sephie, and she was terrified. Big tears ran down her cheeks.

"Johnny! Help me!"

Deb ran over and took Sephie's hand. "Come with me, Sephie. We have to find our families. Then we'll go with Johnny."

"Okay," Sephie said, as Deb led her off into the darkness.

They left just in time, for with a resounding crash, a part of the makeshift wall at the far end fell inwards. The sound had barely ended when it was joined by the dark cheer of the Gangers as they poured over it. Soon the air filled with the cries of the Gangers and crashing sounds as they swept through the stores mashing and setting fire to everything.

CHAPTER 9

Johnny ran to the second floor up the steel stairs. He reached the back of the store where he saw most of the Tribe gathered, waiting for him.

"Johnny," Foodcourt said in a daze. "What's all the commotion? It is New Year's Day?"

His father had been sleeping, and missed the whole thing. Johnny smiled at him softly. "We have to leave Sanctuary. Follow me!"

Johnny led the tribe, knowing where they had to go. The shouts of the Gangers reached the second floor, far in the dark behind them. They had to hurry.

"Everyone down the stairs! But be quiet!" Johnny led the way to a door at the very back of the store marked "EXIT" that led to a concrete staircase. Soon a human train fell in behind him.

Johnny scanned the crowd but didn't see Deb or

Sephie. It worried him, but he had no choice but to lead the rest of the tribe to safety.

As they entered the dark chamber with the stairs, the tribe members gazed about in fear. Teavanna, Johnny's mother, said, "it's so dark, Johnny!"

Johnny turned and addressed the whole group. "Just hold onto the handrail and take one step at a time. It will be all right."

Slowly they made their way down the steps. It was dark and cold, and behind them somewhere they could hear shouting and explosions. They reached the ground floor and another door.

Johnny turned to the crowd snaking up the stairs. "Wait while I break the door open. Then I'll signal and you all go out, one by one."

"NO!" A woman from the tribe wailed. "We will all die!"

"If my son says we are safe, then we are safe," Foodcourt said. "So button it!"

Johnny threw his whole weight against the door, but it didn't budge. He tried again, but it still didn't move. Foodcourt saw what he was trying to do and joined him. Soon two other men began helping too. They all threw their weight against the door, and suddenly it burst open. Bright sunlight streamed in, temporarily blinding them all.

The men and women of the tribe oohed and aahed, never having seen such a bright light before. Johnny peered out at the bright day with joy. They were going to make it out alive!

Johnny looked around. This was the side of Sanctuary opposite from the bridge and the way to the Misterwizard's castle. He saw a building far away with a picture on it of a funny read bird-beastie holding some kind of food in its wing. Its doors and windows were gone. It would be a good temporary hiding place to gather, though, before they made their mad dash to safety.

Johnny turned to Foodcourt, who held his hand up to shade his eyes just like the others. "Hurry father! Lead the Tribe to the building with the picture of a funny red bird-beastie on top of it. It is over there, across this sea of rock."

Johnny pointed to the building. It stood a little way away in the distance but still on the concrete lot.

"I'll meet you there after I find Deb and Sephie. Together, we'll take the Tribe to Misterwizard's castle." Foodcourt smiled and nodded. "And then, on to Australia!"

"Yes," Johnny said, looking annoyed, "on to Australia."

"Good, it's about time."

One by one Foodcourt led the people of the Tribe out. They took their first steps out of Sanctuary into the real world. Outside they gathered in a huddled group, looking like frightened sheep. As they came out into the daylight, they covered their eyes and cowered, as if the Red Eye was going to burn them alive. Some gazed with wonder all around them. For the first time they saw what Sanctuary looked like from the outside. And in the distance behind it, they could see the tall, broken tangle of buildings of the Forbidden City. In front of them lay a sea of concrete, dotted with rusted hulks. In the near distance, old buildings and houses lay in ruins.

They breathed shallow, frightened breaths, afraid of the air. Foodcourt peered around, a look of amazement and delight on his face. “Well, it’s mighty nice out here!”

His excitement was contagious, and soon smiles began to sprout on faces.

“Is it really safe?” A woman of forty cycles named Cinnabon said, as she held tight to her six-cycle old son Wheaties. Cinnabon and Wheaties were of the background that what Misterwizard said used to be referred to as “Latino.” Her husband Marlboroman died from the Sickness years ago and now Cinnabon and her son were alone.

“I don’t feel any bad effects,” Foodcourt said to her. Look at it out here. It’s absolutely beautiful!”

Everyone nodded and agreed and reluctantly smiled.

“All right everybody, follow me. Let’s go!” Foodcourt led the way, and slowly the tribe followed.

Back inside Sanctuary, Johnny made his way back up the stairs to the top, having to push his way past tribe members slowly working their way down. He grew impatient at how slow the tribe was getting out. The sound of the Gangers grew closer. Johnny could tell they weren’t all going to make it in time. He realized that he wasn’t going to be able to go look for Deb and Sephie. He had to do something to create a distraction to save the Tribe.

He ran towards the Gangers silently, like he was hunting wild dogs for meat. He found one banging his metal pike on a table, smashing it. Taking his slingshot off his back he loaded a steel ball in it and aimed. He shot! It arced through the air and found its mark, hitting the Ganger in the throat. The Ganger tried to scream but could only gurgle as he pawed at the wound gushing blood.

“It’s Johnny!” Ripper’s voice echoed in the gloom. “A

female to the one that catches him, alive!"

Johnny ran, away from where the tribe was escaping, back down the steel stairs, leading the Gangers away. Behind him, five, ten, twenty Gangers pounded after him. There were more than he expected. He didn't even have time to aim again, only run.

He hurried to the front of the store and leapt over the makeshift barrier, hoping they would follow. Sure enough, the Gangers did; eager to finally find a victim. Johnny grew out of breath and sweaty as like ants the Gangers poured from the store. Still, Johnny laughed; they were no match for his speed.

"Get him, you wrigglers!" Ripper screamed behind Johnny in anger. "What are you, men or maggots?" This made Johnny laugh even harder.

A board smashed into Johnny's face. Bewildered and with stars dancing in his eyes he fell to the floor. Stabbing pain shot through his head and he felt the wetness of blood drip from his forehead.

Through a red haze he looked up to see who had hit him. In his blurry vision, the face of Leader Nordstrom danced like a ghost.

"That will teach you to hit me, young troublemaker. Take a taste of your own medicine! Now they will kill you. And it serves you right!"

Leader Nordstrom ran off. Johnny tried to get up, but he was too woozy. He turned and looked. The Gangers were almost on top of him with Ripper in front. It looked like the end for him. Despair filled Johnny's heart.

Beep! Beep! Something sped past him. Johnny looked.

A man wearing an old pilot's hat, goggles and a long flowing coat sat on a moped. It was Misterwizard!

"Take this, you disturbers of the peace!" Misterwizard stopped in front of the Gangers. He turned a valve on a tank he had strapped to the front of his moped.

Suddenly a giant plume of fire shot out the front of the tank towards the Gangers. In the sudden light Johnny saw surprise and panic on their faces as they leapt back from the heat and flame.

Misterwizard spun his moped around and zipped over to Johnny. Grabbing his arm, he pulled him up and onto the bike. "I witnessed the traumatic events transpiring through my telescope. Dirty villains! It appears as if I showed up just in time!"

Johnny held on as Misterwizard sped off, a big grin on his face and his beard flowing in the air.

"We're leaving Sanctuary, for good. Can we come to your place?"

"Indubitably, Johnny my boy. I will welcome the company. It gets a mite lonely in Castle all by myself. Though it might get a bit crowded, with the hundred or so members of the Tribe all situated in like sardines in a can, but we shall make do."

"They are all waiting at the building with the red bird-beastie on it."

"All hungry for a cheeseburger, were they?"

"What's a 'cheesebooger?'"

"Only the best food ever known to man. I've attempted to recreate one from photographs, but to date my efforts have been woefully inadequate."

Johnny had no idea what Misterwizard was talking about, but he nodded anyway. "Misterwizard, I have to find Deb and Sephie. They went back to get their families."

Misterwizard thought for a moment then said, "Are you certain they aren't with the other families where you left them?"

"No," Johnny said, not sure what to do."

"I will take you to the building with the funny bird-beastie. Then if she is not there, you and I will go on a quest to find them."

Johnny didn't like leaving without definitely knowing they were safe, but he decided Misterwizard's plan was a compromise. But if they weren't at the building with the red bird-beastie, Misterwizard could take the Tribe back to his castle. Johnny was going to stay until he found them, no matter how long it took.

" Hang on tight!" Misterwizard turned the handle and they sped through the empty mall, past the fires and smoke.

Johnny sped along on Misterwizard's moped, once again glad to be with his good friend. The little bike motored down the empty mall, through the dark and past the smoldering fires. As Johnny rode along, he looked at the stores, storing the sight of them in his memory, for it would probably the last time he'd ever see them. Each one held some memory; though he learned to think of Sanctuary as a prison, it was still the only home he'd ever known.

Sadness filled Johnny's heart, mixed with anger at the Gangers who trashed it with so little feeling. And yet, knowing that he was finally leaving Sanctuary for good, he felt an odd lifting of his spirits as well, as if a heavy weight that was tied to his leg had finally been cut free and dropped away.

"That is how I entered, Johnny," Misterwizard pointed to a hole in a door on the second floor of the store with the letters SE_RS on it. "I saw the villains swarming your domicile, and so I abandoned all caution, threw it to the wind, as they say, and used some dynamite that I kept for myself. I suspected it was of little concern if I demolished your domicile, for I surmised, correctly that the Tribe was losing its longtime habitation. But do not despair, for I made some preparations in advance of just such an event, and now we will finally put them to good use... "

Misterwizard kept talking, most of which Johnny didn't understand, but Johnny only half listened anyway. He thought about the future. What he knew his people needed was to make a 'government.' It was something Misterwizard said 'civilized' people did, and how they grew strong and powerful. Misterwizard said once there was a 'government' again, they could make 'progress,' which meant building real places to live, growing food again, getting rid of the Gangers and the Wildies and the animals, and cleaning up the mess left by the great war. Best of all, it would mean no more fear; it would mean peace and happiness could finally return to the world.

But the problem was how do you go about making a government? Johnny didn't know. He had so much to learn yet from Misterwizard. However it happened, Johnny knew down in his heart that he would have to be the one to make it become real. Johnny was one of the only one learning to read and write, other than Starbucks, who didn't take it very seriously. And Johnny wasn't afraid of everything like so many in his Tribe.

Somehow, he knew in his heart, he'd always known, that he was destined to be the real Leader Nordstrom of his people someday and help them achieve a new government.

But if it truly was his destiny, there were problems to overcome. There was the obvious one, Leader Nordstrom. He liked having the people live in fear and ignorance to control them. The Tribe would never be able to progress beyond hiding in one Sanctuary or another until Leader Nordstrom changed his ways or was removed entirely.

Another potential problem was Johnny's age, but that was solving itself naturally as he grew older. The last big hurdle was possibly the largest, and that was the fear of the people and their resistance to change. That was what Johnny had to work on the most, for he had years of superstition and fear to overcome.

"Sorry to say, the hole I made is on the second floor. Hang on while I ride up the escalator!" Misterwizard sped the moped right up the metal steps, almost bouncing Johnny off. Then he zipped down the aisle of the store, past the plastic people who seemed to watch them with shock and amazement.

"So, Johnny, leaving aside for a moment the fact that you can't find her, how is Deb faring?"

Johnny thought this an odd question. He frowned with puzzlement and said. "Fine."

"Good, good. No more coughing then?"

"No," Johnny replied without thinking, and then he did stop to think. She had coughed more, but not that much, or had she? Johnny felt mild alarm grow in his chest. "Why?"

"Just natural concern, Johnny. And now, are you

ready for a little fun? Grab on tight!"

Before Johnny could reply they reached the back of the store and a ragged opening in the wall. Through it, bright sunlight streamed, hurting Johnny's eyes. He closed them and felt the bike whoosh through the opening.

Wondering what was happening Johnny opened his eyes again, and instantly opened his mouth too in shock. They flew and landed on down a makeshift ramp sitting on an old rusted truck. Then they sailed off the back of the truck onto the ground.

"Yee-haw!" Misterwizard yelled. "Just like Evil Knievel!"

Johnny grinned, with no clue who Evil Knievel was, as he bounced up and down from the rough ride. Off they sped with the Red Eye warm on their backs across the parking lot of old rusted old cars. Misterwizard weaved between them, barely slowing down.

Misterwizard looked at one vehicle as they passed it with a look of sadness. "There's a BMW, though you can barely tell anymore, pity. I'd love to find one of those in an old dealership and get it working again. And look, a Hummer. Now that would be a useful vehicle."

Johnny laughed. Misterwizard was always off in his own world, and Johnny loved to join him there.

They made it around the side of Sanctuary. Johnny kept his eyes peeled for more Gangers. He knew it wouldn't take them long to figure out where the Tribe had went. They had to move, fast.

In the distance, Johnny saw a pair of Wildies rummaging through the cars. They looked old, both men, naked except for ragged clothes wrapped around their waists and dirty. One's left eye was gone, and only a ragged hole in its place. The other's face and arm were burned and covered with red scars. They saw Johnny and Wizard. They yelled and ran for them, but the moped was way too fast. Johnny knew that was going to be another concern: the Wildies. There were almost as many of them as Gangers, and they were even less predictable.

They reached the Johnny's Harley and he hopped off. It was on its kickstand inside the truck where Johnny always left it. Even with all the danger and tension of the last few hours, the sight of his bike filled Johnny with joy. He couldn't wait to jump on it and ride. The sight of it seemed to give him a burst of new energy and he ran up the truck ramp and jumped on.

"See you at the cheeseburger joint!" Misterwizard sped off. Johnny turned on his bike and lifted the kickstand. He maneuvered it towards the ramp. Then he heard a loud roar.

He looked up and smiled. It was Starbucks on his Harley, with Super riding behind.

"I thought you two were goners," Johnny said.

Starbucks grinned cockily. "We thought the same thing about you. I found Super and her family, but I couldn't find Deb and Sephie."

Johnny frowned. "I didn't see them either. I hope they made it back to the red bird building like everybody else."

Starbucks nodded and took off. Johnny hit the throttle and his Harley roared to life. He sped down the ramp and after them.

When Johnny reached the building with the red bird, he saw the tribe milling about inside and Starbucks' bike parked in front. He hopped off and hurried up.

Carny hurried up, holding her belly. "Johnny! You're

safe!" She wrapped her arms around Johnny and gave him a big hug. He hugged her back and smiled at her with happiness. "So are you. I'm glad."

Misterwizard walked out and waved at them, then joined them. Then Thegap and Bathandbodyworks, Deb's mother and father came running out. Right behind them, Microsoft and Abercrombie, Sephie's parents, followed. Microsoft was tall with a gray hair, a long, beaklike nose and big ears. Aberbrombie a little shorter than her husband and a little fat, with a round face.

They ran up to Johnny.

"Johnny," Bathandbodyworks said fearfully, "Deb and Sephie aren't here. We've looked everywhere, but we can't find them."

The happiness that Johnny had just felt disappeared like a small raincloud in the sunshine, to be replaced by the same old dread he'd been feeling way too often lately. "What do you mean they're not here?"

"They never came. They must still be in Sanctuary with those monsters…"

Johnny didn't listen to the rest of what she said, he could tell by the tone of her voice what they were both afraid of.

"Go find them, Johnny," Misterwizard called out. "Starbucks and I will play the part of Moses today and lead the tribe to Castle. But first, take this."

Misterwizard held something out to Johnny. Johnny looked down at it curiously. It was a small rectangular black box, a little bigger than Johnny's hand.

"This is called a walkie-talkie. It only has a small range, and I've had to make up my own form of batteries, but it will help keep us in contact. When you want to talk to me, simply hold it up to your mouth, and press this…" Misterwizard demonstrated by pushing a button on the side of the device. "And to listen you release it and put the front up to your ear."

"Misterwizard, will you ever stop amazing us?" Johnny asked.

"That would be no fun, Johnny. Hurry and find our missing members. And if you find you need help, press the button and call me!"

Johnny nodded. He put the walkie-talkie in his belt, turned his Harley around and sped off, back towards Sanctuary, a place he thought he'd never see again.

Deb's and Sephie's parents watched him go.

Microsoft, Sephie's father, held his wife's shoulders and watched Johnny leave. "We're going to wait here for them to return. "We are too," Bathandbodyworks insisted.

"Now, now," Misterwizard said, "it won't do any good for you to be captured by the Gangers. Then what will your daughters have to come back to? Have faith in Johnny. You know he won't rest until they are both back with us, safe and sound."

Reluctantly, the parents let Carny and Misterwizard lead them back to join the rest.

CHAPTER 10

The Tribe began their long and wonder filled trek to Castle. Slowly they poured out of the building with the red bird and walked, in groups of five or ten, behind Misterwizard, who putted along on his moped. Starbucks and Super rode ahead or circled behind, roaring the Harley's engine, delighting the tribe members who pointed and talked about them.

With every step, the people of the Tribe were experiencing a new world. They looked at each other and pointed at things, talking excitedly with eyes wide with wonder. Their voices rose and fell with happiness and laughter, free from the dark confines of Sanctuary for the first time.

Deb's and Sephie's parents couldn't join in the fun. They kept looking back, worried. Misterwizard drove up to Abercrombie, Sephie's mother, and put a comforting hand on her shoulder. "Don't worry. I'm sure they simply managed to get separated and are hiding in Sanctuary, waiting for Johnny to come find them."

Abercrombie tried to smile at Misterwizard, but all she could manage was a weak frown. She said unconvincingly, "I'm sure you're right." Misterwizard rode to the head of the group again, knowing neither of them were sure, both just hoping with all their might.

As they walked the streets heading towards the bridge, the tribe gazed with interest but also fear at the abandoned buildings around them.

"Look! A Beastie!" One of them pointed and the rest looked and gasped with fear. Standing in the doorway of an old house chewing on grass was a deer-beastie. When they realized it wasn't dangerous, the gazed at it with wonder and joy, for none had ever seen such a beautiful animal. The deer-beastie gazed back, on alert, used to being chased by Wildies.

"Look at it!"

"It's beautiful!"

They all smiled and gazed around, like little children on their first trip to a wonderful, exciting theme park.

A man in the tribe pointed to a car on the side of the road. "What are all those strange, orange pieces of metal, Misterwizard?"

Misterwizard motored back and stopped in front of him. "Those used to be called automobiles, and they were very sleek and stylish, in their time."

The man gave the car a haughty look. "Hmm. They sure don't look it now." He walked over and touched it, then looked with amazement at the orange that came off on his fingers.

The children of the Tribe ran around, enjoying the

sunshine and freedom the likes of which they had never known. Even the adults acted like little children, picking up rocks and peering into the old cars.

Starbucks made another circle, making people in the Tribe cheer. Super was having a blast too, hanging on and being part of the show.

Then one of the members of the Tribe yelled and pointed. The whole tribe stopped and looked. A Wildie sat on a piece of the crumbled wall of an old factory, eating a rat-beastie. The Tribe backed away in fright and hurried past him. The man had wild, black hair sticking straight up. He wore what was left of a black suit, with no shirt and pants full of holes. He glared at them with fierce wild eyes.

Foodcourt pointed at him. "Is that an Aboriginny, Misterwizard, like they have in Austrailia?"

Misterwizard smiled and chuckled. "No Foodcourt, we are not in Australia yet. No, that is just a poor, homeless Wildie."

Carny, who walked with Buildabear, looked warily at the man and moved to the opposite side of her mate, away from the Wildie. "Doesn't he have a tribe?"

"No, Wildies have no one, Carny. You should pity the poor man. In the loneliness of this desolate world we have created, his is the loneliest and saddest of all."

The Wildie held up the rat's head and pointed it at them, making some of the tribe yell with disgust and fear. Another woman in the tribe held her little girl close to her side and asked, "Will he hurt us, Misterwizard?"

"If we were in singular numbers, he most certainly would try, for amusement or to purloin any items of value we might conceal. But we should be relatively safe from the Wildies with our numbers, if we keep moving and don't antagonize them."

The Tribe kept going, with each step breathing more freely the fresh air, the smiles on their faces growing as they enjoyed the pleasures of the world they had never known.

Johnny reached the door where he'd led the Tribe out. He hopped off his bike. Cautiously and with fear at what he'd find, he crept to the opening and peered in.

"Deb! Sephie! Where are you?"

"Johnny!" It was Sephie's voice coming from above on the second floor, sounding sad and afraid. "We're here!"

Throwing caution to the wind Johnny leapt inside and hurried up the stairs to find them. When he did, even greater fear gripped his heart at what he saw. Sephie knelt over the body of Deb, lying on the floor.

Johnny ran up and picked up Deb's head, examining her. Her face was red, and she had yellow liquid coming out of her nose. Sephie looked at him with tears in her eyes. "She won't wake up, Johnny. After you left, she just fell over. I can't wake her up."

Behind him Johnny heard the sounds of the Gangers, still partying and poring through the Tribe's belongings. Some of the voices sounded frighteningly close. It wouldn't be more than mere seconds before the Gangers spotted them.

Johnny didn't have time to think about Deb. He wiped her face clean on a nearby rag, picked her up and carried her down the steps and outside with Sephie following along. They reached the Harley. Then Johnny heard what he was dreading.

From inside at the top of the stairs came a ragged voice. "Hey! Look! They went out here! Let's go get 'em!"

Johnny turned to Sephie. "Sephie, get on the front." Sephie, who—despite the danger—smiled with wonder at Johnny's Haley, did as Johnny told her. Johnny quickly sat Deb on the seat behind her. Hoping desperately that the Harley had room for all three of them, Johnny squished onto the very end of the seat.

And just in time, for out the opening poured Gangers. Johnny turned the handle and the Harley took off.

"There's Johnny! Get him!" A Ganger took off in pursuit. With three people on the bike, Johnny had trouble going fast. The Ganger was catching up!

The Ganger reached them. Johnny pulled out his sword and swung it in an arc. The Ganger backed up long enough for Johnny to put some distance between them. Then he wove between some junk cars, hoping to throw off his pursuers.

Deb stirred, filling Johnny with relief. He held her tight so that she wouldn't fall of or cause them to crash.

They began a desperate game of cat and mouse. Johnny moving between the cars, hearing the voices of Gangers everywhere, trying to get out of the parking lot before they caught him. Sephie grimaced and held on tight, her mouth open in a look of fright, but there was a hint of excitement in her face as well. She was enjoying her first bike ride, and her first moments out in the bright sunshine and fresh air.

Johnny wove around a green hulk to find two Gangers coming right at him! He turned and sped off to the right, wove behind a bug-shaped hulk and then up between two long black ones and ran right into-

-three more Gangers. He heard the others coming from behind. It looked like he was trapped. Then the oddest people came to Johnny's salvation: the Wildies! They ran up and beat on the Gangers, who had to turn and fight them off. Johnny sped by the group, his heart in his throat.

Finally, he reached the end of the parking lot and headed for the bridge across the river, never so happy to leave a place as he was then. But Johnny's joy turned to dismay when he looked ahead. There on the other side of the bridge was the Tribe. They were barely moving! The Gangers were right behind Johnny. Johnny sped up to reach the Tribe.

As Johnny approached one of the stragglers at the end saw him and pointed.

"Here comes Johnny!"

As a whole they turned and looked at him, like a pack of sheep at their shepherd. Johnny sped by them to the front. In front, Misterwizard led them holding a staff just like a Misterwizard should.

Deb's mother and father and Sephie's parents ran up with looks of joy.

Abercrombie said, "Thank goodness! You found them!"

Sephie jumped off the bike and into her mother's arms. "Look, Mommy, I rode on Johnny's machine!"

"That's wonderful, Sephie," Abercrombie said, tears of joy on her face. Then she and Microsoft led Sephie away to join the rest of the group.

"Johnny! Thank heavens you made it. I've had a devil of a time getting them to move. They're like a herd of stubborn wildebeests. I don't think they felt very comfortable with me in charge."

Johnny stopped the bike and climbed off. "We have to hurry! The Gangers are right behind me! But Misterwizard, Deb seems worse."

Deb's parents walked up and studied her with worried looks. The smile that had been on Wizard's face, vanished. He walked over and studied Deb. She lifted her head. "I'm fine, just a little tired." Then she closed her eyes again.

Misterwizard felt her forehead. "I'll be able to do some tests at Castle. Meanwhile, let's get this herd rolling!"

Johnny turned to the Tribe. "Listen, the Gangers are right behind us. We have to move fast. Men of the tribe take up positions on the outside of the Tribe. And start moving!"

Johnny looked at Deb's parents. "I'll keep her on the bike with me, so she doesn't have to walk, if that's okay." They both nodded.

"Johnny, "Misterwizard said, pulling on his goggles, "You take the lead of this treacherous sight -seeing tour. Meanwhile, I'll see if I can't provide a slight distraction to our unwanted followers. I have a few tricks up my sleeve that just might put a kink in their armor."

"We'll see you at Castle, Misterwizard!"

"Tally-ho!" Misterwizard zipped off back the way they'd come. Johnny, with Deb on the front of the bike, rode to the front of the procession and led them across the bridge, and now the Tribe was moving at a quicker pace. Foodcourt walked up with a look of blank delight. "My, it's almost as nice here as Australia, isn't it?"

"Yes, Father, "Johnny said to appease him, not having time to deal with him then.

They reached the other side of the bridge. Deb seemed so quiet it worried Johnny. He hoped they were done with the Gangers, at least for a little while.

Then something worse came along. From around a building nearby, Johnny saw the first head of a wild dog-beastie. He knew it meant there were more following.

Johnny turned to the men behind him. "Get your weapons ready! If we keep moving, we can scare them into staying away."

A murmur of fear swept through the Tribe. One man in the back said, "We never should have left Sanctuary. It's so bright out here!"

"We're going to die!" Another wailed.

"The air! The air! I can't breathe!"

Johnny sighed with irritation. "Just relax. There's nothing wrong with the air. You're just afraid and it's making you panic. It's making it hard for you to breathe. I've been out here for years, and I'm healthier than all of you."

This created a new murmur. Johnny just hoped he wouldn't lose them, now.

The passed by the dog-beasties slowly, the whole Tribe staring at them with fright. The dog-beasties saw the men with their knives and guns. They snarled and studied them, but there were too many men and the dog-beasties didn't move, afraid to attack. Finally, the Tribe passed by them. The fright seemed to energize the Tribe and they moved faster, but now Deb was getting very heavy. Johnny worried that he might drop her or be forced to stop.

Deb stirred again, almost as if hearing Johnny's thoughts. She woke up and looked at him. Johnny smiled at her, trying to hide the concern he felt.

"Johnny, where am I? Are we safe?"

"We're on our way to Misterwizard's. How do you feel?"

"I'm fine, silly," she said, smiling back at him. But then she began to fall off the bike, and Johnny had to grab her.

"I'm just a little dizzy, I don't know why. And I feel so cold."

A stab of pain lanced through Johnny's heart. He grabbed her around the waist and touched her hand. It was cold.

"Deb—"

She smiled. "I'm okay. Just so sleepy." She closed her eyes again. Up ahead, Johnny saw Castle. They were almost there.

In the dark interior of Sanctuary, Ripper watched the last of the Gangers pour out the opening where the Tribe had left, leaving him with only a few Gangers nearby. One of them was Leaker.

In a sing-song voice, Leaker said, "Lookie what I caught."

Ripper turned, and what he saw made him smile with pleasure.

It was Leader Nordstrom, the head of the Tribe. He looked terrified and shook all over.

Ripper strode up to him. "Well it seems your Tribe has left you behind."

Leader Nordstrom scowled with fright. "It's that rotten Johnny. He's trying to steal the Tribe away from me. What are you going to do with me?"

Ripper walked over and stared at Leader Nordstrom, stroking his chin. "That depends. How would you like to have real power? I'm going to take over this whole city, maybe even the world. The Gangers are the Leader Nordstroms of the future. We will own this world soon, and I will rule it with fear and torture. We will have everything we want: women, food, and cringing subjects. If you help me take over your Tribe, I will give you a position of power in my new order.

"And best of all," Ripper smiled darkly, "we will make an end of Johnny Apocalypse."

Leader Nordstrom smiled just as darkly. "Perhaps we can make an arrangement."

They both laughed in ugly unpleasant ways that made the blood in the other Gangers grow cold.

CHAPTER II

The Tribe walked on. From behind a building four Wildies ran out, waving broken sticks in the air.

"You are deadish! We curse you!"

"Children of the cursed fathers. You brought this on us!"

"Give us food or we cook and eat you! Don't make us beg!"

The Wildies looked old and they were stooped over, their skin wrinkled and burned from the radiation and exposure. They wore filthy rags and had bloody cloths wrapped around their feet. One's left eye was gone; another had one arm shorter than the other that hung at his side, useless. A third had burns all over his face; he was the oldest.

Johnny knew right away that they were mostly harmless, men with no wits about them and without the strength to find food for themselves let alone beat a stray dog, but to most of the members of the Tribe they were a terrifying vision. The women instantly cringed, grabbed their children and held them close. The men looked scared, but they took out their weapons and advanced on the four hapless crazies as if they were an army of attacking monsters.

Johnny stopped his bike, hopped off and quickly positioned himself between the Wildies and the men of the tribe. He turned to the men of the Tribe and raised his hands, not even afraid of the Wildies behind him.

"Stop! These are harmless Wildies. Some are dangerous, but most are to be pitied, not feared. They live out here and pick through the trash for food. They are crazy in the head and have the Sickness."

The Wildies reached a point ten feet from the Tribe and stopped. They waved their arms and tried to scare the Tribe, but Johnny saw the desperation, fear and emptiness in their eyes. Johnny felt sadness in his heart for them; they had no one and they didn't live long, for most spent nights shivering and throwing up what little food they'd eaten. Death to them was a relief from pain.

The tribesmen now saw what Johnny was saying was true, and they relaxed. They acted braver and even pointed and laughed at the Wildies who stood there looking pathetic and miserable. This made Johnny angry. He motioned for the Tribe to keep moving, hoping to put the poor, unfortunate men behind them and leave them a small amount of dignity and peace. When it seemed like the Tribe was far enough away, he climbed back on his Harley and drove on, giving the poor, lonely men one last sad glance.

Johnny looked ahead. He could see Castle now; its

tall, white spires stuck up into the sky like knife blades cutting the sky. They were almost there.

Then Johnny heard something even more frightening than the bark of the Barkers. The sound took him back to his first adventure outside Sanctuary, for it a growl. The tiger-beastie he'd tangled with so long ago was still alive, and it was near.

Johnny looked around nervously and spotted it. On a second story ledge of a building with no front wall, it watched them with hungry eyes. Johnny knew that there was not deterring this enemy; it looked hungry and desperate. He would have to fight it or scare it away. He pulled out his sword. Then he looked around wildly for Starbucks. "Starbucks!"

Starbucks drove up with Super behind him. "What's up, Johnny?"

Johnny pointed with his eyes. Starbucks looked up and saw the tiger-beastie. He whistled.

Johnny turned in his seat and looked for his father Foodcourt. "Father, I need your help!'

Foodcourt ran up with eyes wide open. "What can I do, Johnny?"

Johnny hopped off his bike. "I need you to keep pushing my bike towards Castle with Deb on it. I have to do something very important."

Foodcourt nodded, looking serious. He grabbed the handlebars of Johnny's Harley and started pushing it, careful to make sure Deb didn't fall all off. It was hard going with Deb's limp body on the bike, but with a look of determination, he dug his feet in and moved the bike along. Johnny didn't like asking him to do it, but he had no choice. He had to take care of the tiger-beastie before the Tribe saw it, or they would panic and scatter.

Starbucks hopped off. "You can't fight it alone. Super can ride my bike, can't you, Super?"

Super grinned with delight. "You bet I can!" She took off, and promptly fell over. Johnny and Starbucks grinned at her as she righted the bike and scowled at them. "I bet you fell too, your first time." She got back on, and soon was puttering slowly to the front of the tribe.

Johnny and Starbucks ran to the building, swords drawn. When they were inside, they hurried to the broken, rotted stairway to the second floor. As they reached the door leading to the open floor where the tiger-beastie stood, they slowed to a crawl.

Johnny heard its loud eager pants first. Carefully he slipped around the corner he saw it. It lay on the edge, paws dangling over. Its eyes were transfixed on the Tribe below, looking at one after another, picking out a likely victim.

Johnny made sure to position himself so that the tiger-beastie had a way to escape. The last thing he wanted to do was to corner it, for he knew it would have no option but to attack them then. Starbucks seemed to sense this too, for he too moved to a spot leaving the tiger-beastie a way out.

It started rising. Johnny knew it was about to strike. He readied his sword and nodded at Starbucks.

"Hey! Furball! Mangy cat-beastie! Over here!" Starbucks yelled, waving his arms.

The tiger-beastie turned around and saw Starbucks and Johnny. It crouched, ears pinned back, and snarled, showing sharp pointed fangs. It tensed, readying to leap on him. Johnny gritted his teeth and rushed the tiger-beastie. He yelled and thrust his sword out, stabbing the tiger-beastie in the side.

The tiger-beastie howled and spun in midair, clawing at the sword and snarling. Johnny yelled and stabbed again. Starbucks yelled too, louder.

Caught between the two of them, the tiger-beastie crawled backwards and swiped at Johnny with its paw, claws extended. Johnny hoped desperately that it would run instead of attack. He continued thrusting his sword forward, pushing the tiger-beastie back.

Johnny looked over the ledge. Most of the Tribe had passed. Now all he had to worry about was him and Starbucks, getting away with their skin intact.

"Back away! Let it go!" Johnny began following his own advice, hoping Starbucks would do the same.

The tiger-beastie shifted its gaze from one of them to the other and back again, a silent snarl frozen on its face. Its tail twitched swiftly. Even thin and haggard, it was a beautiful animal. Johnny couldn't help but feel admiration and wonder for it, and a quiet joy at being so close to it, even if it meant his death.

Ever so slowly, the tiger-beastie began backing away. Johnny let go a silent sigh of relief. The last of the tribe was down the street. A few more seconds and they could back away, leaving the tiger-beastie alone to look for other prey.

"The Tribe's gone, Johnny. Let's get out of here!" Johnny nodded, enthusiastically agreeing. Slowly the two backed up, leaving the tiger-beastie staring at them with lidded eyes full of menace.

When they got out the door they took off running down the stairs like they'd never run before. They grinned at each other and then laughed, sharing a glorious moment of danger and camaraderie. They reached the outside and looked up at the ledge. The tiger-beastie wasn't there anymore.

Starbucks looked around worriedly. "Where do you think it went?"

Johnny scanned the horizon too, trying to spot it. "I don't know, but let's get back to the Tribe and make sure it wasn't after them. I think I've had enough adventure for one day. I just want to get to Castle and get some sleep."

Starbucks grinned, looked as tired as Johnny. "Me, too." As they hurried back to the Tribe, Johnny hoped the tiger-beastie wouldn't find the Wildies. He hoped it would find the Gangers instead and maybe slow them down.

Johnny looked back. He saw the first of the Gangers coming over the bridge far away. What had happened to Misterwizard?

The Tribe finally reached Castle after what seemed to Johnny like a journey of a thousand miles. Johnny told the Tribe to wait while he raised the fence by himself. He didn't want anyone knowing where the opening was, just yet, for he didn't trust them not to give away the secret by accident to the Gangers.

When he was sure the Tribe was far enough away, and it was just him and Starbucks, Johnny faced the gate. He and Starbucks grinned at each other. Then Johnny spoke.

"Open Sesame!"

Sure enough, the gate raised. Johnny and Starbucks

grinned at each other some more, feeling like they were minor wizards themselves. Then they went back to the Tribe.

After the door was opened Johnny let them in one after another. He told them to go right inside the big doors in front. The men and women of the Tribe cried out with joy at finally arriving at their destination. Some even wept. They ran across the large courtroom without even looking at it and passed through the large wooden doors into the castle as if the sky was falling any minute or the Red Eye was burning them.

Johnny felt an enormous sense of pride at having saved the Tribe from danger, though he tried to hide it. Deb saw though, for she was awake, and she smiled at him. She walked over and put her arms around him. "Johnny, my hero." She reached up and kissed him. He would have enjoyed the kiss immensely, except her lips felt hot, and it instantly put Johnny into a worse panic. Deb was sick! His heart felt sick, and he felt frustrated at not being able to do anything to help her.

Starbucks and Johnny hid their Harleys in the courtyard. Starbucks and Super, holding hands, gaily skipped toward the doors. "Yippee!" Super said. "We get to see Misterwizard's Castle again!"

Johnny and Deb entered last, but before they did Johnny looked back one more time at the road in the direction of Sanctuary, wondering where Misterwizard was, and worrying about his friend.

Johnny entered the castle to find the people of the Tribe standing in the huge room past the small entryway, staring up at the ceiling with its fancy colored glass windows and lofty columns reaching up into the gloom above. Johnny admitted to himself that the first time he saw the room he stood and gawked too, for it was like walking into the doorway to a magical place.

Misterwizard filled the room with all kinds of weird and fantastic things that he called "relics" from the past. When Johnny was very little, Misterwizard had showed him around and explained the names of things, though Johnny didn't know what any of them meant and had forgotten most of them. There were Fake People dressed in all kinds of different outfits, from "army, navy and marine" uniforms to something Misterwizard called "scuba" gear. There was one dressed in a suit with stripes, a hat with flat rim and a black ribbon and carrying a "tommy-gun" that Misterwizard said was a "mobster." There was even one wearing giant shoes, a polka-dotted outfit and a huge rubber nose, its face painted white with a big red smile on its mouth. Misterwizard called that one a "clown from the circus."

There was a red machine with glass walls against one wall that Misterwizard said used to make "popcorn," and another square metal box with a round top that he said played music and was called a "Jukebox." There was lots of fancy furniture in different colors and shapes. There was a booth that you sat in and looked at a glass panel. Misterwizard said it took "pictures of you, if you had a dollar," which made absolutely no sense to Johnny. Then there were also the old cars, the suits of armor and the paintings all over the walls.

The whole room was filled with strange and wonderful things, and the Tribe wandering around looking and touching, murmuring to each other. Johnny watched nervously, hoping they didn't break any of Misterwizard's stuff.

Sephie ran up to Johnny. "Johnny, look at all the

wonderful junk!"

Johnny smiled, and he bent down and gave Sephie a squeeze. "I'll tell you all about it someday. For now, go find your mommy and daddy, Sephie, and stay close to them, all right? "

Sephie nodded happily and wandered off.

Carny walked up to Johnny, rubbing her belly. "Johnny, where are we going to sleep? Miracle and me need rest."

Foodcourt and Teavanna, Johnny's parents, walked up. Foodcourt smiled, his face lit up with excitement. "My, this Misterwizard is an amazing character. Is this our first stop on our way to Australia? It should be, you know. Why stay where there's danger, when we can go where everyone is still safe?"

"Maybe father," Johnny said, humoring him. "We'll stay here and get organized. Then maybe we'll move on."

Foodcourt nodded with a smile of happiness. "Wonderful! We're finally on our way."

Deb walked up, grabbed Johnny's arm and cuddled up to it. "We're safe now, Johnny, thanks to you. But I'm so tired. Where are they all going to sleep?"

"Everybody's tired. But first," Johnny replied, "we have to set up patrols. It won't take too long for the Gangers to find out where we are. And then they're going to attack again."

Johnny did a little trick he'd learned from the Wizard. He put his fingers in his mouth and blew, making a loud whistling sound. It had the desired effect for the members of the Tribe gathered in front of him.

Johnny stood on a wooden box, so everyone could see him. "Listen, everybody. We are safe for now in Misterwizard's castle, but we can't relax yet. The

Gangers are out there, and as soon as they find out where we are, they will try to attack us again."

This produced a murmur of worry to ripple through the Tribe. One man in his early teens said in a melancholy voice, "Why don't they leave us alone? What do they want?"

Super answered for Johnny. "They don't want anything. They're just creeps who have nothing better to do than get their kicks out of hurting people."

A woman named Victoria'ssecret with long, stringy white hair wearing a ragged red bathrobe and shiny black shoes walked up. Her long, pinched face was drawn with worry. "You've brought us here just to die here instead of Sanctuary. The air is probably already killing us, and the Red Eye is turning our skin to ash!"

Her words caused another ripple of fearful murmuring to go through the Tribe. Johnny raised a hand. "That's not true. I have been outside many times. Look at me. I am stronger and healthier than all of you. I drink the water from the flowing river. I eat the deer-beasties and raccoon-beasties. And I have fun walking in the light of the Red Eye. You will too!"

Some of the Tribe looked more hopeful, but others still frowned, unconvinced.

"Is Leader Nordstrom really dead?" A man said.

"I don't know," Johnny replied. "All I know is, it's time for us to stop living in fear and start building a new country. And we can't do that living in fear in the dark, in Sanctuary."

This produced another round of murmuring, but most of it seeming to be positive.Then, just as Johnny felt things were finally beginning to come together, they heard a loud, whiny shout outside the gate.

"It's me, Leader Nordstrom! Let me in! I know you're in there! Hello!"

A wave of excitement and relief rippled through the crowd. The man named Richardmillhousenixon stepped forward, pointed a big, fat finger like a sausage at Johnny and spoke with narrowed eyes. "Leader Nordstrom isn't dead! Now you'll see, Johnny Apocalypse. Now we'll know what to do."

The crowd surged forward to the door and Johnny felt the situation getting out of control. Carny stepped forward and blocked them. "Listen to me!"

The crowd stopped and looked at Carny. "Look, I don't know what's wrong with you people, but Leader Nordstrom has kept us all locked in that dark cave for all our lives. Now Johnny has freed us. If you let Leader Nordstrom lead again, things will go back to being as they were. Are you people really that stupid?"

"Get out of our way, Carny," Cinnabon said. "You think with your baby brains." This made the whole Tribe laugh. They walked past Johnny and Carny, wearing smiles and chuckling.

Carny and Deb walked up to Johnny. "What are we going to do, Johnny?"

"Don't worry," Johnny said, but inside he wished Misterwizard was back.

Johnny hurried out to get to the gate before the crowd did. As some walked outside, they glanced up fearfully at the sky but kept going.

"Hello! Let me in! Where are you?" Johnny stood at the gate. The Tribe looked at him.

Cinnabon frowned with anger and stared at Johnny. "Let him in, Johnny."

Richardmillhousenixon said in a grumpy tone, "He's

Leader Nordstrom. You're not!"

Victoria'ssecret wailed, "Leader Nordstrom will tell us what to do. He always knows!"

Starbucks walked outside to stand next to Johnny. He glared at the crowd. "Johnny's going to let Leader Nordstrom in all right. But before he does, I want to know what you intend to do. Leader Nordstrom wanted to make us stay and all die at Sancturary. Without Johnny's help, you would have."

Richardmillhousenixon stepped forward and put a hand on his big double chin. "So, you think we should just let the Gangers kill Leader Nordstrom? What's wrong with you?"

Starbucks turned to Richardmillhousenixon. "No, of course not. I just want your word, as a tribe, that you won't let Leader Nordstrom hurt Johnny or his family. You owe Johnny that much."

The Tribe members all looked at each other and talked. Then Richardmillhousenixon answered for them, shaking his head up and down and making the fat rolls under his chin wobble. "You're right. Johnny had done right by us. We won't let Leader Nordstrom hurt him."

Johnny turned to Starbucks, gratitude on his face. Starbucks saw it and he grinned impishly at Johnny. "Looks like we avoided another tiger-beastie today." Johnny nodded and the two knocked fists.

Preparing himself mentally for what would come next, Johnny opened the gate. Leader Nordstrom strode in, full of indignation. He glared at Johnny, his mouth set in a grim line.

"It's about time, you little upstart! Trying to take over, are you? Well, we'll see about that. Where are my Enforcers? Arrest Johnny right now!"

The Tribe stared stony-faced at Leader Nordstrom. He looked from one face to another, the realization dawning on him that some things had changed. "What is going on? Why are you not obeying me?"

Richardmillhousenixon took a step forward and put up a big hand, palm facing forward. "You are still Leader Nordstrom, but Johnny Apocalypse saved us from the Gangers. We promised you would not harm him."

Leader Nordstrom looked thoughtful, his white eyebrows furrowed over his dark eyes. "So, because he saved his own skin and took you along with him you think he's some kind of savior now, is that it? All right. Let him alone for now; but soon Johnny Apocalypse will show you who he truly is. Then you will know who really cares about you and who is lying."

Leader Nordstrom strode forward towards the door to the Castle with his usual scowl. The confrontation over, the Tribe followed laughing and talking about what just happened. Johnny and Starbucks joined in, grinning at each other and patting each other's back.

The next few hours were some of the hardest for Johnny to endure. Leader Nordstrom took over as if he'd never left. He ordered all of Misterwizard's things to be hauled outside. Then he began divvying up the room; giving each family a small area of their own. At least Carny and Deb were finally able to lie down, but Johnny could barely contain his anger at the way Leader Nordstrom treated Misterwizard's prized possessions. He wished Misterwizard was there to help defend his home.

Deep inside, feelings of worry swirled in Johnny like the twisting winds of a tornado. Where was Misterwizard?

The Red Eye slipped over the distant mountains and

darkness filled the sky. Leader Nordstrom did set up patrols along the fence, which was one of the only things he did that Johnny thought was smart.

But when Leader Nordstrom headed up the stairs towards Wizard's private quarters, Johnny had had enough. He hurried and blocked his way.

The Tribe was far below, settling down for the night, and couldn't hear them. "What do you think you're doing, you little dirty whelp?" Leader Nordstrom snarled. "Get out of my way."

"No. You will not go into Misterwizard's room. It belongs to him and I won't let you touch it!"

Leader Nordstrom stared for a moment with barely concealed menace, but when he saw the look in Johnny's eyes he thought better than to try and defy him.

"All right, you rotten little rebel. I won't touch your wonderful Misterwizard's junk, for now. But if he doesn't show up soon, I'm going up there and clear it out. I'll make it my office."

"You won't touch one piece, whether Misterwizard returns or not," Johnny replied, his hands balled into fists.

Leader Nordstrom's eyes opened wide with fear, for he knew he'd pushed Johnny just a little too far. Then he scowled. "I'm not done with you, Mister. Sleep lightly, Johnny Apocalypse. Your days with the Tribe are short."

Leader Nordstrom's lip curled one more time and he flashed one more look of hatred before he spun and tramped down the stairs.

Johnny had to find Misterwizard, for his friend had been gone too long. He didn't dare leave though, for he knew Leader Nordstrom would sneak up into Misterwizard's room the moment Johnny left.

Johnny saw his father Foodcourt, and soon he had a solution. After talking with his father, Foodcourt promised he would sleep upstairs in Misterwizard's room, and if Leader Nordstrom tried to get in, he would, "teach him a lesson he wouldn't forget."

Johnny thanked him and headed for the gate. There he found the Enforcers making rounds, just as if they were still at Sanctuary. It gave Johnny the creeps. He walked to the secret gate and was about to leave when he heard a voice behind him.

"Hey, stupid!"

Johnny turned to see a friendly face. It was Starbucks. "Where are you going?"

Starbucks hooked a finger behind him. "Don't you know Leader Nordstrom wants to hang you from the nearest tree? You leave, and maybe you won't get back in."

"I have to go, Starbucks and find Misterwizard. Something's happened to him. You stay and keep an eye on things for me."

"Uh-uh," Starbucks said, shaking his head. "'Cause I'm going with you. You can't wipe your butt without me to help you."

They both laughed. Johnny nodded. "Well, come on then."

They climbed back on their Harleys and rolled them to the gate.

"Open Sesame!" The gate swung open.

Together Johnny and Starbucks rolled their Harleys out the door without starting them.

"Close Sesame!" The gate closed again.

The boys started their engines, and quietly motored away.

Starbucks looked at Johnny. "Do you have any idea where to go, Johnny my man?"

Johnny turned his head and looked at Starbucks. "Back to Sanctuary, I guess. That's where Misterwizard was going."

Together Johnny and Starbucks drove through the dark night.

As he rode, Johnny gazed up at the stars. They were so bright they felt like pinpricks in his skin. Misterwizard said once that one of the few positives of the bombs falling was no lights at night; you could see the stars. Johnny didn't understand how lights could make you not see the stars, but he didn't ask about it.

The starlight lit up the bridge just enough to barely see it. The Yellow Eye wasn't high in the sky that night; Johnny noticed it peaking over the side of the horizon. The cool, night air felt good on Johnny's skin.

As they crossed the bridge, Johnny heard a now familiar but alarming sound: a loud growl. The tiger-beastie was out there in the dark, somewhere.

Johnny turned to Starbucks. "Be careful; I think we have a follower. Tiger-beastie is still hungry."

Starbucks turned the handle on his Harley and sped off. "Well, let's ride faster then!"

Johnny and Starbucks put on an extra burst of speed. They looked at each other and laughed at their predicament and mutual fright. The cool air felt good on their skin, and the steady thrum of the bikes under them gave the boys a thrill as they wove between the dark, black hulks of old cars.

As they grew close to Sanctuary, what Johnny saw made his heart run cold. The night was lit up with orange light. Sanctuary was on fire.

Johnny and Starbucks stopped for a moment and watched the flames dance in the blackness.

"I sure hope Misterwizard is not in there," Starbucks said.

"Come on." Johnny started riding faster.

They reached parking lot and wove their way stealthily through the cars. When they were close enough, Johnny saw that all the gates and doors had been torn down, and now Sanctuary was wide open. The fires burned from the windows and the roof, but the hallway inside was clear.

Johnny and Starbucks parked their Harleys behind the big truck box where they used to hide them and made their way to the nearest opening into Sanctuary. Careful to watch for Gangers, they crept into the Main Hallway. Then they snuck along next to the fronts of the stores, eyes watching for Gangers.

They heard shouts of cruel laughter. Sensing the worst, Johnny and Starbucks crept along until they grew close to the large area near Johnny's old dwelling place. What they saw froze the blood inside them.

The Gangers stood in a group, surrounding something, laughing and drinking. On the ground around them lay all the tribe's belongings, some smashed, others just opened and spilled out.

But it wasn't the destruction of the tribe's possessions that bothered Johnny. It was what the Gangers looked at.

There tied to a poll on top of a pile of junk was Misterwizard! He glared down at the Gangers with righteous wrath, but Johnny also saw fear in his eyes.

And Ripper stood in front of the Gangers. He held a torch. They were going to burn Misterwizard alive.

CHAPTER 12

Johnny couldn't believe his eyes. Panic and desperation gripped him.

"Johnny! What are we going to do?" Starbucks looked as upset as Johnny did.

They had to act fast. Johnny knew that he had to rescue Wizard, even if it meant his own death; Misterwizard had done so much for Johnny, Johnny owed him his life, at least.

"You create a distraction, while I set him free."

"What if they catch you?"

Johnny grimaced. "Then you have to save Misterwizard, no matter what."

Starbucks nodded somberly. Johnny surveyed the scene before him. The area was wide open, in the middle of the mall. On one side stood the J C. Penney's store. On the other side was an open hallway leading to other stores. Johnny saw one place that hid a small amount of cover. It was a small rolling cart, long since empty of whatever it sold, next to the wall by the J. C. Penneys. If Johnny could make it there and then give Starbucks the signal...

Then Johnny thought of something and he smiled. "Listen. I'm going to try and find our "friend" outside. You keep them busy somehow, so they don't hurt Misterwizard before I get back."

Starbucks looked confused, not knowing what Johnny had planned, but he shrugged and nodded. Starbucks snuck forward while Johnny ran back outside fast.

Back in outside again, Johnny was struck with the coolness of the night air. He looked around the parking lot, hoping the tiger-beastie had followed them.

Johnny whistled. "Hey! Tiger-beastie! Come get some dinner! Here I am, all alone, waiting for you! Very tasty I am! Come get me!"

Johnny walked around the dark shapes of the rusted hulks, repeating his invitation over and over in a loud voice. "Tiger-beastie! You're hungry, aren't you? Dinner on the foot, right here!"

Johnny didn't have much time, and he began to panic. He was so engrossed in his thoughts that he wasn't even looking up as he yelled, which almost cost him his life.

As he rounded an old, black car talking loudthere in front of him stood the tiger-beastie! All Johnny could see were its green eyes sparkling in the starlight and a huge giant slinky shape, black against the night sky sitting on the top of a car.

Johnny stopped and stared up at it, frozen in place for a moment by fear. The tiger-beastie moved, and it snapped Johnny out of his state. With a yell Johnny turned and ran.

His heart in this throat, Johnny didn't look back, sure that at any moment he was going to feel sharp claws in his back. On the other hand, he had to know the tiger-beastie was following or his plan wouldn't work. He had to take a chance and look back to make sure.

Johnny ran around a large box-like hulk that said "Humvee" on the side. Breathing hard, he stopped and looked back, straining to hear any sound. He knew tiger-beasties were silent when they hunted, and he really shouldn't hesitate, for it could pounce on him before he even knew it was near, but he had to be sure it was following him.

He peered out at the darkness but saw nothing but the night sky and old, rusted hulks as far as the eye could see.

Then he heard a loud "clump" from on top of the Humvee. He knew what it meant and didn't hesitate but ran again. The tiger-beastie was with him, all right!

The next few moments were some of the scariest of the last few days. He saw the opening into Sanctuary ahead, inviting him in like what it's name meant, a Sanctuary. He knew that the tiger-beastie was much faster than him when it wanted to be. Johnny put every ounce of his strength into running, not saving anything for later, because there might not be a later if he failed.

Just when he was sure he could feel the tiger-beastie's breath on his neck Johnny reached the doorway. He bolted inside without stopping and ran around a corner to hide, and watch. Sure enough, the tiger-beastie loped in, looking for him. It was a magnificent animal, and Johnny couldn't help but wonder at its strength and quiet beauty. A thrill of excitement went through him as well as a pleasure at knowing he had escaped.

The tiger-beastie stopped and surveyed dark Sanctuary. Johnny held his breath and hoped with all his might that the tiger-beastie would keep going. He tried to be silent, so that it wouldn't hear him, but hopefully hear the Gangers ahead.

And it did. The sound of the Gangers' yells and laughter echoed through the mall. The tiger-beastie was instantly interested. It looked towards the sound and began silently padding in the direction of the commotion.

Johnny cheered silently. Then he chuckled, thinking what a nice surprise the Gangers had waiting for them. Johnny crept towards the Ganger camp again, careful to give the tiger-beastie a wide berth.

Johnny made it back to the spot he'd occupied earlier and looked once again at the Gangers. He hoped desperately that all his hard work was going to be worth something, that Starbucks had been able to stop the Gangers from hurting Misterwizard. If the Gangers had killed his friend, Johnny didn't know how he could ever be happy again, knowing he'd let the great man down.

But Johnny didn't need to worry about Starubucks creating a distraction. When he looked at the scene in front of him, he groaned. Misterwizard was still tied to a stake in the middle of the Gangers, but now Starbucks was next to him! Johnny shook his head. Now he had to save both of them!

As Johnny thought about what to do, the tiger-beastie struck. A Ganger on the fringes of the group screamed, and it was obvious from the sound it was in sheer terror. The rest turned to look, and the effect of the fear in the man's voice wiped the smiles and humor from their faces.

Johnny looked too, and what he saw would stay with him forever. The tiger-beastie had its jaw clamped on the shoulder of the Ganger and he was dragging the poor man away as the man screamed and flailed weakly at it.

Instant pandemonium ensued. The Gangers all yelled in fear and ran in different directions. Johnny didn't wait for them to come back. He bolted for Starbucks and Misterwizard as the Gangers ran past him.

Starbucks and Misterwizard saw Johnny. They smiled joy. Johnny pulled out his sword, getting ready to cut them free.

"Not so fast, Johnny boy."

Johnny turned. It was Ripper, his face a mask of hatred and anger. "You ruined our little party, but I'm still going to roast your friends."

Johnny didn't stop or even answer. He reached Starbucks and cut one rope free. A bullet whizzed by his ear. He touched his ear with his fingers and felt blood; luckily, the bullet had only grazed him. He spun around and ducked, just in time to avoid a second shot that tore up the wood between Starbucks' feet.

Starbucks yelled. Johnny sprinted for Ripper. Ripper pointed the gun at Johnny, but Johnny swung his sword, just missing Ripper's arm. Ripper raised his arm out of the way and Johnny swung his sword again. Ripper staggered back, trying to bring his gun to bear. Johnny swung his sword again and again, making half circles, trying to reach Ripper, and Ripper kept backing up and trying to aim his gun.

"Coward! Using a gun on unarmed man. Fight me like a man!"

Ripper laughed; it was an evil, crazy sound. "Why would I do that when I can put a hole in you instead? Get rid of Johnny the Annoyer and little Scrabbler once and for all."

"Hold still so that I can cut you into pieces like you deserve for what you did to our home!" Johnny knew if he stopped swinging, Ripper would be able to aim, and Johnny would be dead, so he kept it up, even though his arm grew tired and heavy.

"Ah, your home, so sad," Ripper said, staying just out of reach. "Now it's home for the Doomsday Prophecy. Soon the whole world will be our home, and Johnny will be a memory people laugh at. And your girl will be mine."

A group of Gangers ran by screaming. Johnny looked up to see the tiger-beastie chasing them. He grinned. "Not much left of Doomsday Prophecy. All tiger-beastie food now."

Ripper laughed too, not able to help himself. "Always more where they come from. Let tiger-beastie eat its full, then I'll find more."

"Hey, Dripper." Ripper turned. Starbucks slugged him in the face, hard. Ripper yelled and staggered back. "Count your losses, friend, and run away before you end up a memory and a joke yourself."

Johnny leapt at Ripper and wrenched his gun away.

Johnny smiled. Starbucks stood there, with Misterwizard behind him. Ripper scowled. He backed away.

"This is just the beginning of your sorrows, Johnny Apocalypse. You got enemies you don't even know about yet. You won't be around much longer. Soon your tribe is going to call Ripper their Leader Nordstrom, and I will take care of your family, and your girl."

"You better shut up, or I'll shoot you right now!" Johnny shook with anger and raised Ripper's gun, even though he knew he was a terrible aim.

"Hey! Gangers! Johnny's here! Come kill him!"

Johnny saw Gangers running back towards them. Johnny, Starbucks and Wizards ran away as Ripper yelled after them, taunting them.

Starbucks grinned. "One thing's sure, Johnny, I always have an adventure when I stick around with you!"

"Run!" Johnny said. He looked at Misterwizard. "Are you all right, Misterwizard?"

Misterwizard looked tired and sweaty but he grinned jauntily, trying hard to keep up with Johnny and Starbucks. "Absolutely splendid my boy, thanks to your timely intervention. A night of thrilling battle, exciting danger and amazing plot twists, don't you think? But I suggest we make our egress before our tormentors regather their wits and forces and capture us again."

Johnny just nodded. After all that had happened, Misterwizard's puzzling words gave Johnny a head-ache.

They ran into the cool night air, jumping up and down with joy at their escape. Weaving between the old cars, they laughed and joked about their success. When they reached the Harleys, it was Misterwizard's turn to take a ride on Johnny's mode of transportation. With whoops like men who just won a war, the two boys sped off, not caring if their Harleys filled the night with the roar of their engines.

CHAPTER 13

They made it across the bridge and a few more blocks and then both their Harleys sputtered and died. Johnny and Starbucks looked at each other and then at Misterwizard. Misterwizard was snoring soundly. Johnny grinned at Starbucks and then climbed off his bike. Starbucks did the same thing.

"Looks like we're out of the water Misterwizard put in them."

Johnny nodded. "Lucky we're far enough away from the Gangers. I just hope we don't meet another tiger-beastie or dog-beastie pack."

"Let's get moving!" They started pushing the Harleys, Misterwizard still on Johnny's. Suddenly Misterwizard awoke with a start, looking around and saw what they were doing.

"Ah!" He said, yawning wide. "Looks like you need a

stop at the petrol station. That is located at my Castle, in a large tanker truck I managed to procure. I'm sorry, I should have reminded you to fill up before you left."

"It's okay, Misterwizard," Johnny said, grinning. "We don't mind pushing."

"Then let me make your burden less wearisome. I will disembark, for there is no reason for me to get a free ride at your expense."

Misterwizard hopped off and soon walked next to the boys as they wheeled their bikes along.

As they walked, they filled each other in on the day's events. Misterwizard told Johnny how he played cat and mouse with the Gangers on his moped, until a group of them managed to set up a trap with a sheet in front of him.

"When I accelerated to pass them, they scooped me up like a sparrow in a net. It was quite embarrassing, if I were to speak candidly, to be so easily duped by such mental inferiors. If one observed their celebration, one would believe they had just won a world war against a veritable army vice capturing one, tired, short old man. It's a good thing you arrived when you did, Johnny, for I really think they planned on making me the main entrée at a luau."

Johnny laughed. He really loved Misterwizard and didn't want to think what the world would be like without him. He told Misterwizard about the tiger-beastie and their adventures on the way to Castle. He finished by telling Misterwizard how Leader Nordstrom had returned and how he had taken over. He told Misterwizard how Leader Nordstrom had taken all of Misterwizard's things in the main floor and moved them outside. Johnny assured Misterwizard that he had kept

Leader Nordstrom out of his room upstairs and how glad was now that Misterwizard was with them now to help deal with the cantankerous man.

While Johnny talked, Misterwizard listened attentively, nodded and saying, "I see" over and over. Misterwizard held onto Johnny's waist and sometimes it was a long time before Misterwizard replied. Johnny swore he heard a soft snore now and then. He smiled, not blaming his friend for being tired, after what he'd been through.

Misterwizard spoke in a serious tone, full of thought. "Johnny, now that the Tribe has been forced to depart the shackles of Sanctuary, it is time to begin rebuilding society. If we fail in this task, the world will continue its destructive descent into anarchy and we will regress on the evolutionary scale back to the level of our ancestors the monkey-beasties. The human race, imperfect and fragmentary as it is, must not die out. We need to recreate a form of government in the democratic form and reinstate law and order. And to accomplish these goals, we need someone to lead the people, someone that will be able to command respect, but who is not afraid. We need a man of courage and determination."

Johnny nodded. "We need to be organized, or the Gangers will kill us or make us slaves. We will have to discuss this with Leader Nordstrom."

"Johnny," Misterwizard said, "Leader Nordstrom has some very minor good qualities, but he is in essence a fatally flawed human being. He is rooted in the past and full of mindless fear. He is not the leader the Tribe needs. He has no dsire to change but is content with the status quo where everyone genuflects to him and he has control over them. The Tribe needs a new Leader

Nordstrom. It needs a Leader Johnny."

Johnny looked at Misterwizard, realizing his mentor was saying the same thing he had thought himself. He decided to bring up his own objections to himself to see what Misterwizard would say. "But I am still—"

"A young man, I know. But you are courageous and wise, far beyond your chronological age. You will be a great leader, because deep inside, you are a man of good character who has great empathy for others."

Once again, Johnny wished Misterwizard could speak more plainly. "But I have no idea how to lead a tribe or 'rebuild a nation.'

"Nonsense! You led the people out of Sanctuary, didn't you? You took charge and saved them. With a true leader, leadership comes naturally when it is needed, and is never a thing sought after or orchestrated beforehand. You have the ingredients inside you for what you require, Johnny."

Johnny stared at the buildings in the distance, thoughts tumbling around in his mind.

"I'll do whatever I can to help the tribe."

"Good. It will not be easy to depose Leader Nordstrom, though someday that is what you will have to do, for the Tribe's own good. You will need to get the Tribe on your side first. And you will have to watch your back. If Leader Nordstrom discovers your intentions, he will be like that tiger-beastie you encountered tonight. He will fight to keep what he has, with no regard for the safety or welfare of others."

Leader Nordstrom watched Johnny leave Castle with pure hatred. He knew perfectly well Johnny planned on taking over the tribe; he also knew Johnny was more popular than he was. Johnny was young, strong, and handsome too, and he'd just saved the tribe. He'd also showed the tribe that they could make it out of Sanctuary and not die. If Leader Nordstrom didn't do something soon, he knew that he would be nothing but the old man that no one paid any attention to anymore, and then he would never be able to give the Tribe over to Ripper. Ripper would surely have him killed then. For betraying the Tribe is what he'd had to promise, to save his own neck. He'd agreed to find a way to let the Gangers capture them. When the Tribe was in Ripper's hands, Ripper promised to let Leader Nordstrom be an important member of the gang and continue to be Leader over the Tribe. But Leader Nordstrom was not stupid; he knew Ripper's promises were worthless. He'd made a deal to save his own neck. He had no intention of giving the Tribe over to Ripper. But if Ripper managed to capture the Tribe on his own, Leader Nordstrom knew he'd better make it look like he helped Ripper, or he'd suffer the same fate as the rest of the Tribe did.

But what could Leader Nordstrom do about Johnny? He'd underestimated the lad. He should have eliminated Johnny long ago, when he first saw the boy breaking the rules and showing such independence.

Leader Nordstrom looked to see members of the Tribe lounging around the main floor. They played with Misterwizard's toys like they were all little scrabblers. They laughed and talked, happier than he'd ever seen them, as if they were tasting freedom for the very first time. Leader Nordstrom had to put a stop to that, and quickly, or they'd realize how much more Johnny had done for them than he did.

He rounded up his Enforcers, irritated to find them relaxing and enjoying the new gadgets as well. Then he stood in front of the Tribe with the Enforcers behind him.

"Listen to me, my people. This Johnny has brought you here, and he meant well I'm sure, but we are all now in real danger. For one thing, this place is exposed to the bad air. It is not enclosed like our Sanctuary. Also, it is too small for all of us. There is no way we can all live and sleep here, and what about food? As for the crackpot that lives here who calls himself Misterwizard, we cannot trust him, for he has lived in the air for too long. He is surely touched and diseased.

Our only choice is to gather our strength and retake Sanctuary, even if we die in the attempt. It is either that, or we will surely perish.

"Don't listen to him!" Deb stood in the front of the Tribe, looking proud and defiant, even though her face was flushed, and she trembled. "Johnny told you the truth. Sanctuary is nothing but a grave. If you return there now, you might as well give up living. The Gangers have surely destroyed it by now or set traps in case we return. There is a whole world out here for us. It's time to stop being afraid of old superstitions."

Leader Nordstrom sneered. "So, are we listening to little children now, a girl and boy of only fifteen seasons and who looks as if she is weak from the Sickness already? Is that who leads the Tribe?"

"I am not a child." It was Foodcourt, Johnny's father. Deb rolled her eyes and grimaced, but Leader Nordstrom smiled. "And I say, Johnny is smarter than all of you, especially Leader Nordstrom! He's going to take us to

Australia, where we will be safe forever!"

Leader Nordstrom knew an opportunity when he saw one. He sidled up to Foodcourt and put on a mock serious look. "And just where is Johnny taking us again, Foodcourt?"

Foodcourt frowned, as if a child would know. "To Australia, of course. The bombs didn't fall there, you know. It's a paradise."

The Tribe exploded in tittering and Deb's face colored.

"Australia," Leader Nordstrom grinned. "A nonsensical land of fantasy. This is Johnny's father. Is it any wonder Johnny led you out here to die? He's reckless and crazy, just like his old man."

Deb's eyes flashed. "That's a terrible thing to say. Johnny cares about the Tribe. He only wants to see them free, and—"

Suddenly Deb felt faint. She reached out to a column for support and held onto it, her eyes closed. The people looked at her with concern.

"You see?" Leader Nordstrom pointed a hand towards Deb. "Being outside is already making her sick. How many more of you will die because of this foolishness?"

A murmur of concern and agreement rippled through the Tribe. Leader Nordstrom had not arrived at his position by accident; he knew how to work a crowd.

"That's not true. I'm not sick, I'm just, I've got—" Deb sank to her knees. People gasped and pointed.

Leader Nordstrom couldn't believe his good luck; surely Fortune smiled on him. He rose to his full height and pointed at her, horror on his face. "She has the Sickness. She will infect us all! How many more will get it?

I will tell you what we will do. We will stay here tonight. But we will keep the doors closed and all the windows bolted tight. We will keep watch for the Gangers and the Wildies, and tomorrow we send out a scouting party of courageous men to Sanctuary to plan our return. Once the Gangers see that we're not there, they will surely leave, and we can reclaim it. For now, no one will go outside, or they will not be let back in. As for Johnny and his crazy Misterwizard—"

"No!" Deb protested weakly.

"-if they return, they will no doubt be contaminated. They will have to find their own place to stay outside, not with us."

Leader Nordstrom turned to sneer at Deb. "And as for you, young lady, you shall be banished to the outside, so you don't infect us all. If you live, which is doubtful, you had better learn your place, and some common sense."

Leader Nordstrom pointed to his Enforcers. "Grab her and take her outside!"

"No!" Deb's mother Bathandbodyworks screamed in anger, running to Deb's side and standing in front of her. Her homely face with its large round nose and big ears looked even more unpleasant when she scowled, in fact it made her look dangerous. At this moment, that was exactly what she was.

"Any one who comes near my daughter and lays a hand on her will not have a hand that works anymore."

Leader Nordstrom looked afraid and so did the old men Enforcers. They looked at Leader Nordstrom to see what to do.

"Fine," Leader Nordstrom said, waving a hand. "But let her stay far away in the corner, far away from anyone.

If she dies then, she won't infect anyone else."

Bathandbodyworks seethed with anger and her eyes narrowed. "You are a terrible man, and someday I hope you get what's coming to you."

Leader Nordstrom's eyes went wide, and he frowned. Then with the Enforcers close on his heels, Leader Nordstrom strode away.

As her mother led her over to a corner of the big room, Deb clutched her stomach, for it was cramping, and she willed Johnny and Misterwizard to come back fast. Tears filled her eyes and she closed them to try and keep the tears from welling out. Was it true? Did she have the Sickness? The very thought filled her with a sick dread, fear and anger. The specter of Death loomed in her mind's eye. She thought of all she would miss, of the life with Johnny she wouldn't have. It couldn't be true, could it? No. She was just sick. She'd tried to do too much that day; the excitement had been too much that was all. On wobbly legs she lay down on the blanket her mother laid on the floor for her.

Johnny, Misterwizard and Starbucks didn't talk, for they had already said everything they could think of. Now they just walked and pushed the Harleys, keeping watch on the surroundings for Wildies and Beasties.

Ahead Johnny saw the spires of Castle, black against the night sky. His eyelids felt like boulders hanging on strings, so heavy. He couldn't wait to get back so that he could sleep. He couldn't remember ever feeling so tired.

He looked over at Misterwizard and Starbucks and

grinned. They walked like they were asleep on their feet too. *Good thing the Gangers were far behind, or they would be easy prey,* Johnny thought.

With relief and a quiet pleasure Johnny realized they had reached Castle. Jonny said the magic word. The gate opened, and they walked in. Then they enjoyed a moment of silence as they stood, simply enjoying the nice, cool night and the view of the jagged dark hulks that had once been buildings against the backdrop of stars.

Suddenly the bright light of a torch sprang from the other side of the gate. A gruff voice called out, full of menace.

"Go away! You are not welcome here!"

It was an Enforcer, one Johnny knew Misterwizard named Onsalenow, a short old man with a big head who shook from old age. He was not exactly intimidating, and Johnny didn't feel like having to deal with him, being so tired. "Onsalenow, it is me, Johnny, and Starbucks and Misterwizard."

"I know who you are, Johnny Troublemaker," Onsalenow shot back. "Go away before you contaminate us all."

"Hmmm," Misterwizard said, stroking his beard. "It seems Leader Nordstrom has been busy while we've been occupied. A minor coo has taken place."

Then as if it was planned, they heard another voice from behind the wall. It was Leader Nordstrom.

"So. You made it back. Too bad for you, and us. This is Sanctuary now, and I am still Leader Nordstrom. If you try to get in, you will be killed, so turn around before we fire on you. You are surely contaminated and insane, and we don't want you giving us your disease."

Johnny felt his head swim. He was so tired he barely had any fight left. An uncharacteristic sob of despair rose up in him. He turned to Misterwizard, hoping his friend had a quick solution.

"Come, let us reason together," Misterwizard said in a calm and friendly tone. "Dear Leader Nordstrom, we humbly bow to your authority, and only wish to assist you and the Tribe. And surely if I were contaminated you are as well by now, as you've spent the whole day in my domicile. In which case, we are all in it together. Keeping us isolated can do you no good, and only weaken your numbers."

"Don't try to confuse me with your superior intelligence old man," Leader Nordstrom snarled. "We are not contaminated, you are! Contaminated in the brain, where it cannot be seen but affects the judgment and reason. I now see why Johnny is so strange. You are the reason Johnny is such a rebel. You have taught him all your tricks and enchantments. But you will not put us under your evil spell. We are returning to Sanctuary tomorrow, where we will be safe, and you and Johnny can rot here, for all we care!"

"Sanctuary is gone," Starbucks said. "The Gangers have burned it. There's no going back there now."

"You lie!" Leader Nordstrom's glaring eye shone through a crack in the wall. "Go away in two tongue clicks, or we open fire."

"Johnny!" A new voice, soft and small. Johnny recognized it as Sephie's.

"Sephie! What's wrong?"

"It's Deb, Johnny. She's real sick!"

"Be quiet!" Leader Nordstrom said, glaring at SEphie. "Someone, take this little girl back to her parents."

"Don't you touch her!" Suddenly Johnny was energized by anger and fully awake. He walked up angrily to stand in front of Leader Nordstrom.

"Don't you worry about her, or anybody anymore," Leader Nordstrom snarled. "As for the girl you call Deb, I suggest you forget her. She will never be yours. I will make sure her parents never let her even talk to you again. At least for as long as she lives, for she has the Sickness. She won't last very long, thanks to you."

Johnny didn't know how long he was going to be able to keep from grabbing Leader Nordstrom and throwing him out of the way to get to Deb. "What are you talking about?"

Johnny looked at Misterwizard, only to see a sorrowful look on his friend's face. "Misterwizard?"

Misterwizard didn't answer. He turned to address Leader Nordstrom one more time. "Please Leader Nordstrom, listen to the voice of reason. We are not your enemies."

"You have one tongue click left. Enforcers get your guns ready."

"The very revolvers I supplied to you," Misterwizard said, clicking his tongue in disapproval.

"Let me in!" Johnny made fists and shook in impotent rage.

"Johnny," Starbucks said, "we better go, or this Wildie is going to really shoot us."

Misterwizard gently grabbed Johnny's arm and pulled him away. "At this moment I think retreat is the better part of valor."

Johnny stared daggers at Leader Nordstrom. "No! I have to get to Deb!"

Leader Nordstrom raised his hand, his eyes wild.

"Open fire!"

"Run!" Starbucks took his own advice and ran out of range. Misterwizard and Johnny followed slowly, Misterwizard pulling Johnny away as Johnny stared back with a look of anger and frustration.

Misterwizard bent over and whispered in Johnny's ear. "Don't worry, friend, we have options open to us."

Johnny looked at Misterwizard curiously and finally allowed himself to be led away. When they were out of sight and earshot of Leader Nordstrom, Johnny turned to Wizard. "What did you mean, Misterwizard?"

Misterwizard smiled somberly. "You didn't think I only had one entrance into my domicile, did you? There's another passage into my personal habitat from the other side."

"Good. I'm going to go in there and—"

"No, no, my boy. We must reconnoiter in my room and come up with a plan first."

"Misterwizard, do you really think that Deb—"

"I don't know, Johnny. I know how you must feel, and I'm sorry. I promise that I will give your friend a thorough examination as soon as I can. But first, we have to deal with our little Leader Nordstrom conundrum."

"He's a conundrum, all right," Starbucks said, spitting on the ground for emphasis. "A dirty, rotten conundrum."

CHAPTER 14

Ripper trembled and squeezed his hands into fists as he watched Johnny, Starbucks and Misterwizard run away. Johnny was constantly making him look like a fool. He knew that every time Johnny beat him, the Gangers saw it, and their respect for him went down a little more. How long before they decided he was weak and one of them decided to challenge him for head of the Doomsday Prophesy?

He knew that most of the Gangers were afraid of him and only a few would even dare stand up to him, but still he had to show them; he had to kill Johnny. Then they would know without a doubt that he was the meanest and toughest Ganger on the planet, and the right one to be Gang Leader Nordstrom of the World.

As if reading Ripper's mind, Leaker walked up and said, "He beat you again, Ripper." Ripper spun around and with a lip curled in fury he hit Leaker on the side of the head as hard as he could. Leaker yelped and fell to the ground. He lay there looking up like a whipped dog. Ripper glared at him with unconcealed contempt and stepped over him on his way to the rest of the gang.

The rest of the gang stood around waiting for orders. A short, fat member called Pork-beastie picked his nose and asked, "Are we going after them?"

Ripper smiled; the wheels in his head turning. For a moment he forgot all about Johnny. "First, we burn this place to the ground. Then they'll be trapped out here, in our world. "

The Gangers grinned like wolves. "They'll either serve us, or we'll kill them one by one." Ripper smiled. "Trust me; things are pretty quick going to get real fun. When they're out looking for food, we'll sneak in and steal their women."

The men hooted. "And pity the fool of them that goes out alone." As Ripper basked in the adulation, the Gangers cheered and gathered their weapons.

Leader Nordstrom strode back into the castle with a feeling of true accomplishment. Visions of Johnny being eaten by animals or killed by Wildies, or better yet being caught by the Gangers, filled his head and warmed his heart.

He stopped in front of the tribe. "Listen to me, my people. I have just seen the great Johnny and his cohorts. They were running away. They have deserted you. It's a good thing you have me and the Enforcers to protect you. From now on, we are on our own, and that is a good thing. Tomorrow, we will go back to Sanctuary, and things will be just as they were, just as they should be."

A murmur rippled through the crowd, and Leader Nordstrom was pleased to sense agreement in it. Now, if he could only get the tribe back to Sanctuary without the Gangers seeing them. The thought of being outside and so exposed to who knew what danger sent a thrill of fear through him that was so strong he felt his bladder weaken. But he had to look strong. With any luck, he could get the Tribe back and double reinforce the doors and windows. Then he could forget his agreement with the Ganger thug Ripper.

"Your Majesty!"

Leader Nordstrom turned to see one of his Enforcers, a man named Radioshack. His face was pale, and his eyes were opened wide with what looked like fright. It had the effect of making Leader Nordstrom afraid, but he tried his best to make the feeling go away.

"What is it?"

"Come see, quick! It is terrible! What are we going to do?"

The Enforcer, who normally pretended to be fierce and courageous, shook in his robe and looked like a frightened, weak old man. As he led the way, Leader Nordstrom followed him, wondering what new calamity was befalling them.

Radioshack led Leader Nordstrom up the stairs of one of Castle's towers to a window that overlooked the city. The Enforcer pointed a finger out the window.

"Look at it, Leader Nordstrom. We are doomed! Why, oh why won't they leave us alone? They're animals!"

Leader Nordstrom peered out into the darkness to

see a bright orange light dancing on the distant horizon. With a sinking dread he realized what it was: Sanctuary burned. The Gangers detroyed it.

Panic filled Leader Nordstrom's brain and sweat instantly broke out on his forehead. Now what? Where could he take them? There was no other place. A sick terror of the Gangers filled his heart. They were monsters. They wouldn't leave the Tribe alone until they all surrendered and agreed to be the Gangers' slaves.

Dark images of the Gangers raping the women and torturing the men while they laughed filled Leader Nordstrom's mind. He was the Leader Nordstrom of the Tribe. Without any thing to barter with, Leader Nordstrom knew Ripper had no reason to keep their agreement. He'd surely kill Leader Nordstrom in a most gruesome way just to show the Tribe that he was their new master.

"Oh, we're doomed!" The Enforcer bent his head and grabbed it with his hands. With disgust Leader Nordstrom realized beneath the cowl the man was sobbing. "They're going to kill us one by one. There's no place to hide."

"Stop your sniveling!" Leader Nordstrom snarled crossly. "They're nothing but mindless animals. We'll stay here and defend this place."

The Enforcer looked up and Leader Nordstrom saw the man's face was wet with tears and worse, slimy snot. "But what about food? When we go out to forage they'll pick us off one by one. We're doomed I tell you!"

Leader Nordstrom suddenly hated the sniveling coward. "No, we're not!" But Leader Nordstrom knew, really, they were. He began to wonder silently if the best thing would be for him to sneak off on his own and leave the Tribe to fend for itself. Maybe he shouldn't have turned Johnny away. Johnny could have dealt with the Tribe rabble and Leader Nordstrom would have only one person to worry about, himself.

Misterwizard led Johnny and Starbucks around to the very back of the castle. Johnny looked up and saw that they were directly below the window of Misterwizard's room. As Johnny and Starbucks watched, Misterwizard smiled impishly. He positioned his hand over one of the bricks of the wall.

"Rapunzel, Rapunzel, let down your hair!" The Misterwizard pushed on the brick, and it moved inward beneath his hand.

"Who's Rapunzel?" Starbucks asked, but Misterwizard didn't answer for his attention, and Johnny's and Starbucks,' was seized by the rope ladder that suddenly dropped in front of them.

"A story for another time, my fine fellow conspirator. I, ah, trust that two young bucks such as you and Johnny will have no trouble climbing a conveyance such as this."

Starbucks snuffed with disdain, grabbed the ladder and began climbing. Before the others could barely blink he was half way up to the top. He looked down with a proud smile. "That answer your question?

Johnny looked at Misterwizard. "How about you, Misterwizard? Can you make it?"

"Of course, my boy," Misterwizard said with a laugh as he grabbed the rope, put one black-booted boot onto a rung and began to ascend. "I am amazingly fit for a man approaching three quarters of a century in age."

Despite Misterwizard's words, Johnny watched carefully until both Misterwizard and Starbucks disappeared inside the window at the top. Then Johnny followed them, scampering up in less than a minute.

When Johnny arrived inside the room he saw Starbucks looking around with wonder and Misterwizard sitting down catching his breath.

"I must say, though I do feel physically up to the challenge of Rapunzel's hair, I am still grateful that it is not the primary means of access to my chambers. And after the day we have had, I will find my bed chamber to be particularly inviting tonight."

Now that they were safely inside, the exhaustion in Johnny's body made him feel twice as heavy. Even Starbucks was yawning.

Johnny's thoughts returned to Deb. His face clouded with worry. Misterwizard noticed and he knew right away what Johnny was thinking. His own brow wrinkled as his face darkened with a frown. "I feel for you boy. But first things first. We must deal with our egregious opponent downstairs. Then we will have time to think about-more important matters."

Johnny nodded, a lump in his throat. As he watched, Misterwizard strode to the door of his chambers. Opening it slightly, he looked down at the assemblage below. "Possibly we are in luck. It seems that most of the Tribe is asleep, and hopefully that includes our esteemed Leader Nordstrom. If Lady Fortune smiles on us, and I do believe she does, we can wait until morning to face our next challenge. And this suits me just fine."

"Me too," Starbucks nodded. "I'm beat. Where do I sleep?"

Misterwizard made Johnny and Starbucks beds on the floor and gave them pillows, and it wasn't long before Johnny and Misterwizard could hear Starbucks snoring loudly in a corner.

Johnny turned to Misterwizard. "I have to go check on Deb, make sure she's all right."

Misterwizard nodded in understanding. "Please do it without creating a disturbance. Return here when you're finished, or Leader Nordstrom will surely discover our presence. Then none of us will get any sleep tonight."

Johnny nodded. He crept to the door and slowly on tiptoes, walked down the dark passageway to the door at the bottom.

Peeking out, he scanned the large room. Everyone slept in groups all over the floor. The cars were too big for Leader Nordstrom to move, so families slept inside them on the seats. Against the walls in a few places long benches with backs sat. Members of the Tribe lay on them, for they had soft padding.

Johnny couldn't see very well in the dark, but finally he spotted Deb in the corner. She lay on a bed on the floor, asleep. As Johnny gazed at her, his love for her came to him full force. He wanted more than anything in the world to walk over and hold her all through the night.

Even though it tore him apart inside, he retreated and closed the door, feeling miserable. He couldn't wait for the morning when they would deal with Leader Nordstrom and he could be with Deb again. He walked back up, his heart heavy.

Johnny lay down on the mattress Misterwizard had placed on the floor for him. But though Johnny lay exhausted, he couldn't sleep. He lay still, staring up at the darkness above, and the faint outline of the stones of the ceiling. Not far from Johnny, Misterwizard lay in his bed, a large four-poster wooden contraption with silk sheets and big, fluffy pillows. Underneath his bed Misterwizard had a funny black pan that radiated heat. It warmed not only Misterwizard's bed but Johnny as well.

Johnny sighed, a sad, plaintive sound. "Misterwizard?" Johnny listened, hoping Misterwizard was still awake.

An answer came back in a soft whisper. "Yes Johnny?"

Johnny smiled inside with a quiet relief. It seemed as if Misterwizard was having a hard time sleeping as well, and Johnny was sure it was for the same reason as him.

"What if Deb-I mean what if she has... "

"People do have colds, Johnny. They do feel ill, and it's not always the Sickness."

"What if it is? No one survives the Sickness."

"Misterwizard," Johnny's voice trembled with emotion. "If Deb-I-I couldn't, I mean I wouldn't—"

"Johnny," Misterwizard said softly. "I promise you. If Deb has the Sickness, which I sincerely doubt, but if she did, I promise you as your friend I will do everything in my power to save her."

"Is there a way Misterwizard? Any way at all?"

"Good night, Johnny. We'll talk more when we know for a certainty that we have something to be concerned about. Now go to sleep!"

Misterwizard stopped talking, and not long after Johnny heard him snoring. Johnny's eyelids began to feel heavy, and despite his best efforts to stay awake and worry, he soon fell fast asleep, but it was a sleep full of dark nightmares.

Johnny woke up early and couldn't get back to sleep. He was plagued with a fear that blew through his soul like the wind through an abandoned building. And the main reason for the fear was the thought of Deb being sick.

No matter how many times he tried to reassure himself with Misterwizard's words, it didn't help. The more he told himself the reasons not to worry, the more panic and desperation he felt. Johnny was beside himself with sorrow, for deep inside, no matter what Misterwizard said, Johnny knew Deb had the Sickness.

He had seen others with it. They grew weak, and then sweaty, and soon they lay around doing nothing, until one day they just stopped moving. The Tribe was terrified of the Sickness, and as soon as someone began to show signs of it the Tribe treated them like they were Wildies, or worse. The Tribe kicked them out into the Forbidden City to fend for themselves. Johnny could remember times when helpless, sick people were forced out. He could still see them shuffling off away from Sanctuary, weeping and alone. Johnny hated the cowardice and cruelty the Tribe sometimes showed. If anyone tried to make Deb leave or treated her badly, Johnny would fight them, no matter who they were.

Finally, Johnny gave up trying to sleep. He walked over to the small window in the shape of an arrow and gazed at the red horizon where the Red Eye was just beginning to show. Red and yellow colors mixed in the blue sky, and Johnny thought how beautiful it was. For a moment the pain inside him eased. And then he thought how he'd like to share it with Deb. And that brought him back to thinking about her sickness, and quickly he was back to feeling bad again.

He felt so helpless. He paced the room listening to Misterwizard's loud snores. Starbucks snored too. Both were sound asleep. Johnny envied them and grew angry at them at the same time. How could they sleep so soundly when Deb might be…?

Johnny heard something at the door and turned instantly towards the sound. It was a slight scrabbling, like a mouse scraping on the wood. As quietly as he could he padded over to the door and stood on one side, listening. Then he heard whispering outside.

"I can't get it open."

Johnny recognized the voice. It was Onsale!

An irritated voice answered. *"You're not trying hard enough. Just break it in. The old fool is gone now. His things now belong to me."*

It was Leader Nordstrom! He was trying to get in to steal Misterwizard's things!

Johnny hurried over to Misterwizard. He put his hands on Misterwizard and shook him, but all Misterwizard did was mumble crossly and roll over.

Johnny moved to Starbucks. He kicked him soundly in the side.

"Ow!" Starbucks' eyes opened, and he peered up at Johnny. "What was that for?"

"Someone's breaking in!"

In a second Starbucks was fully awake. He jumped to his feet full of excitement. "They've got a surprise waiting for them! Who is it?"

"It's Leader Nordstrom."

Starbucks took in this information with a frown. "Then I bet he's got the Enforcers with him. Looks like our troubles are coming to us."

"I tried to wake Misterwizard, but he sleeps better than old man Rollercoaster."

They both grinned. Johnny took out his sword. Starbucks looked at it with wide open eyes. "You can't use that on Leader Nordstrom. He's one of us."

"I only want to scare him. But if he tries to hurt us or Misterwizard, I'll do what I have to."

Starbucks nodded and pulled out his sword too. Johnny hurried over to the door just as a loud crash came from it. They were smashing something against the door to make it open, but the door was made of good, thick wood and didn't even budge.

Leader Nordstrom didn't attempt to be quiet anymore but spoke in a loud and irritated voice. "Open it! Come on, what are you men or little scrabblers?"

Loud grunts came from beyond the door and then another loud crash. From behind him Johnny heard a snort and a snuffling sound. Misterwizard finally began to wake up.

Misterwizard sat up in his big bed, scratched his bald head and said "What's all the infernal cacophony? Has World War Four started now?"

"Leader Nordstrom's trying to break in!" Starbucks whispered loudly. He put his sword away and picked up a golden statue of a nude man holding a hollow globe above his head and swung it experimentally like a club.

Misterwizard woke up quickly and swung his legs out of bed. Dressed in a flannel nightgown, slipped his feet into two slippers with ducks for heads and hurried over to door, just as another loud crash sounded.

"Ha ha!" Misterwizard said with a chuckle. "That's solid oak, you varlets, reinforced with steel bands, a heavy crossbar and set into a groove in the wall. You'll never break that down. You might as well try and break the wall down around it."

Misterwizard grinned at Johnny, but then he saw the look of concern on Johnny's face. "But I suppose we're only postponing the inevitable. We knew it had to come to this, though a few more hours of sleep would have been preferable. Still, the bitter pill doesn't get sweeter with procrastination. Let's greet our visitors, shall we?"

Misterwizard walked over to the door and removed the cross bolt. Johnny tensed and his stomach cramped. Starbucks walked over to stand behind Johnny, the golden statue held above his head ready to strike.

Misterwizard leaned the crossbar against the wall and lifted the small black pin that latched the door. As Johnny and Starbucks held their breath, he pulled the door open.

Standing in front of them were three old men in Enforcer's red robes, sweat pouring down their faces and with looks of utter surprise. From behind them on one side Leader Nordstrom's face appeared with a look of confused unhappiness on it. When he saw Misterwizard, the look was replaced by fear. Quickly Leader Nordstrom tried to cover it with a look of haughty arrogance, but it only partially worked.

"How did you get in there?" Leader Nordstrom saw Johnny and Starbucks too, and his lip curled in anger. "I should have known an old trickster like you and your two criminal youth would find a way back in."

"This is my home, Leader Nordstrom. I invited you and your charges in to save you from the ruffians outside, but I didn't expect you to be so unappreciative."

"Don't try to fool me with your fancy talk." Leader Nordstrom shook with rage as he pointed a crooked finger at Wizard. “I’m not google-eyed over you like so many others. Now you’re going to wish you didn’t come back, because this is going to be your end.”

Johnny stepped forward seething with an anger of his own. “You touch one hair on his head-,” Johnny looked at Misterwizard and remembered he was bald, “er, chin, and I promise you you’ll pull back a bloody stump.”

Leader Nordstrom blanched and pulled back slightly. It was the first time he’d seen Johnny so angry, and he realized just how dangerous Johnny could be when he wanted to be.

Johnny glared at the Enforcers. “And that goes for you too. You’ll hurt him over my dead body, and I’ll take a lot of you old men with me first.”

The Enforcers smiled weak smiles at Johnny and looked mildly terrified.

Leader Nordstrom decided it was time for some of the diplomacy that had helped him fool others so many times in the past. He smiled and said in a silky voice, “Now, now, let’s not be like Beasties, shall we? I’m just naturally upset, for you disobeyed my direct orders, and I am the Leader Nordstrom of this Tribe. Even you, Misterwizard, must understand the need for the order of law and authority.”

Misterwizard stroked his beard and pulled his nightgown closer to him, for he was feeling a chill. “I most certainly do, you devious and cunning politician. But dishonest government is less desirable than no government at all. And a dictatorship will never a democracy be.”

Leader Nordstrom grew angry again; he hated it when Misterwizard said words he didn’t understand and made him feel stupid. "I claim this building for the Tribe. You have two hours to leave, or we will force you out. How do you like that, you and your fancy words?"

"And how to you propose to force us out, Leader Nordstrom? We can easily barricade ourselves inside and there is no way you will be able to enter."

"We can simply starve you out then," Leader Nordstrom said. "Sooner or later, you will have to cap-capulate." Leader Nordstrom rose up to his full height; he knew some big words of his own.

"Capitulate," Misterwizard corrected, making Leader Nordstrom's face flush with embarrassment. "It seems we have what is commonly referred to as an "impasse" All right. As you wish, we will vacate the premises. But you must let me take some of my possessions with me. After all, you're not a thief, are you?"

Leader Nordstrom smiled, relishing in his victory. "You can take all your trash, for all I care. Take all your stupid doo-dads and wingy-thingies. I have no use for your ridiculous toys."

"Fine. Then we have agreed on a cessation of hostilities. "

"We haven't agreed to anything!" Leader Nordstrom barked. "You have two hours, or we come up and push you out a window!"

"Good day."

Misterwizard closed the door. Starbucks relaxed with a sigh of relief. Johnny strode over to stand in front of Misterwizard, visibly upset.

"Misterwizard, how can you let him win like that? You can't leave. This is your home! What about all your things? Where will we go? And I'm not leaving, not without Deb. Or Carny, or Foodcourt, or Teavanna. And what about the others, Sephie and the other families?"

Misterwizard placed a hand on Johnny's shoulder. "Relax, my boy. That was only the first round of negotiations, to buy us time. Believe me when I say, if I wanted to, I have enough chemicals in here to force your whole Tribe to run out of my home with their eyes watering and their stomachs attempting to turn themselves inside out. What we need now is a way for you to talk to the Tribe without Leader Nordstrom aware of it. Despite what Leader Nordstrom thinks of you, you are a hero to your Tribe and they look up to you. With the Tribe on our side, it will be much harder for Leader Nordstrom to force us to leave."

Johnny nodded, relieved. Misterwizard grinned at him but with eyes full of concern. "First, however, I would like to run a comb through my hair and get out of my duck slippers. If I am to die, I would prefer it to be with a slight more dignity."

With the smoldering ruins of Sanctuary behind them and the Red Eye rising behind the distant hills, the Gangers shuffled back towards the city, their arms filled with loot. Ripper led the way, a ragged sneer of dark joy on his face. He carried a strange object he'd found in Sanctuary. One end was flat and round. On the other end, a flat stick jutted out with strings on it. Ripper didn't know what it was, but it was red and when you plucked the strings it made sound, so he took it.

This night was the best of his whole life. At long last

he and the Doomsday Prophesy destroyed Sanctuary. They smashed doors of glass, watching them shatter. They knocked the heads off the Fake People and burned their bodies in big heaps. They piled up all the Tribe's clothes, and after laughing and trying them on, they burned them all. Best of all they killed ten Tribe members, even gotten to torture one before finally hanging him from the ceiling and watching him dangle in his death throes.

Ripper would revel in the memory of this night for as long as he lived, rehearsing it in his mind over and over and enjoying the dark feelings of pleasure it brought him.

And yet, it was a hollow victory, for the Tribe had escaped and once again Johnny had beat him. It was infuriating. How could one boy, barely past being a Scrambler, constantly tweak his nose and make him look like a fool? He was almost twenty seasons, and yet Johnny seemed, smarter than him, always one step ahead. It was like an itch that you couldn't scratch, and if you didn't soon you knew it was going to turn into a deadly disease. Ripper wanted to kill Johnny so badly that it made his teeth ache.

"Where'd the Tribe go, Rip? Where'd they go?"

It was Leaker. He stumbled along next to Ripper, wearing a ridiculous fur coat he'd found and carrying the arm of a Fake People. Ripper looked over at him with disgust. Now there was someone who was stupid. Leaker was so dumb that even some of the Beasties were smarter. But he was also one of Ripper's loudest fans, so he had his uses, at least for a while.

Ripper smiled coldly, holding the strange object by the long stick and resting the other end on his shoulder. As he walked he scanned the horizon. In the distance the ragged square shapes of the building darkened the sky. Searching with his eyes he found the one he was looking for: the strange building with the dark towers jutting up into the sky. He smiled.

"I know where they went, Stupid. They thought they were smart. But now they're trapped, like fish in a bucket. They have no place to go. We'll surround 'em and never let 'em leave or get no food. Soon they'll beg to be our slaves. Then we'll call the shots. We'll make 'em give us all the girls. And Johnny. And the old man, and anyone else we want."

Leaker laughed raggedly. "I can't believe it. We just might beat Johnny after all."

Ripper laughed too, an ugly sound. ""'Course we're gonna win. But it's the doing it that's gonna be fun. We're gonna turn their day time into a nightmare."

CHAPTER 15

Leader Nordstrom cursed silently as he descended to the main floor again with the Enforcers following like loyal dogs. Why did nothing ever go right for him? He had given his life to help others, sacrificing his own personal happiness to help the Tribe survive in the deadly world they were born into.

True, there had been personal benefits, such as always getting first pick of the food they grew, living in the most luxurious place in Sanctuary with the softest bed, the finest clothing that wasn't rotted and his choice of the females, though there wasn't much of a selection to choose from in the Tribe, only a few without mates who didn't have missing teeth or the looks of a hyena. But he deserved a little extra consideration, didn't he, for spending all his time worrying, planning and leading? He had spent his life taking care of them, like a shepherd for his sheep, and now Johnny and Misterwizard were acting like he was a wolf in sheep's clothing. Hadn't he protected the Tribe from the dangers of the world? And now look at where they were, just where he'd feared they'd be, pursued by the Gangers, without a real home and in danger from the bad air and poison. He was so like a suffering servant, misunderstood and oppressed, just for being good.

He had no doubt that Johnny and the Misterwizard wouldn't leave after two hours. There would be a confrontation, which worried Leader Nordstrom a lot. He had no illusions about his own intelligence compared to Misterwizard, or even Johnny. Johnny had been trained by the old man to be just as devious, and Misterwizard was just what his name implied, a wizard, knowing magic from the old world both marvelous and frightening.

They were smart and tricky those two, and Leader Nordstrom knew that at that very moment they were devising a plan to take over. It was only a matter of time before they had the whole Tribe against him, maybe even talking the Tribe into hanging him as some sort of traitor. He wouldn't put it past those two to see to it the Tribe burned him at the stake. The thought made Leader Nordstrom's insides quiver.

Well, if the Tribe could be that ungrateful for all the years Leader Nordstrom had spent slaving over them, then so be it. There was only one choice now. Leader Nordstrom would turn the Tribe over to the Gangers if the Gangers guaranteed him safe passage away, and maybe gave him something of value. Then the Tribe would be at the mercy of Ripper, and they'd be sorry they chosen Johnny over him. When Johnny was dead and the tribe members all being tortured by the Gangers, they would cry out for him, but he'd be long gone, looking for someone else to lead, a people worthier of his help and protection.

Leader Nordstrom stopped a few steps above the main floor where he had a good view of it. The Enforcers stopped behind him. The people milled about talking, laughing, and preparing their cold breakfasts. Leader Nordstrom noticed Johnny's family huddled together. The girl, Carny, fat with a wriggler, sat uncomfortably on the floor. Leader Nordstrom had wanted her once for himself, but Johnny's father had refused. Then her first mate Timex had been killed by the Sickness, and still her father refused to let Leader Nordstrom have her. She chose the stupid and lazy Buildabear instead. He would make sure the Gangers had a special treat for Carny's parents before he left.

Leader Nortstrom stood at his full height and put on his best formal frown. "Listen to me, my people!"

The talk in the room quieted and all eyes turned towards him. "It seems that this malefactor Johnny and his troublesome Misterwizard did not leave after all but snuck into the old trickster's lair above me when we weren't looking."

A chorus of shouts came back in reply.

"Johnny's back!"

"Hurrah for Johnny!"

"And Misterwizard too! We're saved!"

"He'll know what to do next!"

"What did he say? Does he know where to go?"

Leader Nordstrom raised his hands with panic as he felt the situation slipping out of his control. "Stop! Listen to me. Johnny and Misterwizard did not come back to help us, but to take things from us and leave again. They have no intention of helping us. They only think of themselves."

"That is a patent falsehood and a disparagement of our character!"

All eyes looked behind Leader Nordstrom to see Johnny, Starbucks and Misterwizard standing just above Leader Nordstrom. It was Misterwizard who spoke. A ragged cheer went up. Leader Nordstrom turned and stared, his mouth open and his mind racing to try and keep up with events.

Misterwizard turned to Leader Nordstrom. "Dear Leader Nordstrom. You are a capable, self-sacrificing and courageous man, though duplicitous and insidious by nature. You have toiled tirelessly all your life to keep the Tribe safe from misfortune. I admire that, as I know Johnny and Starbucks do as well. And, under the current dire circumstances, I can understand if the strain of recent events has led you to mistrust the motives of even the most loyal of your supporters, such as Johnny, Starbucks and I."

Leader Nordstrom stood a little taller, not being able to hide the fact that he appreciated the compliments, and how they might help his image in front of the Tribe. "Well, I—"

"And, Johnny, Starbucks and I would like you to know that we are here to support you and your endeavors on behalf of the Tribe, to the utmost degree, and with our whole hearts."

A cheer went up and Leader Nordstrom couldn't help but smile, though he really wanted it to be a frown. Things were not going as he wished, and yet they seemed to be going in his favor, somehow.

"I am the Leader Nordstrom—"

"Most assuredly you are and will remain so until the day you leave this mortal coil. We would never employ the slightest machinations to depose you."

Leader Nordstrom opened his mouth then closed it again. Then he said, "I would surely hope not, for any attempt to depose me will end up deposing you first!" Leader Nordstrom didn't know what "depose" meant but he was sure it wasn't something pleasant.

The Tribe turned to Johnny and Wizard.

"Johnny! What do we do?"

"We're trapped! Sanctuary, did you see what they did to it?"

"We're running out of food and water. My baby's hungry!"

Misterwizard turned to Johnny with a fatherly smile. "The sheep always recognize the true shepherd, eh Johnny?"

Johnny frowned. "Shepherd?"

Misterwizard turned back to the Tribe. "Do not be afraid, good and gentle people. I'm sure Leader Nordstrom has a perfect plan for your protection and survival."

All eyes turned back to Leader Nordstrom. Oh, oh, Leader Nordstrom thought; he was on the hot spot again. Things were happening too fast for him to keep up. He wrinkled his brow and opened his mouth, but his mind was a blank. He realized he was appearing stupid, but he had no idea what to say.

Misterwizard stepped in to save him. "Leader Nordstrom has told me his plan, and it is a sound one. There is another mall, or shall we say, Sanctuary, not far from here in the middle of the city. It is even more spacious and luxurious than your old domicile. It will also have the advantage of being ten stories high, allowing the Tribe to keep watch on the surrounding area. It is also centrally located in the city, which will allow room for expansion and exploration."

"What is he saying, Leader Nordstrom?" Cinnabon asked.

"Is he saying that we are never going back to Sanctuary?" Thegap questioned.

"What is a domicile?" Carny said.

"What is expansion? What is explo-ration?" This came from Sephie.

"Will we have to walk? Is it a long way?" the Enforcer Onsale inquired in a wavery voice.

"That last, my friend, is a very intelligent question, and one I will answer immediately," Misterwizard said with a confident grin. "I have been planning for many months to move the Tribe to the new Sanctuary, a safer and healthier environ closer to food sources and with a much greater opportunity for reconstruction of society."

"Leader Nordstrom, I don't understand half of what he says," Richardmillhousenixon complained.

"You move the Tribe?" Leader Nordstrom said with a curled lip.

"With your permission, of course, dear Leader Nordstrom. To that end, I have procured three rather large modes of transportation, and spent many hours repairing and restoring them. They are called, "Buses," and I think you will find traveling in them quite enjoyable and entertaining."

"What is 'enter-taining'?" Cinnabon asked. "Does it hurt?"

Leader Nordstrom put his hands up to the crowd. "It doesn't matter. Listen to Leader Nordstrom. All will be explained in time. For now, let us simply rest. Leader Nordstrom will make sure what happens to Tribe is the right thing."

"But Leader Nordstrom, what about the bad air?" Cinnabon asked. "The poisons? The Sickness? You told us if we left Sanctuary we would die instantly. Weren't we supposed to wait for the 'all clear' from the magic box?"

Leader Nordstrom turned to Misterwizard, hoping he would explain. Misterwizard smiled at Leader Nordstrom and then turned to the Tribe. "Leader Nordstrom has since discovered that time and the elements have greatly reduced the danger to a point where as long as one is cautious, most toxins and dangerous levels can be avoided. Wash the outsides of cans, the skins of fruits and vegetables, drink only water from the river that is flowing and not stagnant and do not intentionally walk into any cloud and you will receive very low doses of radiation, no more than tolerable levels. The half-life for the contamination is now at acceptable, though there are still some hot spots to avoid, but as long as you don't stumble upon any loose Plutonium 235 in old bomb casings laying around you should be fine. And the fresh air and exercise will actually make you stronger and less likely to get the Sickness."

Heads nodded and smiles flourished, even though they only understood half of what he said and hope once again sprouted in the hearts of the Tribe people. A woman with a wriggler turned to her friend. "I'm going to name my scrabbler Toxin. It's beautiful and must be important."

Leader Nordstrom looked at Misterwizard, and on his face there was gratitude, though he tried to hide it. He put on a crooked smile. "So, you have found a way to redeem yourselves, for the moment. As long as you realize that I am, and will always be, Leader Nordstrom." He turned to Johnny. "And that goes for you, too, troublemaker."

Johnny put on a crooked grin of his own. "I don't want to take your place, as long as you lead fairly. All I want is to see Tribe happy and healthy, not trapped in the old Sanctuary graveyard. And now, if we follow Misterwizard's advice, we will be."

Leader Nordstrom huffed. "Maybe we will, and maybe we won't. I will decide what happens to the Tribe, and I alone. I only know what's best for my people. And this doesn't mean I won't be rid of both of you someday."

Johnny strode past Leader Nordstrom, who followed him with his eyes. "All I care about now is making sure Deb is all right."

Misterwizard and Starbucks walked past Leader Nordstrom and the Enforcers as well. Starbucks waved jauntily as the Enforcers scowled darkly at him.

Under his breath, Leader Nordstrom said, "You'd better hurry. She's not going to be around very long. Pity. I wanted her for myself."

Johnny wound his way through the Tribe, having to endure many pats on the back and questions as he went. He didn't care about any of them, only Deb.

A hand on Johnny's arm stopped him. He turned to see Carny smiling at him.

"I'm so proud of you, Johnny. I always knew you

would save us, someday."

Johnny's face colored and he looked uncomfortable. "I have to go." He tried to pull away, but Carny didn't let go.

"I'm glad to be out of Sanctuary, Johnny. I've always wanted to see the Forbidden City. I love you, Johnny, and so does Miracle."

"Okay, let me go!" Johnny gently pulled her hand of his arm, gazed into her eyes with a smile of gratitude for a moment and then walked on.

Sitting on the floor in a corner and eating a loaf of bread, Foodcourt wore a big smile as he talked to Johnny's mother, Teavanna. "We'll be leaving for Australia any day now. Johnny's a good boy. They have things called kangadoos there, did you know that? And calas. And bingos. I can't wait to show them to you. I knew we'd get started soon. The Tribe will like it there. They never had the mushroom monsters there, did you know that? They're still just like they were before."

"Yes dear," Teavanna said, patting his arm. "Any day now."

"My Johnny is a good boy. He's a good boy, my Johnny. He's going to kick that Leader Nordstrom in the bottom and out the door someday. Someday Johnny will feed that old goat to a Beastie, and I'll laugh so hard I'll bust a gut, you watch."

"Now, now, you settle down and rest. You've had a hard day."

Johnny finally found Deb sitting on the floor by a window, resting her head against the wall. Her eyes were closed, and she looked tired. A pang of fear shot through Johnny like an arrow through his heart. She looked worse than when he saw her last.

Johnny knelt down and took her hand. It was cold, and yet her face was flushed and beaded with sweat. Johnny tried to keep the concern from his face, but all he could manage was a smile that looked more like a man about to fall in a hole.

"Deb, I'm here."

Deb opened her eyes and smiled weakly, but her eyes shone with joy at seeing him again. She tried to sit up, but Johnny stopped her, and she lay back down again. "Johnny, you're safe! I was so worried! But I shouldn't have been. I know how strong and brave you are."

Johnny smiled and pushed her wet hair from her face. "You're brave too, Deb."

Deb frowned. "Leader Nordstrom said some terrible things about you. How did you get back in?"

Johnny breathed deeply, his chest feeling heavy with concern. He sat down next to Deb and she cuddled up under his arm.

"It was Misterwizard. He is so smart. He tricked Leader Nordstrom into thinking that we are on his side, at least for now. He even has a plan of where to go, where we will even safer than Sanctuary. It is right in the middle of the city. The Tribe will finally be safe and be able to start living."

"That's wonderful, Johnny!" Deb's eyes widened with excitement. "And then you and I, can—"

Deb's words were cut off by a round of coughing. "Can—"

Johnny put a hand to Deb's face. "Deb, don't talk. Rest. I have to find you a better place. Come with me. I'm taking you up to Misterwizard's room—"

Deb took Johnny's arm, stopping him in mid-sentence. She looked deep into his eyes. "Johnny. I want you to know something."

Johnny moved his face to within inches of hers. He could feel her breath on his lips and feel her warmth.

"Johnny. You are the only man I've ever loved. You know that, don't you? I've never really wanted anyone but you. Even when I was a little scrabbler."

Johnny's insides turned all gooey and love for Deb filled his heart. Suddenly it was hard to swallow, and he tried to keep the tears welling up in the corners of his eyes from falling out. He gazed at Deb's face and they smiled at each other. Then she kissed him, hard. Her lips were hot but even though he was concerned about her, he found himself only thinking about how lovely her lips felt against his.

They parted lips, and Johnny put his face against hers. Her face was hot too. Johnny decided it was time for him to let down his guard and tell Deb just how he felt. "And I've always loved you, Deb, since the first time I saw you with your little white curls and smile that lip up Sanctuary like the Red Eye at mid-day. I would go back to my room and dream about you. I never dreamt you could love me too."

Deb grabbed Johnny's neck and pulled him close. He put his arms around her and they hugged, just holding each other tight.

"Johnny, let's leave here, just you and me. Let's have grand adventures in Australia, just like Foodcourt is always talking about. Let's go now, while we have time, before it's too late."

Johnny noticed that Deb's hair was stringy and wet, and she shook. His eyes grew moist and he felt like a little scrabbler who'd just been punished. "We're going to Misterwizard. He's going to find out what's wrong with you. And then we'll have a whole lifetime of adventures. Together, forever."

Deb didn't reply, but Johnny could see in her eyes that she understood and agreed. Gently he put his arms under her and lifted her up. Slowly and with the utmost care, he carried her up to Misterwizard's room.

The Gangers gathered back at their base in the city. Ripper chose the place because it looked more official and fancier than the buildings around it. In front a green metal statue of a funny looking man in strange clothes stood. He had a friendly but dignified look on his face and being in the building with him out front made Ripper feel important. The building had a huge steeple on top and in front of it ran a huge strip of overgrown grass. On either side of the grass were more fancy buildings. The plaque on the building had the words, "Independence Hall," which meant nothing to Ripper, but he was sure it was someplace where big things happened once.

The only problem was whenever he entered the building he had a weird feeling that he should be quiet and show respect. He hated that feeling so whenever he entered, he made sure to cut a new notch in a column or rip a new hole in a painting.

Now Ripper sat on the big chair in the middle of the

main room like a king as the Gangers gathered weapons and supplies for their next big attack. One leg dangled over the edge of the chair, and he swigged from a bottle that said 'rum' on the side and puffed on a big long stick-like thing he'd found in a box with the word "cigars" on it. Behind the chair on either side of him stood two girls, holding bottles and food for him if he wanted it. Occasionally a Ganger would walk in and show him a tool or weapon they'd found, and he'd nod with approval.

A girl Ganger came in. She wasn't like the girls behind him, for she was tough and mean, like the boy Gangers. Even Ripper knew not to cross her, for she could fight as good as the men and many of the Gangers had the scars to prove it. Her name was Lady Stabs.

Long blond hair hung down on one side of her head. The other side of her head was shaved. In place of her hair she sported the red tattoo of a skull. She wore black leather pants, a black leather jacket and a glove on her right hand with spikes on the back. She walked up to Ripper and stood in front of him, her hand on her hip, looking bored.

"What do you want?"

Lady Stabs spit on the ground. "I want to know when we're gonna eat. Who's supposed to be out hunting?"

"We got the food from Sanctuary," Ripper said, wishing she would just go away.

"It's all mushy vegetables and rat-beastie. A dog-beastie eats better than that. I want some good deer-beastie or raccoon-beastie, like we're used to."

"Then go round up some guys. Tell 'em I said to go out and get some food. We need to get full up, so we're good and strong when we attack that old man's place."

Lady Stabs frowned. "And why are we doing that

anyway? Why don't we just take over Sanctuary?"

"'Cause I said so, that's why! Now get out of here and get me some food."

Lady Stabs scowled and left. Ripper smiled. He loved being the Gangers' Leader Nordstrom. The feeling of power was almost as good as the feeling he got when he was destroying something or watching someone be tortured. He couldn't wait until they had the Tribe at their mercy. In his mind's eye he pictured them cowering in fear, the little ones terrified and the old people begging for their lives. He sat up and leaned forward, playing the scene over and over in his head as he puffed on the cigar.

Leaker ran up. "Is this what you wanted Ripp?"

Ripper looked at the ragged box Leaker held up. Then he cuffed Leaker on the side of the head. Leaker winced and blinked, putting a hand to where he'd been hit.

"No, stupid. The BIG box that's blood color and has squiggles on the side and a picture of a stick with a string coming out the top. I told you which building it was in. You are so dumb. I swear, when this is over, I'm going to cut you up for a treat for the Wildies."

"No, don't do that, Ripper. I'll try again." Leaker hurried away.

Ripper chuckled. He turned to the girl on his right and she immediately bent down to snuggle her face against him. Once again, he tried to ignore the fact that she was missing one eye from birth and had only half her teeth. She had all the important parts anyway, and even if she did creep him out, she didn't talk much.

She gave him a new bottle of rum and he sat back in his chair again and grinned. Someday, he'd have Johnny's Deb. She was beautiful, without any weird facial features or missing parts. She'd be his girl, or he'd make sure some of her parts started missing.

Leaker ran up, holding another box. Ripper nodded with glee. "That's it."

He put down his glass, opened the top of the box and pulled out a stick with a rope coming from the top. These were weapons of special power, ones that could light up the night and destroy whole buildings. When Misterwizard threw some of them at him, he remembered seeing some in an old building. He sent Leaker to find it.

He laughed loud and hearty, with such an evil sound to it that Leaker and the girls looked at him with looks of mild fright. When the Red Eye was gone again and the Yellow Eye rose in the sky, they were going to have lots of fun at Misterwizard's Castle.

CHAPTER 16

The events of the last few days had left Leader Nordstrom exhausted. With the Enforcers in tow, he searched the main floor until he found a corner that seemed to suit him. A family of four had already camped out there, but it was no effort to force them to take their belongings and find another spot. He sent the Enforcers to find him some soft pillows and blankets. When they returned and had made him a nice bed he lay down and closed his eyes, hand behind his head.

"Find me something to eat. And some water."

"Sir," one of the Enforcers said, "the Tribe is complaining. There is very little food and water. And they are cramped together with no room."

Leader Nordstrom scowled without opening his eyes. "Serves them right; it's their own fault. If they hadn't listed to that rebel and his wicked old mage cohort and listened to me instead, we would still be in Sanctuary. Johnny brought those Gangers upon us. Well, they can just suffer for a while. It will teach them a lesson."

The Enforcers frowned. "They are our families too. They are growing impatient to go to the new place the Misterwizard spoke of, and so are we."

Leader Nordstrom opened his eyes and flashed the Enforcers a dark look of fury. "Have you learned nothing? Does no one hear a word I say? Go to this Misterwizard's new place, where we will surely face new dangers and most assuredly all die? It is insanity! Why, we are all being exposed to the Bad Air right now and will probably all come down with the Sickness. But no, Leader Nordstrom knows nothing, does he? Only Misterwizard knows what is good. Bah!"

The Enforcers looked at each other and then back at Leader Nordstrom. "What do you think we should do, Leader Nordstrom?"

"I'll tell you what we're going to do. We're going to sit here and be miserable until the Gangers have lost interest. Then we're going to sneak back to Sanctuary and rebuild it. Then things will be back to the way they were, the way they should be."

"But Sanctuary was burned. There is nothing left there."

"Don't argue with me. Who is Leader Nordstrom here? Who protected the Tribe, all these years? Was it Johnny? Was it Misterwizard?"

The Enforcers nodded, but one said, "Misterwizard has always been a friend to the Tribe. He brings us things and delivers our wrigglers. He helps us with the Sickness."

"And why do you think he does that? To take over the

Tribe from me, that's why. He and this Johnny have been planning this since the day that scrabbler was born. Look at the trouble they have brought upon us. Look at the girl Deb, how sick she is. Do you want us all to be like that?"

The Enforcers were silent, and Leader Nordstrom took this as an agreement with him. He lay back and closed his eyes again. "Now go find me what food and drink are left. I don't care if you have to grab it out of some fool's hand. I need strength to lead the Tribe back to safety."

The Enforcers left to do Leader Nordstrom's bidding. He was soon asleep. He dreamt of being Johnny, and having Deb as his girlfriend, and fighting the Gangers and beating them. And then he saw himself as he was, small, weak, unloved, deformed and pitiful, lying in a pit at the bottom of a well, surrounded by black dogs with teeth bared about to eat him.

Johnny carried Deb towards the stairs to Misterwizard's room, but half way there his way was blocked by two very angry tribe members: Deb's parents. Her father's name was Thegap. He was a small man, even shorter than Misterwizard, only four feet tall, making him always look to Johnny like he was still a boy instead of a man. He had brown hair and finely chiseled features though, and was a pleasant man to talk to, always seeming very intelligent and thoughtful when he spoke. Her mother's name was Bathandbodyworks, and she had always been the ugliest woman Johnny had ever seen. Much taller than her husband, she towered over him. Her nose was big and bulbous, as if a swarm of bees had stung it and her ears were the biggest Johnny had ever seen. Her face was round, and her hair was short like brown grass that had been cut with a dull knife. And her eyes were large and round too, making her look like one of the fake people in Sanctuary. Johnny always wondered how someone as beautiful as Deb had come from a mother who was so homely.

They stood in front of Johnny with narrowed eyes and deep scowls, and Johnny knew he was in for it.

"Well, well," Bathandbodyworks seethed, "Where do you think you are going with our daughter, Johnny Apocalypse? The one who you have made so sick by running out to who knows where and doing who knows what with her?"

"We have never given her hand to you, Mister High and Mighty," Thegap added in, wearing a deep frown of indignation and staring up at Johnny, "though you seem to act as if we did long ago and you two are already mates."

Johnny tried to look unfazed by their words, but inside they hurt him. "I would never do anything to hurt Deb. And I know that you never, I mean I was planning on someday—"

"She is our only daughter." Tears moistened Bathandbodywork's eyes and Johnny suddenly understood they really weren't mad at him, just very concerned for Deb. "She is an angel sent to us from the gods in the old books. Our perfect little angel."

"I know she is. I would never do anything to hurt her. You must know that. I love her."

Thegap's eyes were moist now too, and he wiped his eyes with the back of his small hand. He looked up at

Johnny and nodded. "We know you do, Johnny. We're sorry. Please forgive us. We know that you are the best mate Deb could choose. We are just so upset, so worried..." Thegap blew his nose on his sleeve and wiped it back and forth across his nose.

"But if we lose her," Bathandbodyworks spread her big hands out in a helpless gesture, "We might as well die." Her face was not improved much by the red eyes and tears moistening her cheeks.

"I am taking her to Misterwizard. He will make her better, I promise."

Deb's parents nodded in unison. Bathandbodyworks said, "Yes. If anyone can help her, it is him."

Thegap gave Johnny's shoulder a pat. "I'm sorry for what we said too, Johnny. We're both just so worried we aren't thinking straight. We are lucky that you have chosen her. We know that won't rest until she is better."

"I promise you this. I will do whatever it takes, even if it means my own life, to save her."

"Of course you will," Thegap said. "And Johnny, ignore what I said before. Sometimes we let that dumb Leader Nordstrom confuse us. We want Little Debbie to be your mate, we always have. We were just waiting for you to ask for her. We never planned on giving her to anyone else."

Johnny smiled, touched. They both hugged him around Deb and then let him pass.

Johnny carried Deb up the stairs and into Misterwizard's room. He laid her gently on Misterwizards's big, soft bed. She fell into a fitful sleep as Johnny stroked her hair and watched her breathe.

When he was sure she was asleep, Johnny looked around the room and spotted Misterwizard. His old friend was sitting in a chair at his workbench, which lay against the wall and was full of the strange tools he was always tinkering with.

Johnny walked over and stood next to him. In front of Misterwizard stood one of his strange instruments, a curved metal stick with a base at the bottom and a small tray in the middle that held a little square piece of glass on it. Misterwizard bent over and had one eye looking through a hole in the top of the device. He turned a small black knob on the side ever so slightly.

"Misterwizard, I brought Deb up here to sleep. I hope that is okay."

"Of course, my boy. The poor girl; she is obviously in great distress."

Johnny sighed, asking again, "Is it too late for her?"

Misterwizard looked up at Johnny with a mischievous grin. "Of course not, Johnny." Then he frowned and looked towards Deb. "But it might be soon, unless we find a remedy for her condition."

"So, she does have the Sickness," Johnny said with a sigh.

"Well, yes and no," Misterwizard said, stroking his beard. "You see Johnny, what you and the Tribe call "The Sickness," is actually many sicknesses all coalesced together."

Misterwizard stood up and walked over to gaze down at Deb, and Johnny followed him. "Some of the sicknesses were at one time fairly mild and treatable, while others were very dire, even before the "Great Day of Dying" that happened after the Great War, as you people like to call it. However now, with so little medicine available and such poor health conditions, even the common Cold can become as deadly as the Plague."

Johnny's eyes opened wide. "Is that what Deb has? The common cold? Or does she have the Plague?" "That is what we will have to determine, Johnny. We need to take a sample of her throat culture and examine it under the microscope. That will tell us a great deal. But I suspect she has what is commonly called, 'Influenza.'"

"Her throat culture? Will that hurt?"

Misterwizard grinned. "I shouldn't think so. But since you are her chosen paramour, I will let you collect the sample."

"What do I do?"

"Here." Misterwizard handed Johnny a swab. "Simply open her mouth and swab it with this, making sure to collect a sample of her saliva, or should I say the water in her mouth. Then I will place it under the microscope and look for pathogens."

A look of alarm jumped to Johnny's face. "Pathogens? What kind of Beastie are they?"

Misterwizard's eyes twinkled. "Very tiny ones. Go ahead and swab her, Johnny. You won't hurt her I promise."

With a look of dread, Johnny walked over to Deb with the swab in his hand. He gazed on her beautiful eyes and watched her chest rise and fall with sleep for a moment, love and worry holding hands in his heart.

As gently as he could, Johnny pried open Deb's lips. He placed the swab on her tongue and wiped up some of the moisture there. Then he took the swab out and brought it over to Misterwizard, who had gone back to his chair in front of the microscope.

Taking the swab, Misterwizard said, "Well now, let's just see what miniature worlds we can discover, shall we?"

As Johnny watched Misterwizard slip the swab between to small pieces of glass and then clip it to the small tray, he talked. “Old man Laptop had the Sickness. He shook all the time. At the end he coughed up blood before he died. Do you think Deb has that kind of Sickness?”

“That was a particularly nasty disease called Tuberculosis, Johnny, and no, I don’t think Deb has that type. She is not exhibiting the same symptoms.”

“What about Mistertidybowl? Do you remember him? You took him from the Tribe, saying that he had to go somewhere far away, or he would make the whole Tribe sick.”

“He had a terrible disease called Leprosy, Johnny. I was fortunate that I didn’t contract it from him.”

“What happened to him?”

Misterwizard glanced at Johnny then peered into the glass at the top of the microscope. “I took him to a wooden shack on the other side of town, where I made him comfortable until he passed away. Then I burned the shack and everything in it to the ground, including his body.”

“Does Deb could have that kind?”

“I doubt it, for she has not symptoms indicative of that disease either.”

Johnny looked hard at Misterwizard. “If she did, could you cure her?”

Misterwizard paused and looked at Johnny. Their eyes met in a sad understanding. “No Johnny, I could not. I’ll be frank with you, my boy. The fact is, unless Deb has a very mild cold or fever, there is not much that I can do at all. I’m sorry. You see, on the Great Day of Dying, most medicine was destroyed or looted. What is left has become so old that it is no longer of any use. The only thing left now are the small bottles of aspirin and other drugs that I have managed to collect, ones that haven't turned to dust or rotted. And in some cases, the pills might actually make someone sicker than just a good rest and plenty of fluids."

Johnny sighed with dismay and Misterwizard went back to looking in the microscope.

"Ah hah... yes, just as I surmised."

"What is it? What is it?" Johnny asked.

Misterwizard looked up. "Your little friend simply has a strong case of Influenza, also known as the common flu."

"Influ-en-za? Is that bad?"

Misterwizard sat back in the chair and stroked his beard. "I can't say for sure. It depends on what strain she has, and how severe. What she really needs is a good dose of antibiotics."

Johnny became instantly energized. "Well, where do we get them? I'll go get them right now."

"I wish it were that easy, Johnny. Do you remember how I told you that most medicines had rotted away? I'm afraid any source of antibiotic, unless it was refrigerated constantly, would have become useless years ago, and even if it was refrigerated, it would possibly too old to do any good."

Johnny became exasperated and his voice took on a desperate quality. "So, what do we do?"

Misterwizard stood up. "We wait and see. We make Deb as comfortable as we can and keep her cool. We give her lots of water and rest. And we wait and see."

Misterwizard started to walk away but Johnny stopped him. "And what if that doesn't work,

Misterwizard? I told her parents I would do whatever it took to save her. And I meant it. There must be a way. I don't care if I have to go to Australia. I will find her some an-ti-biot-ics."

Misterwizard thought for a moment, as if weighing in his mind whether he should say something or not. Then he shook his head and said, "There's one place far away I discovered on my personal journeys far and wide. A stronghold deep in the ground and bound by strong steel walls and layers of security. It is possibly the location of a veritable mountain of useful and valuable treasure. I'd given up hope of gaining entrance, for it is a veritable labyrinth of locks and steel doors. I virtually surrendered to the notion that I would never gain its secrets, for it was too hard a nut to crack, but now, it may be our only option, and yet to reach it will be a journey fraught with peril, and one that may end in failure..."

"I don't care about all that," Johnny said. "Let's go there!"

Misterwizard put an arm around Johnny and led him towards Johnny's own bed.

"We will cross that bridge if and when we must. For now let's hope that after a few days of rest, she will be fine, and then she won't need any antibiotics at all. We're grabbing a tail and sure that it's a tiger-beastie, when it is probably just a tomcat-beastie. Let's let her rest. You need to stop worrying about her and think of something else. And I know just the ticket!"

Misterwizard led Johnny over to the large table in the middle of the room. It was covered in maps and papers. Misterwizard picked up on drawing and held it before them. "Here is a schematic of the mall that I told the Tribe about, their new home in downtown Philadelphia.

Help me plan out the defenses, property division, everything. Then when I eventually have to discuss it all with that pompous Leader Nordstrom, it will go much more smoothly."

"Skematic? It looks like what you called a map." Despite his misgivings, Johnny was glad of the distraction. Then began to talk over the layout of the mall, and Johnny found himself getting very interested in it. But in the back of his mind, a dark corner remained, full of fear for Deb.

CHAPTER 17

As night fell, Johnny tried to sleep, but every time he drifted off, images of Deb sick and coughing woke him up in the grip of fear and sadness. In the end, he just sat, staring out the tiny, thin window into the darkness.

And that is why Johnny saw the dark shadows creeping towards the Castle. Immediately he knew who it was. He jumped up and ran to Misterwizard.

Misterwizard lay curled up in a ball, a smile on his face, snoring loudly.

Johnny shook him gently. "Misterwizard! Misterwizard!"

With a snort Misterwizard opened his eyes and opened and closed his mouth, making a slurping sound then looked around, though he didn't seem to really see anyting. "Who dares interrupt an old man's repose?

Depart, ye accursed persecutor!"

Johnny shook him again. "I am sorry Misterwizard, but you must wake up! The Gangers are attacking!"

Misterwizard's eyes popped open and he sat up. "It's you Johnny! Forgive me, I was having a most pleasant dream about a unicorn and a mermaid."

"Misterwizard, the Gangers are coming!"

Misterwizard scowled with disapproval. "Confound the infernal villains! Like all scoundrels, attacking at night."

Misterwizard sat up and rubbed his eyes. "Wake your valiant compatriot Starbucks. Then we must inform Leader Nordstrom post haste, err we all perish." Misterwizard hopped up as Johnny ran to wake up Starbucks.

Johnny passed a window and glanced out. The shadows were closer now; they didn't have much time. He ran to Starbucks and gave him a good kick in the side.

"Huh! What?" Starbucks sat up, an unhappy frown on his face. "Who kicked me?"

"Wake up," Johnny said.

"Can you just once find a different way of waking me up?"

"We've got trouble headed our way."

Starbucks rubbed his eyes and smiled up at Johnny. "So what else is new?" Then he quickly rose and threw on his clothes. "What's going on, Johnny?"

"The Gangers are attacking us in the dark. I have to go tell Leader Nordstrom."

Johnny headed towards the door. He called out to Misterwizard as he ran. "If they surround us, we'll be trapped! They can starve or burn us out."

Misterwizard donned his cloak as he replied. "This

church, er I mean Castle is a stalwart fortress, but is does have the disadvantage of being easily encompassed. I'm afraid any plan of action involves some risk, but I believe our best strategy will be to engage them on one front while the Tribe flees in another direction in the buses, preferably towards the new Shopping Mall, er, Sanctuary."

Johnny stopped at the door and said, "That sounds like a good plan to me. We need to get the Tribe there as fast as possible. Leader Nordstrom is going to think this attack proves he was right."

Misterwizard grabbed Johnny's arm and Johnny turned to look at him. "Don't worry about Leader Nordstrom. He is not truly a leader at all and will do whatever we say to guarantee his own well-being. But Johnny."

"Yes, Misterwizard?"

"We will lead the Tribe to the new Sanctuary, but you and I can't stay there. There is another place you and I, and Deb, must go."

"Where is that?"

"After you left me Johnny, I did some more research. The place I spoke of, it might be Deb's only hope."

"What is it, Misterwizard?"

"It's an underground facility called the President's Bunker, created by the Leader Nordstroms of our country, before the Great War. It is in a city not far from here that used to where the government of this great country resided called Washington D.C. There is an underground tunnel from the Capitol to it, but that one is secured and still impregnable. However, there is also a secret entrance into it from basement of the Museum of American History and the egress to that passage was inadvertently exposed by the fighting. I have been researching it for years, thinking it might be a better place for the Tribe than Sanctuary, for the very reasons that you, I and Deb must go there. It will likely have medicine, weapons and other necessities for survival, ones preserved just for survivors of a nuclear attack. I've taken many private journeys to Washington D. C. to locate it, and finally succeeded. To date I have been unsuccessful at deciphering the final barrier into the Bunker the secret entrance code and the door panel which is made to be operational indefinitely. I had hoped to find the solution to the mystery before broaching the subject to Leader Nordstrom and the Tribe, but circumstances now being what they are, that possibility is now rendered untenable."

"Decipher? Tenable?"

"Never mind that for now. We will cross that hurdle when we reach it, but try we must, for it may be the only place that will have stored medicine to heal your dear Deb."

"Then that's where we go!" Johnny's face set in determination.

"First let's get the Tribe settled in a new home, after getting out of our present predicament of course. And then we can make our plans. "

"If we get out of it," Starbucks said.

"We will," Johnny said. "I've beaten Ripper every time. This will be no different."

Ripper grinned like a wolf, his teeth gleaming in the light of the torch he carried. Beside him, just visible in the dark, Leaker grinned too, a look of pure evil on his face.

"We gonna get 'em this time, Ripper! We gonna get 'em good! Oh man, this is gonna be great!"

Ripper reached over and backhanded Leaker's shoulder, more out of excitement than anger.

"Keep your voice down, Stupid, or they'll hear us. I'm going to pay Johnny back for that Beastie that he led to Sanctuary to attack us. I'm going to take hours to kill him."

"Yeah, yeah. Hoo hoo, it's gonna be great."

Like wraiths in the darkness the Gangers glided along, each carrying guns and clubs, and each with evil grins like Jack-o-lanterns. Some carried the sticks with the strings Ripper found.

In the near distance, the Castle stood out, black against the night sky. A few lights flickered through the windows, but all seemed quiet. The Tribe appeared to be sleeping. Ripper couldn't believe it. Was he actually going to win this time? Did he really have the Tribe surrounded? It almost seemed too easy, in fact he felt a slight disappointment. It was almost as if the final winning was not near as fun as the constant fighting had been.

Then he grinned. It wasn't over yet. They had a battle ahead; a fierce, exciting battle with people screaming in terror and burning buildings and little children running. He couldn't wait. He hurried his pace, eager to get to the fight.

Johnny ran down the stairway and bumped into an Enforcer. "What are you doing down here?" The man asked suspiciously with a glare.

Johnny tried to slip by, but the Enforcer blocked his way.

"Where's Leader Nordstrom?"

"He's sleeping. Don't bother him."

Johnny glared at the man, knowing what he was about to say would change his mind. "The Gangers are attacking."

As Johnny suspected, the man's eyes instantly opened wide in terror. The man fell back, all thoughts of resisting Johnny gone. "We're dead! We're all dead!"

"No, we're not! Help me find Leader Nordstrom, now!"

The man quickly turned and ran into the dark, stumbling over sleeping bodies that groaned in protest. "He is in the corner. Johnny, what will we do?"

Johnny grinned in the dark and thought humorlessly, "*Why don't you ask Leader Nordstrom*?" But he replied, "We'll fight them on one side, and escape to the new Sanctuary from the other. Go wake all the men and tell them to get weapons. They fight for their families tonight!"

The man ran off, mumbling incoherently to himself as Johnny ran on to find Leader Nordstrom. He finally spotted him in the corner, snoring loudly on a velvet pillow.

Without being gentle, Johnny kicked him in the bottom. Leader Nordstrom yelled and sat up with a start. When he saw Johnny, he immediately scowled with anger and hatred.

"What are you doing, sneaking up on me? Are you

planning on killing me in my sleep?"

Johnny grinned darkly. "If I wanted to kill you, I'd do it in the daylight, where everyone could enjoy it."

Leader Nordstrom frowned with fear. "Then what do you want? If you think we're going to have a talk about the Tribe's future now, you're mistaken."

"Be quiet and listen. The Gangers are attacking."

Leader Nordstrom's eyes opened wide in fear, just as the Enforcers had. "I told you. Didn't I tell you? You've led us all to our doom! I shall make sure everyone knows it was you that caused this!"

"And I hope we live to let you do that. For now, we need to fight, and flee to the new Sanctuary as soon as we get a chance."

Leader Nordstrom shook. "We will never make it. We will all die."

"Not if we act fast. Get up and get the women and children ready to move!"

As Johnny ran off, Leader Nordstrom watched him with hatred. Their problems were all Johnny's fault. If Johnny had left well enough alone, they would still be in Sanctuary and everything would be just as it always had been. He would be Leader Nordstrom and life could have remained quiet and peaceful. But no, Johnny had to go on adventures, stirring up the Gangers against them, and causing them to lose their home. Now Johnny would be the hero, and Leader Nordstrom would be nothing. Well, that was enough. Leader Nordstrom decided it was time for him to worry about himself. At the first opportunity, he would get away, and the Gangers could do whatever they wanted with the ungrateful and troublesome Tribe. Leader Nordstrom just hoped that no matter what happened, the Gangers at least stuck a knife in Johnny's heart, ending his meddlesome ways once and for all.

Johnny ran back towards Misterwizard, shaking people and waking them as he went. “Everyone. Wake up and get ready to fight! Gangers are attacking!”

Soon the Castle filled with the sounds of groggy, frightened people and the shadows of ghostly forms rising against the light of the torches, for Misterwizards ‘electricity’ wasn’t on. Johnny heard Starbucks somewhere in the darkness waking people up too.

Suddenly an arm gripped Johnny’s. He turned to see the face of Misterwizard, dark and covered in shadow. “Johnny. We need to create a distraction. Something to occupy the Gangers while the Tribe escapes. I can do some ‘magic’ that will send discourage them temporarily, but it will not last very long.”

Johnny thought for a moment, then he smiled grimly. “I think I know just what to do.”

“Good! Utilize your idea posthaste, for our margin of time for safe passage is quickly dissipating. I will ask Starbucks to wake Leader Nordstrom. Together they can work on getting the Tribe to the buses.”

Johnny shook his head, not even planning to ask what “posthaste” or “dissipating” meant, knowing better. As he turned and ran for the secret entrance, he called to Wizard. “Take care of Deb.”

“Of course, my boy. She will be my highest priority.”

As soon as Buildabear heard Johnny announce that the Gangers were coming, he smiled from where he lay next to Carny, a dark, evil smile. He lay still, hearing Johnny talking to the sleeping mob, waking them up. When he heard Johnny head towards the Secret Exit, he knew he had to move fast.

Sitting up, he shook Carny with his hand. She moaned and rolled over. He scowled and shook her harder. "Wake up, you fat, lazy pig!"

Carny's eyes opened, and she looked at Buildabear. "What is the matter?"

Quickly Buildabear put on a look of care and concern. "Carny! Carny! Wake up! The Gangers are coming!"

Carny struggled to sit up, but her large belly made it difficult. Buildabear didn't bother to help her, just waited impatiently until she finally managed.

"The Gangers?" Carny said, fear in her voice. "Where's Johnny?"

"Johnny is outside, getting the buses ready. We must go quickly. He wants you there first, to protect you!"

Carny smiled, touched, but then she frowned. "Johnny shouldn't worry about me. He should worry about Tribe."

"Johnny's worried for Miracle," Buildabear said with an overdone frown of concern. "He wants to make sure Carny and Miracle don't get hurt. Let's go!"

Carny nodded as Buildabear stood up. She struggled to rise, and once again he didn't help her, secretly loathing her fat body, hating her slowness, but mostly hating that she was Johnny's sister. *Soon,* he thought, *she will be scared, even terrified.* He couldn't wait to see it.

Finally, Carny was able to rise. Buildabear led her

through the dark, his heart racing with excitement and evil pleasure. He couldn't wait to get her to Ripper and see what he would do to her.

The Tribe members were all awake and standing now. Pulling Carny behind him, Buildabear wove through the yelling, bustling Tribe members running this way and that, not sure what they were supposed to be doing. Some saw Buildabear and spoke to him, but he simply ignored them.

Buildabear and Carny made it through the small front room to the two double doors at the front of Castle. "Hurry your fat self!" Buildabear barked at her. "Johnny is waiting by buses and he wants you on first!"

Buildabear pulled the heavy bolt that sealed the doors and the doors opened slightly, free. "Wait!" Carny said. "Won't that let the Gangers in?"

"That's exactly my plan," Buildabear thought, but what he said was, "The Tribe will be gone before they get here. Now stop talking and hurry!"

He pulled open the door on the right and a rush of cool air swept over them, blowing back their hair. "Are you sure we should go outside?" Carny said, looking fearfully out at the darkness.

"Don't argue with me!" Buildabear snarled. "You always argue. You and Johnny think you're smarter than Buildabear. Just be quiet and do as you're told!"

Buildabear pulled Carny outside roughly, making sure to leave the door open. "Wait! Are you sure the buses are this way?" Carny peered into the darkness, trying to see the buses.

"Move! Stop arguing!"

Buildabear pulled Carny into the darkness, towards the distant torchlight heading swiftly towards them.

The trail of orange lights in the darkness grew close. The Gangers ran now, like wolves smelling blood.

Suddenly a huge explosion and a blast of yellow light came from the top of Castle. The Gangers all stopped and looked up, their mouths open in curiosity. As they watched a strange arc of yellow light lit the sky, shooting high in the air, and then coming down to land-

"Look out!" Ripper yelled, as he dove to the left. The other Gangers, Leaker included, were not that quick on the uptake but stood still watching.

The ground in the middle of the Gangers exploded, and the first two Gangers flew in the air, screaming in fear and pain. The rest turned and ran backwards in terror.

In Castle, Misterwizard watched the results of his mortar fire with pride and pleasure. "A little too much to the West, but still quite effective. I will have to adjust my aim slightly." He began fiddling with a knob on the front of the weapon.

"Oh yeah?" Ripper said, grinning. "Let's see how you like it!"

Ripper turned to Leaker. "Give me one of those sticks!"

Leaker brought him a stick.

"Now find me some fire."

"Fire?" Leaker said.

Ripper cuffed Leaker's face. "Fire, stupid! You have to light them!"

"Fire," Leaker yelled, running off into the darkness.

Ripper watched him, and mentally yelled at himself. He'd forgotten they needed fire too. It was Leaker's fault; his stupidity was catching. Ripper looked nervously up at Misterwizard's Castle, wondering when Misterwizard was going to launch another of his magical attacks.

Meanwhile, Johnny ran through the dark as if his life, and the lives of all the people he cared for depended on it, which it did. He moved quickly but silently, his eyes like a cat's in the darkness, knowing just where he was going.

He passed building after building and began to get winded. He started to worry that he would slow down and waste precious time, but just as he was beginning to panic, he saw the building he was looking for in the distance.

Not wasting a moment to look at it he ran inside the dark interior, knowing right where he intended to go. He headed for the "African Tundra" exhibit, and what he knew was waiting inside.

Because of the urgency of the moment Johnny didn't hesitate or feel fear, but threw the doors open. "Hey Barkers! Still hungry?"

In the dark, he saw five, six heads come up, and gleaming eyes. Barks and whines of excitement filled the air, and then dark, lean bodies rose quickly.

Johnny knew he had to run, fast, for the Barkers were surely twice as hungry now. This knowledge filled Johnny with adrenaline and made him run twice as fast. And it was a good thing too, for the Barkers, mad with hunger, ran desperately and swiftly.

Johnny leapt out into the dark and took off towards Castle and the Gangers. He turned once, making sure the Barkers were following. What he saw made him know he didn't need to worry about that, but instead worry about staying ahead of them, for they were only a few yards behind him. They howled and snarled, their teeth bared, hunger in their eyes. Johnny smiled. They would be good and hungry when they arrived, and Johnny had just the snack for them, some good, tasty Gangers.

Ripper ran back to the Gangers, his face a mask of fury. They were spread out, hiding behind buildings and the rusted hulks of cars. He grabbed one by the hair. As the man yelled, Ripper dragged him back into the open. Then he turned and called out to the rest in the darkness.

"Everybody get back out here and stop being chicken-beasties! Did you forget we have magic sticks too? When we get to Castle we will destroy it until there's nothing left." The Gangers all grinned and come out of hiding. They turned and continued their march towards Castle, their courage restored.

Ripper looked around for Leaker. "Where's that idiot with the fire?" Then he heard something strange in the dark, far behind them, drifting on the air like the half-remembered sound from long ago. It sounded like barking, but something urgent, desperate in it that started alarms in Ripper's mind and made his heart skip a beat. Ripper stood still, wondering what it could be, listening. The sound stopped finally. He began to wonder if he had just imagined it. He dismissed it, turned and ran after his gang.

Starbucks ran to Leader Nordstrom, who now stood by the front door. Two Enforcers stood on either side of him. As soon as they saw Starbucks approach, they crossed their spears to deny him access to Leader Nordstrom.

"Halt! What do you want?"

"You braindeads! We have to get the Tribe to the buses Misterwizard has waiting!"

"I am still Leader Nordstrom," Leader Nordstrom said to Starbucks with a haughty look. "I will lead them to the "buses."

"Then do it already! We don't have much time."

Leader Nordstrom turned to the Tribe, who were milling about, weeping and talking in frightened voices.

"Come and follow me! We will go to the buses!"

The Tribe nodded as one as Leader Nordstrom led them out into the small outer room and towards the doors.

Once outside, Starbucks saw the buses on the far side just outside the gates. They stood, three in a row, their doors open. Starbucks worked on herding the Tribe into the buses as Leader Nordstrom stood safe inside the gate near the door, watching. Leader Nordstrom kept scanning the horizon, looking for the Gangers, ready to bolt back inside at the slightest sound of them.

The Tribe acted once again like frightened sheep-beasties, slow to get inside, fearful of the big yellow metal containers.

Starbucks frowned with impatience. "Hurry! Into the buses! They won't hurt you! There's no time for being frightened by something new again!"

"What about our things?' a woman asked him. "Once again we're leaving everything behind. What about food?"

"Johnny and Misterwizard will take care of that. The Gangers are coming. Get in the buses, fast!"

"How will we make them go?" Foodcourt asked.

Starbucks rolled his eyes. "Misterwizard will worry about that. Please, on the bus!"

Foodcourt nodded and climbed on the second one.

Slowly, too slowly for Starbucks, the Tribe filed onto the buses. Once on board they milled about, packed in like firewood, making it hard for more to get on board. Starbucks groaned and grit his teeth. Didn't they understand that their lives depended on it?

In his room, Misterwizard let fly another mortar out the small window, aimed towards the shadows below. The night sky lit up like daytime as it arced through the sky. Misterwizard chuckled with joy, watching it streak across the dark night. "This is just how my grandfather described Fourth of July, before the Great War. I've never been fortunate enough to enjoy fireworks until now!'

Misterwizard looked down at the street in front of the castle and saw Starbucks herding the Tribe onto the buses. He calculated in his mind how many more shells he could launch before he had to hurry down to drive one of the buses. He knew he needed time to recruit and train two more drivers. He knew it would literally be a crash course in automotive operation, but all they had to do was make it far enough to reach the new Sanctuary without running off the road or smashing into a building. With some simple instructions, he believed he could impart enough knowledge to make them successful.

He gazed out past the buses and spied a lone figure, across the street near the next building, heading away from Castle. Misterwizard picked up a pair of green colored goggles with a strap on them. Peering through them he could see at night in a greenish tinge. He strained his eyes and finally made out who it was. "Well, well, the plot thickens. A rat, deserting a sinking ship, ay?"

It was Leader Nordstrom, running off alone into the darkness, deserting the Tribe for his own safety! Misterwizard lowered the goggles but continued to look out at the darkness towards the retreating figure. "From now on, Leader Nordstrom, I declare you the enemy of not only myself and Johnny but the whole Tribe. We shall not rest until you get the comeuppance you deserve. Meanwhile, you have done us a favor, for now we won't have to deal with your constant hindrance. Thank you, Leader Nordstrom, for finally displaying your true nature to us all."

CHAPTER 18

As Castle came into view in the darkness, the Gangers let out a ragged cheer. There were fifty of them left after the fight at Sanctuary, and they wanted revenge. They hurried forward faster, but Ripper stopped and raised a hand. The Gangers stopped and waited to find out why.

Two figures approached, their faces white darkness. As soon as he recognized them, Ripper's heart soared with dark, evil glee. It was Buildabear, and he was leading Carny, Johnny's sister with him!

As soon as the pair grew close, Carny struggled, realizing she'd been tricked. She pulled back, yelling in fear, but Buildabear gripped her arm hard, yanking her viciously. "Stop fighting or I will beat you."

Carny stared at him with hurt and amazement. "How can you do this? I am your mate. You're betraying me. I thought you loved me."

Buildabear sneered at her. "I never loved you. You complain all the time. 'Buildabear, get me water. Buildabear, find food. Buildabear, stay home.' You're fat and you eat too much. I'll get a new mate, maybe two, when I am a Ganger."

Tears fell from Carny's eyes and she wiped them away with her hand. "Johnny was right. He said you were evil. He will come. He will make you pay. He will kill you!"

"That's just what we're hoping," Ripper laughed. "We have you, soon we will have Johnny too." The Gangers laughed, as Buildabear handed Carny over to Ripper. She didn't fight anymore but simple allowed herself to be led away with her head down.

Ripper handed Carny over to Leaker. As Leaker tried to rub his hands over Carny, she struggled and fought him.

"Oh, we're gonna have fun with you," Leaker chortled. "And when your wriggler is born, we'll eat it!"

"Don't touch her," Ripper warned with a scowl. Then he smiled. "Not yet. Not until we have Johnny." Then he turned to Buildabear. Buildabear grinned, his eyes lit up with anticipation.

"What is the Tribe doing?"

"Misterwizard and Johnny are leading them to a new Sanctuary not far from here. It is a tall building with many floors and rooms, just like the old Sanctuary."

Ripper smiled, for he thought he knew the place Buildabear spoke of.

"I know where that is. Well, we'll make sure when they get there, they will find it inviting."

He turned to a Ganger named Rototiller, a short, squat man with big arms and short black hair. "Go to the big place with the Fake People, where all the good stuff was found."

Rototiller "But I'm afraid to go in there. The Fake People watch us. They'll eat us!"

"Stupid! They're not alive. Do what I say, or I'll give you something to really be afraid of. Take ten of the gang and burn the place down. Then when the Tribe gets there, they'll have nowhere to go. They'll be helpless."

Rototiller nodded unhappily. He turned and walked off, a group of gangers following him. Soon they disappeared into the darkness.

Ripper made a fist and raised it in the air. "Let's go get them! They won't even make it to their new Sanctuary!"

"Yes!" Buildabear said, a dark gleam in his eyes. "We can make them all slaves!"

Buildabear grinned at Ripper, but then he saw a strange look on Ripper's face that worried him. When Ripper spoke, his fears were confirmed. "Look, Gangers, the first of the Tribe to die."

The Gangers cheered and surrounded Buildabear. His smile disappeared to be replaced by a look of fright. "Wait! You promised me I could join the Gangers! I gave you Carny!"

Ripper spit at the ground. "How can I trust you, you who not only betray your Tribe but turn over your own mate to me? I have Carny. She will lead me to Johnny. And you, you cowardly snake. You get to die like the cowardly worm-beastie you are!"

"No!" Buildabear screamed and tried to turn and run. The Gangers raised their weapons and gave chase. Ripper watched as they quickly overtook him. They beat him with their clubs and knives, and Buildabear fell to the ground, screaming in fear and pain. Soon he lay still and silent, as the Gangers finished him.

Carny turned away, but on her face, she wore a satisfied smile of fury. She stared to where Buildabear lay on the ground, dead. “You deserved that.’ Then she turned and looked back towards Castle. “Johnny,” she whispered. “Come save me, Johnny!”

Leaker ran up holding a stick with fire burning on its end. He grinned with evil joy at Ripper. Ripper grabbed it from him roughly. “It’s about time.”

Then Ripper grinned. Ripper and the Gangers ran towards Castle, bloodlust in their eyes and smiles of pure evil on their faces. Leaker dragged Carny along, holding her wrist and making her go so fast she kept stumbling. Then he would curse at her and drag her along, happy to have someone he could be mean to, instead of always being the one at the bottom. And from somewhere in the darkness behind them came the sound of Barkers, getting closer.

Johnny ran fast with the Barkers right behind him. Excitement and adrenaline spurred him on coupled with fear, for the Barkers were not more than a few seconds behind him. He saw the dark shadows of the Gangers ahead of him, and he smiled, looking forward to what was about to happen. He could hear their voices talking excitedly ahead, not knowing what was about to happen from behind. It almost made Johnny laugh.

Then he heard something that made fear grip him like a cold hand on his heart. It was Carny’s voice! What was she doing with the Gangers? Amazement and dismay filled Johnny. He couldn't lead the Barkers to the Gangers if Carny was there, they would attack her too!

Johnny saw something on the ground. It was a body. He ran to it and instantly recognized the bloody face. It was Buildabear, or what was left of him. What had Buildabear done? Had he and Carny been outside for some reason and been captured? Or had Buildabear betrayed his sister and given her to the Gangers?

Johnny suspected the last one was the truth. He always knew Buildabear was a rotten, evil man, and now he'd proved it. But now Buildabear had been given his reward in the way he deserved, and that made Johnny very happy. But how was he going to save Carny? If the Barkers attacked the Gangers, they'd hurt Carny too.

Johnny yelled to the Barkers. He heard them coming from the darkness. *Good,* Johnny thought; they could feast on Buildabear, and that would give Johnny some time to get Carny away, before the Barkers moved on, hopefully to the Gangers.

As soon as Johnny saw the first Barker, he turned and ran. But looking back he was happy to see it stop and investigate Buildabear's body. Soon the Barkers surrounded Buildabear. Johnny had no illusions that they would eat every bit of him, and there would be nothing, not even bones, left. Johnny almost regretted Buildabear dying and distracting the Barkers, almost. Would they still be hungry afterwards, or would they turn back? And how could Johnny get Carny away from the Gangers?

Misterwizard let off another volley towards where he saw the dark shapes of the Gangers. He smiled as he watched the pretty yellow arc through the night sky. "Enjoy this present, you evil malefactors!"

Starbucks ran up the stairs. "Misterwizard! People are on the buses. Time to move to new Sanctuary!"

Misterwizard turned and gave Starbucks a pat on the arm. "And so, we shall, Starbucks. I will have to give two Tribe members a quick lesson on driving. I am thinking it will be Johnny's father, Foodcourt, and Deb's father Thegap, they seem like the most stable and reliable choices. Foodcourt, despite the Tribe's opinion of him, is really a very intelligent and capable man. And Thegap, though diminutive in size, is also a smart and good man. Then it will be like a field trip from school. Off to our new home!"

"And I will follow along on my Harley, now that it has the liquid in it again." Starbucks shook his head. "You talk funny. But you're the best guy in the World, Misterwizard. I don't know what Tribe would do if you didn't help us."

"And I'm eager to do it, my boy. Now let's get going!"

Johnny followed the Gangers, keeping hidden from sight. He saw that Leaker was watching Carny. Leaker would be easy, but only if Johnny could keep Ripper and the rest of the Gangers from seeing him.

They were almost at Castle. Johnny figured when the fighting started, he could grab Carny in the confusion. But now that the Barkers were occupied eating

Buildabear, what would keep the Gangers from capturing the Tribe? Johnny hoped Misterwizard had another idea.

"There it is, gang! Attack, and don't let anyone escape!" Ripper waved his sword in the air. As one, the Gangers yelled and rushed at Castle. Leaker held back, having to watch Carny, who struggled and fought against him.

Suddenly another of Misterwizard's mortar shells hit the ground, this time much closer. The Gangers panicked again and scattered, though not as far. Carny twisted her arm, but Leaker held her tight, even though he was terrified of the explosions.

The Gangers saw the front door to Castle and rushed in eager for blood, only to run into the barbed wire and strange skeletons hanging from the fence surrounding the fortress.

"Ripper!" Leaker moaned. "Bad magic here. Misterwizard put a spell on this place."

"Don't be wriggler," Ripper snarled. "These only old bones and sticky metal." Then he smiled evilly and lit the stick. "We have a way in."

The Gangers walked the exterior, looking for an opening, unaware that on the opposite side of Castle, the Tribe was already loaded in the buses and about to leave.

Carny pulled back from Leaker. He turned and showed her his most fearsome and angry face, which didn't scare her at all. "Stop that strugglin,' or Leaker knock your teeth out. Maybe I punch you and make Wriggler die." Leaker twisted Carny's arm savagely.

The string at the end of the stick in Ripper's hand sizzled and hissed. It scared him, and he dropped it. All the Gangers ran in fright, not knowing what it would do. Ripper ran too.

Leaker stared at the sizzling stick, his eyes wide in terror. Carny screamed in anger and kicked him in the shin. Leaker howled in pain and let her go.

The stick exploded, sending rock and dirt flying in the air. Leaker and Carny were far enough away not to be hurt, but two Gangers weren't so lucky. A big rock hit one in the head and he went down in a heap and didn't move. The other was thrown backwards and impaled on a piece of beam sticking out of a building. He hung there, dripping blood, dead.

In the darkness behind them, Johnny laughed. Now was his chance. He ran at Leaker, his mind blank with anger.

Leaker and Carny both saw him at the same time. Carny smiled with joy. Leaker's face showed another emotion: pure terror.

"Johnny!" He backed up, hands held in front of his chest, palms up, in supplication. "I was just keeping her safe for you!"

Carny ran to Johnny and grabbed him around the waist, tears in her eyes. "I knew you'd come for me, Johnny."

Johnny grabbed her around the shoulders and held her tight. "We have to get away. Barkers are coming!"

Leaker heard him. "Barkers?" He turned and ran towards Ripper and the Gangers. "Johnny's here! And he says Barkers coming! Run!" And Leaker did just that, turning and running towards the other side of Castle.

The Gangers were too spread apart to hear Leaker, but Ripper did. He turned and saw Johnny holding Carny. He smiled. "There you are! Time to kill you!" Ripper ran towards Johnny.

Johnny saw him coming. He turned to Carny. "On the

other side of Castle, Misterwizard is loading the Tribe into buses. Go fast and join them before they leave!" Johnny pointed to where the buses were parked.

Carny nodded and ran in that direction. Johnny turned to face Ripper, his sword ready. He didn't have to wait long.

Ripper ran towards him, his own sword held high. "Finally, you stop running like a Cowardie. I'm going to cut you into pieces, so all the Gangers and the Tribe can see Ripper get his revenge."

Johnny and Ripper circled each other, both tense as bowstrings, looking for their opening. "Why don't you leave Tribe alone? They done nothing to you," Johnny asked.

"Because you want it," Ripper shot back. "I'm gonna kill them all, starting with your little Girlie. Deb, is that her name? After I take her for myself."

Johnny's lip curled. "You are evil. I'm going to rid the world of you, and everyone, even the Gagners, will thank me."

"Then come on, what are you waiting for?"

Johnny held his sword high. "I may be only fifteen seasons, but even a Crawler could beat you."

The air filled with the barks of the Barkers. They both turned to look. The first Barker appeared, but just then a Wildie stepped out of the darkness. He yelled and grabbed the Barker, which yelped and snarled. The Wildie bit the Barker and it bared its fangs and bit back.

Soon the rest of the Barkers arrived and attacked the Wildie. He dropped the Barker and ran off, with the other Barkers chasing him.

Ripper grinned. "That Wildie is going to be meat for the Barkers. Now my Gangers will get the Tribe for sure."

"You won't be alive to see it!" Johnny lunged at Ripper.

At the buses, Misterwizard found Foodcourt sitting next to Teavanna in the second bus. As Misterwizard approached, Foodcourt looked up at him with curiosity.

"Dear Foodcourt, there is a task that I need assistance with. It requires someone both courageous and intelligent. The first person who came to my mind was you, for you have both qualities. Would you be willing to assist us, dear friend?"

Foodcourt's eyes widened with pleasure and surprise. "Of course, Misterwizard! I'd jump off a bridge if you asked me to. Just tell me what I need to do, and I'll do it right!"

"Excellent! I knew I could rely on you, fine fellow. And you will get to do something rather exciting and exhilarating. You will drive the bus!"

Foodcourt's mouth opened in delight and surprise. "Drive the bus! Do you think I can?"

"Of course! I will teach you! Come with me!" Misterwizard led Foodcourt to the front and sat him down in the driver's seat. He went over the basic controls. "The most important thing to remember is this pedal that you push when you want to stop. And steering where you want to go."

Foodcourt turned the wheel and pushed both pedals. "I have it. I will drive the bus!"

Misterwizard chuckled at Foodcourt's enthusiasm. "Here, you start it by turning this key. When we signal you, you will put your foot on the brake pedal and turn it. Then release the brake pedal, push the other pedal called the gas pedal very slowly, and you'll be off!"

Foodcourt bounced in the seat with excitement. "I am ready!"

Misterwizard chuckled and patted Foodcourt on the shoulder. "Remember, you turn the wheel in the direction you want to go, and the bus will travel in that direction."

"Got it!" Foodcourt said, his face lit up with excitement. "Pedals to stop and go, turn wheel."

"And try your best not to run into anything."

"You can count on me, Misterwizard!" Foodcourt said, bouncing up and down on the seat. Misterwizard smiled. At the least, the episode ahead was going to be entertaining.

Misterwizard left the bus. Starbucks walked up to him.

"Did you give Thegap driving instructions?" Misterwizard asked.

"I sure did," Starbucks answered. "He may hit a few things on the way, but I did on my Harley too when you taught me. I think he'll make it."

"Then let's be off!"

And just in time, for just as they finished speaking, the Gangers came running around the Castle from both sides.

"Quickly, Starbucks. Now is the time for our hasty departure!" Misterwizard ran to the first bus as Starbucks signaled to Foodcourt and Thegap to start their engines. Then Starbucks ran to his Harley and roared it to life.

Noise and confusion filled the interior of the buses as all the Tribe yelled at once on seeing the Gangers coming.

Sephie ran up to Misterwizard in the driver's seat and pulled on his arm.

"Misterwizard, we can't leave without Johnny." Misterwizard smiled at Sephie and touched the side of her face with his palm. "Don't you worry about Johnny, Little One. Johnny is a strong courageous hero. He is out paving the way for our escape, and he will meet us soon."

Sephie grinned, her eyes bright. "I love Johnny. You know, someday Johnny and me will be mated."

Misterwizard patted Sephie's head. "Of course, you will. Who else would Johnny marry but you? Now go find a seat, Dear. We have to go."

Sephie nodded and hurried back to her seat as Misterwizard turned the key and the bus roared to life.

Then Gangers reached the door of the bus! Quickly they surrounded all three buses. They banged on the doors and sides. The people of the Tribe stared out the windows in terror and screamed.

Faces leered in the windows. A grizzled man of thirty with a short, left arm and missing teeth named Oldnavy hurried up to Wizard.

"What will we do, Misterwizard? We're surrounded!"

Misterwizard turned to the Tribe, who stared at him with wide eyes of fear.

Speaking loudly so that they could all hear he said, "Men of Johnny's Tribe. It is time to put on the Mantle of Courage! Defend what is yours against the barbarians that would take it from you! Johnny, Starbucks and I have helped you as much as we can, but there comes a time when men must come to their own aid. It is time for you to step and up show what mettle you are made of. There is a bag full of weapons in the back of each bus. I suggest that now is the time to utilize them!"

The men of the Tribe looked at each other fearfully, but then a look of determination, of steely resolve began to come into their faces.

"Misterwizard is right," Oldnavy said. "I'm tired of hiding from these Gangers. Let's kill them all!"

With a yell, the men of the Tribe struggled their way through the tribe to the back of the bus. Oldnavy opened the bag and handed out swords and knives.

Oldnavy lifted a sword up in the air and gazed at it with admiration. "Misterwizard, where you get such beautiful weapons?"

Misterwizard smiled. "You can thank Johnny for that. Though I know it was difficult for him, he emptied his hidden treasure trove, the Sword Shop, of all the weapons that were left there, just so that you people could defend yourselves."

Oldnavy smiled with gratitude. "Yay Johnny. Let's go men!"

Yelling with bloodlust, the men of the Tribe poured out the back of the bus, ready to kill or be killed.

CHAPTER 19

Johnny lunged at Ripper, but Ripper slipped backwards out of the way, laughing. Ripper picked up a rock and threw it at Johnny, who hopped and easily dodged it.

"I'm going to enjoy your girl Deb," Ripper sneered. "Think about me with her. She'll enjoy being with a real man, not a little boy."

Johnny yelled and rushed Ripper, sword raised. Ripper sidestepped Johnny waited until Johnny's sword arm had passed, then jabbed Johnny's arm with his knife. Johnny fell back, holding his bleeding arm.

"After what you did to me and my Gangers, I'm going to make sure your girl suffers. After we're done with her, we'll give her to the Wildies."

Johnny rushed Ripper again, swinging his sword in an arc. Ripper stepped back, enjoying baiting Johnny, watching him hit only air.

A new sound came from behind Ripper, one that at first, he didn't recognize. He turned his head to look, but then Johnny was on him. Their swords clashed, and they pressed their bodies against each other, struggling, both trying to raise get their weapon past the other's and land a stab.

With his free hand, Ripper slugged Johnny in the face. Johnny yelled and tripped Ripper with his foot. Ripper staggered backwards, momentarily losing his balance. Johnny pressed in, swinging his sword.

But Ripper recovered and leapt towards Johnny, his sword clanging against Johnny's. But now Johnny struck Ripper with his free fist, and blood started pouring from Ripper's eyebrow.

Johnny landed a cut on Ripper's hand, and Ripper dropped his sword. Johnny swung down to cut Ripper in half, but Ripper grabbed Johnny's arm. They struggled for a few minutes, and then Ripper bashed Johnny's arm against a lamppost. Johnny dropped his sword and threw another punch at Ripper. It hit Ripper in the jaw, but Ripper threw a punch too that struck Johnny in the stomach. Johnny doubled over as Ripper rushed him, butting his head into Johnny's chest. Both fell on the ground, writhing and fighting.

The sound came again, and this time Johnny recognized it. He knew that he had to get away, and fast. Struggling against Ripper, he rolled over so that he was on top. But Ripper had hold of both Johnny's arms. Johnny pulled at his arms and kicked, only to meet Ripper's kicks coming at him.

"Let me go! We have to get away from here!" Johnny yelled.

"You turning cowardie, Johnny? Little Scrabbler is getting scared." Ripper kicked harder, and Johnny kicked back.

Then a voice came out of the darkness and it sent chills up Johnny's spine. It was Leaker.

"Let me help you, Ripper. Let me help you get Johnny!"

Ripper grinned at Johnny with a smile of victory. "Johnny's sword is lying there somewhere. Find it!"

Johnny struggled mightily, but Ripper held him tight. Desperation gripped Johnny as he felt his arms grow tired.

"I found it!" In the corner of his eye, Johnny saw Leaker holding Johnny's sword high in the air.

Ripper stared at Johnny, his eyes dark as midnight. "Stab him!"

Leaker's face twisted in hatred. "You bet I will!" Leaker strode over and Johnny felt hope begin to ebb. He thought about Deb, and his heart drowned in a well of sorrow.

"This is it, Johnny."

"Please," Johnny said, his voice full of sadness. "Don't hurt Deb."

"She'll have fun, I promise." Ripper's face contorted with evil.

"This is for the bug-beasties you poured on my face at Sanctuary!" Leaker strode over, Johnny's sword angled down towards him.

But suddenly a huge, dark shadow lunged, and Leaker disappeared. Seconds later they heard a bloodcurdling scream.

Ripper loosened his grip on Johnny and Johnny broke free. Both men stood up and looked towards where the scream came from. Quickly both forgot their fight at what they saw.

Leaker was on the ground, or what was left of him. Over him stood the Tiger-beastie. It was feasting on Leaker's insides.

Johnny turned and ran one direction, and Ripper the other. Over his shoulder, Ripper yelled, "This isn't over!"

In the second bus, Foodcourt saw the men of the Tribe pouring out of the other bus. He turned towards the interior of the bus. "The men of the Tribe are fighting the Gangers! Let's get out there and help them!"

As one the men in the bus yelled a war cry. The grabbed the weapons from the bag at the back of their bus and hurried to the bus door. Foodcourt opened the door and they piled out.

Outside the bus, the Gangers greeted the onrushing Tribesmen with amazement. Starbucks dismounted his Harley and joined the Tribesmen as they fought like wild animals. Caught totally by surprise, many of the Gangers turned and ran away, but enough stayed and fought back that soon a pitched battle began.

Yells, screams, the clash of knives and swords and an occasional blast of gunfire filled the night air. Men fought back and forth, and soon cries of pain and fear joined the rest of the cacophony. The Gangers were tough and seasoned killers, but the men of the Tribe fought for their families with determination and courage.

Misterwizard hopped out of the bus wielding a rifle with a night scope on it. He took aim at a Ganger and fired, and the Ganger fell, dead. Soon the Gangers learned to back up to where they were not targets for Misterwizard, but Misterwizard followed the fight as it moved and tried to get off shots when he could.

Soon bodies littered the sidewalk next to Castle, those of both Gangers and Tribesmen. The battle began to spread out, with Gangers chasing Tribesmen or Tribesmen chasing Gangers. But the Gangers were stronger and better equipped, and soon the Tribesmen began to get overwhelmed.

Misterwizard and Starbucks watched the battle with dismay, seeing what was happening.

"Misterwizard, we're losing!" Starbucks said.

"It appears so, though there is always hope, until hope vanishes."

As if to prove Misterwizard's words true, the Barkers finally arrived. Starbucks and Misterwizard heard them first. Misterwizard hurried out to where he could yell.

"Men of the Tribe! Get on the buses! It's time to retreat!"

The men of the Tribe heard him and ran back. To help them, Misterwizard took aim as the pursuing Gangers and shot at them, making them run for cover.

As the Tribesmen came, bloody and covered in sweat and grime, Starbucks and Misterwizard hurried them back onto the buses.

And just in time, for out of the darkness came the Barkers. As Starbucks and Misterwizard hurried to get the stragglers on board, a Barker leapt onto a Ganger. The man screamed and fell, the Barker on top of him. Soon the other Gangers scattered.

"I have been proved right again," Misterwizard said to himself with a smile. "You never know what how the tide of battle shall turn, until it is concluded. I never liked those mangy hounds, but now I could kiss each one of them right on their shaggy noses."

Johnny caught up with Carny, only to see her bend over in pain. He hurried up to her and put an arm around her. "What is wrong, Carny?"

Carny smiled at Johnny. "Nothing is wrong. Miracle will come soon. The excitement is making him want to come faster."

"We have to get you to the bus and a safe place soon. Miracle can't come here." *And,* Johnny thought to himself, *we need Misterwizard to make sure Miracle comes at all.*

Johnny supported Carny as she stumbled along, anxious for how long it would take them to get to safety. Then he saw something that filled him with dismay.

All three buses took off, chased by a ragged group of Gangers. Carny saw it too.

'What are we going to do, Johnny? The Buses left."

"I'll have to take you on my Harley. I just hope you can ride."

Johnny led Carny towards his bike, watching warily for Gangers to see them, or for Ripper to reappear. As he held Carny with one arm, he pulled out his sword with his free hand, to be ready.

But they reached Johnny's Harley in safety. Carny gazed at it with wide eyes. "What is that, Johnny? It's beautiful! Is it yours?"

Despite the danger, Johnny couldn't help but feel a

sense of pride and pleasure. "It is my Harley. Get on, quick!"

"I don't think I can!"

"I'll help you." Johnny partially lifted Carny up and helped her get on the back of the bike. It was hard, in her condition. Johnny hoped the jolting of the bike ride wouldn't cause Miracle to be born. Then he would have big problems.

Johnny leapt on the front and started the bike. It roared to life, and Carny grinned with exhilaration. "Johnny, this is exciting!"

"Hold on tight!" Despite their current situation, Johnny couldn't help but smile. He felt Carny wrap her arms around him, reminding him of Deb doing the same thing. It made him wonder how Deb was doing. They had to get the tribe situated soon, so he and Misterwizard could go looking for the medicine.

Johnny took off slowly, making sure Carny didn't slip then he gradually accelerated.

They were on their way to the new Sanctuary.

"Thegap, please begin our journey."

"Okay, here we go." Thegap pushed down the gas pedal in the third bus, and the bus begin slowly creeping forward. The people of the tribe oohed and aahed, never having ridden in a bus before, and watched the landscape slowly pass by. Sephie sat at a window and bounced up and down next to her parents, who looked as excited as she was. Behind them, the Gangers who were not being attacked by the Barkers chased them and banged on the back of the bus, but the people of the Tribe just stuck out their tongues or made faces at them, no longer afraid.

Foodcourt started driving too, and Misterwizard watched him through the back window. The old buses coughed and lurched, even though Misterwizard had worked on their engines. Their shocks squeaked and groaned, and the buses swayed slightly. Many of the tribespeople looked around in fright. They had been through too many new experiences in the last twenty-four hours, and their lives had been turned upside down.

Inside Misterwizard's bus, celebration of victory began. The Tribesmen yelled a ragged cheer, their faces beaten but full of pride and happiness.

Oldnavy grinned at the tribe from the front of the bus. "We stood up to them men! We showed the Gangers that we are not afraid to fight!" The rest of the men cheered. In the driver's seat, Misterwizard smiled with pleasure and turned to listen.

"From now on, those Gangers will know to stay away from our tribe, or they will know Death!"

Another cheer went up.

"I dare say, you men fought with exceptional bravery and intestinal fortitude," Misterwizard said. "I am proud of you. And you didn't need Leader Nordstrom to tell you to do it."

"Where is Leader Nordstrom?" a tribesman asked. "He wasn't with us."

"I'm afraid Leader Nordstrom deserted you men in your hour of need and proved the true color of his nature."

"The what?" Oldnavy asked.

"Nothing, dear friend. Please, do me a favor and see

how Deb is doing. Tell me if she seems to be in good spirits."

Oldnavy walked to the back of the bus where Deb was lying, with her parents on either side of her. He studied her for a moment. Then he met Deb's father's gaze. It showed worry and fear. He touched Deb's forehead, and immediately pulled back his hand with alarm.

Oldnavy hurried back up to Misterwizard, his face grave. "She is wet with night sweats, but she is cold to the touch. She has the Sickness, Misterwizard. She should be moved, before we all get it!"

Misterwizard frowned deeply, his eyes sad. "She doesn't have much time. Johnny and I must reach Washington and the hidden bunker soon, or I fear she will succumb to her illness. But my first priority is to deliver you to your new domicile. I will accelerate my speed as much as I can, and hope the others can mimic my actions, for time is the substance in which we burn!"

Misterwizard heard Deb's coughing from the back of the bus, and it worried him, but not as much as the coughing he heard from other Tribes members. If they didn't get Deb isolated soon, she would spread her flu to the whole Tribe.

Foodcourt's bus drove all the way over to the other side of the road and almost went off, but he corrected at the last moment. Misterwizard could hear the people in in Foodcourt's bus yelling directions to him, and Foodcourt yelling back grumpily. He smiled, mildly enjoying their first road trip.

Finally, both drivers behind Misterwizard seemed to be getting the hang of it, and the buses moved slowly down the middle of the road. Misterwizard finally breathed easliy, but he wondered how the men were going to do when and if they had to turn. It would simply have to be learning by trial and error, and a lot of minor collisions, just like Johnny and Starbucks learned. The thought made Misterwizard grin.

Back at the Castle, the Gangers scattered as the Barkers attacked. Ripper ran up and saw what was happening. Full of fury, he ran up to a Barker and stabbed it dead with his sword.

"Come back here, you cowardies! They are only Barkers!"

Slowly the Gangers ran back, the ones that weren't being eaten by the Barkers. Now thirty remained, what was left alive or not maimed. As the Barkers came at them they attacked them in force, until the Barkers gave up and ran off.

Ripper kicked a dead Barker, full of rage.

"Now what do we do, Ripper?" A Ganger named Facegash asked, named for the gash that went from the left side of his face down to his chin. "The Tribe is gone. We lost."

Ripper strode over and slapped Facegash on the face, hard. Facegash yelped, backed away and covered his face with this hand. "We didn't lose. You see the dead Tribe people lying around? We have taken Misterwizard's Castle. It is ours now. And we have all these dead Barkers for meat."

The Gangers nodded, cheered.

"And soon they are going to find their new Sanctuary

is already burning!" The gangers cheered.

Facegash grinned at Ripper. "So now that Leaker is dead, can I be your next second in command?"

Ripper smiled and thought about it. Facegash was dumb and he was ugly, but he had no compunction about killing. "For now. But you'll have to show me you're worthy."

"How do I do that?" Facegash's face scrunched up as he tried to think.

"But helping me kill Johnny."

"You bet I will." Facegash raised his sword high.

Lady Stabs walked up. "So is this our new place, Ripper?"

"Yes, but we are not staying here. After we've rested and fed up, we go after the Tribe."

"But why, Ripper?" Facegash asked, his face a mask of innocent confusion. "We own the city now! There's hardly any of them left! We can have everything we want!"

Ripper walked over and stared into Facegash's face. "You just became my second in command, and already you're making me regret it."

Facegash looked down, a look of shame on his face.

"Because no one gets away from the Doomsday Prophecy and lives to boast about it. We will kill them all, so everyone knows to fear us."

The Gangers all nodded and cheered again. Then they began gathering the Barkers for food and looting the dead Tribesmen's bodies.

As daylight faded again and the Red Eye dipped close to the horizon, the weary travelers approached their new Sanctuary. They were all exhausted, and most slept. Misterwizard's eyes threatened to close as well, and his beard touched his chest as his head dipped.

Thegap was tired as well, and his bus kept banging into old cars and weaving down the road, but no one cared anymore, as long as he kept going. The streets were lined with trash and old cars, and old half destroyed buildings flanked them on either side.

Often they passed a Wildie, who would stare up at them from the darkness, wondering about the strange yellow metal things creaking and groaning down the usually deserted road. They passed Beasties, too, rat-beasties that ran in front of the bus, an occasional raccoon-beastie watching from a patch of grass in an old building, or even Barkers who would follow the buses for a while and then finally trot off.

The buildings loomed dark and spindly against the night sky filled with stars, like giant metal spiders or crooked old men. In the dark the hulks of cars or trolleys looked like dead beasts slain on the sides of the road. The only lights came from the stars above and the headlights of the buses, shining a yellow beam in front of them and lighting up the street.

They passed a building with many open floors and rusted cars on each level. It seemed to go up to the sky. Another building whose front was all glass had half the glass broken and lying in a pile in front. Where the glass was gone, dark rooms could be seen full of old, moldy furniture.

Oldnavy spotted a large, rectangular building straight ahead of them that seemed relatively intact. He pointed.

"Misterwizard, is that it?"

Misterwizard opened his eyes and smiled. "Yes, my dear man. That structure is called the Shops at Freedom Place Mall, now rechristened New Sanctuary. One of the few intact buildings left in the fair city of Philadelphia. There we will start anew."

"Good. I'm so tired, I don't know if I can stay on my feet much longer."

Misterwizard smiled and closed his eyes again. "I too, find myself a weary traveler, welcome to be home." He closed his eyes and the bus continued to crawl forward, even as Miisterwizard took a quick nap.

But as they drew close to their new home, Oldnavy shooked Misterwizard's shoulder. Misterwizard awoke with a start and slammed on the brake, stopping the bus with a jolt. Behind him, Foodcourt tried to stop and did, but not before bumping Misterwizard's bus. Thegap stopped better behind Foodcourt, his brakes squeaking. Most of the Tribe in Misterwizard's bus were asleep and didn't even notice. Misterwizard rubbed his eyes and looked ahead to see what the matter was. Oldnavy stared, his mouth opened wide with dismay. "Oh, no! Misterwizard, look!"

Misterwizard peered out the front of the bus. From the broken windows of the tall building, smoke poured out. Through the holes left, they could see fires inside, casting shadows on the street and other buildings. Their new home was ablaze. And worse yet, they saw the dark silhouettes of people inside, dancing and jumping. The Gangers had arived there first.

Oldnavy turned to Misterwizard, looking like a man defeated. "How did they know where we were going, MIsterward? And what do we do now?"

Before Misterwizard could answer, a ragged cheer erupted from the people at the back of the bus. They both turned to see what was happening. Misterwizard looked in the rearview mirror and smiled. Johnny rode past the second bus on his Harley, with Carny riding behind him.

The Tribesmen smiled with joy. "Johnny's back!"

"Hurrah! Our hero!"

"Johnny! Johnny!"

Sephie looked out the window and smiled, tears of joy in her eyes.

Misterwizard climbed out of the bus and waited for Johnny to reach them. When he did, Misterwizard strode over to him, arms wide, to find Starbucks already giving Johnny a hug. Johnny and Starbucks joined Misterwizard in a three-way hug, and then Misterwizard stood back and shook Johnny's hand.

"Johnny my boy, you don't know how thrilled you make an old man's heart, just to see that you are safe and of sound limb. I missed you terribly."

"Johnny smiled, touched, and then frowned. "Carny is in a bad way. Miracle is coming, Misterwizard. We have to get inside New Sanctuary soon."

Misterwizard frowned. "I'm afraid I have some bad news, Johnny."

Johnny scowled. "When do we stop having bad news?"

Starbucks looked past them and saw the smoke. "Oh, oh. Somebody knew where we were going."

Johnny looked and saw New Sanctuary burning. His face filled with anger and frustration. "How did they know?"

Misterwizard looked Johnny in the eye. "Leader

Nordstrom, possibly."

"No,' Johnny said. "It was Buildabear. But he already paid for his treachery."

The people in the buses began to get out and gaze ahead at the smoking building, and Johnny knew that they had better come up with a new plan.

"What do we do now, Misterwizard? Where do we take them?"

Misterwizard strode back and forth, deep in thought. Johnny and Starbucks watched him, waiting.

"I see only one alternative. And it is probably for the best in any case."

Both Johnny and Starbucks watched Misterwizard intently, waiting for him to tell them.

"There are no more safe havens in Philadelphia. We must press on with all dispatch to Washington D. C. We must find the President's secret bunker, find a way to break into it and hope it is full of medicine and supplies. Even if we can't, we will be in a new city where we can create a new home, free from the Gangers. It is a longer journey and may be fraught with unknown factors, but it is the best choice."

Johnny looked back at the weary tribe, all sleeping as best they could, even the ones lying on the floor in the aisle. "But they're all so tired already," Johnny said, "and Carny may not make it."

Misterwizard nodded. "If Carny's wriggler comes, we will deal with it the best we can. I'm afraid the Gangers have burned our bridges for us. I don't see any other place to go."

"How far is it, Misterwizard?"

Misterwizard stroked his beard, thinking. "Oh, I'd say, only about one hundred and fifty miles or so."

Starbucks' mouth fell open. "And how long is that?"

Misterwizard smiled, enjoying having a mental problem. "I'd say at our current rate of speed of say, twenty miles an hour, approximately eight or nine hours."

"How much is an hour?" Johnny asked.

"Let's just say, we can make it there before the red eye sets tomorrow, if we press on and don't make too many stops for sightseeing and necessities."

"Well," Starbucks said, shrugging, "Let's get going, before the Gangers inside the building see us."

They all nodded and went into action. Misterwizard looked at Carny. "Let's get Carny to one of the buses where she can lie down."

Together he and Starbucks helped Carny off the bike and Starbucks walked her to the first bus.

Johnny walked with Misterwizard back towards the one in front. "How is Deb?"

Misterwizard knew Johnny was going to ask that question, and he was not looking forward to having to answer. "We must get to Washington quickly. She does not have the Sickness, but the flue is also contagious, and if the others learn this fact, they will insist she leaves the bus. I've tried to keep her isolated, but there is only so much I can do on a crowded bus."

They climbed on the bus and all eyes turned to them, anxious to hear what was going on.

"People of the tribe," Misterwizard said, "it seems due to a traitor in our midst our journey to a new home is going to be a little longer than anticipated."

A groan of misery came from all the people.

"Johnny's here!" Sephie ran up and hugged Johnny's legs. He smiled and knelt to give her a real hug. The rest of the Tribe smiled.

"Don't worry," Johnny said. "I know you're tired, but we'll make it. We haven't come this far to fail. We just have to hang on a little longer."

Thegap, who had walked up and peered in the door, smiled wearily. "If you say so, we believe you, Johnny."

"I want to see Deb," Johnny said.

Johnny walked to the back of the bus and Thegap followed him. They found Deb, lying on the seat. Her eyes were closed. She was covered in sweat but wrapped up in a blanket and shivering. Her nose was red from blowing it, and her breath was raspy. Johnny felt so worried he wanted to cry but kept it from his face. He knew that Deb was real sick now; if they didn't find medicine soon, it would be very bad.

Even in the crowded bus the others had tried to put as much distance from Deb as they could, and he could see them eyeing her with fear in their eyes. Then Johnny heard something that worried him. Deb's mother, despite the danger, sat next to Deb and held her hand, and as Johnny watched Deb, her mother Bathandbodyworks coughed. It made Johnny's heart jump.

"I don't care if I get sick, I'm not leaving her."

Johnny nodded, understanding. "We're going to find medicine, as soon as we get to our new Sanctuary."

Thegap nodded somberly. Deb opened her eyes and smiled when she saw Johnny and her father. They smiled back, trying not to show what they were both thinking.

"Johnny! I was so worried about you, but you're safe. Thanks to you we all are." She tried to rise up but Johnny gently pushed her back down. Johnny grabbed her hand, kissed it, and held it close.

"I love you Deb, and care only about you. I save the Tribe, just for you."

Deb smiled wider. "Deb loves Johnny too, but knows he's not telling truth. Johnny is too wonderful to care only for Deb."

"Rest now, sleep. Soon we will be at a new place and we'll get you the medicine you need." Johnny bent down and kissed Deb's hot forehead. Deb protested. "Stay away, Johnny, or you'll get sick too."

"I don't care."

"Don't say that, Johnny. The tribe needs you. Someday you will be the new Leader Nordstrom."

"With you by my side."

Deb smiled, and Johnny reached down and kissed her cheek. She gazed up at him, eyes full of love. They shared a moment together. Then Deb closed her eyes and laid down.

"I'll watch over her, Johnny," Bathandbodyworks said. "You go help Misterwizard."

Johnny nodded and watched her for a moment, his eyes full of pain and worry. Then he hurried to the front of the bus.

While Johnny and Thegap talked to Deb, Misterwizard ran to the second bus and helped find another driver so Foodcourt could also get some rest. He found a man named Footlocker, who was a fat man with straw colored hair and a big nose. But he was a cheerful fellow who had been watching Foodcourt drive and so seemed ready to pick up driving quickly. Thus encouraged, Misterwizard ran back to the third bus and talked Richardmillhousenixon into driving so Thggap could get a break. Then he hurried back to the front bus and sat down again in the driver's seat.

"Onward!" Misterwizard said aloud to himself as he started the engine again. "Tired though I am, I will once again assume the driving position. I just hope I stay awake long enough to make the trip without incident."

Johnny jumped off the bus and onto his Harley and soon he and the buses were off again, heading for their new Sanctuary in a strange new city, Washington D.C.

CHAPTER 20

After five hours of hard driving, slowed because of the old, rusting hulks on the road they had to weave around or push out of the way, Washington D. C. finally appeared over the horizon. Johnny and Starbucks rode ahead on their Harleys with Super on Starbuck's bike with him. Johnny saw something, stopped his bike and raised a hand. Starbucks and the buses stopped too. Johnny climbed off his bike and looked ahead. Starbucks joined him, and then he too saw what Johnny saw.

"Wow," Starbucks said. "Look at that."

They both turned and walked back to the first bus. Misterwizard opened the door and smiled at Johnny, curious to know what he wanted.

"Misterwizard," Johnny inquired, "do you know where this new Sanctuary is?"

"Most certainly, Johnny. When we grow close, I'll contact you on the walkie-talkie and tell you where to turn."

Johnny nodded, frowning. "Good. But there is something ahead of us you need to see."

Misterwizard hopped out of the bus and followed Johnny to his bike. Johnny pointed in front of them.

Washington was devastated by the Great War much worse than Philadelphia. Few tall buildings remained, and rubble and debris lay strewn as far as the eye could see. And in the middle of all the trash and twisted steel...

"Wildies," Misterwizard said gravely. "Thousands, all milling about. Many more than in Philadelphia. I'm amazed there are so many of them who survived after the Great War. This will prove to be an unpleasant hindrance to our progress."

"We will take care of it," Johnny said. "Starbucks and I will ride ahead and draw them away, and then you and the other drivers can drive the buses through. When you reach the new Sanctuary, call me on the walky-talky and we'll circle back around and join you."

Misterwizard clapped one hand on each of their shoulders. "It might be dangerous. I hate to see you boys have to once again risk your lives for us."

"It'll be okay," Starbucks said. "We'll stay far ahead of them. Our Harleys can go way faster than they can run on foot. We've been chased before."

Misterwizard put an arm around both boys and gave them a hug. "I want you boys to know how much I appreciate what courageous lads you are. The Tribe is lucky to have you."

Johnny and Starbucks smiled. Then Johnny said, "Tell us that when we're safe in our new Sanctuary, Deb is not sick anymore and Carny has had her wriggler."

They all smiled and headed back to their vehicles, but first Johnny paid Deb one more visit. She was asleep, so he simply kissed her on her hot, sweaty forehead, and once again felt the urgency of time. He hurried off the bus to his Harley.

He found Starbucks and Super already mounted and waiting. They started their Harleys with loud roars. The tribespeople on the buses poked their heads out the windows and gazed ahead, watching them and looking at the new city on the horizon.

Johnny and Starbucks drove to the front of the first bus.

"All ready, Misterwizard!" Misterwizard waved a hand and started his bus. Behind them the other buses started up again. Johnny and Starbucks took off with the buses not far behind.

As the Red Eye peaked over the horizon, it found the Gangers in high spirits. Having spent the night in Castle, they had pawed through all of Misterwizard's things and claimed treasures, most of which totally foreign to them, but looked shiny and important.

On the grounds of Castle, they had built a huge bonfire and used it to cook and eat the bodies of the Tribe people who had been killed, for they were not only killers, they were cannibals. They also set up a spit and used it to roast the Barkers. Two were on it now, being turned by a Ganger as he pulled pieces off and chewed on them.

Ripper gazed out from Misterwizard's room, happy but not content. Having slept in Misterwizard's sumptuous bed with the canopy over it, Ripper felt like a king in his castle. And like a child on that holiday that was on longer celebrated but tradition said was special, Christmas, he had spent the night finding new toys in Wizard's collection that were fascinating and amazing. And yet, still, there was a weight in his heart that would not lift, a nagging doubt that couldn't be wished away.

Once again, Johnny had escaped him. No one in the Gang said anything, but he knew they thought he was weak. They thought Johnny was better than him. He was losing the respect of the Doomsday Prophecy. That burned Ripper like a hot knife twisting in his insides. If he continued to fail, other gang members bigger and stronger than him would start challenging him. Then it might go bad. He might even lose. He had to find a way to prove to the Gangers that he was still the toughest and the meanest or, just like a pack of wolves, a fiercer wolf would try and take over.

From out in the distance came a yell of fright. Ripper peered out the window. What he saw made him grin. He hurried downstairs. When he arrived, he found a Ganger coming out of the ruins, and in his grasp was a very frightened, very unhappy Leader Nordstrom.

"Let me go! I didn't do anything to you! I didn't fight, I let you have them!" Leader Nordstrom's eyes were big saucers, his face white with fear. It made Ripper laugh, a good belly laugh, like he hadn't enjoyed in a while. He sauntered outside and a Ganger threw Leader Nordstrom at Ripper's feet. Leader Nordstrom lowered his head and groveled, hands folded. The Gangers gathered around, laughing.

"Please. I will do whatever you want. Just don't kill me. I'm just a weak, old man. I never did anything to fight you. It was all Johnny. He stirred up the trouble. I'm your friend."

Ripper saw this was a perfect chance to reassert his leadership, if he played it right. "Well, well, what you think, Doomsday Prophecy? You ever see such a sniveling dog before?"

The Gangers laughed so hard they held their bellies. "Or is it a flea who we should throw in the fire and burn? We have a nice fire there. He would do good on a spit, roasting."

The Gangers cheered, and Leader Nordstrom tried even harder to grovel, his face to the ground. Ripper yanked his face up to be within inches of his own. As Leader Nordstrom stared wide eyed at him, Ripper spit in Leader Nordstrom's face. The Gangers roared. Ripper threw Leader Nordstrom on the ground, and Leader Nordstrom crawled over to a curb and curled up into a ball.

"Prepare a spit. We shall have roast Leader Nordstrom for dinner tonight." The Gangers cheered. Leader Nordstrom sobbed, a pathetic sight in the corner. Ripper walked over and grabbed a bottle of booze and took a swig. He was having a grand time, and it almost made him forget about the Tribe and Johnny.

"Please. I can still help you. Don't kill me."

Ripper walked over and poured some booze on Leader Nordstrom's inert body, making the Gangers hoot with laughter. "How can you help us you pathetic little worm-beastie?"

Leader Nordstrom looked up, his face imploring. "I can help you find Johnny. I know where Tribe is going."

Ripper thought about this, scratching his chin. He wanted to kill Leader Nordstrom to show the Gangers that he was still ruthless and in charge, but what Leader Nordstrom said might be true. They really didn't know where the Tribe was heading, and if Leader Nordstrom did, he might be more valuable alive.

"All right, pathetic excuse for a man. Tell us, and maybe we won't eat you tonight."

Leader Nordstrom looked up, and this time the cunning that he was so known for shone in his eyes again. "If I do that, you will just kill me anyway. I will take you there, but only if you promise me two things."

Ripper looked around at the Gangers to see if they were beginning to think him weak, but none of them seemed to even be looking at him. They were all watching Leader Nordstrom, intent on his words. Ripper decided it was worth the risk.

"What two things?"

Leader Nordstrom sat up, looking exhausted but more like his old, wily self. "First, when we get there, you will let me go."

Ripper took another swig of whiskey. "And the second?"

Leader Nordstrom smiled darkly, his eyes full of hatred. "You will kill Johnny, Wizard, Starbucks, Carny, Deb and Johnny's whole family."

Warmth spread through Ripper's heart. He sensed a kindred spirit in Leader Nordstrom, and it almost made him like the man. "That, Leader Nordstrom of the Tribe, is a promise you don't even have to ask for."

Leader Nordstrom and Ripper smiled at each other, eyes meeting. Maybe, thought Ripper, this Leader Nordstrom might be a good person to keep around. He had a nice, dark, devious mind, and together they might make a good team.

Johnny and Starbucks reached the outskirts of Washington D.C. They stopped where they couldn't be seen by the mob of Wildies. Both Johnny and Starbucks dismounted. They walked over and peered around the corner.

In the distance, the mangled remains of skyscrapers and houses dotted the landscape. In the streets, Wildies wandered aimlessly, fought with each other, chewed on pieces of meat or simply slept on the ground or leaning against the rusted hulks of cars.

"What do you think, Johnny? Do you think we can really lead them away?"

"We have to do something not very smart. We need to make one of them angry. Then the rest will chase us."

"You're right," Starbucks said. "That isn't very smart. But when have we been very smart?"

Starbucks turned to Super. "Super, you need to go back to the bus with the others."

Super scowled, angry. "I will not! I can face the danger too!"

Starbucks stubbornly answered back, "I don't want you to get hurt!"

"I'm sticking with you, and that's that. You're wasting time, poop-brain."

Johnny smiled at Starbucks and shrugged. Starbucks shrugged back.

"Guess you're stuck with her, Starbucks."

They all laughed. Then Johnny ran back to the first bus. He stepped inside when Misterwizard opened the door.

"Do you know which way you need to go, Misterwizard?"

"Absolutely my boy. We need to head in a western direction towards the very heart of the city. Near the big, tall white buildings in the center, that's where the underground bunker is located. Its entrance is under what used to be called the Museum of American History. An amazing building, still full of fascinating artifacts from life gone by. Electric guitars and Ruby Slippers."

"I don't know what you're talking about, as usual."

"Never mind, Johnny. You just lead the Wildies toward the East and when it's as clear as you can make it, we'll make a dash for it. By the way, East is," Misterwizard pointed, "That direction."

Johnny headed for the door, then turned. "You may still have to fight."

Misterwizard smiled and held up a rifle. "Don't worry my boy. I abhor violence, but if the necessity arises, the men of the Tribe and myself are up to the challenge. They proved that against the Gangers."

Johnny shook Misterwizard's hand and they smiled at each other. "Once more into the breach, my dear boy," Misterwizard said with cheer, "Good luck, and May the Force be with you."

"The what?"

Misterwizard chuckled. "Another tale for another time, Johnny."

Johnny climbed out of the bus and hopped on his Harley. He looked at Starbucks, who was already back on his as well.

"Just follow my lead, okay Starbucks?"

"You're the boss. Just don't lead us into any more buildings with dead beasties."

All three laughed. The boys started their Harleys with a roar and Super held onto Starbucks tight. Then the boys took off towards the Wildies.

Back at Castle, the Gangers prepared for the long journey ahead, and they were not happy about it.

Facegash strode up to Ripper as he stood outside, leaning on a statue of a man on a horse. "Why do we have to go? It's nice here, warm and lots of food. We don't care about Johnny. We don't care about the Tribe. You stupid over this Tribe and all you talk about is Johnny this, Johnny that. The Ganger say stay. We will stay."

Ripper knew a challenge when he saw it. He looked behind Facegash to see the rest of the Gangers behind him, waiting to see what Ripper would say. He looked at Facegash again. Facegash was much bigger than Ripper, with bulging muscles. But he was slow, and if Ripper beat him good enough, he would turn cowardie. Ripper had seen it happen before.

Ripper walked up to Facegash and without a word, slapped him hard across the face. Facegash gasped and fell back, holding his cheek and glowering, but there was fear in his eyes as well.

"Who is the Leader Nordstrom of the Doomsday Prophecy? Is it not me? You want to be Leader Nordstrom? You are a slow-witted fool better at hauling supplies like a horse-beastie than trying to think."

Ripper walked around Facegash to confront the rest of the gang. "I am Leader Nordstrom. If you doubt that, come here and challenge me. I will hand you your heart."

The Gangers stared, looking cowardie, and Ripper was encouraged.

"So right now, we are safe and warm, with full bellies. But we leave the Tribe alone, and someday they come back and kill us, kill us all."

Ripper strode around in front of the Gangers, enjoying his audience. "Do you think Johnny will leave us alone? We who have killed his people and burned their home? No. Johnny will be back, after he is set and safe, with a new Sanctuary and more, better weapons. But if we strike now, while they are on the run and alone, we can easily beat them. They will be our slaves, and we will be the Leader Nordstroms of this new World."

The Gangers nodded and cheered, and Ripper smiled inside, knowing that he had won the Ganger's confidence back, for the moment. He had to get them moving quickly, before they had time to start thinking again. He hurried to find Leader Nordstrom.

He found Leader Nordstrom, huddled next to a fire under a blanket like an old woman, chewing on a piece of jerky. Ripper tore the blanket off him and Leader Nordstrom looked up at him with fright.

"We are leaving. You show us the way to Johnny and the Tribe, now."

Leader Nordstrom snorted. "You're leaving. And how are you going to get there? It's a long way to where they are going, and unless you're blind, you saw them riding in big metal-beasties. We need some of those Beasties. And we need to learn how to control them. That will take time, lots of time. Go do that, and then get back to me."

Leader Nordstrom grabbed his blanket to cover himself again.

Ripper grabbed the blanket and yanked it away again. "You think Johnny the only one who can control the metal-beasties? We saw him riding, and we know how he did it. He found his in a building with lot of metal-beasties, all different kinds. We found some big ones and learned to ride them better than Johnny a long time ago. You just be ready to go when we are." Ripper threw the blanket at Leader Nordstrom. It fell partially into the fire and Leader Nordstrom yelled and grabbed it out. As he watched Ripper with scared eyes, he patted out the flames on the blanket.

Ripper walked off, thinking to himself. He knew where metal-beasties were. But he had to admit, it would take some time to make them roar again. Even though they had toyed with the metal-beasties, they never really tried to drive them very far. It would take time to be sure they would go, time he hated wasting. Every minute longer meant more time for Johnny and the Tribe to get settled, and that meant it would be harder for the Gangers to beat them. Ripper had to get the metal-beasties working, fast.

The Wildies heard the roar of Johnny and Starbucks' Harleys before they saw them. As a group they turned towards the sound. Johnny's plan was to ride up to a Wildie, knock him over, roar their engines, and then take off when the Wildies came after them.

But as they came over the crest of the road, the

Wildies were already in full charge towards them. The Wildies brandished clubs and knives. Some even had guns. Johnny didn't expect this, and he turned his Harley and stopped. Starbucks stopped next to him.

'Let's get out of here!" Starbucks yelled above the screams of the Wildies. Johnny pointed. "That way, fast!"

Johnny and Starbucks sped off fast, the Wildies only ten feet behind them, down a side road. Super turned her head and watched the Wildies running after them. Ahead of them, Johnny saw more Wildies. They had only seconds before the Wildies cut off the road ahead. He sped up and Starbucks followed suit.

On either side of the road, Wildies poured out. Johnny didn't realize how many there were. He'd never seen so many Wildies in his life. He began to feel a little scared inside. Something was wrong, strange. There shouldn't have been so many in one place; they almost seemed organized.

Johnny drove as fast as he could. The gap ahead between the Wildies was narrowing. At the last moment, he roared past them. The Wildies were so close that one's hand brushed Johnny's cheek. He hoped that Starbucks and Super had made it through but didn't dare stop to look and see. He sped ahead, looking for a clear route.

Ahead the road curved between two tall skyscrapers. As Johnny approached the turn, two Wildies ran out. One was a huge man in ragged clothes with a long, bushy beard. He held a club in his hand waved it in the air. The other was an old woman, one of the oldest Johnny had ever seen, almost Misterwizard's age, in a long, dirty dress. Her long, white hair and wrinkled face made her look frightening.

The pair ran right in front of Johnny, and he had to swerve. Being only fifteen years old, the Harley was big for Johnny, and it slipped on the pavement. He almost went down, but at the last moment got his foot down. But he did have to stop, and before he could get going again, the pair were on him.

Johnny pulled out his sword and swung at the man's leg as the man reached him. He hit the man's leg, not enough to cut deep, but enough to make the man back off, grasping his leg. Then the old woman was on him. Johnny didn't want to hurt her, but she came at him, fingers spread, looking like she was going to dig them into his face.

Johnny waved his sword in her face, causing her to hesitate, and long enough for Johnny to throttle the Harley and get going again. He risked a glance behind, but to his dismay there was no Starbucks and Super. Johnny feared the worst. Had they made it? Were they right then being torn apart by the Wildies? Johnny wasn't sure what to do. If he went back, he would surely be overwhelmed too, and it wouldn't save his friends. He sped on ahead, hoping Starbucks could escape and meet up with him.

As soon as Misterwizard saw Johnny and Starbucks take off with the Wildies in tow, he hit the gas pedal and the bus lurched forward. Behind him he could hear Footlocker and Richardmillhousenixon doing the same thing, their buses following close behind.

As Misterwizard turned the bus to the left, he

watched Footlocker anxiously to see if he would negotiate the turn. At first the second bus continued forward, and Misterwizard feared that Footlocker didn't know how to turn. But at the last moment, the front of the second bus laboriously turned to follow Misterwizard's direction.

Silently Misterwizard cheered Footlocker on as the second bus continued forward, quickly running out of turning room. Finally, it finished the turn, but not without jumping up the curve with a sickening lurch. Misterwizard sympathized with the Tribe people inside, it had to be quite a jolting experience. The second bus continued around, however, and came down off the curb again. After a few more weaves and wobbles, it began to make a crooked line in the right direction.

"Good man, Footlocker!" Misterwizard said with a chuckle. "We'll make a bus driver out of you yet!"

The third bus managed to follow along behind. Misterwizard turned his attention to the road ahead. There were still quite a few Wildies. He was surprised to see so many. The other times he had come to Washington D. C., there weren't near as many, or he would have been better prepared. He wondered why there were so many. Misterwizard was puzzled and intrigued.

Washington D.C. had not taken a direct blast from a nuclear device, but one had impacted outside the city, destroying many buildings and leaving the rest broken and damaged. The Bunker they were headed for was in the very heart of downtown, inside the Museum of American History. The bright yellow buses would stand out like sunbeams as they labored through the streets, very hard for the Wildies to miss. Misterwizard just hoped that Johnny and Starbucks could gain the Wildies' interest enough that the buses could make it relatively unnoticed.

Five Wildies stood in the road, right in front of Misterwizard's bus, a woman and four men. One of the men was really just a boy, and as Misterwizard gazed at him, he felt a pang of sympathy. All of them wore ragged, dirty clothing and their hair and faces were dirty. Once they were safe in the Bunker and began rebuilding civilization, Misterwizard vowed they would come back for the Wildies, and help all that were rational enough to be saved to join them.

The five Wildies wandered aimlessly, not seeing the buses bearing down on them. Misterwizard decided the best thing to do was simply to angle around them as fast as they could, and not give them time to block the buses' way.

Misterwizard turned the big steering wheel, angling the bus as close to the right curb as he could. It didn't help matters that all throughout the streets, old hulks of rusted cars blocked parts of the road, making driving a constant path through an obstacle course. Luckily at this moment, the road was clear near the Wildies. Misterwizard stepped on the gas and the bus lurched forward.

Behind him, the Tribe people in the bus talked excitedly, pointing out the windows and moving around. Misterwizard called back to them, "Sit down, please, the trip is about to get a little bumpy."

Misterwizard roared past the Wildies. As soon as he did, they turned and saw him and started yelling. They took off after him, but he was too far ahead. The other buses weren't so lucky. As they approached, the Wildies now blocked the road. Misterwizard watched the second bus in the rear-view mirror with trepidation. What would Footlocker do?

CHAPTER 21

Johnny sped ahead, and he took his radio out of his pocket. He pushed the button, just the way Misterwizard had taught him to, and put it up to his mouth.

"Misterwizard! Are you there? I think I lost Starbucks!"

There was no answer. Johnny repeated it again, but still only static responded. He placed the radio back on his pocket and thought about what to do.

Wildies still lined the road, a few on either side, but not as many as before. He had no idea where he was, and a feeling of panic tickled at his mind. He was alone in a strange city, and he had no idea where Misterwizard was headed. If he didn't get in contact with him, he could wander the city for days and never know where to look. And his friends Starbucks and Super, did Johnny just leave them to die?

Johnny stopped his Harley in the middle of the road, ignoring the danger from the Wildies. He was going to go back, no matter what, and find them. He had to or hate himself for the rest of his life. He couldn't leave his friends to die.

As Johnny was pondering these thoughts, he looked back to where he'd left Starbucks. His mouth opened in surprise and dismay at what he saw.

A hundred Wildies walked slowly up the street, packing it from side to side. And in the middle of the pack, Starbucks walked his Harley with Super at his side. They were the Wildies' prisoners.

The mild panic in Johnny turned to full blown fear. They were caught. Would this be the end for them? Would the Wildies kill them and eat them? That was the most likely scenario. Or did they have something even more gruesome in mind?

The mob reached Johnny, surround him and then curiously they stopped. Starbucks rolled his Harley until he was next to Johnny. Johnny looked at him and Starbucks smiled sadly back.

"They knocked me down, Johnny, and we couldn't get away. Sorry."

Johnny eyed the crowd. "It's not your fault, Starbucks. But what do they want? Are they going to kill us and eat us?"

"I don't know," Starbucks said, eyeing the crowd. Super stood close to him, her arms around his waist, watching the Wildies nervously. "I thought they were going to kill and eat us right away, but instead they just picked up my Harley, gave it to me and motioned for us to follow them."

The Wildies drew closer, watching them, studying their clothes and Harleys. Johnny noticed not only men in dirty clothes with dirty faces, but women and children amongst them, all in rags with wild hair. Most had missing teeth, and many had deformities, some even missing arms or eyes.

A little girl walked up to Johnny. She reminded him of Sephie. Johnny smiled at her. She smiled back. A woman in the crowd ran up and snatched the girl back, her eyes full of suspicion.

Johnny frowned and studied the crowd again. For Wildies they didn't act crazy, in fact they almost seemed intelligent. Most had some sort of deformity, but there were a few that looked normal, almost healthy Johnny began to wonder just what they had stumbled into.

As if to answer Johnny's thoughts, the mob of Wildies ahead parted like a curtain, leaving a path. The three prisoners looked ahead down it to see what was going to happen.

"Now what?" Starbucks asked.

The eyes of the Wildies all turned towards something coming down the street. And then they did something amazing and a little frightening to Johnny. The all bowed on their knees and raised their hands, towards something, or someone. Johnny, Starbucks and Super turned to see who, or what, was coming.

Misterwizard contemplated, should he stop and wait for the other buses, prepare to make a fight of it? Or should he press on, get the Tribe in his bus safe first, and then come back? The second choice smacked of cowardice to Misterwizard, and he instantly dismissed it. No, they would fight together, and die together, if need be. He stopped the bus and turned to face the Tribe inside.

"It seems our friends on the bus behind us have fallen into some difficulty. Ergo, it may behoove us to stand and alleviate them of their hindrances."

The Tribe stared at Misterwizard, as if he was speaking a foreign language. Misterwizard frowned crossly, and said, "It looks like we're going to have to fight!"

That the Tribe understood. Everyone started jabbering at once. The men jumped to their feet, made noises of bravado and grabbed their weapons. Then the men stomped to the front of the bus, ready for action. Thegap left Deb and ran up, sword in hand. He turned to the other behind him. "It looks like once again we have to fight for our families. Are you all ready?"

A ragged cheer went up from the men. Misterwizard put up a restraining hand. "One moment. I will depart and do a reconnaissance mission. I will determine if indeed our compatriots are in fact in difficulty."

"What?" One Tribe member said, and they all looked at him with puzzled looks.

Misterwizard grinned. "Wait."

The men all nodded their heads, and relaxed. Misterwizard opened the door to the bus and hopped out, carrying two of his best toys, both non-lethal, but both very convincing. The first was a can of mace that he'd found on his journeys. The other was even better; a

Stun Gun that he'd tinkered with and got working. It would give any Wildie a second thought about attacking.

Misterwizard reached the back of the bus. He noticed the Tribe people inside, all gathered at the back of the bus, peering back to where the other bus was. Misterwizard joined them in looking back, as he slowly walked down the road, can of mace and stun gun in his hands.

Five or six Wildies wandered around on the street and in the buildings on either side, but fortunately they didn't seem to be taking any interest in Misterwizard or the bright yellow bus. Misterwizard peered down the street, but it curved slightly, and he couldn't see much beyond a block. He decided to give the other buses a few minutes. If they didn't show up soon, he'd have a decision to make, either to follow them on foot or turn his bus around and try to find them. Neither choice seemed very pleasant, nor did either option hold much chance for a good outcome. But choose he would have to, soon.

The minutes seemed to drag on like hours. Misterwizard paced back and forth, his body aching with impatience. The Tribe stared at him through the glass windows of the bus, wide eyed and with scared expressions. Finally, Misterwizard decided he had no choice, for the Wildies around were beginning to look his way. He turned to remount the bus and retrace their steps.

And just then came a spectacle down the road that he would remember the rest of his days with humor and a little bit of fright. The other bus driven by Footlocker barreled down the street towards them. Misterwizard could see Footlocker inside, gripping the steering wheel with white knuckles, his eyes as big as saucers. But it was what was on the outside of the bus that was bizarre: Wildies hung on to every window, yelling and pounding on them as Tribe people fought them from inside.

Misterwizard turned to yell at the Tribesmen in his bus, but he didn't need to. They had seen the predicament of their friends and were already pouring off the bus, weapons ready, yelling and shouting blood cries.

Before Misterwizard could even react, they ran past him. Things began to happen fast. Footlocker slammed on the brakes of the bus with a loud screech and half the Wildies fell off. The rest saw the men approaching them and jumped to the street.

Behind Footlocker the third bus appeared with Wildies hanging on it. It came to a screeching halt right behind Footlocker's bus. In a second the men of the Tribe and the Wildies clashed in an epic battle. Most of the Wildies had only clubs while the men of the Tribe had knives and guns, but the Wildies fought like mad men and proved to be formidable.

Misterwizard joined the fray. He zapped a Wildie with his stun gun, and the man fell to the ground, writhing and howling. The effect was magical. The other Wildies saw it. They backed away with eyes wide with fear and wonder. Misterwizard, loving the chance for a theatrical performance, waved the stun gun in the air with a flourish and a mean smile. 'Run, you vagabonds! You filthy rabble, or I will strike you with the power of the gods!"

Misterwizard's performance coupled with the knives and guns of the Tribesmen was enough to convince the Wildies. They took off running, pursued by the cheers of the Tribesmen. Inside the buses the rest of the Tribe cheered as well. It was an enjoyable victory.

"Hurry!" Misterwizard yelled. "Let's not waste the time Johnny and Starbucks have given us. Back into the buses with haste!"

The tribesmen ran back to their buses. Misterwizard looked at Footlocker, who smiled back, frazzled but happy. Misterwizard gave him a look of appreciation and praise and put up a fist to say thanks. Footlocker waved a hand back, a silly grin on his face. Then Misterwizard hurried back to his bus. There was no time to waste.

Five miles outside of Washington D.C., a cavalcade of strange vehicles trundled down the road towards the city. In the very front a wicked looking Humvee with a painted skull on its hoot and a dead rat painted on the door drove. Behind it came two old Army transports, painted black and red with skulls and blood and knives painted on them. On the doors of each it said, "DUMDA PROPESY," the closest they could manage writing the ancient words. Behind the transports, a half dozen small, beat up cars and vans followed, all painted the same way. And on either side of the vehicles, Harleys and Honda motorbikes buzzed along like angry bees pestering an intruder.

In the back of the Humvee, Ripper lay across the seat, eyes closed, enjoying a big, fat cigar. The smoke from the cigar filled the cabin, and in the front seat, Leader Nordstrom wheezed, his eyes watering. It had not taken as long as Ripper feared to learn to drive the metal-beasties. It seems some of the Gangers had already been tinkering with them, and one even knew how to drive. After a few mistakes where some metal-beasties were driven into buildings and others into each other, the Gangers finally began to get a hang of it. Soon they had a party as they picked out the metal-beasties they wanted and even painted the gruesome pictures and letters.

Leader Nordstrom waved his hand at the smoke. "Must you do whatever you are doing with that thing in your mouth? It is foul smelling and I can barely breathe."

"Shut up," Ripper said, "or we'll turn my metal-beastie off and you'll be pushing it the whole way. How much longer until we get to Johnny?"

Leader Nordstrom coughed and wheezed out, "I don't know for sure. I can only guess exactly where they are going."

Ripper opened his eyes and glared at Leader Nordstrom. "You told me you knew. Did you lie to me?"

Leader Nordstrom's watering eyes went wide. "No, no. This is where they are going. I just don't know exactly where their new Sanctuary is. But it won't be hard to find them. How many big, yellow metal-beasties can there be in a town?"

"You are a fool and an idiot," Ripper said, closing his eyes again. "If we do not find Johnny soon after arriving, I may get impatient and bored." Ripper smiled, took another drag on his cigar and blew it in Leader Nordstrom's direction, making him cough again. "Then I may want to entertain myself by watching you fight some of my biggest Gangers."

"We'll find him," Leader Nordstrom whined. "But they are not going to be just sitting there, waving a flag that says, 'come get me.' There's no reason to take it out on me."

Ripper opened his eyes and sat up. He turned to Leader Nordstrom. "Put your hand out."

Leader Nordstrom, full of fear, put his hand in the air, afraid of what was going to happen.

Ripper took his cigar out of his mouth and pressed the lit end onto Leader Nordstrom's palm. Leader Nordstrom howled in pain and tried to pull his hand back, but Ripper grabbed it. "Do you feel that? That is only a taste of what you will get, if I don't find Johnny soon."

Ripper lifted the cigar back up and stuffed it in his mouth with a grin of evil pleasure. Leader Nordstrom pulled back his hand and whimpered, cradling his hand to his chest.

Ripper closed his eyes and lay back again, reveling in the memory of his latest cruelty. He would do the same to Johnny and everyone Johnny loved, only worse, much worse.

From the stairs of a crumbled building it watched them. On either side of the stairs, stone lion-beasties stared forward. It looked at one, then the other. Did it recognize what they were? It gazed at them for a moment than looked ahead again at the odd metal things moving away down the street. It didn't know what the metal things were, but it knew inside was the prey. And it was leaving.

It watched with hungry eyes, it's big, red tongue out, panting. Where the prey went, it would follow. On furry padded feet, the tiger-beastie trotted down the steps after the strange parade of vehicles heading out of Philadelphia.

CHAPTER 22

Misterwizard drove on towards the heart of the city. He pulled his radio out and keyed the mike. "Johnny my boy. Are you there, Johnny?" There was no reply. Concerned, Misterwizard placed the radio back in his coat. "I hope you are doing well, Johnny. You and Starbucks are brave lads. I so want to see you again."

Misterwizard knew where he was going; he had been there many times on his journeys to Washington D. C. Being on his own when he wasn't helping the Tribe, Misterwizard liked to explore and go on trips.

As Misterwizard drove, he thought about how it all started. Before the Great War, Misterwizard's grandfather, whose name was Mathew Broadstone, had been a Mathematics and Physics teacher in a high school in city called Boston. His grandfather was thirty when it happened, and his father was only six. From what

Misterwizard's father told him the War did not come on suddenly but slowly, like a slow heating pot of water which finally comes to a boil. Rumblings and warning signs appeared, and it was almost as if the countries of the World grew tired of being peaceful and everyone decided to be ornery and uncooperative at the same time.

His father told him clashes between what was once China and a country called Japan grew, with many other countries between them caught in the fray. A country called Russia became overrun once again with people called Communists who threatened global domination. But the real nail in the World's coffin came when their own country, the United States, turned from the belief in a wonderful thing called Democracy to a dictatorship led by the President who declared himself king, and began plans to take over the country to the South, known as Mexico.

On a fateful day, the Declaration of Independence was declared invalid and the President assumed total power. Misterwizard's grandfather knew then that Freedom was soon to be a precious and rare commodity, and that men would soon have to fend for themselves. He built an underground bunker to hide in, one where he could live for an extended period. He filled it with enough food and water to last for ten years and made it self-sustaining.

Then, his father told him, one day it happened. His grandfather, who was in his yard gardening, looked up towards Boston where they lived to see a mushroom cloud. Knowing exactly what it meant he sat in his rose bed and cried. Then he hurried to the shelter with his wife and Misterwizard's father, and they closed the door.

His father told Misterwizard that fifteen years passed before they ventured out. Life as they had known it was gone. The few people left were all Wildies or Gangers, brutally taking what they wanted by force and killing others for sport or for meat. Misterwizard's grandfather was killed by a Wildie while looking for food. His father, whose name was Abraham, left Boston and learned to live a solitary existence. He finally found a mate, his mother Ruth, but she was not strong and died soon after Misterwizard's birth. Then his father found Castle, where he raised Misterwizard and taught him everything he knew about the world that was now gone.

Misterwizard, whose real name was chosen for romantic reasons by his parents, was Adam. Misterwizard heard stories from a young age of how wonderful the world had been, so full of people and life. He spent his childhood gathering trinkets and old artifacts from the past, tinkering with them and asking his father what they were. Then one day, a roaming tiger-beastie, very young but strong and fierce, killed his father, and Misterwizard was all alone. Misterwizard used to hunt the city, trying to find the tiger-beastie and kill it for taking away his father, but he was never able to find it.

Then one day, Misterwizard stumbled upon the Tribe. He did it totally by accident, as he was wandering around looking for new objects. He happened to be strolling through the parking lot, looking through the old cars, and decided to go into the old mall and see what he could find.

What he found was a large group of half savages eating rat-beasties and drinking rain water to survive. They were eking out a miserable existence, and half of them were starved and about to die. Even then, Leader Nordstrom was in charge, but he didn't have a name at that time. It was Misterwizard who gave them all names, from the stores and object in the mall, mostly for fun but also to encourage them to learn to read, an attempt that for most of them failed miserably. He became their teacher and guide, and it was due to Misterwizard that they were now a civilized, organized tribe, though Leader Nordstrom took all the credit.

And then Misterwizard met Johnny. Johnny was only five when Misterwizard met him, and he was already a tough, ornery little boy. He stumbled, or should he say, was ambushed by Johnny, as he searched the store called Radio Shack, looking for batteries that might still have a charge, or at least be in good enough shape to be recharged.

Misterwizard walked up an aisle in the dark, dusty store, holding a basket, just as he would have had he been shopping there almost a hundred years ago. Suddenly he heard a growl, and a little, mangy, dirty boy in ragged furs jumped on him. As Misterwizard tried to overcome his shock, the little monster tried to bite his arm. Misterwizard grabbed Johnny and held him up in the air as Johnny growled, kicked and yelled.

Misterwizard chuckled and found himself liking Johnny right from the start. "You are quite the ball of fire, aren't you, young man? I shall name you Johnny. Johnny Apocalypse, the hero of the nuclear wasteland."

From that point on, Johnny and Misterwizard became the best of friends. Misterwizard made teaching Johnny his highest priority, for he saw in Johnny the strength and courage to be a leader. Johnny was unafraid, and yet he saw a quality of goodness in Johnny, an understanding of right and wrong that wasn't present in a lot of the survivors.

It was Johnny's mother Teavana who named him Misterwizard, after Johnny told her the story of Merlin from a book called King Arthur and the Knights of the Round Table that Misterwizard had read to Johnny and Starbucks. Misterwizard half suspected that Johnny and Starbucks really thought he was Merlin, King Arthur's wizard. More than once Starbucks had accidentally called him Merlin and quickly corrected himself. He didn't mind; if the Tribe wanted to compliment him by naming him Misterwizard, or even Merlin, it was fine with him. He couldn't wait until Johnny was the true leader of the Tribe. Then the Tribe could finally begin building a new civilization, based on the principles of democracy and freedom. Misterwizard just hoped it didn't take too long, for he himself was no spring chicken, and Time marched on, no respecter of any man or tribe.

Misterwizard knew they were getting close when he saw the remains of the Washington Monument ahead. Once a proud spear jutting into the night sky, now it reminded him of a broken stick, half of the building sheared off and turned into rubble around its base. Misterwizard had been to Washington D.C. many times, but it still filled him with sadness when he saw what had become of it. The roofs of the Capitol and the White House were both broken and fallen in, and the Lincoln Memorial had simply disappeared into a hole in the ground.

Even sadder to Misterwizard was that the men in

power at the time when it all happened brought it on themselves, for if they had only remained true to the ideals of Democracy, the Great War may never have happened.

The museums and historic buildings in the middle of Washington D. C. were all situated around an area that was called in the ancient days the National Mall. The Mall was a large, rectangular grassy area. On the front side of the Mall stood a building called the Capitol. It was where the man in power in the United States held court, a man called the President. On the far opposite side of the Mall was the Washington Monument, a building created to honor the first President of the former country. The museums of what used to be called the Smithsonian, of which the Museum of American History was part of, were situated on the sides of the grassy Mall or close by on streets near it.

As Misterwizard approached the grassy Mall on his way to the Museum of American History, he saw something on the grass that seemed strange and mildly alarming. Hundreds of ramshackle buildings occupied the lawn. A shanty town had sprung up made of scrap lumber and trash. The whole grass area was filled by it, and as he looked more closely, he realized that Wildies roamed in and out of the shacks, hundreds of them, maybe thousands.

Nothing like it had been there the last time he had visited. Were the Wildies rebuilding a form of government of their own? Were they rational enough now to be organized and orderly? Up to that point, all the Wildies Misterwizard had run into were either insane, wild animals because of the radiation and years of solitude, or mercenary cutthroats looking to prey on whomever came their way. It seemed impossible to imagine that they could possibly be turned into a rational, organized group of people with a common goal. And yet, there was what looked like a makeshift town in the making.

Misterwizard feared that if the Wildies in the ramshackle village spotted them, the Tribe would easily be overwhelmed by sheer numbers. He drove his bus to lead Footlocker and Richardmillhousenixon to the back of the Museum of American History and parked the buses there, hopefully out of sight of the shanty village.

As soon as Misterwizard stopped, the Tribe talked excitedly all at once, like children from what used to be called "school" on an adventure that used to be called a "field trip." Misterwizard turned to them and raised a hand. The noise quieted somewhat and Misterwizard spoke.

"Well, my friends and fellow travelers, we have reached our destination. However, there is something new in the equation that was not anticipated. It seems the Wildies have some sort of rudimentary camp not far from here, and it would not do to have them discover our intentions. To that end, I need you all to egress the vehicle as quietly and quickly as you can and make your way into the Museum."

"What did he say?" A middle-aged woman asked with a confused frown.

Deb answered from the back in a weak voice. "He said be quiet and get into the building."

"Oh, well why didn't he just say so?" the old lady replied, and a smattering of laughter filled the bus.

Misterwizard walked back to check on Deb. She was covered in sweat and breathing hard. Misterwizard frowned, knowing that her time was fleeting. And then he heard something that worried him even more. As the old lady left the bus, she coughed as well. The sickness was spreading. He had to find a cure fast.

Misterwizard helped Deb up. Then he walked her, but mostly carried her off the bus. He brought her to the door of the building and sat her down. She closed her eyes and lay back, as if the simple effort of getting off the bus had exhausted her. Misterwizard cast one more worried glance in her direction and then made his way to Footlocker's bus. There he found Footlocker, Foodcourt and the other members of the Tribe from the bus already out and chattering loudly. The members of the third bus were out as well, talking and milling about.

Misterwizard waved a hand with a grumpy frown. "SHHH! Please, my friends, keep the revelry to a minimum. I know we are all very relieved to finally disembark from these uncomfortable and laborious vehicles, but we must quietly endeavor to enter the Museum as fast as we can. We are not alone!"

"What?" a Tribesman said.

"Get inside, and shut up," Foodcourt replied. The talking subsided and a more muted group shuffled towards the building.

Misterwizard turned to Footlocker, Foodcourt and Teavanna, for they had stopped to talk to him.

Misterwizard shook hands with all four of the men who drove and said, "I am immensely impressed, my fine and courageous companions, with your driving skills and willingness to step up to the challenge. Johnny will be proud of all of you."

All four men beamed and stood a little taller, and Teavanna smiled with pride at Foodcourt and squeezed him from the side. Foodcourt tried to act nonchalant and said, "It was really nothing. I must say, it was much easier than I thought it would be. A child could have done it." Then he looked at the building with wide eyes full of interest and excitement. "Is this place like Australia?"

Misterwizard smiled and patted Foodcourt on the shoulder with his hand. "It is better, dear Foodcourt, immeasurably better."

Misterwizard frowned. "For now, hopefully, it is salvation, for the Tribe and especially for our dear Deb. The only obstacle in our way, and it is a formidable one, is my lack of the code to access the underground bunker. I was hoping in one of my visits I would be able to decipher it, but up to now, I have been unfruitful. And then events forced our hand, the Gangers, and Deb's condition, to be specific."

Foodcourt just stared at Misterwizard, and Misterwizard knew Foodcourt barely understood half of what he said. "We have to get inside the Bunker, dear friends. And I don't have a clue how we are going to do it."

Teavanna smiled and grabbed Misterwizard's arm. "You'll figure it out, Misterwizard. We have faith in you."

Misterwizard, touched, nodded at her with affection.

"Let's get inside the Museum!" Footlocker said, and they all hurried to comply.

Foodcourt walked off towards the building. Misterwizard watched him, stroking his beard. "I have always been touched by the Tribe's faith in me, I will not cause them to lose it and discover that I really am no Misterwizard after all."

Then he followed them all into the Museum of American History.

CHAPTER 23

Johnny, Starbucks and Super waited for whatever was coming, but when it did it took them totally by surprise. Ten Wildies, five on either side of the opened path, marched forward in solemn fashion, each behind the next. The three prisoners could see these Wildies seemed different from the others, for they were dressed in silk robes with hoods of bright, beautiful colors, red and blue and green and purple. Their hair was combed, and they looked as if they had even bathed. In their hands they held strange, bright yellow sticks of metal, each about the size of Johnny's forearm. The metal sticks looked hollow and had buttons on top and weird loops of metal on the bottom.

The fancy Wildies walked up slowly, somberly, taking one step at a time, as if they were doing something very important. When they were a few feet away from Johnny and his friends, they stopped and turned to face the middle of the pathway. Then as Johnny, Starbucks and Super watched in fascinated curiosity, the men held the metal objects to their lips and blew through a hole in the back.

Suddenly the air was filled with beautiful and strange sounds, like the thunder before the rain, or the call of the birds Johnny had seen high up in the sky. It was loud and hurt their ears, but it was wonderful as well. The three looked at each other with surprise and elation. None of them had ever heard something so pleasant before.

"What are they doing, Johnny?" Super asked, amazement on her face.

"I don't know," Johnny said, grinning, "But it sure sound pretty."

As the music filled the air the rest of the Wildies bowed low, and it became evident the strange sounds were meant to herald the arrival of whomever was coming.

Johnny put his hand on the hilt of his sword. He cast a meaningful glance at Starbucks, who nodded back, and put his hand on his sword as well. Super looked at them. Starbucks slid a knife to her behind his back and she took it with a furtive nod. All three understood that they might be fighting their way out, or to their death.

A man appeared at the end of the path. He was tall, with long black hair, his lean face was handsome, with a long, sloping nose and a scar running down his cheek from just below his eye to the side of his chin. His piercing blue eyes were alert and showed a haughtiness and pride. He wore an elegant, long black robe that looked like it was made out of bear-beastie fur, but tied to it were shiny gold and silver pieces of metal carved in fancy designs. It was the most beautiful coat Johnny had ever seen, and made the man seem regal and magical. Under his fur coat he wore a blue outfit of shiny material that had folds and rumples in it. Somehow the weary travelers knew right away this man was the Wildies' Leader Nordstrom.

He walked slowly towards them in measured strides, head held high, and as he passed the Wildies they bowed low to the ground with their eyes looking down. Behind him strode two of the hugest Wildies Johnny had ever seen. Dressed in nothing but cloth shorts, they both had rippling muscles and carried large swords. They scowled dangerously, and Johnny could tell they wouldn't hesitate to use their swords to kill someone and feel nothing while they did it.

The strange man and his guards stopped in front of Johnny and his companions, and the Wildies with the strange metal objects stopped blowing them. Quickly the only sound was the whistling of the wind up and down the street, a weird howling like a vengeful ghost. The strange man studied them, turning his head this way and that, as if sizing them up. Johnny, Starbucks and Super looked back with defiant gazes, but inside all three of them were a little scared, feeling alone and defenseless. The path had disappeared and the Wildies crowded around, making a circle around the strange meeting, watching intently, silently.

Finally, the man spoke. His voice was weak and wavery, but Johnny could tell he tried to sound important and proud, just the way Leader Nordtrom used to speak. "Avast! Who be ye varlets what have come to invade my kingdom with such wanton arrogance? Speak quick, for I cut off your heads and mount them on spikes for the buzzards to feed upon. Like yon poor knaves!" Another man walked up, and in his hand, he held a steel rod. On it was the bloody head of a man. The street filled with sound as the Wildies cheered and yelled.

Johnny, Starbucks and Super looked at the grisly visage with disgust and fright. Super looked away, and Starbucks put an arm around her to comfort her. The strange man grinned at the crowd, enjoying the sensation he had made. Then he waved, and the head was taken away.

The cheering died down and the Wildies waited for a response. Johnny steeled himself and answered back. "We are simply travelers, meaning no harm or offense to anyone. But who are you to claim this land for your 'kingdom'? This is Washington Deecee, the capitol of America the Beautiful." Johnny knew these things from talking to Misterwizard. He hoped his knowledge might shake the man's confidence. He quoted something else Misterwizard had said. "This land is my land. This land is your land. From Cal-forna to the newark eyelan. This is the Land of the Fee and Home of the Bave, the birtpace of Democraty. It belongs to all men!"

The Wildies yelled in anger until their Leader Nordstrom-man put a hand up, instantly silencing them. He glared at Johnny, Starbucks and Super, his eyes filled with what to Johnny thought looked like an insane anger.

"How dare ye sail your vessels into my presence and parlay with me in such rude arrogance? You are not even men but dog-beasties. This be no Washington Deecee ye speak of. From two full cold cycles past and to the end of time, this land be the Kingdom of Algonia, and I be Lord Algon!" The Wildies cheered again.

When the cheering had died down once more,

Starbucks said, "You talk funny. Are you a crazie?" Johnny put up a hand to silence him. "Please forgive us, Lord Algon. We are not looking for a fight. As I said, we are simply travelers, passing through. If you allow us, we will simply leave in peace."

Lord Algon smiled, happy at Johnny's apparent acceptance of his Lordship. "Know ye, I could have such lowly worms as thee torn apart limb from limb, but thou art fortunate. I am of a truth feeling of a kindly nature today." Lord Algon waved a hand casually. "If ye willingly pledge your loyalty and undying servitude to me and bow in trembling supplication, perhaps I may have mercy on ye and spare your miserable hides from torture, for today."

The Wildies nodded and smiled, enjoying the spectacle. Super whispered to Johnny, "He talks even funnier than Misterwizard. What nonsense is he babbling?"

Johnny whispered back, "Misterwizard read a book to me he called, "Treasure Island" where they talked like him. It is really old talk done by people called Irates, long before the Great War."

"Do you think he's touched in the head?" Starbucks whispered.

The three grinned at each other, all agreeing, and Johnny shrugged. Super whispered, "I'm not going to bow to this creep. I'll stick this sticker in his eye first."

"Me either," Starbucks said. "What do you think, Johnny?"

In answer Johnny turned to Lord Algon. "We have no quarrel with you, but we have a leader of our own in a far-away land. We cannot serve you, for we would be disloyal to our own king. Please let us go our way. No one has to die."

Lord Algon turned to the crowd and grinned. "Forsooth, he says no one be needing to die!" They all laughed so hard some fell down and rolled on the ground. "The only ones what shall perish be you three, though maybe we take the fine lass to be one of my maids. You two will die in the throes of agony. And then we shall all feast on your flesh until we pick your bones clean."

His words made Starbucks furious. He raised his sword and started towards Lord Algon, but Johnny restrained him. "He isn't going to touch Super. I'll kill him first."

"We won't let him, I promise you that," Johnny said.

Lord Algon's words made the Wildies howl even louder, until it hurt the prisoner's ears. Johnny figured that at one time, this 'king' had been just an ordinary Wildie like the rest. Somehow, he had convinced the Wildies to make him their king. Washington Deecee was now a very dangerous place. If only they had known about Lord Algon and his kingdom, they could have been more prepared, but it looked like even Misterwizard hadn't been aware of it. Johnny hoped that the buses had made it through and were somewhere that the Wildies couldn't find them. If the whole Tribe were captured, things could go very bad indeed. He knew that somehow, he and Starbucks had to keep this 'king' occupied until Misterwizard could get into the Bunker and get the Tribe to safety.

Ripper and the Gangers in their ragtag cars and trucks reached the outskirts of Washington D.C. As if on cue, they all slowed down at once and drove slowly into the city. Ripper's Humvee led the pack. Ripper saw that they were now close. He sat up, fully alert and intent, and stared out the window.

Ahead of them the streets were filled with Wildies. Ripper had no way of knowing that only five blocks ahead, Johnny and Starbucks were having a confrontation with Lord Argon.

The driver of Ripper's Humvee looked back at him. "Look at all them Wildies roamin' around, Ripper."

"So, what?" Ripper said. "You scared of a bunch of lowlife rabble? Run 'em over if they get in our way. And keep an eye out for them yellow things called buses."

Suddenly the door to the Humvee opened and Leader Nordstrom leapt out. Ripper looked out the window just in time to see Leader Nordstrom pick himself up off the ground and limp off. His driver grinned at him. "Shall we go after him?"

Ripper smiled. "Why bother? The Wildies will take care of him. We got all we could out of 'im. I hope they cook him and eat 'im while he's still alive."

Ripper and the driver laughed, and Ripper looked out the front window again.

As the Tribe filtered into the Museum of American History, Misterwizard helped Deb to the marble entry hall where she sat on a bench. On the way in, he took one more glance towards the Wildies in the distance. They didn't seem to have seen the Tribe, and the buses just looked like more abandoned vehicles on the street. Still, Misterwizard knew that they had only a little time before they were discovered.

As the last member of the Tribe made it in, Misterwizard closed the doors and tried to jam a bench in the door handles to block them.

There were really no places that looked very comfortable, for the room held nothing but glass displays with an open floor in the middle. Deb didn't seem to care, she simply laid her head down on the hard, cold bench and closed her eyes. Misterwizard studied her with concern, knowing he had to find some medicine soon.

The other people from the Tribe wandered up and down the aisles, gazing at all the strange objects behind the glass. Misterwizard listened to their exclamations of amazement as they looked at each new strange, unfamiliar object. Foodcourt ran up to Misterwizard. "Misterwizard! Please come! You must explain some of these things to us!"

Misterwizard smiled with amusement, but then frowned again. "First we must make Deb more comfortable. You see that room over there?" Misterwizard pointed to a doorway. Foodcourt nodded. "That is what is called the 'Gift Shop.' Go inside and see if you can find any blankets or pillows inside my good man, or anything soft that might make Deb more at ease in her discomfort."

Foodcourt nodded eagerly and ran off to do what Misterwizard asked. Misterwizard joined the Tribe at the display cases, stroking his beard and wearing a grin.

He walked up to see Sephie standing on her tiptoes

peering into a case. When Misterwizard arrived, she smiled at him with eyes full of wonder. Misterwizard picked her up and held her where she could see. She pointed to the strange object in the glass. "Misterwizard, who is that funny, small green man?"

Misterwizard chuckled. "That man is supposed to look like a frog-beastie. And his name is Kermit."

"Is he dead?"

"No, Sweetheart, he is a puppet. He is made of cloth and thread, and he was used once in a much gentler time to make people laugh."

Sephie smiled. "He makes me laugh."

Misterwizard looked in Sephie's face. "I tell you what. When we're all done with our little adventure, you can have Kermit for your very own. Would you like that?"

Sephie's eyes went wide with joy. "All for my very own?"

"Why not? I don't see anyone else laying copyright claim to Kermit in the foreseeable future. From now on, he is yours!"

"Whee!" Sephie put her hands up in celebration. Misterwizard set her down and wandered back to see what the others were discovering. Teavanna ran up to him, grabbed his arm and dragged him over to a display case. "Misterwizard, look at this. It is so colorful and strange. What is it?"

Misterwizard smiled at her. "It is something that your son Johnny or Starbucks, and surely Super, would enjoy, if and when they are afforded the opportunity. It is called an "electric guitar."

"E-lec-tric Geetar," Teavanna parroted. "What does it do?"

"It makes music. You first must plug it into some sort

of electrical power, and then you strum the strings on the top. Then sound comes out. Some say the sound is beautiful, others are not so enamored with it."

Foodcourt hurried up to Wizard. "I found a blanket and a pillow for her, just as you asked. She doesn't look very good, Misterwizard."

Misterwizard nodded. What Foodcourt said reminded him of his mission. He had to get to the basement of the museum where the Bunker hid, to the secret panel, and try to gain access.

But before Misterwizard could act, another member of the Tribe grabbed him, and soon he was fired with one question one after another:

"What is that symbol with the yellow mountains?"

"That is known as the "Golden Arches." It represented a quite successful eating establishment in its day."

"What is that chair? It is a holy chair?"

"No, that chair belonged to a character on a thing called Television. It says here his name is Archie Bunker. He must have been quite popular and famous in his time."

"Who is that man, and what is he doing in this picture?"

"That, so the sign says, is Louis Armstrong, and he is blowing an object called a "Trumpet." There it is, next to the picture. He must have been quite a talented musician in his day."

"What are those things?"

Many of the things they pointed out to Misterwizard, he had never seen or experienced either, only heard about in stories from his father, but he tried his best to act knowledgeable and answer their questions.

"They are, um, ice skates. If I understand the picture correctly, you put them on your feet and glide across water when it becomes frozen. Now no more questions. I must hurry."

The members of the Tribe didn't listen, instead they dragged Misterwizard into a room with one huge display case on its side. They pointed to the object inside with avid curiosity.

"Please tell us, Misterwizard. What is that big piece of cloth doing there? Is it holy?"

This one Misterwizard knew. He touched the display case and gazed at the red and blue tattered item beneath, his heart stirring with emotion. "This, my dear friends, is called a 'flag.' It is what nations flew in the air to represent themselves. This one represents the nation that was here before us, the nation that I hope to resurrect, and I believe Johnny too. It was called the "United States of America." Though when we resurrect it, it shall be as it was intended, based on freedom and liberty, not as it sadly ended, in sorrow and oppression. This flag inspired a great song, known as the National Anthem. It is very old and very precious."

Hushed and respectful the Tribe peoples walked out. Misterwizard gazed at the flag for a few more moments, thinking back to the past, and wondering about the future. Then he too left.

He walked outside, only to be grabbed again. He was led to a large room where the Tribe gathered around a huge metal object in the middle of the floor.

"Misterwizard! Misterwizard! What is it?"

Misterwizard gazed on the shiny, beautiful contraption. It had huge round, metal wheels and a smokestack on top. Misterwizard smiled with affection, remembering pictures and stories his father had told him about them.

"That, my friends, is known as a locomotive. It was propelled by energy from heated water referred to as "steam," created by burning a rock called coal or by electrical energy. It moved on two metal rails laid on the ground everywhere it went."

Foodcourt snorted. "I don't believe it. Sometimes Misterwizard, I think you make things up to make sport of us. How could something this big move on two steel pieces of metal? And run on hot water?"

"There are many things that seem impossible, dear Foodcourt, but I assure you they were fact. If I told you some of the things that were before, you would think me a raving idiot, and yet I would be telling you the truth."

Carny waddled up to Wizard, her face contorted with pain, and immediately alarms went off in Wizard's brain, for he knew what it was.

"Misterwizard," Carny said, doubling over, "I felt the pushing. Miracle will come soon!"

Misterwizard turned to Foodcourt. "Quickly, find a spot for Carny to rest. I have been recalcitrant in my duties. Instead of gawking along with the rest of you like a tourist, I should have been endeavoring to find a way out of our present predicament. For that, I am truly repentant. Foodcourt, you are in charge. I must go to the basement. I have never been successful in determining the access code for the underground base, but it is our only salvation. I simply must redouble my efforts, though I'm afraid even dynamite will not affect the strong metal protecting the entrance."

Foodcourt did not understand half of what Misterwizard said, as always, but he nodded anyway, leading Carny over to a bench, while Misterwizard turned and looked for the stairs to the lower levels. He saw them and ran towards them, but a sound made him hesitate one more time. It was the Tribe. It sounded like all of them in another room. They were "ooh-ing" and "aah-ing" at something, and though he knew his time was fleeting, Misterwizard couldn't help himself from checking to see what had caused such a reaction.

, Walking into another room, he saw the whole Tribe staring into one case. Their eyes were all wide open and they gazed with rapture and what looked almost like worship at something. Misterwizard walked over to see what it was. When he saw, he couldn't help but chuckle.

Abercrombie looked at Wizard. "Misterwizard, what is it? A god?

Misterwizard stroked his short beard and chuckled. It truly was an amazing item they gazed at, strange and otherworldly, and yet looking like a person, just like them. Misterwizard read the inscription and then said, "No Abercrombie, it is not a god. It is what was once called a "prop" for a thing called a "movie." My father told me about them, though I've never had the pleasure of viewing one. Hopefully once we've begun to rebuild our domicile, I will be able to rectify that for our amusement. A movie was a moving story portrayed on a big screen, one as big as that wall over there, a pretend story made up to entertain, like telling stories by the firelight. And props were things they made to make the story seem real."

Abercrombie asked, "But it is so beautiful! It looks like a person, only one made of gold!"

Misterwizard nodded. "The movie makers were enormously talented at their profession and very good story tellers. This particular prop, so it says, is something called a "robot." A robot was a machine made to look and act like a man, kind of like the fake people back in Sanctuary, only ones that could move."

Another member of the Tribe said, "Aren't they scary enough without moving?"

Misterwizard chuckled. "They weren't meant to be scary, but fun. This one's name, so it says, is C-3PO."

"Cee-Threepioh," the Tribe repeated reverently.

"So, he's not alive?" Foodcourt asked. "He looks like he could look at us and talk at any second."

"No, Foodcourt. He is only made to look that way."

"And so, we shouldn't worship him?"

"No, Oldnavy, you should not."

"Life must have been so amazing, before," Abercrombie said.

"Yes, I believe it was," Misterwizard replied. "And it will be again."

CHAPTER 24

Johnny, Starbucks and Super were led to a large white building on the far side of the grassy Mall that was partially demolished. They didn't know it yet, but it was the old Capitol building. They followed Lord Algon to a room at the back, passing large paintings half eaten by bug-beasties or destroyed by age that showed men in funny costumes on them. A blue carpet ran down the middle of the hallway and little tables lined the walls.

In the room at the back stood a large, wooden desk. Lord Algon sat in the big brown chair behind it. The two huge Wildies positioned themselves on either side of him. Johnny noticed two more just as big stood outside the door as guards.

One of the Wildies next to Lord Algon said, "Kneel before Lord Algon or lose your heads!"

Johnny, Starbucks and Super looked at each other.

They all nodded, deciding their pride was not worth dying over, not when they had so much to lose. All three knelt in front of Lord Algon.

Lord Algon smiled at their obedience and seemed to relax. "Prithee, speak ye now of how ye came to my Kingdom, and do it speedily, afore I grow impatient."

Johnny spoke first. "As we said, Lord Algon, we are merely travelers. We are simply looking for safe passage. We seek no quarrel with you, er ye, and only wouldst deign to go on our way."

"Would ye?" Lord Algon said, as an attractive Wildie woman with long red hair in a white toga began feeding him grapes. "And what tribute will ye render unto me, Lord of this here realm, to gain yourself free passage?"

Johnny and Starbucks glanced at each other, thinking about it. Then Johnny said, "We have nothing to offer but our Harleys. You are welcome to them. All we ask is to let us leave in peace."

"Forsooth," Lord Algon said, "ye speak of the strange metal dragons ye rode 'ere we spied you. And, troth, what makes ye think we would want such foul contraptions?"

"They're fun to ride," Super said, "and make a cool noise."

"A cool noise, say ye?" Lord Algon rose from the chair. "We shall see if we believe ye or nay. Outside with us."

Lord Algon walked outside again and Johnny and the others followed. Lord Algon approached the Harleys, which had been pushed along by Wildies to just outside the black gate around the building.

Lord Algon yawned, as if bored and pointed at the Harleys. Show me this, 'cool noise,' if ye be able. I will judge whether it be cool or not."

Johnny and Starbucks grinned at each other and walked over to the Harleys. As the Wildies gathered around and Lord Algon watched with eager anticipation, Johnny turned the key on his bike and turned the throttle. The Harley roared, eliciting a gasp from the crowd. Lord Algon's eyes opened wide and he stepped back. But a smile of joy spread over his face like a little boy with a new toy.

"Aye, these be truly magical things, as ye say."

Johnny roared the Harley again, and the crowd cheered. Lord Algon looked fascinated, his eyes lit up with excitement. "Perhaps we might will be willing to show ye mercy, in exchange for such gifts as these."

The trio grinned at each other. It looked like they might escape with their lives after all.

Leader Nordstrom ran as fast as he could with his hurt leg, not even looking where he was going, frantic with fear, just wanting to escape the Gangers and what he knew would be certain death. He had thought joining Ripper would be of some advantage at first, but his experience with him had shown Leader Nordstrom that Ripper was nothing but an animal.

How Leader Nordstrom wished he was back with the Tribe, back in charge, at Sanctuary, sleeping in his own warm bed. His belly ached with hunger and he was cold and sore. He couldn't remember being so tired or miserable. And it was all Johnny's fault. Johnny had brought the Gangers down upon them. Johnny caused them to lose their home. And it was certainly Johnny's fault that Leader Nordstrom was no longer treated as he deserved, with respect and honor. Leader Nordstrom hated Johnny so much, thinking about it made his stomach hurt. He hoped with all his heart that Ripper killed Johnny. And how he longed to be there to see it! He thought about it all the time, especially now that he was so hungry and scared.

Leader Nordstrom stopped running. His leg ached like it was on fire. He looked around and saw he was on a street in the middle of the city. He'd been running so hard he didn't even stop to look around, but now he saw that he was near a large building much like Sanctuary. The windows of the stores were filled with the fake people in fancy clothes, just like ones scattered around their old home. Their frozen stares always terrified Leader Nordstrom but looking at them now almost made him homesick. He wondered if this place would make a nice new home for him, now that he was all alone.

All alone. The realization of the fact that he was all by himself made him feel wretched. He would become just another Wildie, scrounging for food and slowly going crazy. He wondered if he should try and find the Tribe; maybe Johnny and Misterwizard would let him back in, if he promised not to cause any more trouble and if he let Johnny be in charge. Johnny and Misterwizard were the soft-hearted weak type that forgave easily. Surely if he acted contrite, they would believe his sincerity and forgive him. Then he could plan his revenge, all the while sleeping in a nice warm bed with a belly full of food. Yes, that is what he would do. He smiled and felt encouraged, now that he had a plan. He decided he would look for some food, and then start searching for the Tribe.

Leader Nordstrom's neck itched, for he sensed a presence behind him; someone was watching him. He turned around quickly, his heart beating hard with fear, and peered around. There was nothing there, only abandoned cars and old paper flitting about, driven by the wind. He stood still, listening, until the fear of whatever it was made him move again.

Leader Nordstrom headed up the street, glancing behind himself every few seconds anxiously. He knew something was there, he could feel it. And what was worse, he began to be sure that whatever it was tracked him. Leader Nordstrom quickened his pace, forgetting all about the building that was like Sanctuary, and soon he was running.

He reached another building, this one with the sign of the yellow mountains. The glass in the front of the building was all smashed and lay on the street and inside the building. Leader Nordstrom knew that this place once served food, but there would be none left that was edible, it would all have rotted long ago. Leader Nordstrom stopped in front of the building and looked around. And then he saw it.

It came out from behind an old rusted car, and it was watching him. As soon as Leader Nordstrom saw it, ice filled his blood as if someone had poured ice-water in through a hole in his head. Fear gripped him like it never had before and he felt his bladder weaken and his pants grow wet.

There next to the car stood the tiger-beastie. It must have followed them from Castle, looking for another meal. Its green eyes seemed to hypnotize him, he couldn't stop staring into them. It stood still, watching him. Leader Nordstrom knew any second it would take off toward him; he had only seconds to get away.

Finally, Leader Nordstrom was able to move, and he ran like he had never run in his life. He took off down the street, not even looking back to see if the horrible creature was following but feeling as if its claws and sharp teeth were already digging into his neck.

A scream escaped Leader Nordstrom's lips, and soon he was screaming steadily, at the top of his lungs, his mind blank with terror. He ran and ran, ignoring the pain in his leg, until he ran right into a group of Wildies standing around a barrel full of burning wood in the middle of the street. Leader Nordstrom dove into them, knocking one man over and landing in a heap on top of him. The other Wildies yelled, but Leader Nordstrom was too scared to hear them or care. He jumped up and ran to stand behind another of the Wildies, peering nervously over them, looking for the tiger-beastie. The Wildie Leader Nordstrom knocked over stood up and dusted himself off, glaring at Leader Nordstrom with a dangerous expression.

The Wildies each held a makeshift weapon made of wood with nails or hooks in it. One of the Wildies who seemed to be their leader pointed at Leader Nordstrom and spoke crossly. "Aye? What matter of little mouse be ye, varlet? Be ye touched in the head? Or be ye looking for a good beating?"

Leader Nordstrom turned to the Wildie with a wild look on his face. "I don't know what you're talking about! Tiger-beastie! Tiger-beastie!" Leader Nordstrom pointed down the road with a shaky finger. "Tiger-beastie coming!" With that last, Leader Nordstrom turned to run, hoping the tiger-beastie would be distracted by the Wildies and he would have time to escape. But one of the

Wildies grabbed his coat and wouldn't let him go. "Hold, ye intruder, 'ere we grow incensed and beat ye about the ears. You cannot traverse these lands without our Lord's permission. You must give obeisance to our King and gain his blessing 'ere you travel his realm."

"What gibberish are you talking? A tiger-beastie is coming, you fool! We must escape, or it will eat us!"

The Wildies looked down the street where Leader Nordstrom pointed without much concern. Then they looked back at him with lazy smiles. "We see no tiger-beastie of which ye speak. Only a strange man likely touched in the head from too much sun, or maybe too much wine." They all laughed and pointed at him.

Leader Nordstrom's fear started to abate, and he grew angry. "Fine, fools, you stay here, and you will see soon enough. You will make a nice meal for it, while I go about my business." Leader Nordstrom tried to leave, but the Wildie still held him tight.

"Did you nae hear any of what I spoke?" The apparent Leader Nordstrom of the group said. "You be on your way, 'ere it pleases our Lord. Or perhaps he will find you troublesome and feed to ye his pets. It matters not to us but go to him ye will. Or perhaps ye'd rather die here on this spot."

"I have no idea what you are saying, you idiot," Leader Nordstrom said, trying in vain to pull away. "I am the Leader Nordstrom of a Tribe of my own, and so it may be that your "king" and I should indeed meet and discuss a treaty. Meanwhile, he will expect you to treat me with the respect and dignity deserving of my station."

The Wildies gathered together and talked quietly to each other, while the one Wildie still held onto Leader

Nordstrom's sleeve. Then the Leader Nordstrom walked over to Leader Nordstrom. "Very well. We shall take you to our King. Perhaps he will find ye an entertaining, if fleeting, diversion, and may find interest in this Tribe ye speak of."

The Wildie holding Leader Nordstrom pulled him, and soon he was being dragged towards the center of the city, and Lord Algon.

Ripper looked out the front of the Humvee at the group of Wildies standing in the street. There was about ten of them. He put up a hand and the driver stopped. Quickly all the other vehicles behind the Humvee followed suit. Ripper climbed out of the Humvee, and drivers in the other vehicles got out as well, wondering why they'd stopped. Facegash walked up with a questioning look.

Ripper smiled darkly. "It has been a long trip. Let's have some fun with these Wildies and see if they can entertain us." Facegash grinned with excitement. He turned to the Gangers behind him and raised an arm. "Go get 'em, men!" He pointed at the Wildies ahead, who looked back at them curiously. The Gangers yelled and poured out of the vehicles, weapons in hand. They rushed past Ripper and Facegash, who watched with big grins.

When the Wildies realized what was happening, they turned to run, but they were too late. The Gangers surrounded them and began beating them with clubs and the handles of their swords. The Wildies screamed and raised their arms to ward off the blows. Some tried to fight back with their own clubs, but quickly the small group of Wildies was overwhelmed. They ended up cowering on the ground as the Gangers beat them.

Ripper strolled up to watch the mayhem. As he reached the Gangers he raised a hand, and they stopped beating the Wildies, who lay on the ground whimpering. Ripper walked up to one man who lay on the ground, his hand on his bleeding head. “You were blocking our way. We were heading down this road, and you were standing in the middle of the street as if it was your house. Do you have any idea how annoying that was to me?”

The man looked up with his eyes, not turning his head. “Please, have mercy my liege. We are but simple men, nae warriors such as yerselves. We meant not to encumber your travels.”

Ripper looked at Facegash, who shrugged. Then Ripper knelt by the man. “You talk funny. Why do you talk so funny?”

“I speak the words of my people, my lord. ‘Tis the common speech of this land. ‘Tis the speech of my Lord Algon. ‘Twas he who taught us this parlay.”

“Lord Algon, huh?” Ripper said. “Tell me more about this Lord Algon. Where is he, and how many ‘warriors’ does he have?”

The Wildie shook his head. “I musn’t, my lord. Lord Algon would torture and kill me, if I were to betray him.”

“Well guess what,” Ripper said with a smile. “If you don’t tell me what I want to know, whatever Lord Algon would do to you would be nothing compared to what we’re about to do. We’re experts at causing pain, and we’ll be very happy to prove it.”

Misterwizard finally managed to escape the Tribe and reach the basement of the Museum. He had spent many hours visiting the city and looking for the hidden underground base prepared for the President in the event of a catastrophe just like the Great War that had devastated the planet. During his exploration, he found papers detailing how a secret tunnel from the White House led to the Bunker which was located deep under the Museum of American History. He'd also discovered, however, that there was an auxiliary entrance in the basement of the museum, hidden in a secret place so the inhabitants had two ways in and out in case of emergency. He'd also discovered the technical plans showing the layout and construction of the Bunker, though it had taken him many trips and searches to find them. The plans had been hidden in a heavy vault in a flat, odd shaped building called the Pentagon. Once he'd blasted his way inside the vault, he spent hours reading old documents and papers, learning many interesting facts about the defenses of the country that was before.

That was where he was headed now; the only problem was, though he had uncovered the secret door, it had a key panel on it, and without the code, he couldn't open the door. The code wasn't on the secret papers he'd found, and he suspected whomever had it had died with it long ago. It was possible the door didn't even work anymore, that it had no power. He had planned for this eventuality, however. If the door no longer worked, he planned on using explosives to blow it open, or taking the longer route of drilling through the wall. He'd studied the plans and found a place where the steel and concrete should be the thinnest. There was no reason to worry about doing damage, for any inhabitants of the vault had surely perished years ago. Still, the vault was virtually impregnable, he knew he it would take a lot of explosives to blast a hole in it. Now, with the Wildies outside, he had no time to drill and too much noise could be dangerous.

Misterwizard reached the area where the door was. Hidden behind a statue of George Washington, the door was accessed by pushing a button on the back of the statue's leg. This released catches on the statue, allowing it to roll out of the way. When the statue was moved, the outline of a door could barely be seen. And hidden at the top of the door was a small panel that could be slid up. Behind it was the keypad.

Misterwizard reached the basement and quickly found the statue. He gazed at it for a moment, for George Washington was one of Misterwizard's heroes. From the floor above, the voices of the Tribe members talking filtered down as they continued to marvel at all of the Museum's displays. The basement was cool and dark, and for a brief moment Misterwizard enjoyed the solitude, lost in his own thoughts.

Stirring himself out of his reverie, Misterwizard walked over and found the button on George's leg, just where he remembered it. He pushed it and heard a soft click. Gripping the statue and pushing with a soft grunt, Misterwizard was able to get the statue moving. Slowly he pushed it out of the way.

And just where he remembered it stood the door. Misterwizard scratched his bearded chin and searched for the panel. When he finally spied it, he walked over and slid the metal cover up. There was the keypad. It didn't use simply numbers for the password, but letters of the alphabet as well, meaning that the code could be even more complicated. Trying not to think of the number of possible combinations, Misterwizard pushed a button, simply hoping that the panel would light up.

It did! The numbers and letters lit up with an orange glow. That meant that whatever generator the hidden base had was still functioning, at least with enough power to operate the keypad. Now the only problem was, what was the combination? Misterwizard didn't even know how long the combination was, let alone what the specific numbers and letters were. Somewhere, some General or high official who was long dead held a briefcase with the combination written down, but the chances of Misterwizard finding him would be astronomical. His only hope was to try and decipher the code. He might as well have been trying to fly by flapping his arms. Misterwizard knew it was virtually hopeless, but he had to try. He began pushing numbers and letters at random to see what would happen.

Misterwizard took out a pad of paper and a pencil that he had brought along for the occasion. He tried a combination of five letters and five numbers to start, chosen at random. The keypad blinked twice and then made a buzzing sound. Misterwizard wrote the combination that he'd used down and sighed. It was going to be a long process. He tried another combination, this time one off in number and letter from the one he had tried before. Once again, the panel beeped, and once again he wrote it down. He tried two more combinations, both negative, and wrote them both down.

As he was preparing to try again, Foodcourt came

running down the stairs. His face was grim.

"Misterwizard! Come quickly! Deb has stopped breathing!"

Misterwizard's heart sank and his mind filled with worry. He put the paper and pencil down on the statue's pedestal and hurried after Foodcourt.

What Misterwizard didn't see was the small camera in the corner of the room, high up on the wall. It turned to watch him and Foodcourt as they hurried out of the room.

Leader Nordstrom was led to a huge lawn surrounded by a black metal fence with spikes in front of a white, crumbling mansion. Though he wore a scowl to appear fierce, inside, Leader Nordstrom was scared to death and could barely walk. He didn't know what was going to happen to him, and he wished not for the last time that he could simply run back to Sanctuary and hide under the covers of his bed.

He was brought into a room with a huge wooden desk and big brown chair. On it sat a man in regal clothing. Leader Nordstrom could tell by the man's bearing that he was their king. Leader Nordstrom knew he had to think fast, put all his diplomatic skills to work to get out of the situation alive.

Lord Algon stood up and walked towards Leader Nordstrom, a smile of curiosity on his face. He turned to the crowd of Wildies. "Anon! We are blessed with many a strange visitor today! The gods have fain to play games with us and see what will out. What think ye, my subjects, of all this?" The crowd roared in amusement. Lord Algon turned to Leader Nordstrom, who tried hard not to fall because of his shaking legs.

"Be ye aligned with the strange men and fair maiden and their metal dragons 'ere we just deigned to allow flee our presence? Speak quickly, varlet."

Leader Nordstrom smiled weakly. "I-I-I am Leader Nordstrom, of the Tribe from a place called Sanctuary. I come to discuss peace negotiations, so our two peoples can be allies."

Lord Algon frowned, for this was new information. "A tribe from Sanctuary, here in my kingdom? If so, where be they? Be they hidden, waiting to ambush us whilst we sleep? Speak quickly, or I will see ye drawn and quartered!"

"No, no," Leader Nordstrom said hastily, "our desire is only for peace and friendship with you and your Wildies, er, people."

Lord Algon moved to stand right in front of Leader Nordstrom. He signaled for his enforcers to join him and they stood behind him, looking menacing with their swords held ready. "If this be truth, then where be they? I see only thee, and the three strangers I have met afore. Dost thou love thine head, varlet? If so, speak with haste."

"Well, I don't know where they are, at the moment," Leader Nordstrom whined, "I seem to have been separated from my Tribe. But they are nearby, uh, forsooth."

Lord Algon's eyes narrowed. "Methinks ye codgen me a fool. Ye wouldst have me believe that ye have no knowledge of your own Tribe's whereabouts?"

"It's true, I swear!" Leader Nordstrom said nasally.

"The others you spoke of, were they two men, one with blond hair and the other with dark skin? Did they ride strange vehicles with shiny metal?"

"Of a truth they did." Lord Algon pointed and the crowd parted, revealing the Harleys.

Leader Nordstrom smiled, now feeling as if he had a card to deal. "Of a truth, these two men are evil brigands, come to your land to spy it out and report back to their tribe, one that has attacked mine as well. They are evil, cruel warriors bent on conquering your people and killing you, my lord. You must find them and tie them up. Then you can interrogate them and find out where their army is waiting!"

Leader Nordstrom waited, expecting Lord Algon to react, but Lord Algon simply stared at Leader Nordstrom, as if trying to read into his soul. "Alas and alack, ye say these two are our enemies, and yet they it be that gave us these metal dragons. Ye it could be that is playing a trick and casting the doubt on them. We will bring back these two strangers and their lass, and we will keep thee as well. Soon, I will find the truth verily, if I have to remove all of your hides to do it."

This didn't turn out the way Leader Nordstrom wanted; he was hoping Lord Algon would simply believe him, but now Leader Nordstrom would have to be more convincing than Johnny and Starbucks. He wondered where the Tribe was, and why Johnny and Starbucks were not with them. There were pieces of the puzzle Leader Nordstrom didn't know, and this made the hand he would play more dangerous. And there was the Joker in the deck as well, for somewhere, Ripper and the Gangers were on their way. Leader Nordstrom knew he would have to use all his wits to come out on top, even if it simply meant find the opportune time to run away. Still, he hoped when it was all finished, at least it would see the death of his nemesis, Johnny Apocalypse.

CHAPTER 25

After Ripper and the Gangers finished torturing and killing the Wildies, Ripper gathered them together in front of the vehicles.

"Listen up. Those Wildies all talk funny, like they was touched in the head. But one of them said something about a 'Lord Algon.' Seems like these Wildies have decided to make their own crazy kingdom here." The Gangers looked at each other and laughed. "So, what we got to do, is show them who they really need to bow down to, and that's the Doomsday Prophecy!" The Gangers all cheered and nodded.

"And," Ripper continued, "we got to do it before Johnny and the Tribe meet up with them, and form some kind of bond or something, making it even harder to take 'em down. I say we 'depose' this king of theirs and set ourselves up as the Leader Nordstroms. Then when

Johnny and the Tribe comes along, we'll be even stronger to give 'em what for."

"But Ripper," a thin Ganger with long, dirty stringy blond hair named Hoothoot asked in a whiny voice, "maybe it's too late. What if the Tribe is already aligned with this Lord Algon? We could be walking into a trap, and then we be the ones gettin' what's for."

Ripper walked over to Hoothoot, who couldn't help but flinch and shrink down in Ripper's presence. "What are you, a cowardie? We are the Doomsday Prophecy. If we have to we'll go out in a fighting to the death. But we don't back down from nobody. Get it? Or maybe you want we should make an example of what a cowardie you are and feed you to the rest of the Gangers?"

"No, no, I'm with ya Ripper!" Hoothoot grinned fawningly and he leapt up and down in a show of cooperation. "I was just thinkin, that's all."

"Well, how about you let those with brains do the thinkin' from now on. Mount up! We ride to Lord Algon and his nutty in the head Wildies! Today will be a day in Doomsday Prophecy history!"

The Gangers cheered and ran to their vehicles. Ripper glared at Hoothoot one more time before heading to his Humvee. Hoothoot ran to his ride, grateful just to be alive.

Misterwizard hurried up to where Deb lay on the bench. The Tribe gathered around her but not too close, looks of fear and sadness on their faces. A woman named Jayceepenney, with a thin face, long black hair and a hook nose said, "She is dead. We must get rid of her body, before she makes us all sick!" Deb's mother scowled at Jayceepenney. "She isn't dead! Don't say that until Misterwizard says so!" But there was a hint of fear and sorrow in her voice, as she feared the worst.

They parted as Misterwizard approached. He knelt down next to Deb. He looked at her face and then put his ear to her mouth. To his relief, he heard barely perceptible breathing.

"She is not dead." An audible sigh came from all the Tribes members. The woman, Jayceepenney piped up again. "She will still make us sick! We need to keep her away from the rest of us!"

"She's my daughter! She needs help!" Deb's father, Thegap thundered.

"Well, getting the rest of us sick won't help her!" Jayceepenney shot back.

Misterwizard didn't comment, knowing that Jayceepenney was essentially right. Deb could make them all sick, and if she didn't get cured soon, she would die. "Hurry. Convey her with all gentility to the basement floor of this establishment. There she will be isolated from the rest of the Tribe, and in a advantageous location. She must be the first to enter when I find the correct combination, for she has little time left."

Foodcourt and two other men gingerly picked Deb up and gently carried her down to the basement. The placed her on the cold marble floor and put a pillow under her head. Deb's father, Thegap, sat next to her, stroking her head with his hand. Her mother Bathandbodyworks sat next to her, watching her, a look of concern and sorrow on her face.

From the corner of the room, Carny spoke up in a small, timid voice. “Misterwizard, I didn’t want to be selfish, with Deb having so much trouble, but Miracle is coming real soon!”

Misterwizard hurried over and looked at Carny. Her face was covered in sweat, and she was breathing heavily.

“Keep from pushing, as long as you can, dear Carny.” Misterwizard turned to Foodcourt. “Foodcourt, find some sheets and blankets, just in case, well, in case I am tardy in gaining access to our new abode.”

Foodcourt just nodded and started rummaging around. Misterwizard ran as fast as he could back downstairs to the keypad and stared at it. “I have to find the combination. It is becoming an urgent necessity!”

Sephie had joined Misterwizard at the keypad and watched him with curiosity. Suddenly looked up and pointed. “Misterwizard! That thing up there moved! I think it is alive!”

Misterwizard turned towards it with a smile of excitement and interest. “It did, did it? Well, this is quite an unexpected and hopefully encouraging development. Let’s hope, dear Sephie, that it is not merely operating as programmed long ago, but that there is a real person somewhere watching us.”

Some of the tribe members heard Sephie’s words. They came running down the stairs to see what was happening.

Misterwizard walked to where he was standing right in front of the camera. “Hello. If there is someone there, please help us. We are not vagrants or criminals, but simply citizens of this land that need aid. We have a member who is very ill, and needs medical attention, and another that is about to bring a child into the world. Please, if you are there, have mercy on us."

The whole Tribe gathered in front of the camera, waiting. But it did not move again.

The Wildie was an old man, older than most. His father had witnessed the Great War and lived through the Great Sickness. With white hair and a face wrinkled not only by time but also by the hardness of his life, he wandered on the outskirts of the crowd, not really listening to Lord Algon's thundering. He knew Lord Algon was most probably insane, but their 'king' had organized the Wildies, and that was something that hadn't happened in all the time the old man had been alive. The old man knew it wouldn't last, but he was happy to enjoy the peace while it did. He had spent many days hiding from packs of roaming Wildies, scrabbling for scraps in the trash bins and fighting others for bits of cloth or trinkets. At least Lord Algon had set up a common food area and taught the Wildies to build wooden shacks to live in.

The old man wandered back to his own hut, a lean-to from the rain, and an old, moldy sleeping bag. He thought about taking a nap but decided to take a walk instead. He decided to walk by the old brick buildings and look at some of the strange oddities in them. It was a favorite pastime of his, to look at the old things from the old times. Not many of the other Wildies, even the children, seemed very interested in the artifacts from before the Great War. Most of them were too busy scrabbling for food or fighting over clothes. The old man loved to look at the old pictures and strange junk behind the glass in the old buildings. It let him fantasize about what life was like before, and dream of a time when maybe it would be like that again. Most of the Wildies just thought him a Crazie, and maybe he was, but it was what he enjoyed.

He walked off the lawn with all its huts across the concrete street towards the old buildings. And that's when he saw the buses. Three big, yellow, long buses, all parked in a row. The old man was sure he'd never seen them there before, he would have remembered. Cautiously he walked up to the nearest one. They seemed so big and well, yellow. He stood on his tiptoes and tried to see inside. The bus looked empty.

Carefully, he crept up to the door and peered in. The bus was empty all right. With an excited grin he pried open the door and tiptoed inside. The bus was huge inside. The seats were littered with bits of clothing, junk and...food! With joy he found a half-eaten apple. He picked it up and gazed at it lovingly. Then he ate it slowly, savoring each delicious bite. He spent the next few minutes scouring the bus, eating all the food he could find.

As he was eating the leftover chili out of a can, he remembered where he was, and that the owners might come back any moment. He looked up with fear, scanning the horizon, but no one approached. He thought about what he should do. Surely, there was food on the other two buses as well, and yet, he was taking a chance, for at any moment the owners of the buses might return.

This made him think about where they could have gone. He looked out one of the window and was sure he had the answer. The buses were parked in front of one huge building that said, "M M of A eric His ry" on it. What were they doing inside? Were they planning an attack on Lord Algon and the Wildies? Were they some advanced tribe that could help the Wildies? Or were they a group of Gangers, getting ready to take over the city?

Whomever they were, the thought of them made the old man quiver with fear. He pondered what to do. Should he tell Lord Algon? He would surely get a reward if he did, maybe even extra food rations. He decided that he would explore just one more bus, and then he would run to tell Lord Algon what he had found. Maybe he would be the hero for once, and people would treat him with a little more respect.

Johnny, Starbucks and Super walked, followed by a crowd of Wildies. After giving Lord Algon the Harleys the friends were allowed to go their way. Now they walked aimlessly, heading towards the outskirts of the city. The only thing Johnny didn't want to do was lead the Wildies towards the Tribe and the bright yellow buses. His plan was to simply walk to the edge of the city where the Wildies would eventually stop following, and then circle back, this time being careful not to be spotted, and try to get back to Misterwizard and the Tribe. Fortunately, Lord Algon hadn't noticed Johnny's radio, or things might have gone much worse. Once Johnny and Starbucks reached the edge of town, Johnny would contact Misterwizard, and with any luck, they would be able to find the Tribe quickly.

As they walked along, Scrabbler Wildies, from six seasons old to ones as old as ten, skipped along next to them, staring at them with amazement and curiosity. One was a little girl who reminded Johnny of a young Deb, with blond hair and a cute smile. Her clothes and face were dirty, and her hair was a tangled mess. It made Johnny sad to see her like that. *Lord Algon wasn't doing anything to improve the Wildies' lives,* Johnny thought. He was sure their king only cared about himself, and from what Johnny could tell, Lord Algon was also insane. Someday, unless someone intervened, Lord Algon's 'kingdom' would dissolve into chaos and violence. Johnny hoped before that happened, he and Misterwizard could talk Lord Algon and his Wildies into being friends, so together they could create a true government. Johnny knew that it wouldn't be easy to reason with a mad king. With luck; the Tribe would have a chance to get settled in New Sanctuary before they had to deal with Lord Algon and his followers.

Almost as if reading Johnny's thoughts, a group of Wildies ran up to stand in front of the Johnny and his friends. One in front, a short but strong looking man with short black hair and black eyes put his hand up to stop their progress. He scowled at them a dark, suspicious expression that immediately made Johnny anxious. And he held a short, dull sword in his hand that still looked dangerous.

"Halt, ye two-tongued devils! Ye spoke falsely to our lord and he be vey wroth! Ye spoke not of the others with ye, a whole shipload ye have hidden, and so have earned our lord's anger! Ye will return to him at once to face judgement or I am to split yer gillets here and now!"

Johnny and Starbucks looked at each other. "Oh, oh,"

Starbucks said. "It looks like they found out about the Tribe."

Johnny nodded with regret, sad to see the way things were happening. "We may have to fight now, Starbucks."

Johnny looked at Starbucks furtively. Starbucks looked back quizzically, not knowing what Johnny was planning.

Suddenly Johnny pulled out his sword and pointed it right at the lead Wilide's throat. "Run, Super! Go to the Tribe and warn them!"

Super took off running. The Wildie yelled and the rest watched, but Johnny's sword made him hesitate, and Super was fast. In a flash she disappeared behind through the door of a nearby abandoned building.

Johnny lowered his sword and moved back. The Wildie smiled at him with a begrudging respect.

"Aye, ye have saved thy fair maiden, and for that I respect thee. But 'twill only make matters worse for ye with Lord Algon! Now turn about and start marching!"

Johnny glared back. "Let's go. Your 'king' is waiting."

"Yeah," Starbucks said. "I can't wait to see him again."

Together Johnny and Starbucks turned around and headed back towards Lord Algon's castle, with the crowd of Wildies following and surrounding them, jabbering and pointing.

Johnny and Starbucks looked at each other, both wondering just what was going to happen next.

Made in the USA
Middletown, DE
01 May 2021

38235477R00199